'I'm blown away with the depth of feeling I have for this beautiful, original and affecting story. For me, the most engaging stories are the ones that confront me with questions about myself as a human. Brendan poses deep, fearless questions about decency and honesty and the human condition with humour, heart and a boldness that allows me to feel brave. That's why I love this book. Unforgettable.' Asher Keddie

'Mesmerising. I love your guts, Pete Lum, you glorious rugby league battler dreamer poet king. I didn't know how much I needed this book until I couldn't stop picking it up. Thing broke through my defences like a sneaky grubber. It's Shark Park on a bright Sunday afternoon. It's Sylvia Plath on a lonely Sunday night. Poetry, all of it. Totally unpredictable, wholly adorable and bloody unforgettable.' Trent Dalton

'Plum is a character, and a book, that is going to get people talking about many issues: family, friendship, husbands and wives and fathers and sons and the slow creep of your past creeping up and mugging you from behind. All this is in *Plum*, but Brendan Cowell should really be celebrated for his unabashed love of language: an exuberant Australian dialect busting out of its suburban shell. This is a novel to change the way we think and to enrich our enjoyment of the words we live among – which, in the literary art, come to the same thing. Battered and knocked about and put through hell, *Plum* is a winner.' Malcolm Knox

'A poetic, redemptive story with masterly dialogue and prose that doesn't pull any of its punches – *Plum* examines the bruise on a nation obsessed with masculinity.' Tara June Winch

'I grew up in Newcastle with a rugby league ball in my hands. The game is in my veins, and it has given me everything. I see traits in Plum that remind me of myself and the blokes I played with. Good and bad. The characters are so real. I loved this book. An insight into being admired, the hero worship, and then the struggles when that all finishes. The way Brendan has presented brain issues is spot-on too. The episodes, aura and seizures are painfully familiar. This novel is as real and raw as it gets. Don't hesitate.' Andrew Johns

'I'm a poet character in this book and play myself, which is weird, and got my attention for starters. Brendan Cowell referees a surreal game in his old stomping ground of the Shire, with Charles Bukowski and Sylvia Plath going head to head with the Cronulla Sharks, and it's poetry versus battered blokedom, throwing the dummy to go all the way down the blindside.' Tug Dumbly

'Plum loco! *Plum* sits happily panting like an existential scrum between Hunter S. Thomson's *Electric Kool-Aid Acid Test* and Tom Robbins's *Even Cowgirls Get the Blues*. Cowell has plumbed the depths of the Aussie archetype and laid bare the heartfelt bones of the hero breed. I am reminded by his larger-than-life characters of the collaboration between Bukowski and the underground comic artist Robert Crumb, which elevated and enshrined ordinary lives, picking among them for the golden metaphor of existence.' Ken Granneman, Brendan's Year Twelve drama teacher

Brendan Cowell is an award-winning writer, actor and director for television, theatre and film. He wrote the smash hit *Ruben Guthrie* for Belvoir St Theatre in 2009, and wrote and directed the film adaptation, winning an Australian Writers Guild Award (AWGIE) for the screenplay. Brendan wrote two episodes of the multi award-winning series *The Slap* for which he won the AACTA Best Screenplay prize. He has been named the 'leading light amongst playwrights of his generation' (*Sun Herald*) and has won the Patrick White Playwrights Award, the Philip Parsons Young Playwright's Award and the Griffin Award. His eleven plays have been produced all around the world. He was a writer on the acclaimed TV series *Love My Way*, in which he starred. Many of his episodes for *Love My Way* were nominated for AWGIEs for Outstanding Screenplay. Based between Sydney and London, Brendan is currently in development on two television shows, one with CBS and another with Amazon. Brendan's bestselling debut novel, *How It Feels*, was published by Pan Macmillan in 2010.

PLUM

BRENDAN COWELL

FOURTH ESTATE

This is a work of fiction and is not endorsed by the NRL or any NRL club.

Fourth Estate
An imprint of HarperCollins*Publishers*

HarperCollins*Publishers*
Australia • Brazil • Canada • France • Germany • Holland • India
Italy • Japan • Mexico • New Zealand • Poland • Spain • Sweden
Switzerland • United Kingdom • United States of America

First published in Australia in 2021
by HarperCollins*Publishers* Australia Pty Limited
Level 13, 201 Elizabeth Street, Sydney NSW 2000
ABN 36 009 913 517
harpercollins.com.au

A catalogue record for this book is available from the National Library of Australia.

ISBN 978 1 4607 6050 5 (paperback)
ISBN 978 1 4607 1386 0 (ebook)
ISBN 978 1 4607 8938 4 (audiobook)

Cover design by Darren Holt, HarperCollins Design Studio
Author photograph @BuildSeriesSyd
Typeset in Bembo Std Regular by Kirby Jones
Printed and bound by CPI Group (UK) Ltd, Croydon, CR0 4YY

For my cousin Anthony

Prologue

What are the best things you can feel in your time on earth? Like, if you had to say, what feels the best in terms of human experiences? Of all the ones on offer to us in this life? And keep it above board, please. What would be your top three, say? Getting sweaty on the dance floor at your wedding. Skiing out of a helicopter in Colorado. Eating a pizza with your wife in actual Italy. High at a festival and your favourite band are just there, they are right in front of you. Sex with love. Seeing your first baby be born and everyone is doing well. Dunno. They're all up there. Finishing the half-marathon with your best mate from school. Finishing just ahead of him too. Or after years of toiling away at it − sucking it all up and pushing through the tough times and the inadvertent politics of the workplace − finally getting that promotion and buying that house with water glimpses. Sure. That all feels pretty great. But for Peter Lum, well, it was now. It was this moment, the one before the beginning. The moment where the adrenaline of what he was about to do matched with his fear of the unknown. This psyched-up, fired-up, pent-up surrender to chaos, to competition, to collision. The knowledge you could kill or be killed. The want for that perilous limbo.

The busted neon bar overhead lit up his face then didn't, as he slapped himself with both hands and on both cheeks, took a deep breath and then thought about nothing.

'Let's do this,' he said to the carpet, as he ducked into the thin corridor with the roar of the crowd underscoring his hard-beating heart. This was the best feeling ever − knowing you had what it took, knowing the truth was in you, and knowing that your time had come …

One

'Year of the Shark,' Pete said, before gulping at his ice-cold schooner of New.

'I dunno. I saw John Morris at Cronulla Kitchen getting a coffee yesterday morning and when I asked him how we might go, he just put his hands to his throat, mate – seriously, he just did this.' Brick stuck his tongue out and gripped his Adam's apple with both hands. 'The Sharks are choked. The cap has choked em.'

'Gunna be a long fucken year for the blue, black and white, I reckon,' Magic Matt said, sipping from a half-full beer, his hands so big the glass looked like a test tube.

'You'll still tip em, though,' Squeaky said, and the boys laughed cos of course they would. Even if Cronulla Sharks fielded a team of eight alpacas the boys would tip Sharks because that's what teams is, and that's what loyalty is, and that's what you learn when you play sports, and they'd all played top-level sports at some point.

'Your young bloke's got his grand final this Satdy, doesn't he, Pete?' asked Brick, the pull of gambling leading his eyes down towards his TAB phone app.

'Yeah, the Jersey Flegg final – Satdy against Dogs. They look good too,' answered Pete.

'Mick Ennis still coaching em?' Magic Matt asked, his eyes on the latest barmaid.

'Yeah, Mick's all over em. There's not a weak link. And they're fit.'

'Your bloke starting at 6?'

'Yeah, he is. Five-eighth.'

'Son of a gun.'

'In the Game of the Father,' Matt joked, thinking this one was gold.

'Something like that, yeah,' Pete said.

'Shit ay, no pressure, Gav,' Brick said. 'You're just Peter Lum's son.'

'He'll be right.' Pete was keen to let that topic go. He was already too nervous for his kid, having to fill his own shoes and all, as well as playing blokes a lot older and bigger. Peter just hoped he enjoyed the eighty minutes and had a crack.

'You give him any words of advice?' Matt asked, never one to read the room. Perhaps it was his height, perhaps coming in at seven foot two he missed what was going on down on earth.

Pete shook his head, scrunching his nose as if to say, *He doesn't need it.*

It was 1.26 pm in the cavern of male failure and leering known as the Caringbah Inn – or to 'The Coxless Four', as their WhatsApp group was called, it was the Cazbah – and the dogs were on the big tele, and Brick Wall, who got his nickname from running through an actual wall, turned his brick-shaped physique to face the race. 'Off and racing!' he said, as he always did, in his best falsetto Johnny Tapp voice.

'Racing now,' added Squeaky, who would bet on a leaf in the rain if they let him.

Magic Matt offloaded his keys and cards onto the table like he'd just got home, and reached for his walking stick. 'Beers?' Back in the day, he'd played centre for the Sydney Kings, but unlike Brick and Pete, he'd stopped training altogether and so, now forty-nine, Magic was a limping blimp, waiting on a list to get his hip done again. The bloke was practically unrecognisable as the former Boomer enforcer who'd once dunked on Patrick Ewing.

'Wait till the race is over,' Brick said, eyes fixed on the tele, 'but, yep, you're up, Matty my boy.'

'Yep, I'll have another, s'il vous plaît,' Squeaky said. A stripped-back branch of a bloke, he'd earnt his nickname amid an unprecedented jockey career, and his tiny little glass-cracking voice had not descended a semi-quaver in all the years he'd been off the stallions. If anything it had got squeakier.

'Pete?'

'Nah, I'll hit the waters, thanks Matty.'

'You took the bus, didn't ya?' asked Squeaky.

'Fuck me, you prick of a cunt,' said Brick, as his white and grey greyhound didn't quite get round the final straight straight enough.

'Haha, I told ya! Wait for the trots in Inverell, dogs are rigged, Brick-a-brack.'

'Harness is no more pure, Squeak.'

'You sure, Pete?' asked Matt, waving his NAB card.

'Nup. Waters.'

'Charmayne got ya in the doghouse again?'

'Nah, she's all good.'

'Why you not schooner-ing then?' Squeaky asked.

Pete turned to face the little chap, thinking, *What is this,* 60 *Minutes?* 'I got this competition winner thing tonight at Sharks Leagues.'

'That fucken dog is still running backwards!' said Brick, as Matt hobbled off to get three schooners of New and a water for Peter 'The Plum' Lum.

'Didn't I tell you?' Plum asked Squeak.

'No, you didn't.'

'It's this "Meet the Ex-Players" thing, I dunno much about it … but there's a quiz.'

'Quiz?'

'Yeah, quiz. So better stay fresh. Well, as fresh as I get.'

'Ha, that's it,' Brick said, and tipped in the dregs of his beer.

'How come you weren't asked, Brick?' Squeaky asked him. 'You're ex-Sharks too.'

'Because he wasn't very fucken good!' Matty yelled from the bar.

'Kick me when I'm down, mate! I just dropped a fucken pineapple on the lickers!'

'I thought your missus banned you from the punt?' Pete asked.

'Another reason why I will always be single,' said Squeaky.

'What? Cos you're a flaming homo?' Brick said, getting his own back now.

Squeaky, suddenly overheating, opened his phone apps up for distraction. Betfair, Sportsbet, Ladbrokes – he had the holy trinity.

'How *are* you punting, though, Brick?' Pete asked him.

Brick leant in. 'Look, if you must know, I got me Leb mate Jezza from the gym to give us his card details. I pay him cash per day and he tops it up for me.'

'Sounds healthy,' said Squeak, firing up a multi.

'You can fucken talk, Mr "I'm a professional gambler and I still live in a one-bedroom shitbox on the Kingsway".'

'I like to keep it simple.'

Pete laughed. 'What do they say? Never get a tip from a jockey.'

'And look if I'm honest,' Brick said, his chest rising up, 'me and the old girl are probably on the way out anyway. Neither of us are happy and the kid is sick to death of the arguing –'

'Join the single scene with me, Bricko!'

'Grindr or Scruff was it, Squeaky?'

'Manhunt,' said Squeak. 'More bears.'

Pete loved these blokes. He'd played first grade with Brick throughout his career. The man was like family – as was

Squeak – whereas he'd only met Magic Matt in recent years, drinking beers here at the Cazbah. The four of them were a posse now, the Coxless Four, meeting for half-a-dozen lunch beers on their shared days off, talking about how different it gets post-career and how much things have changed with social media, and strategising over how their shared racehorse, Floodlight, would surely make em all millionaires.

'I got ya a light, Plum,' Matt said, returning to the boys – the four beers on a tray in his left hand, walking stick in his right, 'which has water in it … says the cute new barmaid.'

'You're a prick,' Pete said, lifting the light to his lips and looking around at the scattered tables of other males punting and drinking on a Tuesday. He took a proper gulp, then blinked his eyes and for a second it was like they might never open again. A strange snowstorm-like sensation filled his skull, building and cracking and flowing …

'Oh yeah!' Magic said, snapping Pete back into the room. 'Boys, gather round. You are gathered round, ok. Listen up then, focus. Announcement. Me, Brick and Pete's fiftieths are coming up next year, I'm thinking Thailand for a –'

'Thailand!' Squeak said, fist-pumping the air.

'Reunite with your favourite ladyboys,' Brick said, delighting in his fresh schooner.

'That was not a ladyboy,' Squeak said. 'That was a *lady* who owned a motorbike and simply offered to ferry me home. You ever been drunk on a highway in Phuket?'

'She looked very satisfied in the morning.'

'You gotta pay the Uber driver. We all know that.'

'Rightio!' said Squeak, no longer enduring the joke. 'What's the projected itinerary, Magic?'

'Cambodia, Vietnam, or maybe just Thailand if we can only get a week.'

'Could be a good release.'

'I'd hit Pattaya again, that was unreal.'

'Look, if it was my decision,' Matt said, 'I'd say post-hip op the four of us pool our collective cash, drop it on an Aussie Pub somewhere up the coast from Bangkok, do away with the Western way of life and the bullshit that comes with it, check the fuck out on the Thai beaches, schooner in hand, beautiful, stress-free young ladies waiting for us back in our bamboo huts, for sponge baths and four-handed ...'

'See how many STDs we can collect in one calendar year?'

'Chlamydia just means you're having fun,' Magic Matt declared, just in time for the barmaid to come by, picking up the decimated Twisties packet and the dead schooner glasses. 'In jest, in jest,' Matt added, for her information.

'Stay classy,' said Plum.

'What do we think of my two-tiered plan?'

'I like living in Cronulla – God's Own Country.'

'Pride of the South.'

'Yeah, but fuck it off,' Matt said. 'We *did* our bit, we entertained people for twenty years, took the blows. Let's go treat ourselves for the last twenty.'

Peter Lum was almost impossible to ruffle but this got under his skin a bit, and even with the snowstorm playing havoc in the space above his eyes he felt the need to speak out. 'Nup, I'm going to have to stop you there. We were treating *ourselves*, Matty, as far as I'm concerned. We got to play sport and earn money for doing it.'

'Yeah, no, look, I agree, I'm just saying, there's a lifestyle there –'

'It was for us as much as it was for them – it was an honour –'

'I agree.'

'Really?'

'Ok.'

'You're both saying the same thing,' Squeak said. 'You both played the same. You both left nothing out there.'

'I'm not saying it was a chore, Plum. Geez, I was just –'

But Plum was spoiled now, and for some reason he couldn't stop this blinking.

'I gotta go. Charmayne's trying out this new salad on me before we hit the corporate. Check yas.' He drained his light beer and headed out of the place, not without a few half waves to blokes he knew, or knew knew him, or knew knew who he was.

Pete lived on Kurnell Road in a pastel-blue 70s two-bedroom weatherboard with a backyard, right next to a young family called the Wallaces, who were always having people over to see their fountain. He shared the house with his son, Gavin, who'd recently taken it upon himself to disband the half-a-week-with-mum-half-a-week-with-dad plan – 'it's just easier with footy to be at dads and walk to training,' he had explained by text to his mother, Renee, and oddly enough she'd bought it. The other tenant was Pete's girlfriend, Charmayne, who officially lived in a flat she'd bought with her mother in Como but was also finding herself pretty much full-time at Pete's these days. Ainslee, Gavin's girlfriend, might as well have been living with the Lums too, having spent the last six months basically attached to Gavin's hip 24/7; she crawled out of his bedroom window every morning at 6 am to bolt the seven kays to Gymea so she could be home before her family woke up. It was full of life, the Kurnell Road house, and with the recent renovations opening up the space into one big lounge–kitchen–dining area, well, this was just how Peter liked it: busy. The more noise and movement around The Plum, the more he could get away with not saying a lot and just letting time drift by.

So when Plum arrived home to the sound of Ainslee and Gavin shooting baskets in the backyard, he felt good. He was grinning even as he joined the casual skills session.

'Did you play at school, Ainslee?' he asked, passing her the ball.

'I didn't play this sport, no,' said Ainslee. 'Only when they were missing someone.'

'Right.'

Ainslee set herself for the free throw. 'I did well when I did play, but … I don't know, I never really wanted to play basketball for like a team, even though I liked it.' The ball swished through the hoop.

'And yet you're a dead eye!' said Pete, passing the ball to his son, set deep in the corner.

'I'm hopeless,' Gavin said, and then hit one from the corner with a flick of his left wrist.

The kid was genuinely lanky, probably more suited to a height game like basketball than league. Pete had thrown him in with Magic Matt up at Sutho Police Boys for a weekend camp a few years back, but he wasn't having it, Gav – he simply loved footy, and he dug into the line like no one had told him he was a string bean.

'Nothing but net!' Ainslee said, running over to congratulate her man.

The golden afternoon sun got coy behind the horizon ledge where Shark Park met the mangroves and where Captain Cook once went, 'This will do us, chaps.' Pete spun the ball in his hands, watching the black lines blur together, as Ainslee and Gavin half-cuddled, half-wrestled beside the ring that Pete had bolted into the elm tree when his son turned eleven and was momentarily obsessed with Steph Curry of the Denver Nuggets.

'Nothing but white lace,' Gavin said, in an impersonation of an American commentator.

The ball was making Pete feel sick, so he stopped the spin and looked over to the couple. He was amazed at the ease between Gavin and Ainslee. All his own relationships had such an implicit strain underneath them, even in the good times, his partners inevitably leaving him for a more attentive bloke or just turning the volume down on the whole thing, citing Peter Lum as either 'too vague', 'too non-communicative' or just too into 'the boys, the bets and the beer'.

'Hey everyone!' Charmayne said, elbowing the fly screen open while managing not to disrupt her two vivid and voluminous bowls of salad.

'You right there, Charmayne?' Gavin asked, not really going anywhere, Ainslee around his waist.

'Oh yep, I'm balanced,' she said, as she descended the steps. Her curly blonde hair and her height made a goddess-like silhouette, Pete thought.

'This one's goats cheese, roasted beetroot and pomegranate with chunks of pancetta and grated radish with a balsamic and coconut oil vinaigrette,' she said as they all took their seats at the outdoor table, 'and this is a leafless salad I do with baby squash, pear, cauliflower, walnuts and quinoa.'

'KING WAAAAAAA!!!!' announced Pete, to which no one responded. It was a joke Pete had rolled out a hundred times over and it still wasn't funny.

Ainslee poured some sparkling water into her glass and then Gavin's, as always, and then tucked into the salads. 'These are both so good!'

'Which is your favourite?' Charmayne asked, only nibbling at hers.

'KING WAAAAAAA!!!!' said Pete again – and, again, he was ignored.

Gavin shoved a few chunks of pancetta into his mouth. 'I like this first one, but only because it has meat in it – and beetroot is my favourite vegetable next to sweet potato. I love sweet potato. I could live on sweet potato, like not even joking.'

'And kumara has less GI than the potato,' Charmayne said, 'which is why you find it in Keto diet books and such.'

'Oh right, so it's better for you than say a roast potato?'

'Hundred per cent.'

11

'I love it even more than before and I loved it a lot before.'

Charmayne turned to Pete. 'What do you prefer, darling?'

'Yeah,' said Ainslee and Gavin in unison, 'which salad?'

But Peter had left the table after his second 'KING WAAAAAAA!!!!' – not physically but mentally. He had wandered off, baby squash in mouth, still chewing over the bus ride home from the Cazbah. He was baffled as to how on earth the driver turned out to be an Asian woman when he'd been one hundred per cent certain an older American bloke had spoken to him from the driver's seat.

'Peter?'

The 917 bus from Port Hacking Road to Cronulla Station had just edged past where the old Pizza Hut and BBC Hardware used to be when Pete's name had been called out.

'Peter! Hey cock.'

Pete had looked around to see if anyone else had heard it, but the old Greek couple on the other side of the aisle were unmoved, and the twelve-year-olds up the back had just been to swimming and now sat Siamese and ensconced in a serious Snapchat session.

'I said, hey cock! It's me, up front.'

Pete switched his neck to frontwards. In the rear-vision mirror bolted on above the concertina rubber door frame, he made out the reflection of an older man, his smashed-up face crevassed and split open by life, smoking a ciggie and smiling.

'Yeah, now you got me. How you doin today?'

Peter raised his eyebrows and pointed to his chest, poking his finger at his favourite orange Mambo T-shirt.

'Yeah, that's right, I'm talking to you, cock. You doin ok?'

Peter smirked. He'd never heard a driver speak over the intercom before, let alone use the word 'cock' to refer to a passenger.

'It's a rough life, ain't it? But you know what I say, there's always a light at the end of the tunnel, and if there ain't a light, there's always a broad, a bet or a cold beer!' The American bus driver choked on his own laughter, a lifetime of Marlboro Reds interfering with his outpouring of self-awe.

Keen to not engage, as was Plum's nature, he didn't answer.

The driver continued to eyeball him in the mirror. 'What am I? Chopped liver?'

Pete checked out of the chat, returning to his television of choice: the bus window. Americans were always speaking. *No wonder there are so many talk shows over there*, thought Pete. *The only one we ever had was that Rove bloke.*

When the 917 reached Shark Park, Pete hit the red button, stood up and dismounted the bus. His old paddock brought back too many memories and he preferred to face the golf course and just wait for the right time to cross, like when the bus had gone and the highway was free of cars. He watched the bus chortle back to life and it was only when it passed him that he realised it was not a crusty old yank driving it anymore; it was a tiny Asian woman behind the wheel. But by the time this dawned on him it was too late. He was by the golf course now and the bus was heaving towards Kurnell, leaving a powdery puff of pink and grey pollution for the new Fitness First building to choke on.

'Peter, come back to us!' Charmayne, like so many times before, pinched her man on the earlobe, and just like that he was back in the current set-up.

'I like em both,' he said, grinning madly.

'Ha, yeah,' said Gav, because he hated it when his dad went off like that.

'Will you do both of these for Gym N Trim, Char?' asked Ainslee.

'That's not the business name yet. Plum, don't go telling people draft ideas! That was just one of the options. It's not confirmed yet.'

'Sorry, babe. I was just telling em your ideas. It's all good.'

'I like Gym N Trim,' Ainslee said. 'It says it all – plus it's motivating!'

'I like it too,' said Gav.

'Yeah, I think it's a front-runner,' agreed Charmayne.

'There's nothing wrong with it,' concluded Pete, and the family ate in silence for a bit, leaving space in the air for a small rescue dog to bark up a symphony on the left side of the house, and a friend of the Wallaces, who had clearly just temperature-tested the fountain, to scream out, 'Fuck, Kiegan, it's so cold!'

'Gym N Trim is the best one you've thought up for sure,' Pete said, working hard.

This was Charmayne's fifth career move in the five years Pete had been seeing her. Originally from South Africa she'd been a cheerleader with the Sharkettes since she was a teenager. But after snapping her Achilles before a full Remondis Stadium at the age of twenty-seven she'd moved into dance choreography, but this just annoyed her as she wanted to be on the floor with the girls, so she started working at a wine call centre, then began assisting a make-up artist, before putting herself through a Swedish massage course in Strathfield – the phase Pete liked the most – but this didn't last either, and so now it was nutrition, about which she was completely obsessed. She was constantly counting calories and explaining to Pete what 'role' certain foods played in the body and cooking experimental salads every other night. She'd even suggested that they start a café together called 'Plum's Kitchen', with him as the face of it and her doing the administrative stuff and of course the cooking. But what Charmayne didn't quite understand about her bloke was that he may well have the time to pour into such a venture but these days he actually spent a large portion of his week trying to get away from other humans. Other than his mates and his family, he wanted no human contact, as humans were always looking for a photo opportunity, or they just *had* to tell him about how they knew someone who played with him once, or even worse they had some advice to pass on to the current playing group. Pete got more private every day. Charmayne was hurt when he finally gave her a 'No', because she could see the café – the shop front and the vibe and the way it would bring them even closer – but she got over it because she loved him. And fuck did he love her. He never said it to her heaps, but he would kill for his woman, cos she was the person in his life that he could boldly go outside and say had the biggest heart he had come across, and playing a game like rugby league, you come across a few big hearts. You can't really play without one.

'Gym N Trim it is then!' decided Charmayne, raising her glass to the evening sky.

A wiry man in a leather jacket stood on the small blue carpeted stage talking into a cordless mic with a voice that was bigger than him. This bloke was from the radio, Charmayne suspected, looking around for Pete, who had ducked off 'for a slash' some eight to twelve minutes ago. She located Gavin and Ainslee standing together, arm-in-arm, pointing out over the footy field, fantasising of shared glory to come. Charmayne was never the maternal type – she'd rather eat a chair than end up like half her friends, depressed and ballooning with two screaming lunatics to serve – but these two and their pure love for each other, well, the feeling it gave her as their semi-mum was as close as she had ever come to 'the instinct', and she didn't hate it. She scanned on, women and their half-pissed husbands waving as they passed her, coming up to the members lounge from a session in the bar below. Some of the players' wives remembered her from her time in the Sharkette leotard, but rarely did anyone ever stop to talk to her, unless, mind you, she was with Plum. This used to annoy her, but these days, with her passion for Gym N Trim and her increasing sense of self since turning thirty-nine, she could not give a flying fuck what they thought. She felt sorry for *them* now, in a way, collecting all their happiness from one place, one team, one never-changing scene.

Finally, she spotted her man wolfing down a set of chicken skewers and a few party pies in the corner of the room. She wished she was upset at him, he'd barely nudged either of her salads, claiming to be full, but she wasn't *that* girlfriend and also there was something so boyish and adorable about the way he had snuck out to snack behind her back. He was fifty next year but still just a kid. All those footy players stayed kids, she knew that better than anyone – that's why they did all those silly things. They were just little children hiding out in Goliath's scaffolding.

'Ladies and gentlemen, without further ado, it is my honour and my privilege, not only to be here and host this quiz, but to do so with my favourite player, and the prime minister's favourite player – our local hero, the best 13 that ever was … Peter "The Plum" Lum!'

The hundred or so fanatics cheered as Pete wiped his mouth, threw the napkin in the bin, licked his teeth and made his way through the crowd to the stage.

'Here he is!' the radio guy bellowed. 'Plum, get up here, you legend!'

'Thanks mate,' Peter said, taking his own cordless mic and nodding at the worshippers, trying to remember the guy's name. Was it Whizza, or Whacka, or Wocko?

'Good to see you back at the leagues club, mate.'

'It's always nice to enter this place. I rarely remember leaving though.'

Within seconds Pete had turned on his self-deprecating charm, and ex-players, officials, families and friends of competition winners were eating out of their hero's hands – and Pete, well, he just stood there, effortless in his green chinos and black Sharks polo, his highlights reel on loop behind his head. It wasn't until after the interview, until the quiz part, that he started to feel a dull ache in his head, and the slow return of the snowstorm that he'd felt at the pub.

'Two more questions, Plum, and you're free to have a schooner.'

'I'll deserve one after this. Haven't been asked this many questions since Year Eight Maths test.'

The host let the crowd laugh then deepened his voice for the question. 'Who am I? Born in Inverell, I began my career for the Hull Kingston Rovers ...'

Pete's eyes started glazing over.

'... returning to Australia in 1986 where I joined the mighty Cronulla Sharks ...'

The hubbub was already growing – everyone already knew the answer – everyone except Pete, seemingly, who remained dumbstruck, the snowstorm savaging his frontal lobe.

'Inverell ... has ... trots ...' Plum said, fizzing with oblivion. 'Another clue, Wizza?'

Wacka pushed on, assuming Plum was just building tension with the delay. 'I won two successive Dally M Player of the Year awards in 1988 and 1989 – and my unprecedented skill made Cronulla–Sutherland a formidable side after many years in the doldrums ...'

'Oh, yeah, shit,' Pete said, and the audience also started to think that he was having them all on. The man in question was The Plum's favourite player and mentor, the man he widely thanked and gave credit to for all his onfield achievements. Forgetting this bloke's name was like forgetting his PIN. But still the answer didn't come.

'Australian selectors during my brief but brilliant heyday as a lock forward were often criticised for ignoring me ...'

Pete looked around the room, the snowstorm blurring his vision. The faces were eggs on top of shirts.

'... but it is true I had failed to show my skills in a badly beaten New South Wales side during the 1989 State of Origin series ...'

'Ah, yeah,' Pete said. 'I can just about –'

'GAVIN MILLER!' screamed a voice from the side of the room.

The crowd gasped into their beers and rums, then went silent.

Pete swivelled his head to find his son standing there, water bottle in one hand, the other hand palm up with confusion.

'Dad?'

'Yeah, mate?' Pete said, his head now clearing of its blizzard.

'You named *me* after him, Dad. You named me Gavin, after Gavin Miller.'

Pete didn't have a punchline for this one, and he felt like he might shit himself – something in the salads or the skewers maybe. So he handed the cordless mic roughly to the host, waved to the silent floor and left the room, flicking a look to Charmayne on his way out – as if to say 'Let's hit the frog and toad.'

As soon as they got home, out of the Uber and into the hall, Pete was at her, kissing her neck and removing her floral dress while leading her to the bedroom.

'I wanna be inside ya,' he said. 'Let me get inside ya, love. I wanna be in ya.'

Charmayne loved all this business because Pete was so much more expansive with his body than he was with his words, and so it was here that she felt the confirmation of what she often questioned outside the house: that he loved *her* and wanted *her* all of the time. But now, tonight, after his strange loss of lucidity at the club, she felt something else moving in and out of her; a sense of loss or need in the night, the boy was back, and it was like he wished to never have to go out into the dark on his own ever again, fearing monsters and wolves, and all sorts of ghouls that reality had manifested just to pray on little Plum boy.

As he rose towards the goal line, though, alarm bells rang in her body and brain. 'Plum, stop, Plum, please, Plum, get out of me!' she finally screamed.

'Hey?' he said, rolling to the side of her and panting with more confusion than ever. 'Char?'

'You don't cum inside me, Plum. Remember? That's the rule!'

'What did I do?' he asked, feeling the jizz migrating over and down his inner thigh.

'We get off at Redfern, remember? I don't want no pill and you don't want no condom, so we get off at Redfern!'

'Or Sutho?' Pete joked, reaching for her wet place, but she wasn't playing about.

'No, Redfern. The stop before Central. That's our rule.' Charmayne propped herself up onto her elbows, stern as he'd seen her. 'You know this, right?'

Pete grabbed a pair of Lonsdale shorts off the linen press and headed for the kitchen. 'I'm going to get an OJ. You want juice? Anything?'

'No,' said Charmayne, bewildered. 'No, I do not.'

The next morning came quick. With Brick outside in his Hilux at 5.30 am, Pete slid out of bed and cleared the chamber without Charmayne even missing a beat in her skipping sort of snore. He couldn't put his finger on what he'd done wrong last night but he knew it wasn't his best offering. Being an athlete, a player, meant Pete had learnt and perfected the art of forgetting. Forgetting was a crucial arrow in his kitbag. The ability to delete the last shit pass, bombed try or simple conversion was essential. Just breathe deep, shake it off and look to the next movement – and Peter employed this well-honed skill possibly too often in his relationships. Move on and don't look back, just focus on the current shift and hope to God you don't hear a bloody whistle.

'All good, Plum?' Brick asked, croaky as Madge Bishop from *Neighbours*.

'Doesn't get any earlier, does it?'

'Nah.'

Pete rubbed his cold hands together, half a banana rolling about in his mouth and the other half in Brick's. This was all they needed to fuel the morning beach run – anything more would interrupt things. Half a banana and an Eclipse mint and get in!

Brick switched on Triple M. 'How was last night?'

'Hey?'

'How was the corporate, the competition winner thing, at the Leagues …?'

'Oh yeah, normal,' Pete said, wishing he'd had a shit before departure.

'Charmayne go with ya?'

Pete nodded.

'You're lucky you shook Cazbah when you did. Bloody Squeak tipped us into a Superfecta, next thing we're on the snort back at his. Fucken lunatic stuff.'

'Have you been to sleep?'

'Three bells I think it was. Yeah. I crashed on Squeaky's couch for a bit.'

'How was the surface?'

'Been sleeping on my own couch for the past eighteen months - so not too bad actually.'

'Is that right?'

'That's right …' said Brick, breaking into a heinous cough.

'Well, don't have a heart attack on the beach. I never finished me St Johns Ambulance.'

It was a grey old whipping morning, making small promises of a sunny day, as Peter and Brick flicked their sandals off – wrapped em up in a towel with the car key, shoved the towel into a shrub, and pushed into the soft sand. Brick was a lot heavier than Pete but this didn't stop him getting along the beach. He was fit as fuck – running a boxing gym would do that to you – and he ate pretty good. The only flaws on his sculpture were the twenty daily schooners evident round the hip area. Brick Wall was the living epitome of 'fit and fat', and the soft sand knew of both.

'Jog on!' they said as one, tapping backs of hands.

Pete and Brick did this run every Monday, Wednesday and Thursday without fail, up to Kurnell on the soft sand, back to Cronulla in the wet, quick dip, takeaway coffee and home. This had them in the shower by 7 am with yesterday's cobwebs floating out to sea and thinking that maybe a few cold ones in the arvo were more than deserved, once the chores were done and the missus was on board, of course.

'Morning Plum!' 'G'day Pete!' 'Go you Sharkies!' bellowed the passers-by: fired-up couples letting their tiny white yappers go nuts in the short water; older people walking hand in hand hoping they lived to see another premiership; or just locals, people he'd once met in the twelve items or less line at Coles. Bloody nearly every bastard who went by had some kind of offering to Pete, it was like it was on the syllabus, and for Pete there was no escaping it – his running flow in constant interruption, having to raise a left arm and then a right arm to wave to the breathers with every second step; Brick often mimicked it, privately wondering why they didn't cry out 'Brick' at all.

But this morning the boys were both out of sorts. Where Brick would usually be pushing ahead, running backwards even, enticing Pete to jog harder, faster, he was hiding in a trot, wishing the whole thing over, his body still marinating in beer and gin and cocaine and beer and ciggies and rum and cocaine and beer. Plum ran ahead, head down. He was done with the ritual today, and by the time they reached the curve he swore to himself if one more person called out his name he might just snap and ask them where they'd met, and if they never had, then why the fuck were they talking to him? But this would get back and he knew it. Cronulla was an insular peninsula and keeping up appearances was all the rage, so when a couple in their late thirties waved over at Pete from where they were beach fishing, he went nup and ducked left up the sand dune. Riding the crest of the grassy lip, he spotted a puddle-patched path, leading up towards a cliff face.

Brick, coughing up hell, followed him for a bit, but the dunes got steep and so the still-pissed boxing brute stopped to catch some salt air. 'Plum! What are you fucken doing? Let's work back!'

But Plum wasn't having it. He delved left and further inland with gusto, finding a sweet and steady trot, dodging deep puddles and wonky jutting-out ruts, making his way into sharp pastel reeds and then following an emerging fence line down into a sand valley, where Peter caught glimpses of 'Developing Kurnell', a popular and dividing topic at Sutherland Shire dinner parties. Not having to wave at cunts now, he used his elbows as wings and lost his prop mate way back, picking up pace with every discovered stretch of land. Stranger Country. Like being on the moon but a salt moon. Pete was amazed at the overly spacious, jog-friendly surrounds, wondering why there weren't more people doing what he was, and why he and Brick had never broken off the sand laneways and had a gander at what went on over yonder. He'd come here a bit with footy back in the day, the Kurnell sand hills, those brutal military style drills, and a few times as a teen getting ripped and sliding down the dunes on cardboard boxes, and maybe once with his mum and sister to check out where they shot *Mad Max*, but not here, not where he was, and not how it was now. This was alien. Just so beautiful and alien, just so wonderfully … not like anything he knew in this town, and up until now he believed he knew the lot. He got to a clearing, still with plenty of puff, where a sign to Cape Bailey suggested he veer left and continue up the rocky pathway to where a lighthouse presented itself, white and tall and innocent. Pete said 'Fuck' to himself, and then stopped, looking around the place for human ruckuses, but there was nothin, just a Gore-Tex draped on a branch a bit of a way off, and a snapped surfboard down near the inlet to what appeared to be a petite, perfect beach. As he got closer to the lighthouse, the alien-ness swerved into a new dimension and Pete started to feel like he had been here before, even though he knew he hadn't. The bulging, virginal sensation of the familiar made him start to laugh even, for the more he shook his head in amazement at the strange, other-worldly surrounds, the more he felt like this was something he had done before, in this same body, in this same lifetime.

'Fuck, bro.'

Every fucking step, every fucking breath, every fucking puddle and leaf and seagull and poke of fresh sunlight was from an already day he had already done.

'No,' Pete said to the whipping, salty wind. 'This is all new to me.'

But it wasn't. And as the lighthouse presented itself just metres away now, Pete was trapped in the most intense sense of déjà vu he had ever had.

This is repeating.
This is not original.
This is sequel.
This is already?

Pete pressed his face against the cool white cement of the lighthouse and instantly fell asleep standing up. Minutes passed in somnambulance. Plum's head connected to the lighthouse. Then, out of nowhere, them cauliflower ears on either flank of his cranium caught wind of his best-ever friend's far-off desperate scream: 'Plum! Where is ya, mate? It's me, Brick Wall!'

Plum pushed off the lighthouse, electric with recognition, towards the sea.

Eleven years Plum had been working at Qantas domestic airport, eight of those in the baggage department and now three pulling planes out to the runways. He loved the job, it was mindless and physical, and the boys he worked with were sound. They had an NRL tipping comp, 'the Tarmac Tippers', and looked after each other, even though they were all well aware of how far down the airline pecking order they were. Squeaky had got him the job when post-footy life had reared its ugly head and Pete had found himself not wanting to stay in the game. He wasn't interested in making his way up to the commentary box in a blazer like them other tossers, or hiding out in the sheds with a Powerade and a towel pretending he was of use – none of that caper was for him. So he took the tip, signed on and didn't look back, even though Squeak quit as soon as Pete began and devoted himself to full-time punting by buying a weekly syndicate off a bloke in Perth and massaging outcome via that set of stats. But it turned out a blessing in the end – Squeak quitting, not the syndicate – cos, for Pete, going to work was like diving into a voluntary void: he didn't have to talk to anyone for ten hours. Just head down arse up and sweet blissful anonymity.

So after his toast with egg, bacon and sausage on it, a muesli bar and a glass of cold OJ, Pete jumped in the Subaru Forester and drove past Sans Souci to Botany, watching the planes lifting up overhead, which always made him smile cos it was like he was off someplace too.

Pete swiped in at the staff carpark, proceeding to the domestic terminal airside through a security checkpoint, which involved a hands-in-the-air, how's-your-father full-body scan.

No gloves up the rectus, but a fair bit of inner thigh and tickle. Then it was time to collect his radio, fire up the iPad, insert the three passwords and check on the allocated work. With a flight in waiting, Pete located the vehicle he was to man, and did a quick radio check with Air Traffic Control to confirm driving on aprons and live taxiways was all good with them. Pete mounted the leather seat, praying it wasn't already too warm – nothing worse than another guy's bum energy – and proceeded to the bay on his tug, connecting the tow bar to a plane with the help of Graham, the ground engineer, who was never that nice, to be honest, and wasn't now. Once the plane was fully trimmed and boarded, the pilot contacted ATC for permission to suggest pushback. With the beacon started, the engineer and Pete communicated that all was clear, baggage on and sides locked up, then it was time for Pete to proceed with the brake release and start pushing the plane onto the tarmac. This was his favourite bit, where it was just him and the plane moving away from civilisation. It reminded him of the moment when you broke the defensive line in footy and the crowd took that collective breath.

Once out onto the taxiway, Pete came to rest, disconnecting his vehicle now that the plane's brakes were on. All set to bugger off into the sky. Pete moved away from the plane, confirming completion over his radio and waiting for the next allocated plane. All good fun in an adult-Lego sort of way but a bit ground-hoggish when you thought about it. And today was no different. Pete went about another push, clicking on an Airbus A330 destined for Hobart. He waved to the ground staff, flicked on the beacon light, nodded to Graham and then pulled the lever back to D.

'All locked up here, beacon on, permission to push please,' he said into his radio.

'Push granted, thanks Peter,' said Bel, the only female ATC officer, and off he went, turning the key in the ignition of his humble tug, and beginning his push out onto the smaller apron, just round the bend behind terminal three. Pete liked this push, as it was the one with the most distance to travel, guaranteeing him at least five to seven minutes driving, whereas the terminal one and two-ers would only give you three to four.

Pete led the A330 onto the apron, where an Air New Zealand airbus could be seen bursting through a puffy white cloud above the Harbour Bridge, and a light aircraft for Mudgee or Orange was starting to fire up just to the right of him. He blinked, and started to feel that weird snowstorm sensation again, or like he might vomit. There were spots everywhere he looked.

'Ah, fuck.'

Blinking like a freak now, Pete shrugged it off and kept pushing, the apron stop point now only a hundred-ish feet away. He smiled, turning the wheel to the left as the Hazelton Airlines' seventy-seater began its take-off sprint. The Air New Zealand flight was also now within a minute of landing, and all Pete had to do was stop, stop, stop his tugger ... about now. But he couldn't quite feel his feet to brake and his arms were tingling with the buzz of a billion bees. He felt spit coming down the right side of his chin and his eyes were closing with that harsh static brain blizzard again. *This is a turn of sorts*, he thought, *but it'll be over soon*. His eyes closed to claim a re-set, but instead started watching a slideshow. The lighthouse. Gavin as a baby. Charmayne's eyes. Scoring a try in State of Origin. Mum's funeral in the rain. Bradley Clyde hugging him in the rain. His sister, Sarah, in their cubby. Gavin Miller. Oktoberfest with the boys. Naked tits. A polaroid of his father's face. Bolognese in Italy. Renee at the wedding ...

Everything noisy ...

Everything like childhood ...

Then everything to black.

And the plane went towards the plane.

They would not stop him, they said, but they could not let him drive the Forester home, even though he said he felt fine. It didn't help his case that when they asked him where he wanted to go he kept saying different cities – clearly, still not quite in the room. So Barnabus the safety officer and Lee-Anne from HR called Peter's listed next of kin, who, at the time, was in a mums and bubs screening of *Little Women*.

'Oh God, what's he done now?' Renee shrieked, making sure the other mums knew she had a drama on her hands by putting the call on speaker as she dragged her pram out of the aisle.

When she got to the airport she found Peter slumped on an orange plastic chair in the medical room, sipping on a cloudy apple juice through a straw. He looked like a ten-year-old boy who had lost his parents at Miranda Westfield, where she had just been, gently ensconced in Timothée Chalamet's broken Lothario.

'Where are we going?' said Pete, as he buckled himself into the passenger seat of Renee's white Kia.

'To Sutherland Hospital.'

'Why? Is the kid sick?' he asked, looking around at six-month-old Tallulah in the back.

'No, Pete. You are.'

'I'm not sick.'

'Alright.'

'Where does it say I'm sick?'

'It doesn't say it.'

'So just let me get my car.'

'You're not allowed to drive.'

'I drove a plane out onto the runway. I can drive a car home …'

Renee pulled over, instantly transported to the tone and texture of their marital blues in their big brown house on Woolooware Road.

'You nearly towed a plane into another incoming plane, Pete, plus another one about to take off!'

'Hey?'

'You nearly killed a lot of people.'

'No way. Fake news. Geez, Renee.'

'Didn't they tell you what happened? Before I turned up? Peter, they must have. Are you still unconscious or are you just being an immature shit to get at me?'

'I had a turn. I had a moment. No one got hurt.'

'Well. Good. But the safety officer said we need to see a neurologist.'

'He said we *could* if we wanted to. He didn't say we *had* to. I heard the fucken info!' Pete said, and the baby started crying.

It wasn't the first, second or even third time Pete and Renee had sat in a hospital waiting room together, and there was something about it that seemed to ease things between them. It was a place, historically, where they worked well. Survival mode suited them. Like when Gavin broke his leg surfing off Shark Island, or when Renee had her four miscarriages, or the fifty times Pete had to get scans on his back, or that one time they walked out of a hospital with a pram, no idea and a newborn bloody baby. All of those times brought the husband and wife closer together and something was always gained from the horror or the hope, but this time, well, they hadn't been married for a decade and Renee didn't seem to want to be there, at least in Peter's weary mind she didn't. Plus, Plum was embarrassed that Renee was still listed as his next of kin at work, an observation she was surely dying to make, if given half a chance.

'From what we can gather, Mr Lum, you've had a seizure,' said the junior neurologist, standing next to the other junior neurologist, and Renee could not help wondering how long ago these two puppies were on the razz at schoolies week.

'All good then. Can we go?' Pete said, clutching his Bupa card.

'Just a few more questions, Mr Lum.'

'Call me Peter, please. I'm not your teacher.'

Pete and Renee were sitting and the two trainee doctors were standing, and it was impossible to tell which one of them was more senior as they both had clipboards and neither seemed to even consider what the other was thinking.

'We just have a few questions, Peter,' said the taller one with the iPhone ear bud case on his keychain and a patchy excuse for a moustache.

'What ones? How many? How long?'

For the first time, the two young practitioners looked at each other. 'Fifteen minutes to half an hour?' they chorused.

'I've been in this hospital more times than you've been to the movies so why don't you look at me history, swing us a script for headaches or what and I'll be off,' Pete said, wishing he was hitting the heavy bag at Brick's Boxing Gym right now.

'Have you been experiencing headaches?' asked the junior neuro with the moustache.

'No more than any bloke. You know – couple here and there? Nothing a beer won't fix.'

'How often do you take drugs or alcohol – and what do you take if you do?' asked the other one, slightly shorter but with a protruding jaw like Conan O'Brien.

'Drugs and alcohol? I wasn't drunk, son. I was at work.'

'That's not what he is asking,' said Renee, mopping up pumpkin from Tallulah's chin.

'Do you drink alcohol regularly?' Moustache asked.

'No more than anyone.'

'So you drink normal amounts of alcohol?'

'Yes siree.'

'Bullshit,' sneezed Renee.

'How many units a day?' said Conan.

'Depends …'

'On what?' helped Moustache.

'On whether it's a day ending with Y,' Renee said. 'Now just be honest, Peter, or I'll tell them.'

'How would you know how much I drink, Renee? You're not in my life.'

'How would I know? Because your fucking drinking is one of the reasons why one of us isn't wearing a wedding ring anymore! Now tell the kids the truth!'

Pete looked down at his ring finger and, even though the jewellery was gone now, the lines were still evident up close, and so too the feeling of being linked to this woman.

'I'd say I have five, sometimes six or even, yeah, more beers a day … and like, maybe a few wines at night? Share a bottle with my girlfriend if she's up for it.'

Conan wrote it down. 'Do you have any AFDs?'

'What's that?'

'Alcohol Free Days,' said Renee, Conan and Moustache as one smug force.

'I didn't drink for the first fourteen years of my life, and since then I think I've had a few days off with the flu. How's them facts?'

Renee tried to hide the fact she was amused by suddenly burying her face into the chest of her baby. *The cheeky prick*, she thought.

'And what about drugs,' Conan asked. 'Do you take any prescription or party drugs?'

'The more honest you can be here the better,' Moustache confirmed.

Pete was all set to approximate when Kanye West's 'Gold-digger' hit came bursting out of Conan's pocket in the form of a ringtone, which the young doctor quickly shut down, apologising with a crease of his gills to Moustache.

'You done with your dance party there, son?' said Pete,

snarling like he once did when footy was footy and scrums were scrums.

'Sorry.'

'So. Drugs, Peter?'

'I'm not the drugs bloke but, yeah, I'll smoke a vegan cig every now and again, the odd line of rack and roll, pop a biccy at the races maybe two or three times a year, but no, that's a young man's game these days – isn't it, boys?' said Pete, looking up to find two blank-faced 25-year-olds who he guessed had never, to this day, ever been slightly tipsy let alone high.

'So it's safe to say you do burn the candle, Mr Lum?'

'The candle is out – I think it's safe to say,' Renee proffered.

'Candles are expensive,' Pete said. 'Scented candles.'

Conan chose to ignore this. 'Is your life stressful?'

'No more than anyone else's?'

An onslaught of interrogation ensued, with each blow making Peter more and more sure he was doing life wrong: 'How much sleep do you get?' followed by 'Do you have a history of brain issues in the family?' into 'Have there been any recent incidents you can remember that were out of the ordinary?' via 'Do you suffer from vertigo?' onto the pinnacle of 'Did you ever play contact sport at all?'

'Ha!' said Renee, and then peered down the back of her baby's nappy and took a big whiff.

'Why?' asked Plum, coy now, and also afraid for himself – and, yeah, afraid for Gavin, whose grand final was now only days and hours away.

'Well, sir, seizures are tricky. Look, two per cent of the population will have them in their lifetime. It's a thing that *does* happen –'

'So how do they ... how did I ... if I got one then why did it happen to ... me?'

'Oh, darling Plum,' said Renee, ultimately happy to be his next of kin.

'They can be genetic or they can be caused by risk factors. Stress and a bad lifestyle is the most common cocktail.'

'And if you played footy for a living?' asked Renee.

The youths looked to each other, realising what they were dealing with and that it was pretty much out of their reach in terms of medical experience. Conan knew he recognised the patient from somewhere, but Moustache was still looking at him as a collection of atoms and arteries draped in a shirt and shorts.

'Just tell me what now and then we can go, ok?' said Pete, being an adult finally.

'We suggest you don't drink or operate heavy machinery, including a car, for at least six months … but Liz will do some scans and an EEG when you see her.'

'Six months?'

'Who is Liz?' Renee asked.

'I can't work, or drink piss? At all?'

'What happened to you could be anything, Peter, but our early conclusion is that regardless of what caused the seizure you had this morning, you can't push it to the limit any longer. The brain is a vulnerable organ, and it sounds to us like your brain in particular is trying it's best to let you know that it is not coping.'

And then Kanye West started up in Conan's pocket again and the millennial medics were gone, sending Pete and Renee off with a screaming, pooey baby and a contact for Liz Lombardo, Doctor of Neurology, specialising in strokes and epilepsy.

On the way back to Kurnell Road it was imperative that Renee drop past De La Salle to pick up Zoe and Tyson, her husband Ollie's kids, whom Pete was not a big fan of. Pete sat in the back and, as a storm talked itself into business over the coastline, Tallulah's six-month-old hand looped itself around his little finger, which made the former NSW Origin player and Cronulla Sharks immortal feel less doomed and like it might be ok. He just needed to go easy for a bit.

As soon as he got inside the house, Peter flung open the fridge and cracked a cold tin of New. He was onto his third in a flash, then fourth, then fifth, chopping up carrots and onions with a spring in his step. Wednesday was his night to do the cooking and Gavin always appreciated a few serves of Pete's spaghetti bolognese – so giddy up and hold the parmesan.

A howl of 'Dad!' rolled down the hallway with the inevitable clang of the screen door and Ainslee and Gav burst into the kitchen lathered in sweat.

'Hey, Mr Lum, did Gavin tell you we're going to go to Bali?' Ainslee asked.

Gavin pulled out the jug of iced water and lemon wedges from the fridge. 'We're not going yet. Ains just looked it up.'

'Oh yeah?' said Pete, ducking into the fridge behind Gavin, seeking out the sweet chilli sauce, his secret ingredient – a bit of sweetness amid the savoury.

'Well, yeah,' Ainslee said, 'if you win Jersey Flegg on Saturday – but that's a given.'

Gavin tried not to catch his dad's eye, cos Pete and Gavin didn't like to talk about games too much until it was game day. That's when Pete went in for the pump-up. Just the two of them in the Subaru, 'Monsters' by Something for Kate on the stereo, and Plum telling his son stories of how he won what seemed to be unwinnable games. Prior to this, there was not much use going on about it. It only made you overthink things, and Pete was always on about the danger of overthinking things.

'Bali, ay?' Plum said to his son.

'Thinking about it.'

'How's that work?'

'Few players from the girls league are going … and a few players from our side.'

Pete took a slug of his beer. 'Year Twelves?'

'Well, yeah, Ainslee and her team are mostly Year Twelves, but ... So I'd be, yeah ...'

'And so yeah you're in Year Ten still. Not Year Twelve. Like Ainslee and her mates.'

And it was true, Gavin was the youngest player in his Jersey Flegg team, the Sharks under-19s pathways side, and he had beaten out kids two or three years older than him to claim the number 6 jumper, and there was no disputing the decision.

'You can travel by yourself at sixteen,' Ainslee said, 'if you have −'

'If you have what?'

'If you have permission, Dad.'

'Yeah, if you said it was ok, Mr Lum.'

Ainslee looked to Gavin. They'd discussed the game plan. He just had to convert the effort.

'And you did, um, once you did ... say ... you said if I wanted I could not do Year Eleven, like if I didn't want to. Like Kane and me other mates who dropped out for labouring, you said I could drop out for footy, because also you said you dropped out of school for footy and −'

'Hey hey hey!' Pete said, stirring the bog and clicking his neck from side to side. 'One minute we're talking holidays, now it's dropping out of school?'

'Who's dropping out?' Charmayne came in from the back deck with her iPad and her headphones all connected up.

'Good timing,' Pete said and cracked open the bottle of riesling he had ready to go: a splash for the sauce and a glass for his missus put the world in good stead.

'Lovely,' Charmayne said, looking into the pot and for a second thinking about sticking her pinkie into it before Pete pre-empted her with a sizeable shove of 'no' to this notion.

'Ok, don't shove me,' she said, not quite annoyed but close to it.

She took the glass of wine and started setting the table properly, not the half-arsed Peter version that was on offer: cutlery bunched and wet with some plates stacked up beside them, and newspapers, socks and chaos all dotted about the eating place.

'I'm not dropping out ... I just was saying that ... I was just ... Ainslee?'

'We were just thinking about going to Bali for schoolies with some of my friends and some of Gavin's friends from footy – if everything goes ok on Saturday and you give the nod.'

'Your parents have given you the nod?'

'Yeah, as long as they know where we're staying, and we can get a cheap place there. It's kind of been a healthy alternative to the Gold Coast for years now, ay.'

'Just ask Schapelle Corby that,' Pete said, to which Charmayne scoffed.

'I'm still just thinking about Saturday, Dad. But yeah if we win, I've got money saved up from working at Woollies, so I could mostly afford the flights and shit.'

'But you're still just thinking about Saturday?' said Pete, locking eyes with his son.

Ainslee pulled off her sweaty T-shirt and put on a clean one over her sports bra. 'He's been talking about nothing else.'

'I'm sure, I'm sure,' said Pete, looking at the two sweaty, horny, loved-up youths.

Charmayne jumped in, closing down her pink iPad by holding that one button. 'I went to Ubud once with the girls. It was really beautiful. I didn't go to Kuta, though.'

'Mr Lum? Did you ever go to Bali?'

'No, it's not on my list, Ainslee. I don't need to drink illusion shakers in a bar in Indonesia –'

Charmayne rolled her eyes. 'But you do go to Thailand with the boys.'

'That's for golf.'

'Oh, yeah, golf. The great game of golf. Where are your clubs?'

'Provided!'

'I think you're swinging a different club over there. At least I know some of you are.'

'What happens on tour ...' Pete said, winking at his lady and shaking his hips.

She slapped him across the ribs, laughing in disgust. 'Wrap it up!'

'We're not going to take drugs or anything, Dad, we're just going to go on bushwalks and swim in waterfalls and, like, have fun together.'

'And canyons!'

'Yeah, like canyons. It's not like daredevil shit or nothing. Just pleasant aspects?'

'Focus on fucken Saturday and then you can come back to me about Bali and its pleasant aspects, ok?' said Pete, and a chilly wind whipped through the kitchen–dining area. 'Ok?'

Gavin looked to Ainslee, who looked to Charmayne, who raised her threaded eyebrows with faint positivity. This allowed Pete to check himself by spinning round and returning to the pot, sucking on his sixth beer and wondering why he felt a bit like his own dad all of a sudden.

'Darl, where's your car?'

'That'd be a good movie, Char,' Pete joked. *Darl, Where's Your Car?*'

'It's not in the drive.'

'Oh yeah, it's just your one in the drive, Charmayne,' confirmed Ainslee, all over everything that ever happened.

'Dad,' said Gavin, still rattled by Pete's outburst.

'Darl, where's my car?' Pete joked in an American accent, grabbing a hunk of buttery bread and sliding it through the meaty puddle of bolognese left in his bowl.

Charmayne loathed these late-night carb loads Pete dished up but at the same time she had never dated a bloke who ever bothered to cook, so she complied. 'Are you going to answer me, love?' she asked him, trying to get more sauce than pasta onto her fork.

'It's still at work.'

'Why? Did you have a few beers afterwards?'

'No, I just … Um, yeah no, it was just …' With the whole seizure and everything, plus the session with Renee and the junior neurologists, Pete had not spared a thought for the Subaru and its abandonment, let alone the time to draft a good excuse. 'A bloke at work is thinking of buying a Forester, so I said he could, um, he could, um, have a go at mine for a few days.'

'Really?'

'So he's got it until the weekend, I think.'

'Oh. Which guy? That's pretty generous.'

'Just this young bloke. Greek, I think. Stavros.'

'Stavros has your Subaru?'

'Yeah, that is correct. Stavros has my Subaru. Good movie title there too.'

'And so how are you going to get to work?'

'Stavros is going to pick me up. On the corner.'

'Does he have the same shifts as you this week?'

'Not all of them, no.'

'Ok, then.'

'Yeah.'

'So he won't drive you all of the days?'

'Not all but most.'

'Well, that's not that convenient for you.'

'It's all good.'

'Is it?'

'Who wants ice cream?'

The family ate in relative silence, enjoying a few slices of pineapple with vanilla diet ice cream on the couch in front of

Married at First Sight. It was the last episode of the season, and Pete could easily believe the idiots getting married would do so without meeting their other half but he could not believe anyone would take advice from the boneheaded hosts. They never got it right and they didn't exactly look happy themselves; in conclusion, the hosts were the A1 clingers. He voiced this belief once more as the show wrapped up, and then the teenagers shuffled off to bed like they always did, with Pete once again wondering how his teenage son was so utterly relaxed in a relationship. Never a worry for the lad. Whereas Pete was always bumping into walls with love. He and Charmayne had been together a stretch, but it had been far from a smooth ride – and Renee, well, she was always slamming doors back in the day, screaming at him to be out less and around more, to listen and understand, for it to be two-way traffic not just one in the caring departments, and, geez, she had lungs on her. She could really go when she wanted to. Whereas Charmayne, she just went quiet, but you knew inside she was hurting when they fought. And he hated that, he hated hurting her because she was good, this one. She had a good heart and would do anything for anyone. She was that fucking special, Char, and a serious looker. She'd win all them shows.

As he and Char got ready for bed, Renee's words configured in Pete's head, the ones she repeated when she drove him home this arvo, all three kids in the vehicle: *Tell your girlfriend what happened. Don't be a dick, Pete. Communicate with this one.*

'Do you mind putting your phone in the other room please, love?' asked Charmayne, taking off her panties and bra, then throwing on one of Pete's old St Helens training shirts.

'Phone out? Yep rightio.'

This was a new thing. Ever since one of her friends had had a breast cancer scare she'd been all about not having anything digital in the sleeping space. Pete flicked up the silent switch then lobbed his iPhone into the hall, shutting the door.

'Thanks, oh, I'm cold,' said Char, getting in and under, feeling full and regretful from all the carbs and ice cream she'd sent down the tunnel again.

'One tick,' Pete said, trying to work out the alarm clock.

'What are you doing with the clock?'

'I have to set me alarm cos my phone's in the hall.'

'Just scroll to the time you want then hold down "alarm".'

'Yeah, I know how to do it,' Pete said, not really ever knowing how to do it, just fluking it once or twice since they bought the item three weeks ago.

Why couldn't he just keep his phone on aeroplane mode and do the alarm that way? But the thing with women was, you had to let them have the easy ones. That was the tip from his old man, as well as 'don't fight with women at night – wait till the morning', and this should have been an easy one, if Pete had read the manual before throwing it in the recycling.

'Hurry up, I feel like a cuddle.'

'Hold your horses.'

'You've probably only got about thirty seconds, Plum, and I'll be asleep.'

'That's ok,' said Pete, wondering why the numbers were flashing at him now and if he had maybe just changed the actual time. 'I don't need to have it anyway.'

'That's pretty sexy, babe – you *don't need to have it?*'

'I reckon that's a win,' said Pete, climbing into bed and quickly rolling his wide right arm around her slim waist, plunging his face and then eyelids right into that slender neck of hers.

'I'm wearing your old training shirt again.'

'I like it, I'm smelling plums.'

'All you footy players just wanna fuck yourselves anyway, right?'

'Or each other, that's why we have scrums. Pack her in ...'

An innocent yelp, a thud and then a joint giggle drifted in from down the hall, and Charmayne paused, her left hand now firmly clenching Pete's shaft. 'What are they doing down there?'

'What do you think?' said Pete, just about full bone.

'Feels weird to have sex at the same time as the children.'

'If we went by that protocol, we'd never have sex.'

'Why is that?'

'Because they're always at it those two! You'd think a fifteen kay jog before dinner might tire them out a little, but –'

Another giggle and yelp emanated, and Pete rolled onto his back. Charmayne flicked the hair out of her face, equally happy to call it off, bloated as fuck.

'Are you going to let him go to Bali with her?'

'Look, I think we both know I'm a pushover. But getting past Renee will be a different issue. She already thinks they're way too serious.'

'Have you seen her lately, Plum?' asked Charmayne, her head now resting on his chest that sprouted long golden-brown hairs from within its faded Tahiti singlet.

'Who?'

'Renee?'

'Why do you ask?'

'Just curious. Can't I –'

'Few texts, that's about it, I think –'

'I want to see that baby of hers again, Tallulah, she's sooooooo cute.'

'Getting big too, and strong.'

'Did you see her?'

'Who?'

'Tallulah!'

'No.'

'Then how do you know?'

Plum blinked. 'Gavin showed me a photo from when he stayed there.'

'He hasn't stayed there for ages.'

'Visited. What's with the Angela Lansbury tonight?'

'The what?'

'The Spanish Inquisition.'

'I'm sorry. I just think her baby is —'

'Well, I think there's going to be a christening, so you can do your ogling then.'

Ainslee omitted a glass-cracking scream then a giggle.

'She better not get pregnant,' Charmayne said, peering up at Pete.

'Get off at Redfern, you reckon?'

'Oh, you remembered that one today, that's nice. Maybe you can remember it the next time you're inside me.'

'When will that be, do you think?'

She took her hand and placed it round his floppy cock and then let it go; there was to be no army today, no force to be reckoned with. Pete was a footy player when it came to sex: whistle blew and it was on, if not then he was in the ice bath. So instead of rooting he craned his neck around once more to check the alarm clock.

'What's the alarm for?'

'Thursday tomorrow. Sand sessions with Brick.'

'I thought you weren't doing it tomorrow?'

'Hey?'

Charmayne knew she was on uncertain ground here but she pushed on regardless. 'I spoke to Brick this afternoon and he said he'd sent you a WhatsApp, said he was pulling the plug — because you nearly killed him … running off into the sand dunes or something.'

Plum was blinking fast, the snowstorm in his head collecting momentum again. 'Why were you talking to Brick on the phone?'

'Why are we accusing each other of things tonight?'

'You tell me,' Pete said, trying to breathe good breaths and to keep both his eyes open.

'He's interested in my salad.'

'He's fucken what?'

'Don't get funny, please. He just said he wants to taste my stuff next week, because he says he is looking to put a pop-up café in the outside entrance bit with, like, fresh juices and, and salads, or like healthy wraps, and you told him I was doing the nutrition and the salad-making course at TAFE, so he was just keen. He's keen –'

'I'm sure he is keen.'

'Isn't Brick your best friend?'

Pete was fucking raging. The storm in his skull was fucking raging. He swallowed hard because never in his life had he felt this out of his depth, without any sort of understanding or set of skills to take the pain away. He wasn't in the places he liked: pub, gym, stadium. He wasn't dressed and ready, he did not have the ball in hand.

'Hey, Pete, are you going to answer me or are you just going to lie there like a log?'

And then Ainslee yelped again from down the hallway and the alarm started pulsing with low, bass-like repetitions and that was it. Pete was out of bed quicker than Andrew Ettingshausen, and the alarm clock – that quiet boxy piece of time-technology that fit inside his gorilla-scale mitt like an orange – well, it was mightily flung, shot-putted one could say, into the bedroom door with terrifying, gladiatorial intent, separating into red and black pieces, then flopping about and buzzing to its end. Pete grunted gusts of confusion and quiet undealt-with man-pain into the carpet – a short, off-white shagpile that he had picked out with the help of Renee's schoolfriend Phoebe who knew the Cassacelli family well and got him quite the deal at Cronulla Carpets.

'I'll just get up when you do,' Pete said, turning back to the bed, but Charmayne was now up and about, shoving her stuff into a calico bag and dressing, tears and sweat forming one thick and salted line of liquid down her face. 'Charmayne? Where are you going? Your salads are great, it's no surprise that Brick wants to whack em on his premises. I'd snap em up too if I –'

'You barely eat my salads. You're full of shit.'

'Babe, what's going on?' he said, on the move towards her now. 'It's just a clock.'

'Don't you dare touch me,' she said, pointing at the bit between his eyebrows. 'You know I grew up with that shit. Don't you dare.'

'Possum?'

'No "possum"! I'm going home now and please do not try and stop me or I will call the fucking cops. I'm not even kidding.'

And he didn't stop her. He just stood there in his shredded old singlet, balls swinging in the cold air, as her RAV4 could be heard making its way out of Cronulla, past Gymea and Sutherland to Como–Jannali, where her Cape Town-born psychiatrist mother would wake up on her daughter's arrival and they would sit at the kitchen table drinking gin and tonics until 4.31 am, trying to decipher why men, even the good ones, had to go and scare the shit out of women like this.

Pete hadn't had a dart in eighteen months but as he lay awake in the bed his girlfriend had just said hooroo to, he couldn't stop thinking about lighting up and ripping down a coupla coffin-sticks. Coupla shifting hours later Pete was in his tracky-dacks and his Brick's Boxing windbreaker, trudging down to the 7-Eleven for a deck of Winnie Blues, or whatever they called em these days: 'Ultra fucken Slim Light Smooth'.

Pete paid the unfathomable price and sat on the curb across from the cop shop, looking out over the empty Kingsway and smoking until 6 am. Then he went to walk back home but remembered that Ainslee would be up about now, and Pete knew if she saw him like this she would tell Gavin and then Gavin would be worried about him, and Gavin had his Jersey Flegg grand final on Saturday and Pete wasn't about to upset the focus, so he turned back towards the water.

Pete knew about the strategy in place for Ainslee. Her parents had three other kids younger than her and so they'd stopped caring what she did a year or two ago. As long as she was at the breakfast table to help out then she could be an actual owl for all they cared. She was a good kid, never had to call them at 3 am to collect her – snapped high heels in her hand, adorned with a tall story of how she lost her Opal card at the party and couldn't get a bus. That was not Ainslee. Plus, she was also an insanely diligent athlete and student, with a smile that would cheer up a children's cancer ward, and often did when the senior league headed there. And so off she went most mornings round 6-ish, jogging the half hour home with a pink 'JUST DO IT' knapsack on her person, her elbows right up near her ears. She loved it and she could have pushed on with the running, she was state schoolgirl's long distance champion at thirteen and fifteen, but footy and hockey had got her. She loved hockey best, and so she should, with all sorts of talk going on that she could well be the next Rechelle Hawkes if she didn't lose her athletic focus on such things as Gavin, or actually Gavin, or, you know, getting too intense with Gavin.

Pete walked towards the sea. And as much as he wasn't a fully blown idiot, as much as Pete did read the odd book, the ex-champ still couldn't quite make head or tails of his brain situation. Shit like this happened to ex-players. It happened in films. Just the other day, Squeaky had been talking about that Will Smith concussion movie – but that was a Hollywood film and the facts in it were way overblown. And Pete Lum didn't play fucken NFL; he didn't tackle with his skull. He was a ball-playing forward. A rugby league guy. Braced for collision! He felt fine! And so did Wally Lewis after his

44

moment on the news where he lost it. He wasn't old Turvey, staring down the barrel of dementia or ... what was the Cowboys player again? Fuck, what was his name? He wasn't Mark Coyne. They were only just discussing it at the Cazbah. There was a soccer chick impacted by headers, and Christ, what's the guy who killed himself ... the poor AFL guy? Shit, maybe his brain was done for ...

Plum loved this beach area. Ever since the Lum family shifted south east in the late 70s, Pete felt thrilled to be alive. As kids, he and Sarah used to play at the park in front of Northies, jumping from sandstone boulder to boulder, while their mum waited in the car till they were defeated, which was never, which was when it got too cold and dark and the Christian Surfers were starting up their rowdy bonfires on the sand. North Cronulla was the centre of the universe: a blue and golden wonderland when he was young; a surfing paradise and place to pash chicks when he was a teenager; and as an adult there was beer gardens and clubs aplenty. It never stopped being a carnival, no matter what age he was.

And now, as a 49-year-old man with brain issues, it was a place to set sail. So Pete put the cigarette butt in his pocket, picked up a huge rock from under a palm tree beside them same swings and walked down to the sea, wondering if the boulder in his clutch was enough to sink him. He had seen it in a movie on SBS, one of those ones they play at 2 am on the weekend. Was it Norwegian maybe? A blond guy called Lars tried to sink himself in a fjord. Was that what he was about to do? Sink himself like Lars? He didn't know. He was just taking it one step at a time as he crept round the ridge of the rocks where the pavement curved above his head, using his shoulders against the wall and trying not to slip when the waves sprayed up into his legs. When he got further round the wall, he heaved the rock up to his chest and then rolled his windbreaker in and around it, so it couldn't disconnect from his person, so it was tied to him. He wished he could have one more smoke but he needed both hands now, and the wind was that sharp, there'd be no chance of lighting up. Instead, he looked up at the moon, disfigured by cloud, and tried to follow a seagull for a bit, but it kept disappearing in the mist. After a while he just looked down at his drenched trackies and his black NBs, and then into the rock pools that probably held stuff for crabs and small fish to live off, then he looked up, took a deep breath of salted air and bent right down like he was doing a weighted lunge. Man, he'd never seen a bloke do a weighted lunge like Brick, the guy could seriously rise up with five hundred kilograms on his shoulders. Fucken maniac. Prick was trying to edge in on Char, always edging. Whatever Plum had, he had to have it too. Well, Brick could have her now, couldn't he? Better off with someone else, Charmayne was. So was Gavin. With Plum out of the way, with Plum gone to the real-life sharks, everyone could get on with the job, and none of the shit to come would have to bother em. Renee, too. Sweet Renee, what did he fuck up there? All of it, probably. She was a punisher, without a doubt, but he was the one who'd stuffed it. Wouldn't change his ways, wouldn't listen to the pleas, and wouldn't get help.

With dumb old Plum in mind, and the plum-shaped face of his father, Albert, another gutless prick, somehow appearing in the backdrop of the charcoal sky, Pete leapt into the air with the boulder in his jacket and for a moment there was peace. Like when that young pommy forward knocked him out in Wigan – came flying out of the line, trying to make a name for himself, roided up and shoulder first – there was peace in the concussion. Soft, chiming sounds and honey-like bliss. Concussion. A return to innocence, like blankets on the couch with Mum, and there is lemon cordial and there is cuddling. And Pete felt it now. The naive nothing. Peter Lum was going to meet the bottom of the sea like it was his closing head knock, and this soft yet solid thought built a churlish smile across his face. He could taste the end … bubbling in the darkness round his mouth … within reach …

The world turned black as plums and quiet.

Until a scream from the depths broke the divine descent and a single word broke through the blackness.

'PLUM!'

Peter Lum was saved.

Conscious and somewhere in Lilli Pilli, wearing nothing but a gown and slippers, Peter followed the angel through his rather large residence.

'My old man died a year and a half ago, and we owned a company – family company – called Hose It Down. Heard of us? Basically if you've ever replaced a rubber hose or put some sort of piping in, yeah, that would maybe be one of our products. We're Australia's largest producer of four-inch rubber hosing.' Trent led the way down a spiral staircase, past a vintage Kawasaki motorbike and into a glass wine cellar, through an open-plan bedroom with a cinema-sized screen on the wall and a view of an infinity pool. 'Instead of, you know, I don't know, carrying on with being a financial person, I chose to have a complete nervous breakdown,' Trent continued. '"Untreated grief and childhood trauma, met with a pretty serious cocaine problem", according to my $475-an-hour psych, and so I got out. I sold the whole franchise and pissed off everyone I'm related to. Then I bought the most expensive house in Australia, basically.'

'Jesus fuck me,' said Pete, inspecting the wall of electric guitars in the palatial bedroom.

'I don't even like guitars,' Trent said and pressed a button on a pylon, which made the glass-fronted bedroom wall start moving into the roof, 'but I thought, well, you know, I'm forty-five and if I'm going to have a mid-life crisis and pour all my money into some overindulgent man cave, I need to have some guitars that famous people played.'

'Your mates must love coming over for beers.'

'Well, this is the thing, Peter. It wasn't, unfortunately, till *after* I'd built and decorated this monstrosity that I realised I actually didn't have any mates left. 1) I never had mates at school because I was so rich and everyone thought I was up myself. 2) I've always been quite up myself. And 3) I either fucked all my mates over financially at some point or failed to help them out when they asked me.'

'Right, well, there you go.'

'I have a gym, a bowling alley, a wine fridge that would marvel any French wanker's stash, and basically it's just me here. The only people that come over are Uber Eats guys, and they don't even come in. And that is not because I don't ask them in, Peter, I always ask them in, but I assume they think I'll kill them. I mean why else would a multibillionaire want to open a bottle of 1967 Sancerre on a Tuesday night with a 22-year-old kid named Sanjeed?'

'Can't think why.'

'Exactly!'

The two men had only met a couple of hours ago but somehow Trent's manic friendliness and over-eager demeanour was comforting to the ex-lock forward, and, let's face it, Trent did just pull him out of the sea with a boulder attached to him, then drive him to his house and shove him in the rainforest shower, throw him a terry-towelling robe and sit him down with a Sencha tea in front of the wifi-controlled log fire in the guest quarters.

Peter had struggled initially when Trent got his arms around his neck and started swimming back to the surface. He thrashed hard – trying to reverse headbutt the guy – but then cognitive thinking checked in and Pete realised what he was doing, so he let Trent guide him to the surface then to shore like on one of them rescue shows. By the time he got to Trent's Tesla, it was like the whole thing hadn't really happened, because Pete couldn't remember deciding to do it. He couldn't recall the moment he went, 'Yeah, I might kill myself now.' It just kinda started taking place. One moment he was off for a deck of cigs and trying to avoid Ainslee – the next he was giving it all away.

'This is probably going to be a bit embarrassing,' said Trent, as the lift doors closed and the two men started moving down into the bowels of the beast.

Pete was holding his tea in what looked like a Japanese egg cup. 'Why's that, Trent?'

'Well, I'm about to show you my gym.'

'What's embarrassing about that, mate? It's good to train regularly. I reckon most blokes go downhill after forty because they don't rip in anymore.'

'Look, I can't agree more on that matter. I mean, it was me swimming across Cronulla Beach at 6 am this morning in just Speedos and a pair of goggles.'

'It's true, that was you.'

'Fitness is all mindset. You don't get your head ready, it doesn't matter how many push-ups you do. Doesn't matter what sort of proteins in your shaker, yeah?'

'Mind over matter.'

The doors opened and the men emerged from the lift.

'But training to be a tri-athlete at forty-five years old is not what I'm embarrassed about, right. Shit, I'm literally shaking. What I am embarrassed about ...' Trent led Pete past the sauna and into a plush, carpeted room with a pool table, some rare arcade games and a fully equipped retro bar with a cheese wheel, and flicked on the lights. '... is this!'

There was no hiding it. The wood-panelled gym that connected with a twin-lane bowling alley was one thing. The man cave's outer wall a shrine to Peter Lum's career was another. Two signed Sharks number 13 jerseys, one from his days at St

Helens. A signed and framed Kangaroo's headgear. There was even a pair of Plum's boots hanging down over a framed poster of his Origin appearance in 98. This guy was a little more than a fan but, still, Pete didn't feel alarmed. Instead he just stood next to Trent, admiring the wall like it was a sunset.

'You're my favourite player, Peter Lum.'

'Geez, I'd wanna be.'

'There's still one Origin jumper I want to get.'

'The 96? Where I scored the winning try? That's in my living room.'

'Don't invite me over then.'

'I never will. Not now. No way.'

Pete scanned the emblems of his playing career and, as vivid as they were, for some reason he felt nothing. He did his duty and pointed out the blood marks and rips that pertained to certain hero plays, but he didn't go on; the museum felt dead to him. He did, though, insist on a beer and a game of snooker, and with Tool's new album on full, the morning drifted by in proper style: two strangers enjoying the other via Asahi and stick. For the first time since Trent's father died – or more accurately since he'd put himself through that expensive rehab just out of Byron – there was someone in his life, someone he liked, and it was Pete who suggested they exchange numbers, not Trent. It was definitely Peter. Peter Lum. The Plum.

'Well, I might head off,' said Pete from the infinity pool. 'People will be worried.'

Trent rose up from the day bed with his iPad and a fresh Asahi. 'Can I give you a lift?'

'Nah mate, I'm all good. I'll just go fetch me duds.'

When Pete finally came back down from the guest quarters (getting a bit lost on the way), he held out his hand to Trent, and with the most awkward, up-and-down handshake known to man, they said farewell.

'No more swimming with rocks,' Trent said.

'Promise,' said Pete, his tracksuit washed and dried like nothing had ever happened at sea, like there had never been a tussle, and like he had never said, 'Let me die.'

These days, the only time Pete found himself in Caringbah was when he went to the doctors, or visited Squeaky for a bong and some intensive Grand Theft Auto, which was usually after a session at the Cazbah. It had been a decade since his mum had died and they'd sold the Combara Avenue house and a little less than that since Sarah and her family had moved out of Dolans Bay and shot up to Darwin, and so it was all quite overwhelming for him to wander the familiar streets of Burraneer Bay and Port Hacking from Trent's joint in Lilli Pilli Bay. To see the new house frontages and landscaped front gardens, and the optimistic young mums getting on with their mid-week rituals, Pete did his usual amount of ducking and waving at passing Holden Rodeos stacked with tradesmen screamin out, 'There's The fucken Plum,' while scoffing toasties and Red Bull on their way to a roofing gig. He walked down Caringbah Road, past Our Lady of Fatima, through and behind the Anglican church, along Jacaranda Road, wondering if he was happy when he lived here. If that childhood he had on this asphalt was a good one, or if the oily, lurking feeling in his throat meant it wasn't at all – and the suburb was trying to tell him that – radically honest hometown. And he was so close to getting home without incident when something caught his eye and stopped him dead in his tracks.

Woolooware Oval was a soccer field and because of this ill-fortune, it wasn't a stretch of local lawn that Plum gave much love to. He genuinely hated soccer. It was always nil–nil between Arsenal and Whoever City, and the fans were a bunch of opera singers, as were the players, getting paid nineteen million euros a second to score a goal twice a year in one of the seven cups or comps they were currently on rotation in.

Like Darling Harbour, Themed Dress-Up Parties and The Bunker, soccer was also a founding item on Plum's 'Things I'd Get Rid Of If I Was Mayor Of The World' list. The only thing Woolooware Oval had going for it was that it was a nice one to pass by when he was trying to get home without being seen. But this time, as he turned left off Castlewood Avenue and strolled past the home of Cronulla Seagulls FC, he was struck by a sort of magnetic anomaly.

There, in the centre of the empty, stud-worn, sun-bleached soccer park, was a young girl, probably thirteen or fourteen, in a long red T-shirt and black shorts, booting a rugby league ball into the air then running to catch it. And even though her catching rate was palpably low, the intensity and the *effort* at which she went to get under the thing locked Pete's retina to her – and for ten to twelve uninterrupted minutes he stood there by the fence line like some sort of creep. Peter Lum was in a dream state, fingers on the wire and mouth open wide to witness the moments. God forbid if anyone saw what he was doing, for he was transfixed, watching this girl, in all her poetic simplicity, kick that footy up into the blue sky then bolt after it, only to over-run it, trip or not quite get her chest close enough. Sometimes she roped that pigskin egg in and Peter would emit a small 'Yes' of satisfaction and respect. Mostly, though, she bobbled it or just misjudged its descent, but her failures were as sweet as her wins because he could see she was taking it all in, as she scolded and then corrected herself after every effort. And this was, he thought, all you could ask for, even when you played first grade or Origin or you were playing for Tonga: that everything you did, every moment you spent on field, was one of pure desire to learn more, and gain more understanding, not only of the game but the game that lived within you, the player, your player, and how you, with what you had inside and within you, could make an impact. And she was. My Lord, she was.

'Good girl,' Pete said, as she kept on training, unaware that one of the world's best-ever players was just twenty feet away watching her through a diagonal fence square.

With tears in his eyes, Pete walked the remaining ten minutes home to Kurnell Road, talking to himself in a burst, letting words fall out like droplets of truth and toil:

Simpler times, kick the ball after school.
Simpler times, orange cordial in the pool.
Simpler times, Mum's got dinner on the table.
Simpler times, I'll stay at yours, or you stay at mine if you're able.
Those simple times, like rain on the trampoline.
Pretty girls in the sprinkler, is it Lindell, Melanie or Justine?
Simpler times, spin the footy in your hands.
Simpler times, cubby house and handstands.
Left my mouthguard in the car.
Life's a joke that was pushed too far.
Simpler times, I want you back.
Simpler times, I can't relax.
Calippo after training, lemon-lime, rewind.
To simpler times.
Simpler rhymes.

Two

If the Flegg grand final hadn't been out at Bankwest Stadium in Parramatta, Peter might have forgotten about the car altogether. For the forty-eight hours since the seizure he'd been getting the bus and/or walking from A to B, and, yeah, he had a feeling that something was different, but with everything that was going on in his head lately, it didn't occur to him that the Forester was still in the long-term carpark out at Kingsford Smith Airport.

At this point it was still only Renee who knew what had happened on the tarmac, with Qantas respecting his request to keep the whole ordeal under wraps until they spoke again, which Pete now realised was booked in for today.

There were a few factors at play.

1) Despite the advice from Moustache and Conan about not getting behind the wheel for six months, Pete was still going to drive his fucking car about – his mum drove till she was eighty, for God's sake, and he would do the same. But maybe not just yet. The headache situation still caused him to blink all the time, and he had this added sensation that he was at sea; when he stood up suddenly it took a while for his computer to render, so he needed …

2) Someone to drive his car back home from the airport after his meeting with HR and …

3) Someone to drive them out to the game tomorrow, but without causing Gavin to ask why his dad wasn't behind the

wheel. There was a team bus going, but Gavin was expecting to ride with him because he didn't want to miss the motivational chat. After much contemplation over a few tins of pale ale in the bath Peter concluded that …

4) He needed a mate to go with him to get his car and …

5) Squeaky used to work there. Pete could share the whole shit show with him, swear the cunt to secrecy then get him to drive the Forester home so that …

6) On Saturday morning, Ainslee could take the wheel, cos she was on her Ls now and needed a hundred-odd hours of driving to get off em, meaning Pete could sit in the back giving the fire-up monologue to his son right beside him.

The plan was an absolute belter. And on the text-line Squeak was in off the break, always looking for company and a few bets/beers, besides which anyone that was anyone in racing knew the Friday meets were for desperates only.

'That's all good, Pete,' said Squeak, as they got out of the Uber and headed through the outdoor Arrivals area, round the taxi rank towards a door with a sign that said 'Baggage'. 'I'm sure it was just a turn.'

'Mate, yeah, fucken, like … shit happens to people our age.'

'That's it, that's it.'

'We're in the sniper zone, forty to fifty. It's normal, ay.'

They paused outside some big grey doors with the scan lock and Pete could tell by the pushed smile on his mate's face that Squeaky was a bit shaken by the tale.

'You want me to come into the meeting with you, Plummo, or just hang outside and have a coffee till you're sorted?'

'Look, I um … yeah, can you sit in – with me – just for a bit? I don't really remember heaps of what went on so it'd be good to have someone else in there … hearing –'

'Right on, righto, rightio,' said Squeak, packing shit. He hated confrontation in life; whenever he came near it he'd climb on a horse, both literal and metaphorical, and get the fuck out of town.

But this time it was Plum, so he didn't have a choice. He was earthbound and in, hi ho silver. 'Scan the door, mate. Let's face the music, no drama,' he said, patting Pete on the back that still, after all these years, was carved out of feldspar granite – and he would place that same hand on that same back an hour and sixteen minutes later as they hopped onto the empty staff shuttle bus that looped round to the long-term carpark. 'You right, buddy?'

'Yeah, you?'

Plum hadn't read novels or poems or anything in a book since school really – or at least since his mum died – but one thing Plum *did* read was between the lines, and when the Head of Staff and Operations says things like 'Look, we love having you here, don't get us wrong' and 'We don't want to have to get other parties involved' or the clincher 'Sometimes things like this happen because we all need a freshen up', Pete knew it was exit time. They'd done their best to protect him from the press, Squeaky noted to him as they entered the carpark bay 12A, but some of the passengers wanted to know what had happened, and even though trouble had been averted and the plane in the air with only a 45-minute delay, there had been calls and emails from passengers and their lawyers.

'Do you have any cocaine left over?' asked Plum, the seatbelt like a straitjacket.

'Hey?'

'Nothing, just feel like tying one on, that's all.'

Squeaky nodded. He *always* felt like tying one on, but he knew Pete had his son's final tomorrow, and rolling up with eyes like slits in the snow wasn't good, especially with an ex-wife like Renee and a current like Charmayne. Forget it, brother. 'Floodlight's racing in Moonee Valley on Thursday, remember?'

'Hey?' Pete said, so annoyed at life he couldn't stop smiling.

'Let's have a look at a break-out sesh then, boys' day, dress-up even?'

'What?' Pete's headache was on full crank and his eyes were doing their blink-dance again. 'Is the AC on or is it just not cold enough ... you can't pick what's ... don't do ...?'

Squeaky turned up the AC and the radio, and drove his mate home. He thought about filling his buddy in on the stuff that had been going round about him — how that woman journo Dana was gunna release images and stuff about Plum's demise — but he thought better of it, the bloke had had enough for one day. Plus, newspapers were tomorrow's bog roll.

Back at Kurnell Road, Squeak climbed out of the Subaru that he had, under instruction from its owner, parked quietly and slowly on the pebbled drive. 'You ok, Plumzo?'

'Yeah, all good, Hugo.'

The two mates met round the front of the vehicle for the key exchange. The sun was low over the mangroves, and round here that meant just a touch of chill round 6 pm, but you were still a pussy if you donned a jumper, even mid-winter.

'You'll get a hand-out ...' Squeak said, stroking his thin arms to delete the goose pimples.

'Yeah, no, true, get a pay-out, s'all good there.'

'Qantas won't not look after you — they're the Spirit of Australia and so are you.'

'That's it, that's it. Good old "Qantas never crashed".'

'You going to see a doc about it all?'

'About what, mate?'

'The head stuff, the conk-out, the brain failure episode.'

'Maybe. Yeah. Dunno.'

'Could be something in it?'

Pete knocked on his little mate Squeak's head and laughed. 'Could be something in it for all of us. Catch you Thursday. Go Floodlight!'

Hugo 'Squeaky' Rennick, the first jockey to win the Golden Slipper twice in five years, watched as his buddy ambled up to the front porch, hoping to fuck he wasn't completely fucked.

These days were so golden, he thought. You didn't have to worry about achieving things because you weren't that young anymore, but you didn't have to worry about packing it all up because you weren't so old just yet. Late forties was a sweet spot and Squeak never wanted things to change. This was the holy grail: sucking piss and punting with a smile on your dial and your pals in cahoots. And, look, as much as he avoided confrontation with a leather whip and a stallion to go, the ex-jockey knew brain injuries were far from a joke, and that if anyone was going to have symptoms it was Plum. The bloke played as hard as anyone could play and drank the grog in the same fashion – no off switch – plus he didn't mind an eccie or a snifter either. He was a fucken animal, a brand of animal they did not make anymore because they couldn't.

'Hooroo!' Pete said, as he jiggled the car keys, his way of saying thank you to another man, his way of saying cheers, his way of saying keep your mouth shut or I'll deadset kill you, and Squeak understood this loud and abundantly clear as he crossed the Kingsway, wondering if he could catch the last race at the Cazbah.

When Pete got inside the house it was less cold. Gavin was on the couch watching a replay of the 2016 grand final with a beach towel on his lap and no shirt on. Like so many things in both his sporting and general life, Gavin had adopted this technique from his main man, Plum. Plum did not do napkins beyond the dining table so if he was going to take a drink or a snack to the couch he took a beach towel. He'd then take his shirt off so it didn't suffer a stain and he'd drape the towel across his person, using the ends of it to wipe his mouth to catch falling crumbs and sips; it was failsafe. Charmayne had also got into it, noting that regular bath towels were busy, but beach towels, outside of the odd ocean dip, were screaming out for a second purposing and this was it: 'snack cover'.

'You right, kid?' said Pete, grabbing Gav's shoulder – which was getting harder and harder to squeeze with every season.

'Yeah, just chillin.'

'Where's Ainslee?'

'She's at hers.'

'Night off?'

'Yeah, dunno. She might come over later.'

'Got it.'

'Was that Stavros?'

'What's that?' Pete said, finding this a good time to head into the kitchen and start cleaning up after his son, who liked to use four hundred plates and knives to make a sanga.

'Who dropped the car off? Charmayne said some bloke called Stavros had it.'

'Did you speak to her?'

'Just on Messenger.'

'Oh, yeah, we just got it back off him,' Peter said, eating a cheese slice.

'We?'

'Squeaky and me.'

'I thought Hugo left Qantas.'

'He was visiting, surprising a staff member, whose birthday it was. We done?'

'Yeah, all good.'

'Good.'

'Is Charmayne coming to my game tomorrow?'

'Did she say she was coming?'

Gavin paused the game. 'Are you ok, Dad?'

'Yeah. Why?'

'I saw your alarm clock in the outside plastics bin.'

Pete walked over, putting his hands on either side of his son's scalp. 'You checkin I got a brain still? Just make sure you get eight hours tonight, ok? No messing around with your bird till all hours like the other night.'

'Ok, Dad.'

'And I'll see you in the car at 7 am. Tell Ainslee she can drive if she wants.'

'But what about my pump-up? She's only on Learners.'

'Ladies in the front. Pump-up in the back.'

And with that Pete was done, walking back down the hallway to his bedroom, feeling like the kid who got away with it. That feeling reminded him of an Easter when he was just seven or eight, when his mum, circumspect due to a weather forecast predicting a Sunday morning storm, decided to line the hallways with eggs so that when Peter and Sarah climbed out of their bunks there would be choccies to find, rain, hail or shine. But best-laid plans – and eggs – often go awry, and when Pete's dad, Albert, rolled in at 3 am, blind from the club, on his trip down the hallway he managed to step on all the eggs, crushing them in the caverns of his big bare feet. Instead of turning the lights on and looking at what he'd trodden on, Albert busted into Peter and Sarah's room, switched on the bed light that shone right into the face of the boy in the bottom bunk and shook him, hard, mind you, by the pyjama neck, screaming, 'Why did you line the hallway with stones, you little goose?' until Mum came in and quietly, calmly, convinced the drunk looming man to lay off. 'Albert, leave the boy alone. He didn't do anything. Let him sleep.'

When Peter got into his bedroom he realised he had inadvertently said goodnight to his son just now and it wasn't yet 7 pm so he would have to isolate within his own quarters or look like a crazy man. He lay down on his bed and looked up at the roof, pulling his phone out of his pocket for a scan. Pete went on to the Messenger app, the blue one, that for some vague reason was the main artery through which he and Charmayne seemed to speak. He went up and down their last spat of communication, wondering why she hadn't written back to his last efforts of 'Hey', 'Char?', 'Babe!' and the one he just knew she couldn't resist, the 'I didn't cheat on you' text he'd sent while sinking lagers in the tub a day or two ago. He picked out an emoji to send – the one where the bloke or the sheila has her hands up in the air not knowing the answer, the 'I give up' gesture, or a 'Fuck knows' sort of one – when Charmayne Slocombe came online, and like the first time he saw her in the sheds at Shark Park, ten-ish years ago, dressed in blue and black lycra smiling like a sunflower and fluffing her pom-poms, his heart started racing – and now he was desperately trying to save their relationship only to have his video chat ended before it even began.

'Fuck cunt.'

Pete sent a 'Sorry' text, followed by an 'I miss ya', but once more, nothing came back to him. The snowstorm was coming in strong and he closed his eyes to stop that blasted blinking barrage he was now a brother to, took a few deep breaths and fell asleep with the phone on his chest at 7.23 pm.

'No, we'll be right,' said Pete from the back, as Charmayne climbed into the front passenger seat.

He'd been woken last night by the sound of Charmayne taking off her bangles, and if he was on Sportsbet he would have called it an outside chance at best, but as she crawled in beside him he was just so grateful for the win he feared muttering a word.

'Go back to sleep,' she'd said, as she continued undressing – but not all of it – and they'd fallen back to sleep together, no alarm clock needed, just limbs and breath and forgiveness.

'Are you sure, Mr Lum?' Ainslee said, swivelling in the driver's seat to face the father and son, her eyes near popping out of her head with the inherent stakes of the day now firmly in her hands. She had *some* hours under her belt, close to forty when she'd last checked. Her dad had given her a burn whenever he could get away from work and the itinerary of her younger siblings' dance recitals and excursions, but she would not call herself a 'confident driver' yet. Not at all, no way. She liked parking, but not reverse parking, no way. She liked indicating, but not merging, no way. She liked being in the right lane, but not going fast, no way. This was where she was at, and she was yet to go faster than seventy or indeed complete a whole journey without having someone beep the horn at her at least three or four times. So when Pete had thrown her the keys over the breakfast table, she'd nearly choked on her Sultana Bran.

'I can drive us home,' said Char. 'If you want.'

'Ainslee, we believe in you,' said Pete, nearly over the line. 'Having you drive will help calm the boy's nerves. Plus, it's all pretty smooth once you get to the M4.'

And it was smooth, like Greg Inglis in space. With Charmayne's calming voice providing forecast from the front, Ainslee was able to lead the foursome out of the Shire and into Rockdale, where the fitness-obsessed teenager – who would one day play for Australia in three different sports – found a highway that led to a freeway that curled onto another highway where she could settle into the right lane, just below the speed limit. With crisis averted, Pete turned to his son to issue his pump-up speech. Gavin had skipped the team bus for this and, with his girlfriend driving and his dad being all smiley and strange again, he was starting to wonder why.

'Son, how're you feeling?'

'I'm fine,' said Gavin, not fine.

'Great moments are born from great opportunity.'

'Ok,' said Gavin, his throat going dry.

'And today is a great opportunity ...' Pete said, and then his brain started cracking again.

'Anything else?' asked his son.

Plum never quoted books or used big words in his pump-ups. He just told stories from his own experience and spoke from the heart, but this morning in the back of the Subaru he was coming up empty. 'You should not have any doubt about what you have to do tonight.'

'Today,' Gavin said.

'You only get one shot,' Pete said, with a mildly American accent, causing Charmayne, the involuntary safety officer, to spin around in her seat.

'And?'

With the sun belting through the windscreen, and the sound of car horns raging at Ainslee as she continued to explore her passion for driving in the right lane and never at the expense of the speed limit, Pete closed his eyes, sucked in a few big ones, thought of nothing but sheep and hills and birdsong, then spoke, from a mouth he had never owned, a library he had never thought to join, and a period in history he had never attended. 'We few, we happy few, we band of brothers,' he said, looking now into his son's eyes. 'He will never be vile, my bro.'

'Vile? Who's vile?' Gavin asked him.

'And gentlemen in England now-a-bed shall think themselves accurs'd they were not here, and um, um yeah they would hold their manhood cheap whilst any speaketh? Son. Them that fought with us upon Saint Crispin's day.'

The car was silent until Gavin, the manhood in focus, felt the need to break it. 'Whose day is it, Dad?'

But Peter couldn't remember a thing he'd just said, so he grabbed his son's chin and said, 'It's your day, son, now go and snap a few cunts in half. Ok?'

Before the whistle blew, Pete went down to get a hot dog and bumped into Renee and Ollie and their weird, mute kids, Tyson and Zoe. Ollie, who was always rocking that polo shirt collar-up look that said, *I went to private school*, asked where he was sitting, and so Pete pointed up to Charmayne who was laughing at something Brick had on his larger-than-most-people's phone. Ollie took his teenagers up towards the spot, with Renee saying she'd see them up there in a sec; she had some business with the ex, it seemed.

'Have you told her yet?' Renee asked, biting off a fair bit of Pete's hot dog.

'Hey?' he said, wondering why some people he knew didn't just say 'yes' to a hot dog when you asked them but instead chose to eat nearly half of yours.

'Charmayne? Have you told her about your epileptic fit?'

Pete was busy pushing in the onions that her imposter bite had forced out the other end but after the words 'epileptic fit', he shot her a look and led her away from the food truck.

'You know that's what you had,' she said. 'You had a fit.'

'I had a moment – and I haven't had one since.'

'I spoke to Liz.'

'Who's Liz?'

Renee scoffed. 'Liz is the fucking clinical neurologist who the doctors put us in touch with. I gave her your number. Have you not spoken to her yet?'

'Righto, settle down, people are about.'

'No, I won't settle down, Peter. You're being a fucking child. Has she called you or not, and if she *has* called you, why haven't you spoken to her? And don't give me this *I'm busy* bullshit – you no longer have a job, you only worked three days at Qantas anyway, and everyone knows all you do with your life these days is run along the beach in the morning and go to the pub with your moron mates and talk about how good you all used to be – *when sport was sport and men were men.*'

'I haven't spoken to her, no, but I will,' Pete said, trying to shush her with his own volume.

'*Has* she called you, Peter? It's not a difficult question.'

Admittedly, there had been a few unknown numbers calling in lately, but Pete was not one to answer calls from numbers he didn't know, and he struggled to work out voicemail, so he'd just left it, thinking if they were serious they'd get him eventually, and clearly they weren't cos they only bothered four or five times.

'Peter, has she called you?'

Pete felt in proper need of a beer in a plastic cup now – that's what this woman did to him, she dragged him to the bottle. But, geez, he had to give it to her, she looked tight, cleavage on display, and he couldn't help wondering if Ollie savoured the delights. Probably not, he decided, the bloke was wetter than London in February. He took a bite of the hot dog. 'We keep missing each other.'

'So you called her back?'

'I will tomorrow.'

She scoffed harder and scratchier this time, then grabbed the last corner of his hot dog and shoved it in her mouth. 'One more question and I'll bugger off. Have you told Charmayne about it all?'

'About it all what?'

She spoke as she chewed, and it was not without incident, considering the amount of mustard Plum liked to lay on the shaft of the frankfurters these days. 'Oh my God. About the full-scale seizure you had at work. About how you might have a serious brain issue. About how you nearly killed a few hundred people.'

Pete looked up to the stand, where Ollie and his kids were interrupting Charmayne and Brick's engrossment – and, to be honest, this he did not mind at all. 'No, she doesn't know.'

Renee would have folded her arms here, but she couldn't, she was holding a baby, so instead she just glared at him.

'What?'

'Well, two things. I'm going to get myself a hot dog. And secondly, if you don't call Liz – who is amazing by the way, I learnt so much about the brain from talking to her, and she's a huge league fan from way back, and get this, Peter, she was brought up in a really remote Aboriginal community so it is simply amazing how she has come to be where she is and anyway, ugh, she's so so so lovely – well then, yes, if you don't spill it, then I am sorry to say this but, yes, Peter, I'm going to take Charmayne for a little drink myself and she's going to get the low-down. Call it a threat if you like, I call it a promise.'

'Renee, it's really none of your bus –'

'We share a son. If we didn't, I wouldn't care. But we do. So it is my business. And I'm your next of kin,' she said, powering over to the food truck. 'Go Sharks!'

'Let's go, Sharks,' Ollie yelled, as Gideon Westcott, the lightning centre, stepped his way over in the seventh minute. With points on the board and the Sharks completing sets, Pete could rest back a little, just as Gavin set for the conversion attempt. Watching his son succeed at the game that gave him everything brought Plum a lot of pride, but he would be lying if he said it was fun on the sideline because it wasn't; it was nerve-racking! Pete lived every bloomin moment, every pass, every mid-field bomb – not that he needed to though cos his son had nerves of steel and rarely did he ever make a mistake.

Brick leant around Charmayne to look at him. 'You right, Pete?'

'Yeah, Bricko,' said Pete. 'Surprised to see you out of the Shire, that's all.'

'What else does a newly single bloke do of a Satdy?'

'Single?'

'Yeah, did you hear, darling?' Charmayne said. 'Suzanne kicked Brick out. We have to have him over for dinner.'

The crowd went wild again as Gavin sweetly slotted the conversion and it was 6–0 Cronulla Sharkies over the Bulldogs.

'Don't you think? Nothing like a home-cooked meal to heal a heartbreak. Plum?'

'Sounds good to me,' said Pete, squeezing her thigh with love.

'How was your hot dog?' she asked him.

'Oh yeah, good. Renee ate most of it.'

'Yeah, I saw that.'

Plum and Charmayne peered down the aisle to where Renee was climbing up off her seat and pointing to the Dogs' error with a half-eaten hot dog. 'Smash em, Sharks!'

Plum looked to the field. Gavin, a dummy, then inside ball to Kai, the number 11.

'Bend the line, Kai,' Plum said, but just to his own chest hair.

Going into the line was never a big deal for Plum, it was just part of it. Contrary to popular belief it didn't really hurt either. What hurt was getting hit when you weren't ready for it. Or twisting your ankle in a tackle. Or getting chinned by an upper cut from Brick Wall in an Origin scrum. But really, truly, the other stuff, it didn't even sting. It just jolted ya for a second – and what's the big deal with a jolt, a jolt made a man feel alive if anything. Pete played NRL *for* the impact. He went out there looking for it and as far as he was concerned if you didn't do it that way then you may as well stay home with your mum. But with ten minutes to go in the first half and the young Sharkies up 16–8, the Dogs started to find their bark and bite and suddenly everything changed for Plum, and the game he'd been born to play, the game that had given him everything, took on a completely new meaning.

As if in slow-motion, the artistry and agility of the players disappeared, and all he could see was young boys' heads going into other young boys' heads. Heads that held brains and ideas and futures, heads like ice-cream buckets not built to protect the tiniest bird, were mindlessly crashing into others. Necks snapping backwards, noses splitting and smearing, skulls spilling red ink. The ruck, where Plum had spent half his life in operatic tussle with other burly tenors, was now a theatre of damage; the hit-ups, where true ticker was tested, was now some sort of etch-a-sketch, swiping knowledge away. This was a carnival of carnage, ladies and gents, and although the spectacle tapped into the most carnal of desires, it was all ominous now. Every hard knock he observed, in the innocence of athletic youth before him, seemed to dissolve into the recollection of the ones he had endured himself, just bloody like it. Shoulder into temple. Knee into eyeball. Elbow into teeth. His past was his present but more abundant, and Pete could now see why he had come to nearly do over a plane full of passengers. He'd been in a thousand collisions by the time he had hair on his nuts. Forget professional sport, the damage was done way before then. You just had to open your eyes and see – this should not be legal. And so when Gavin, his only son, his ray of light, his reason for not letting it all just slip – who up to this point in the fixture had been mostly quiet with the pill in hand – slipped through a gap with a dummy and a jink only to be thoroughly cleaned up by a Tavita Rangai Ti swinging arm, well, that was it, the shit show had to stop.

His face burning, his heart racing, his throat dried up with panic, Pete got out of his blue seat and, to the bafflement of his crew, took off right, descended the concrete steps, then walked along the bottom frame of the stand, down onto the tiny hill, pushing past a few blokes he knew and that journalist Dana Crighton with her iPhone aimed at him, and headed out the exit turnstile with his son laid out on the field behind him.

'One more, thanks love,' Pete said to the broomstick-shaped barmaid, who still had not made an attempt to converse with the well-oiled ex-player. Such a glorious woman was she, he handed her three paper slips. 'And I'll whack these bets on too.'

It was a Saturday so the races were thick and fast, providing sweet relief from the battlefield he'd just abandoned.

'I have wasted my life on the horses,' said an American man standing next to him. 'But still I bet every day.'

'Is that right?' Pete said, disinterested.

'I don't know any other thing to do, not me. The numbers, they call and I move in.'

Pete's trifecta, which a second ago looked likely, was now spreading out in the turn, and with the man now standing way too close, Pete became agitated and started flicking the slip – *tap-tap* – on the top of his left hand. 'Fuckin get up.'

'No joy?' asked the man, and then took a long slug from his bottle of Budweiser.

Peter ripped up his ticket and let it scatter in the air, shifting focus to his eighth schooner of pale ale by taking it down in one glorious gulp. 'Do I look like a winner?'

'Name's Bukowski, old cock. Charles. And yes, to me you are a king.'

'Hang on a sec,' said Pete, remembering the expression. 'Who *are* you?'

'You're upset. The loss. I know. It's hard to win at anything. Losing is easy. It's grand to be the Great American Loser – or in your case the Great Australian Loser. Anybody can do it; almost everybody does but not necessarily in style. Losing in style, that's the jazz.'

Bukowski finished his sermon, drank more of his stubbie, the foam forming on his beard like a moth finding rest.

'Yes!' Pete exclaimed, as if there was an appeal from the stewards and the trifecta had indeed come in. 'You were driving my bus! I remember you, you spoke to me on the bus. Do you drive buses in the Shire?'

'Sure I do,' said Bukowski, retrieving a packet of Marlboro Reds from his coat pocket, 'but before we get into the local transport system versus WestConnex, do you fancy a smoke in the beer garden, Mr Peter "The Plum" Lum?'

'How do you know my name?'

70

'Any man who is any man knows your name, cock. Like I said, you are the Great Australian Loser.'

Pete scanned the unapologetically Indonesian-themed tiki beer garden, empty but for a couple – still awake from the night before – chewing their faces off and feeding from a jug of cider in the corner, and an old woman on a bench – jiggling a pram with one hand and sipping a red wine from the other.

'Seriously, was it you on the bus – talking to me over the microphone?' asked Pete, who had taken the liberty of organising the next two rounds before heading outside.

'Peter, I'm on the bus with you from now till eternity. I am the bus, you are the bus, if you know what I mean. It doesn't matter. All that matters is beer, pussy and horses.'

'Ok, but it was you driving the bus from the Cazbah to Cronulla?'

'Sure, it was me. Rocking the Cazbah, baby.' Bukowski twisted his cigarette out, coughed up a lung, nearly died (again), then took another one from his deck and lit it up with glee. 'Tell me about yourself, Mr Lum. You were a rugby guy, right?'

'Rugby league. But, yeah, you Yanks call it rugby, even though league is league and union is union. They're completely different codes –'

'And how's it been for you, cock, since the rugby's been over?'

'It's been good … yeah,' said Pete, sipping his schooner, thinking he had answered.

'You know what? I know you're an Aussie, and a male, and a tough guy, but, seriously, if you ain't going to give me a straight answer, I'm going to finish this Bud and get back on my bus, if you know what I mean?'

If Bukowski's voice was any raspier it would have been an electric hacksaw but, still, Pete could feel the softness of his heart within it, and the way he was looking at Pete, well, he could tell Bukowski was a cardigan of a man. And oddly enough, while Peter Lum usually found himself slicing off the prospect of new friendships, he didn't mind the man's company.

Bukowski stubbed out his cigarette. 'That's why I always prefer to drink with the queers, they got so much emotion in em, it's all alive on the surface even. They just tell you how they are – point blank. They love to drink and fuck and talk. The queers are real men, whereas the straights, it's fucken boring with the *yeah, nah, dunno* answers, that is until they've had ten drinks and a coupla bumps of coke in the cubicle and finally they tell you how their dad used to touch em on the johnson, sobbing and exploding. Do you know what I'm saying, rugby hero?'

'My dad was not that man,' said Peter.

'What kinda man was he then? Old Albert. Was he there for you?'

'Hey?'

'Was he a good dad? Did he turn up? Did he hit ya?'

'How do you know my father's name?'

'This part always bores me so. Just roll with it. Don't ask questions.'

'Are you from the television?'

'Ha! That's the best one I've heard yet. I could barely get them to publish me in the zines, you think I have a head for TV? Maybe for radio, I like that: "TV" ...' Bukowski sipped on his beer like it was a part of his arm, like it was a drip. 'Just answer the question.'

'My father was a good guy. Very charming and funny and always high energy, you know? He was a real character. Naturally funny – not like punchlines, just was. And everyone loved him, all the adults, everyone in Orange, all the kids, well, they was jealous of me, because my dad coached me in cricket and coached me in footy and he was always there, buying us soft drinks after the game, taking us to the river if it was hot. He was the one who told me I could go all the way, you know? He pushed me to play, said, "Make waves, son, make waves, you got it in ya, now go and make waves."' Pete tapped Bukowski on the chest each time he said 'waves', forcing the old drunk to cough.

'Alright, alright macho man.'

'But when the company he was working for sold itself to a bigger freight company — my dad drove trucks, you see, across the Central Tablelands — well, we shifted south east, and Sydney, Cronulla, the temptations, the women, the pubs, the … I dunno, Dad just, he stopped coming home. From when I was fourteen he just lost interest in us and when he did come home he was not really there. Just peering out the window and murmuring things when we talked about school. Or yeah, some nights, he was raging. Full. We'd pack our stuff into garbage bags and the rest is … I mean, I still love him, I'll always love him, but he did just fucking abandon us. Had other kids with some woman, moved out Lithgow way …'

'Most fathers are assholes and it's not their fault. Men are not meant to be home, they're meant to be swinging clubs in the wilderness and making huts, but society has put us all in suits and asked us to be indoors. That's where the violence comes.'

'I didn't say he was violent. Did I?'

'You didn't have to,' said Bukowski, with a chuckle. 'You should read *Ham on Rye*, it's about how my old man beat the hell outta me, and about my skin condition. You see, I used to go and see this nurse who would deal with my facial sores —'

'He loved us, my sister, Sarah, and I. He loved us a lot. And my mother too. He just wasn't educated and he couldn't hold his drink. He'd have one or two and bang —'

'I wrote a book called *Women* once too, I don't imagine you've read that either. I imagine you read one biography a year, perhaps about a golfer.'

'I read the odd book. I used to read everything. When I was young Mum would —'

'Well, read more, asshole!' Bukowski said and slammed his fist down on the bench so hard that the mangled couple and the child-minding grandma stopped what they were doing and looked over.

'I will,' said Peter. 'I promise I will.'

Bukowski laughed, and so did Peter as he offered a cigarette to his new friend, who shook his head and waved them away like they were bad for him. 'I only smoke Marlboro cos they don't sell Lucky Strikes in this godforsaken place. Can you fucken believe it? Call the place the lucky country, but no Lucky Strikes.'

'Seems ironic.'

'It sure does, Alanis Morissette.'

'Huh?'

'So, pussy? Wives? Girlfriends?'

'I have a girlfriend, her name is Charmayne, and I imagine she's, um, she's, um … far from impressed by me right now.'

'Why is that? You been playing up with the whores, Peter? You found a stripper named Candy and persevered until she finally told you her real name? I can empathise with that; every decent man has convinced himself he could save a stripper from herself at one time or another.'

'No.'

'What then? Impotence? That can be awful.'

'I just … No, I just … I had an incident, and I'm struggling to find a way to, um, share it with her,' Peter said, lighting up a dart.

Bukowski could see The Plum was in pain so he gave him some space to breathe. 'You guys wear helmets when you play rugby?'

'League. Rugby league. It's called "League".'

'You guys wear helmets when you play little league?' Bukowski laughed so hard at his own joke, it set off another monumental coughing fit.

'No, we do not.'

'There it is.'

'Helmets don't prevent concussions. They actually provide a bigger target to hit. The only reason they wear em in boxing is to prevent head cuts.'

Bukowski leant in, took Peter's hand and shared something from the canon. 'This is your life, cock. Don't do what you think you gotta do. Be awake, be engaged, see the corridors. There are doorways. They may be hidden, but they're there. We have things to show you, and to tell you, so don't be blind. Eyes open, chest full of breath, play on. Life and death are the same thing, because they are always both on offer. To you, Peter, to you, and that's only because you are marvellous. Did you know that, cock? You are marvellous. It is marvellous to be here with you, and as far as I have been told, three or four of the Gods are waiting to delight in you.' Charles finished, eyes on Plum.

'Did you just make that up?' asked a poem-drunk Plum, trying hard not to cry.

'Yes, I did just make it up but not just now. I just made it yours, from when I made it up, which, as Will says, "If it be not now, then be it …" Ah shit, I'm too hammered to remember the provenance of the fucking falling sparrow. Shall we go get a proper drink, Peter?'

And with that they departed, sauntering down the strand to Uncle Kurt's cocktail bar, where, a war or two older than anyone else in the joint, they rested on half a dozen whiskey sours and requested songs from 1973 to 1977 on the jukebox.

'What do you love most about her? This Charmayne broad? The Saffa!'

Peter endeavoured to answer, but Bukowski was back on the invisible mic already. 'And if you don't convince me? Well, this evening is finishing in the whorehouse for both of us. My treat! Cos there's a couple of larger ladies in the red lighter down near Church Street, and I tell ya, Peter, an hour of fucking these women and you stay fucked for a year. I'm still fucked from last year, what do you think I'm doing all the way out in Parramatta on a weekend? I'm not going to see *Blithe Spirit* at the Riverside Theatre!'

'What do I love about Charmayne?' Peter asked himself, as 'Angie' by the Rolling Stones filled his eyes and heart and ribs.

'Yeah, tell me about her. She got them big sunburnt Cape Town titties?'

'Watch yourself, Hank.'

'How'd you know my name?'

'It's written on your zippo. Hank Chinaski.'

'Respect,' Bukowski said, and ordered a couple more sours with his fingers.

'We have fun. Like, sometimes in bed we will put the sheet over our bodies and pretend we're in the luge team. You know the luge?'

'I love the winter Olympics.'

'We'll do that for a long time, just pissing ourselves, having a fake luge race in bed. I've never had that ... I've never been able to drop my guard with a woman before. Every woman I have been with before Charmayne I've always felt like I was either doing something wrong, had just done something wrong, or was about to do something wrong. I could never meet their expectations.'

Bukowski slapped some coins on the bar. 'Expectations are the enemy of peace.'

Then Pete's brain worked good, showing him a few pictures of where he had been, and why he was no longer there. 'I just left the footy ground. My son, he got knocked down. I didn't hang around.'

'Is your bitch there? Pete. Is your lady there?'

'Charmayne!' Peter put his head on the bar. Bukowski patted the back of it where the bald patch was, and the Rolling Stones tried their best to send hugs from the crackling jukebox. 'You know the strange thing, Hank?' Pete asked, his head back in play. 'I smashed my alarm clock in front of her. Such a small thing –'

'No small things in love.'

'That's what tipped us over. A tiny thing that I –'

'It's not the big things that tip a man over the edge. Death he's aware of, bankruptcy, divorce, addiction – no, it's none of that. Your best friend sleeping with your woman is manageable, AIDS we can manage, tsunamis we can deal with – no, it's the small things, the little things, the phone cords not untangling from the computer cords, the car not starting a week after you collected it from the shop. That's right, cock, it's the continuing series of tiny tragedies that send a man insane – not the death of his dog or dad or daughter but buying the wrong size shirt and only noticing once he's home, turning up the day before an appointment, it's those things, those broken banalities that kill us, and take us down, crocodile-rolling with resentments, a wrong call by a referee, a parking ticket, a broken shoelace. It's that swarm of despair that can kill quicker than karate. And they're always there, lying dormant, prepared for –'

'I just think there's a duty, Hank,' Pete said, homeless drunk now, head hanging and heart bursting. 'There's a duty. From a parent to a child. From a man to his son. There's a duty. To be there, you know? And to not go away. Doesn't matter what, what, what else is going on for you. If you make a kid, if you decide to do it, you gotta turn up, and when life is all static, doesn't matter, cos there's a duty to not just up and leave!'

Pete looked up, but Charles Bukowski was no longer there.

'Did you see where that man went?' Pete asked the barman.

'What man?' said the kid, wiping down the bit of wood in front of Peter.

There was no whiskey sour but his; no coins spilt out on the bar. The only thing that spoke of Charles's presence was that golden Dupont zippo standing erect on the coaster just to the right of him. Pete held it up to the light and read out the name: 'Hank Chinaski.'

Outside Uncle Kurt's cocktail lounge, Parramatta had turned on itself. Gone was the golden sun of Saturdays in the west, replaced by a wicked, whipping wind that had caused café owners up and down the plaza to collapse their awnings and call it quits on all things alfresco. Pete crossed the canal by bridge, jogged on past the Centrelink offices, then wobbled across the six-lane highway – charging with enormous killer freight trucks that nearly claimed him – towards Bankwest Stadium, lighting another fag with the ghost of Bukowski's sturdy lighter.

What a character, Peter thought, *What a loose unit*. And how odd was it that he'd been his bus driver and then his drinking buddy but in two completely different towns so far away from one another. Did he drive all over Sydney? The whole thing didn't make sense, but the whole thing had also made *so* much sense.

As Peter shook the padlocked gate at the stadium's entrance, rain started to collect on his neck, and the whipping wind gathered such sureness it was singing.

Through the wire, Peter could see a groundskeeper, picking up plastic cups with a plastic claw the length of his actual arms. 'Hey, can ya let me in?' Peter called out.

'My brother,' the groundskeeper replied, 'the clubhouse is that way.'

'I want to get in,' Peter said. 'My son is playing here. Gavin Lum, he's five-eighth.'

'No, my brother,' said the groundskeeper, now just feet away from Plum but on the other side of the gates that were tightly wrapped in thick locks and chain. 'The game's over. There are no more games on today. It's 9.30 pm, my brother.'

Pete looked at the tall, beautiful kid. *Is he Nigerian? Kenyan? Somewhere in Africa anyway.* 'Have you seen my father?' Pete asked him, a hundred times as drunk as he'd been in his entire thirties and forties. Drunk enough to believe that perhaps this kid, who escaped from Boko Haram on a boat with his uncle eleven years ago and since then had been living in a housing estate with six other Nigerian people studying ESL and computers in Parramatta TAFE, with three jobs round the clock and a penchant for Cherry Ripes, might just know how he could get a hold of Albert Lum to ask a few of them big health questions.

'My brother, I think you need to get home. It's late and it looks like you've had some alcohols,' said the groundskeeper, happy to try out this long sentence on a madman.

'Alright kid,' Plum said. 'But remember this ... It's not the big things that kill you, it's shoelaces.'

Pete woke up on his front lawn, the harsh morning sun screaming into his eyes. He'd been dreamin of Charmayne and that dress she wore when they went to Paris, and the way she laughed at him as if she wasn't in public, making people turn around but not in a way that meant they didn't love the sound. How she had grabbed him on that bridge in Montmartre and told him she'd never expected to be this happy with a fella. And how even though it was a pretty cliché setting, declaring one's love in France above the River Seine, well, he was just plain into it.

'Fuck.'

His wallet and phone were slopped out beside him and it was proper hot, it was 32 degrees and his head hurt, and why, and when, and what was this burning, busted life?

'Oh Lord.'

Pete looked down his body. His shirt was torn and his jeans, piss-drenched and drying, were halfway down his thighs. The sun was up there, which meant it could be 9 am or even 10. Had the neighbours seen him?

'Oh Jesus.'

A shadow crossed over the sun.

'Dad,' said a voice, six hundred feet tall above him and sun-flared, carrying a tray and what looked like a jug of lime cordial.

'Son?' Pete said, and rolled to his side so he could push himself up off the earth and onto his knees.

'Drink this.'

'I was just … resting.'

'Yeah, good one, Dad,' Gavin said, pouring out a glass of iced lime cordial. 'You ok?'

Peter gulped down the cordial with the ferocity of a soldier just home from the desert sands and then looked at his son again. With the help of a little cloud cover, he could see now that his son had a real blinder of a black eye just above his left cheekbone. 'Yeah, pal. You?'

'I'm ok.'

'Yeah?'

'Yeah.'

'Not sore?'

'Nah.'

'Good.'

'Yep.'

'Strong.'

'Did you even see what happened?'

'Hey?'

'Did you even see what happened, Dad? Like, how I got it? Did you see the stiff arm?'

Pete chewed on a choc-chip muffin from the tray of breakfast food that his son had prepared, half-nodding as if to say *Of course I saw it* but at the same time knowing that there was a chance he could get sprung here.

'Dad?'

80

'I think I was in the dunny when it went down,' he said, mouth filling up.

'When what went down?'

'The stink.'

'It wasn't a stink. It was in the second half. Which was after you had left.'

'Oh? Really. No ...'

'I got collared in the first half, but that was nothing. In the second I got a stiff arm.'

'Yeah,' said Plum, acting lost, and then acting found. 'So what happened in the second half?'

'It was just before I scored. Their hooker got sent off. Then I scored two plays later.'

'You scored, son?' Plum said, beaming now, the last bit of muffin lodged in the back of his throat where the voice and the larynx liked to run their operations.

'I scored three tries, Dad, and kicked six goals. I was man of the match. And two scouts, one from Storm and one from Manly, came and spoke to me after.'

Pete stood up, his hatred for Manly issuing him some long-lost balance and agility but not so much that he still didn't have to spread his arms out for balance. 'Well, you're not playing with the Sea Eagles. I'd rather get root canal with no anaesthetic than have a child of mine play for Manly. Kidding, aren't ya?' He shook his head, inhaled some snot, then refilled his glass of cordial, wondering how on earth he got home and whether Charmayne was here when he did.

'Why did you leave, Dad?'

'Hey?'

'Why did you leave the game? Where'd you go?'

Pete pulled his jeans up, dusting off the muffin crumbs and the grassy wetness. 'Who said I left?'

'Charmayne, Uncle Brick, Mum, Ollie.'

'Oh.'

'And Zoe and Tyson.'

'Got it.'

'Char said you just stood up and then bailed.'

'Right.'

'She drove us all home. Ainslee didn't want to drive in the dark. And Brick was pissed.'

'Brick was there?'

'Yeah, we had a photo. He handed me the trophy.'

Pete looked into his son's face, which was red with hurt and narrow with disappointment.

'It's not ok, Dad.'

Peter wanted to reach out and tell the kid he loved him but instead he reached for defensiveness and aggro as his paper weapons. 'What is "not ok", Gavin?'

'Whatever's going on with you lately. You're getting heaps pissed in the day. You're being heaps aggressive to me and Ainslee and Charmayne. You lied to us about the car. Like, why would you lie about the car? What's the go with the car?'

'Where is Charmayne? Is she inside?'

'She left, Dad.'

'What do you mean she left?'

'She left because you pushed her, Dad.'

'No way, I would never. I don't ever do that type of stuff. Nope.'

'I saw you, Dad. We all saw you. You pushed her, Dad.'

'No-no, no, you did not. Not possible.'

'Don't you recall? You were crazy, Dad, like you were this different person.'

'You're saying I put my hands on my girlfriend, are ya? Is that what you're saying to me? Gavin?'

And then Ainslee came outside with a beach towel and two friends, offering Pete an opportunity to find the gap and break through the wall of defence that was his own shame.

'Hey Mr Lum,' said Ainslee. 'This is Tanika and this is Nadia. We're going for a swim. Do you want to come?'

Plum nodded at the girls, who were seemingly excited by the scandal of Gavin's dad being a bit of a psycho.

'I'll get you some boardshorts,' said Gavin, going inside with a tray of his own shame.

Having executed the journey to Parra, and not exactly under the most stress-free conditions, Ainslee was now quite the sassy L-plater, even adding talking and pointing to her skill list as she cruised past St Aloysius and Gunnamatta Bay in the Forester. 'That's where we had end of year photos. In the pergola there. Was so lit.'

Pete sat in the back between Ainslee's two best friends, feeling like he was either still drunk or had somehow got away with no hangover. But by the time they got there, and with the amount of time it took to lock down an appropriate parking spot that did not require rear-to-curb insertion, the darkness was arriving and Pete hoped for the girls' sake that they could get out soon. He imagined they weren't exactly enjoying themselves either, with Pete's enormous thighs basically pushing them out the windows, and he'd started to notice that he reeked of wee and whiskey.

'Dad, can I go to Bali?' Gavin asked once they were out beyond the family friendly ocean pool, where he'd once seen a woman rescue a young shark.

'Hey?'

'Can I go to Bali with Ainslee?'

'What's your mum say?'

'She said it was ok with her if it was ok with you. That was before the game, though.'

'Maybe you should ask her again.'

'Maybe *you* should.'

Pete and Gavin had been swimming here ever since Gav was brave enough to push out beyond the froth with his old man. Oak Park Beach was the go for them. And this was their system, no matter who was along for the ride. They'd whack their boardies on in the canary yellow pavilion, hide their stuff inside a rolled-up towel beneath the rocky shelf to the right of the pav, then walk round the perimeter of the ocean pool to the front where they'd lift up the rusty chains, creep over the mossy, slippery craters, then dive into the breaking waves, swimming underneath the rolling froth until they were out beyond the break line, always treading water so as not to step on the coral, where many a stinger or a bluebottle had picked off a floating human; and they did not discriminate, those summer creatures, they loved to introduce both tourists and locals alike to severe anaphylaxis.

Today, Peter wished he could have asked Gavin if it was ok if they just swam in the ocean pool with the girls. He wanted so much to feel the water around his battered body, and to clear his heavy head, but being out in the beast itself was something that this time out was not at all relaxing; with the next line of waves looking fatter and more fierce than the last, it was all starting to illicit a sense of impending doom for Plum. He focused on a small yacht out beyond the lip to level out the dizziness. Behind it, Bundeena was just a green myth.

God, shit, no. He couldn't let his panic be known, couldn't let his son see him this way, not after yesterday, not after letting him down in such a monumental manner. Not after whatever he was referring to this morning. He had to man-up now, he had to be in the sea with the boy, and not let the boy see the boy in him.

'You said ask Mum, and she said I can go, so I think I'm just going to go.'

'Go where?'

'Bali, Dad. Bali.'

Pete stood up on a nearby rock covered in weed and cunje. He didn't care a bit it wasn't the done thing; he needed the leverage, and if the stingers wanted to have a crack then pipe up and rip in, he thought. 'You don't think you're going too fast, Gav?'

'What do you mean? Why are you up on that rock?'

'With Ainslee. I know you're having sex and stuff. Are you sure you're not rushing it all going overseas with her too?'

Gavin duck-dived under a wave then popped up right next to his dad, kicking hard beneath the water to maintain the close distance, and he couldn't help grinning. 1) His dad had said 'sex and stuff', and 2) well, Bali looked on.

'Dad, we're not *doing it*,' Gavin said, grabbing onto his dad's natural-born altar.

'What do you mean?'

'Me and Ains. We haven't done it yet. We're waiting.'

'For what? Till you're married?' Pete said from above, the dizziness disappearing with every breath, with every droplet of salted water round his scaffolding, with every moment of being here in nature with his number one.

'No, not that. We don't believe in God and stuff, we just didn't want to get distracted from footy, y'know. But now that I won Flegg, and got man of the match, it's all "go" she reckons. Big V. So, yeah, Dad, can I go to Bali?'

'Well, that's a tough one to say no to.'

'So don't say no.'

'Can I say let me think about it?'

'Yeah, cool.'

'Ok, then let me think about it.'

'But you're thinkin yes not no?

'I'm thinkin I'm thinkin is what I'm thinkin!' Pete said, with quite a bit of lung.

The father and son took each other in for what seemed like a week. Then a sweet little wave came and Gavin took the curl. Pete could see his son's figure through the peeling glass; the way it took him to the shore seemed pre-ordained, his arm straight up from the elbow like a fin shooting out of his own skull. Gavin popped over the shelf and into the ocean pool where his girlfriend was snorkelling. He dived under her, came up in front of her, and with his hands on her ears he then kissed her. Pete saw her face droop as Gav revealed the verdict. She had clearly wished for better news, but it wasn't a 'no', not yet, and that was the main thing. For a couple as young, fit and positive as these two, 'no' was their one enemy.

Pete dried, dressed and then left the kids to it. With the sun now blazing, the beach was starting to get crowded and he didn't want to have to engage with a fan in this state. On top of this he needed a chicken burger and a Fanta and now. Maybe even a slider of Panadol from Cronulla Chemist and one of them Berocca drinks. He'd had a crack last night, a proper look at it, and beyond drinking with Bukowski it was all blackout. He looked up into the sky, where a plane set itself for landing over Botany Bay, thinking, *Man, I nearly slaughtered you and all that you carry.* Then he turned from the sea and the sky to town.

As he approached Cronulla train station Pete felt a vibrate in the arse pocket, only to see that same 03 number coming at him again. He answered, perching on a bus stop bench facing Monro Park and all its quaint pointlessness.

'Peter Lum,' said Peter Lum.

'Peter, it's Liz Lombardo here. From the Brain Centre in Melbourne. Your wife, Renee, gave me your number.'

'Ex-wife,' Pete said.

'Oh, I'm sorry. Oh, yep, she did say that. She has a bub with her new fella.'

'Yeah, it's not my one. Tallulah's not.'

'My mistake, my mistake. Maybe it's *my* brain that's not quite right,' Liz said, laughing heartily at her own joke. 'I tried to call you a few times.'

'Oh, really? Yeah, I think I tried you back.'

'Did you try? Or did you just try to try.'

Liz was a 55-year-old Aboriginal woman brought up in the Western Brisbane community of Logan on a diet of rugby league and river fishing, and her Yugambeh voice could not have been more comforting and warm but Pete still didn't trust her. They were all the same these specialists, they all just told you stuff then took your coin, making you feel like you needed em, like you'd just cark it without em on the payroll – you just had to look at modern footy, the amount of superfluous clowns loitering round the sheds dressed in high vis, calling emselves 'high performance scientists' or whatever the nonsense; they were leaf blowers at best. This one would be no different.

'How're you feeling today?' Liz asked, after delivering her full neuroscience bio spiel.

'Fine, yeah. Yourself, Liz?'

'Nothing out of the ordinary? No dizziness or tiredness or –'

'No, fine. I just had a swim with my son.'

'All good. All good.'

'Yeah, no, good.'

'Well, that's good.'

'That's it.'

'So, um, I don't know how much Renee told you of my schedule, but I do a few days a week in Sydney every fortnight – every second week that is. I'm runnin a program there called Sphere Australia, where I give money to research projects based around strokes and dementia, but I also work in aneurisms, epilepsy and seizures, which I'm not saying is your situation necessarily, ok? But Renee told me what happened at Qantas, and with your history, it might be worth popping into the Sydney Brain Centre if you have a free day? Or even better if you're floating past Melbs – well, I have my own set-up here and we could have a little bo-peep inside your noggin. Does any of that jibber-jabber appeal to you, Peter? Or are you just thinking who is this crazy blackfella telling me what to do?'

'Hey, oh, look,' said Pete, the headache climbing back in. 'What's the bo-peep bit?'

'Oh, just a standard MRI and maybe an EEG to taste.'

Pete wanted to listen up, he did, but at the same time as Liz was going on about memory and how it's just like country – the mind – he could see this woman across the road who was breastfeeding her baby and she had just lit a ciggie. This was one of the harder things for Plum to fathom, how people could smoke darts around babies, and he nearly got up and walked over and ripped it out of her hand but instead he just stayed where he was, thinking, *Yeah, enough mess was made last night without a scene being made just where the riots ran raw.* And so with the snowstorm reappearing, Pete asked Liz if he could call her back tomorrow; he said he had a fair bit on today and he wasn't sure if he needed any of the scans, having had 'zero symptoms since the event', as far as he could tell.

Liz knew his type well and so she kept talking for a bit, something about whiplash and contusion, but Plum had stopped listening altogether by then.

'Cheers Liz, catch ya,' he said, taking the phone from his ear and nearly fainting right there and then in his boardshorts outside the station where a pack of white knob-shiners had chased a few innocent kids with brown skin onto the train in 2005 – racial hatred, the one thing Pete disliked about this beautiful beach town.

It was time for a chicken burger, some kickers, medium chips, barbecue sauce, a Fanta, a Sprite, four advance Panadol and a Berocca Berry. And, yeah, maybe it was also time for a leveller – and, look, the first schooner after a big one usually had nails in it, but the second one didn't hurt, and by the time you got to the third, world order would be somewhat restored ...

The club was buzzing with young families, and people who may have even been gay or Lebanese, God forbid in these waters. Dozens of hip kids were outside in T-shirts of 70s bands they'd never seen, approaching the old art of barefoot bowls with a similar ironic hollowness, everything just grist for the Tinder mill. The whole scene looked like a *Home and Away* cliff-hanger, and the more he looked round the more it brought Plum's cranium throb back on, so instead he ducked under the swinging arm of the wall-mounted tele and fired up the blindside into the pokies room where Queen of the Nile seemed to be calling his name from the corner cradle.

'My queen.'

Pete bought himself a Carlton Draught, a glass of water and a whiskey on the rocks from the quieter, more clandestine gambling bar, and took a seat before the flashing, twinkling Cleopatra – the last active ruler of the Ptolemaic Kingdom of Egypt.

And for a bit it *was* all shits and giggles, Pete sliding a fresh hundo in the tank and, yeah, he was merely pecking away, slapping at the pads without a real care, almost drifting off and then back again, it was a Sunday meditation, really. But then he cracked a scatter, and on his next slap a random feature – and hang on a sec are we not in business, sire!

'Let's go disco,' Pete said, a few more empty schooners by his side.

He slid another hundo in thinking if he could isolate an Extra Bet, then hello baby, we'll be buying Charmayne a business-class trip to Tokyo, all sins forgiven. *Luge time!*

But with the lines all leaning on jackpot for the journey, gravity had its wicked way and as fast as Pete kept doubling up for the main feature, slapping red and black in unison like Rachmaninov at his bumblebee peak, the hundreds kept disappearing with the schooners, and pretty soon Pete was cut off, declined at the altar, having exceeded his internal withdrawal limit of eighteen hundred bucks in only twenty-five minutes of steady, relentless slap-slap-slapping.

Pete bummed a fag on the pastel deck to laugh it off and was all set to go home when he found a fifty in his top pocket, and thought, *Well, I dunno, what the heck? Why not see what one last pineapple can do? Not chasing my losses if I found it on the way out?*

Pete swapped machines to solve the problem, pushing that magic fifty into Lucky 88, wondering if he should have chosen More Lucky, which he swore was also smiling at him from across the tartan-carpeted, bourbon-breath room of hope and heartache.

Five minutes later Pete was walking across the roundabout with cars and utes beeping at him.

Forty minutes later, after a bit of an annoying ordeal with the dude before him at the Bendigo Bank ATM, Plum was in front of More Lucky, with a pocket full of hundreds, some twenties and a stack of still-warm fifties.

SLAP. TAP. SLAP SLAP TAP.

Seventy-five minutes later he was walking towards the exit, wishing he was unconscious again, wishing he was six and chasing the milkman, wishing he could call his dad and say, 'I'm fucked.' Wishing it wasn't true that he'd missed his son's game and pushed his lady.

The bouncer, a massive unit from the South Island, asked him to kindly leave behind both the half-full and half-empty schooner glasses he was carrying, and even though Pete understood and would definitely oblige, still, he had to first alert the bloke to an innate hypocrisy prevalent in his place of work: 'What about those kids drinking on the lawns? Look at em, they're outside. Look at that one, he's wearing a Rodriguez T-shirt, and does he even know "Sugar Man"? Was he even around when "Sugar Man" came out? Ask the little prick, I dare ya!' Pete sucked down the dregs of his latest draught, placed it on the cement and sprang back upright with his hands in the air as if to say, 'Look, officer'. Then shit got a bit messy, limbs and voices raised, but cos of who he was, it levelled out before the cops were called in. 'Call the cops, I don't care. I'm Peter Lum. Hear me?'

It was Pete's life's work to keep the dirty work of his life from Gavin. Devastating as it was that his son had seen the chaos of last night and, yeah, a few earlier blow-outs with Renee, Pete was proud that Gavin had never found out about his eighteen days in the big house. It was a promise Renee had eventually agreed to keep. She'd told seven-year-old Gav that his dad was just away at a training camp in Brisbane when he was actually in Maitland Gaol for a third drink-driving charge. His second drink-driving charge was only an hour after his first one, when Pete had simply walked out of Sutherland Police Station only to get right back into his car.

He left the club and groaned all the way back into town, wondering why what had just happened had indeed happened. He didn't have a lazy eight grand to hurl about, either. Qantas had put him on a fifteen per cent furlough until his contract ran out, and after the divorce going mostly Renee's way, the Euro trip, the Kurnell Road reno and Gavin's swelling footy expenses, he'd pretty much spent the last of his playing-day savings. The 8-ish K he just spunked *was* their rainy day coin and, well, the fucker just pissed down.

Plum entered Home, Timber and Hardware with an unjustified swagger, not really knowing what he was doing there, but sensing it would reveal itself soon.

'Do you sell rope?' he asked the sales assistant, who had that prerequisite 'Why are you even talking?' vibe of any self-respecting teenager working in retail.

91

'Eight,' the girl replied, pointing to a place in the air above her head.

'Aisle eight?' Pete asked, but she was down in her phone now.

Twisted rope, sisal high-strength rope, blue rope, wire rope, flexi rope, polypropylene rope, rope chain, wet rope, rope for cub scouts and handy crafts, bungee rope, sea-fairing rope, heavy duty grunt rope – who knew there were so many options of rope?

Play on, said Pete inside his aching head, lifting off a nice bundle of high-strength braided construction. He slipped the loop out of its packaging and held it in hands that were lightly shaking. The rope claimed to resist abrasion, petrol, oil, mildew and sunlight. Which was positive news as far as he was concerned. *Yeah*, he thought, *this is the real stuff*. The rope looked a bit thin but its breaking strength was 2400 kilograms, and Pete, at just over a hundred, reckoned it would be alright when it mattered most. White with double black trace, the product was only sixty-four bucks, which was about what he had left in his bank account. And considering the rope was apparently ideal for a multitude of uses including boating, farming, truck and transport, Pete agreed he should look no further, even though what he was getting it for didn't really fit under those categories. What Pete was getting it for, put simply, was a lot more bespoke. He could swing it over the basketball ring, he thought, or perhaps just drive to Bundeena and find a nice quiet tree in the nasho there. *Or! Oh! Yippee!* The mangroves behind Shark Park, that might be nice – *hoohoo yes*. That'd be a real honouring of his time there as club immortal; though how would Gavin feel about that if he ended up with the Sharks as a player? He wouldn't want to be chipping over the top in that direction – no way that would work. *Bundeena it is*, thought the 49-year-old, all set to hand the twine over to the over-it sales assistant, when he received one of them tap on the shoulders that can only be described as really fucking annoying.

92

'My new best mate!'

Pete turned to find Trent standing behind him with some hosing and a small cage, and looking stoked in an open Hawaiian shirt and Waratahs shorts. He squinted at him. Trent's energy was like neon light in the 7-Eleven; Plum felt exposed in its presence.

'You never SMSed me,' Trent said, unsure why he had said 'SMS' and not 'texted'.

'Oh, yeah, I was gunna.'

Trent, clearly struggling to hold all of the loot he was getting on with, flicked a nod down at the bundle of opened rope in Plum's hands. 'Doing a bit of DIY?'

'Yep, nah, just thought I'd ... do some, um ... tying off ...'

If only Pete had stayed in the sun with his son. If only he was still there. Listening to Ainslee's friends' stories, to their crackling voices and high hopes. If only he hadn't lost all that money at the bowlo. *If only, if only, if only ...*

'I bought a cat!' Trent said, putting the cage on the ground. 'Figured I needed something to share the space with. And check this out, Plum – this is the piping my dad used to make. This is the legacy of the great man.'

Plum had to admit it, it looked like good hose.

'Thought I'd test out the new batch, whack some of it in at my new bar and then compare it with our old stuff. I have a feeling it won't be as durable!'

'Your new bar?'

'Huh?'

'What's your "new bar" mean? Your bar at home?'

The sales assistant, growing weary of their chat, requested they stand aside to let an Italian family purchase their lattice and potting mix.

'Oh, yeah, didn't I tell ya?' Trent said. 'I bought a bar, kind of a little hobby project. I always wanted to run a bar, or a boutique hotel, you know, for my family and friends to drink and hang at, but then same issue as always – family hate me and I've got no friends!' Trent laughed heartily at his own gag and then seemed to breathe in deep at the truth of it all.

'Where is it, though? Is it in Cronulla? I know every bar in Cronulla.'

The Italian family left the counter and Trent slid the cat cage along the floor with the edge of his thongs. 'How about we wander down now, mate, and I'll show you?'

'Where's the cat?'

'Oh, she's at home. My cleaner, Flavia, takes four days to do a lap of the whole house, so she kinda hangs with the cat and feeds it and stuff. Means I can do things without having to worry if she – the cat, not Flavia – has drowned in the pool.'

'Can you drown in an infinity pool? And if so, does it go on forever?'

'Geez – I like the way your brain works, Peter. You forwards don't get enough credit. Deep down you're all big thinkers trapped in a philistine's body.'

'Something like that,' said Pete, wishing he didn't have to hand the rope over now. But taking it back may make it worse, so he laid it down on the counter and let Trent think what he wanted to think. Everyone bought rope, and rope had heaps of uses. Rope was common as.

'How good is this?' Trent said, flicking on the lights. The place was pretty big but it felt not that big at all – kind of like Leichhardt Oval. It was decked out with booths on the sides and a small stage with a curtain up the end. There were some tables in the middle of the room, covered with red paper tablecloths, and an old BMX was hung up on one wall.

'Shit,' said Pete. 'Is this yours?'

'Yeah, yeah, it's my new bar. Well, to be honest, I've never had a bar before so I should just say, "It's my bar," even though, as you noted at the hardware outlet, I do have a bar at my house.'

'Your house is not a house, it's a suburb, it's a planet.'

'Nah, it's still just a house. The same as a Lamborghini will always be just a car, and a private jet will be just a plane. The brain normalises everything, that's why money will never make you happy. The brain won't let it, the only thrill of buying shit like a PJ or a mansion or a Lambo, is, firstly, in the research, but mostly it's the moment *before* you buy it.' Trent ducked round behind the wooden bar where a line of small fridges revealed themselves below the golden spirit shelves, immaculately organised and shiny. 'A couple of days after that, it's all just what it is. It's nothing but functional. Normalised by the brain not wanting to go overboard, like how when you go on a rollercoaster and you get that rush that feels like your head just might explode. That's your brain telling you that it's having too much fun. The thrill is your brain actually burning with overload. Same with here. It's just a bar.'

'When did you buy this joint?' Pete asked, not too keen to discuss the brain right now.

'Beer?'

'Be rude to say no,' Pete said, whacking the rope down and pulling up a stool.

'I bought it a few months ago but I've only just opened it, soft open!'

'This place is operational?'

'Yeah mate, it's what I do now,' said Trent, handing over an ice-cold lifesaving frothy. 'Cheers.'

'Cheers. You're an international man of mystery,' Pete said, lifting the cup of reliability to his lips.

'Or just a Shire-based one?'

'Fuck, I love beer,' said Pete, gulping at it hard, both with focus and with need.

'Yeah, beer is good.'

The two men spent some time with their beers, then when the beers had done their respective jobs, they returned to the other for company.

'What was this joint before? I don't tend to walk down this alleyway. Gavin does but –'

'It used to be an old bike shop,' said Trent, 'but they got so popular that they moved out of the alleyway and up into Cronulla Street for more visibility. I don't want visibility, you see? I want this to be a joint you find, not like JD's or El Sol.'

'What's it called?'

'The Old Bike Shop,' Trent said, proudly nodding at his implicit creativity.

'Right!' said Pete. 'Makes sense. The Old Bike Shop.'

'Yeah, because you know, everyone can ride a bike. All walks of life. Bikes don't discriminate, they're just like, "Get on me!"'

'And how's business? Do you pack it out or … or what's the go?'

'Well, not many people know about it yet, cos, um, you can't really see in from the street, the alley, I mean, and it's not open in the day, so people seem to walk past it at night thinking it's a closed bike shop. So, yeah, it's not like … pumping. But that's intentional, in a kind of New York speakeasy kind of bespoke way, know what I mean?'

'So does anyone come in?'

'Not really,' Trent said, as if he'd just realised it. 'No. No one comes in.'

'Well, I'm here and I love the joint. Dark, with beer and no people. The perfect bar!'

'A waterfall starts with one drop of water and look what comes from that. Anyway, we've got the poetry night on tomorrow. It's called Lost for Words. So we should get some characters rolling through the doors then. I'm going to throw the spotlight up on the little stage back there, which was where the workshop was in the bar's previous life.'

A pulse of excess joy and anxiety ripped through Pete's system. 'Poetry night?'

'Poetry night first Mondays of the month. I got a blues jam night every Tuesday, a trivia night every second Wednesday. Thursday's is Queer Night – our most popular evening. Sundays I'm thinking I'll just give it a bit of a tidy. Of course you'd have to be in the know to know that that's what is happening which means no one *does* know that that's what is happening because I don't even have a website – basically I only want people in here who get the spirit of the place, which is warmth and, like, yeah … acceptance of difference?'

Pete's eyes could not unlock themselves from that little thrust stage up the back, and the curtain that framed it. The whole set-up reminded him of primary school and how often he'd get roped into a showing. Pete was partial to that play *Oliver*. How good was it! The Artful Dodger – geez, he was a goer. And that tale about the guys in the canoe. What was it, *Huckleberry Finn*? Pete remembered playing Huck, and a gum tree – and he even played Jesus once in the Easter show. Alan Bertram usually got the main part cos he was tall but after he left to Joeys in Year Nine, Pete got elevated from Judas to Jesus, and he thought he'd hit the big time until he realised that they were the chunkier parts – the Judases – and that all Jesus really did was act smug and wave his arms about for the miracles.

All these thoughts, and the cold beer, and, yeah, Trent, who was putting on some old Smiths records, then New Order and The Cure, seemed to take the hell away and allow him to block out what just went down at the pokies, and block out the flashes of that hallway and the look on Char's face as she went away, dragging a striped bag full of clothes.

Trent offered Pete a position: 'Official security guard to the Old Bike Shop, starting tomorrow with Lost for Words.'

Not that they'd ever had a scuffle at the joint, but maybe they would one night and, if so, Plum would provide both the hustle and the muscle to keep things in check. Having just poured 8K down the drain and bought some suicide twine, he accepted.

'Security, I gotta install some piping to the AC. You wouldn't mind giving me a hand for a second, would ya?' Trent threw his shirt over the Pac-Man arcade game, revealing quite the washboard six-pack situation. Pete couldn't help but be impressed by the effort.

And so with the two fast friends working in tandem, the ductless split-installation air-conditioning system Trent had purchased online a week ago was up on the back wall – just outside the ladies dunnies – and the piping, well, it was not showing any signs of a decline in quality. Trent had to accept his successor was on top of it.

By nightfall Pete had mopped and wiped down the tables, hoovered, and affixed shower doors in the staff quarters – and the two-man squad could not deny it: the Old Bike Shop had come up alright.

It was getting late and Pete was struggling. He'd been wearing the same T-shirt for two days now and he was so tired that the blinking was coming back. Plus, he couldn't stop thinking that maybe he should try a call or even a 'sorry' text to Char. 'Right, well, see you tomorrow boss?'

'Yes, and don't be late, ok?' said Trent, in a faux boss voice.

The next afternoon Pete arrived, shit-shave-showered, and grateful for the distraction. While they set up for the night, Pete noticed how Trent became more and more nervous, and when their first patron walked in the doors – an older gent in a cord jacket with elbow pads stitched on – Pete could see Trent as a young boy in his private school clothes and imagined just how nervous a kid he would have been, and this only endeared

Trent to Plum more. Trent too lived life as an imposter, albeit a heaps fucking loaded one.

The man with the patches approached the bar. 'Is this the poetry night?'

With no idea where Trent had suddenly disappeared to, Peter improvised. 'Yeah, Lost for Words it's called. Starts at 8 pm. Beer, champ?'

'House wine,' said the academic, then jolted back in his skin as 'Eye of the Tiger' came blaring through the speakers, shaking the walls.

Pete found a bottle of Poet's Corner, unscrewed the lid and filled up a wine glass. The song reminded Peter of *Rocky* and Rocky's love, Adrian – *Adrian!* – which then led Pete to thoughts of Charmayne and how she too had stuck by her bloke when others would not have. He had most likely done that one in for good now. Just like Stallone's embattled character, he'd pushed his luck too far. Luckily, the misery was short-pondered, with some acid-jazz replacing 'Survivor' and the re-emergence of Trent, who was now wearing a black beret, a mustard polo-neck sweater and a pair of high-waisted stonewashed jeans.

'Miles Davis, Rebirth of Cool!' said Trent, pretty confident this was the kind of shit poets would be into.

Plum spotted his rope still on the bar, slung it over his shoulder and made for the door. 'I'll set up outside. Make sure punters are wearing the appropriate footwear.'

'Stay inside. Lost for Words is about to begin. You can't miss the poems!'

'Oh mate, you're a legend, but poems ain't really my thing. Plus I'm security.'

'What's a poet going to do?'

'We hurt with our words,' said their only patron, sipping his dry red and starting to pep up, a manila folder of original metaphysical works under his arm.

'Hooroo,' said Plum, and he was practically out the door – practically saved from the dark angel of the written word and all that would fall out of a pen – when a wheelchair with a live woman in it collided with his shins.

'Fucking hell,' Plum said.

His hands landed on the wheel rims to protect a further head-clash and the loop of sixty-four-dollar rope fell into the woman's lap. Their faces were only inches apart.

'Sorry,' Pete said, breathing hard into her ebullient eyes, her strangely unflinching face.

'You've seen into my soul now,' she said, without the slightest hint of forgiveness or apology.

'I didn't see you coming.'

'Well, men never do.'

'I was waving goodbye.'

'Well, men always are.'

'Did I hurt you?'

'Men usually do.'

'Can I do something?'

'Can you?'

Pete pushed off the wheels and stood up. He was embarrassed as, but for some reason he didn't bolt. The woman picked up the rope and read out the label in a clipped English accent: 'Ideal for a multitude of uses including boating, farming, truck and transport applications.'

'Yeah, it's versatile,' said Pete, looking around and noticing a bunch of people in black smoking near a pot of tulips.

'Are *you* versatile, though?' she asked.

'What?'

'Are you as versatile as this rope?'

'Why?' Pete asked, reaching his hand out for the twine.

Instead of providing the product, she placed her hand in his, gridlocking his gaze once more. 'I need someone to assist in getting my wheelchair, and me, into the bar.'

'Oh, yeah. I can do that. I'm the security guard after all.'

'Then secure me.'

Plum bent down and lifted the whole chair up and carried it around the bend of the doorway and down the three steps into the Old Bike Shop, where Trent and the wine-drinking old man turned around and saw a poem in itself, a visual poem of connection.

'Hello, my name is Jupiter, and welcome to Lost for Words.'

The tiny audience applauded their host, as did Plum, awestruck at the energy in the room. Jupiter was big and beautiful in a dress made of staplers and other Officeworks products, and not only was Pete unwilling to lay a bet down on gender, he also couldn't quite work out if Jupiter was twenty or forty.

'We first started this night at JD's, but it was loudly disrespected by Shire philistines, so, yeah, fuck that …'

The crowd stomped its eighteen feet in solidarity – and as Pete looked around, it was like each person in the joint had crawled out of a different period in history, like the bar was now a real-life museum to the oddness of time, and Pete couldn't help but smile at it all; the flamboyance, the commitment to outfit, and the poise. There was an older woman with bright pink hair, smoking from a cigarette holder. A young blonde woman in a space suit with bleeding red eyes. A black man with his head half-shaved swanning about in a girls school uniform. There were jazz hats and twirled moustaches, gothic young people in layers of black eye make-up, the girl in the wheelchair, and a hippy couple in the corner with their foreheads touching – moaning, stroking each other's arms.

'… and so I'd firstly like to thank that gorgeous, open-hearted, inspirational and downright fucking sexy Trent – for taking the night on and giving us poor misunderstood poets a home.'

The club of misfits stood for Trent, who raised a glass of white wine from the corner then pointed it over to Pete, who was happy to be sitting at the bar on his own with an Asahi to call his friend. Pete had never seen anything like this. Lost for Words was really making sense to him now, as a title – for the first time in Plum's long life in Cronulla, *he* was the one who stood out in the crowd, *he* was the misfit, in his jeans and shirt, in his sad and dripping Plum-ness.

The first poet was a middle-aged woman named Windchime who read a piece called 'Your smoke offends me', about an ex-boyfriend who, as far as Pete could tell, didn't appreciate her smoking. Her next poem was a shorter, punchier offering, about life as a single sixty-year-old:

I thought being single at sixty would be easy peasy lemon squeezy
But it's not, it's difficult, difficult, lemon difficult

There were at least thirty people in the Old Bike Shop now and this line just killed em.

'Looking for a poet to rent? I choose … Trent!' said Jupiter, mic'd up from backstage – meaning behind the red curtain that hung from a makeshift frame on the edge of the rostrum that was the modest Lost for Words stage.

Trent got up, so Pete ducked round behind the bar, ready to serve. No one approached, though. Pete guessed they were either too broke or simply too into poems. But he liked standing there. He was helping out. He was the muscle and the hustle.

'Bridget suggested I do a haiku as my first poem,' Trent said, looking over to the young woman in the wheelchair, who was rolling a cigarette beneath the hanging bike. 'So before I wrote this haiku, I thought I'd better google "what's a haiku?" And, look, most of you may or may not know this but a haiku is a Japanese poem that consists of seventeen syllables in three lines. The first line has five syllables, the second has seven, and then the third one has five – that's a haiku …' A simmering of laughter filled the room, and Trent, looking like Neil from *The*

Young Ones in his mustard turtle-neck, continued on. 'So the next thing I did was google "what's a syllable?"' At his utter sincerity, the Lost for Words audience exploded with laughter, as did Pete, taking the liberty of re-filling his Asahi, heart bursting.

'This haiku is about the bushfires.'

> *Sco-Mo you are dire*
> *What if the Sharks were on fire*
> *Pray for Cronulla*

'Thanks, thanks,' Trent said, as the applause trickled in then away.

Peter made vodka sodas for a couple of girls who had walked in off the street, enjoying the admin of inserting the lemon wedge and then the straw and swirling it all together.

'This next haiku is also about the bushfires, it's about the damage they did and about the koalas who died.' Trent took a deep breath. 'It's called "Fallen Idol".'

And Pete heard the title. He heard it in the deepest of his man chambers.

> *Cute Aussie icon*
> *Hides a terrible shame*
> *Sad chlamydia*

After Trent, a high-energy, ultra-Aussie guy called Tug got up and read a crazy poem about how his dog shits out works of art, followed by a short and sombre offering called 'Swoop'.

> *One day*
> *the police came*
> *to our infant's school*
> *and shot the magpie at playlunch.*

They'd been swooping us.

I thought about them lots after,
those babies in their nest
high up in that gum
starving.

'Last but not least, Bridget!' Jupiter announced, now dressed in
Hello Kitty overalls.

Pete turned to see the woman in the wheelchair appearing
through the curtains. He had no idea how she'd got up there,
let alone made her entrance, but it was enough to make him
stay where he was.

'Hello, my name is Bridget,' she said, sliding the mic down
its stand. 'And this is a poem called "Swap with Me, I'll Swap
With You". It's about how everyone shares the same amount of
pain, no matter what their life's like. So yeah.'

'Settle in, son,' Trent said, sliding a tequila shot to Pete.
'This should be a belter.'

Bridget sat in the silence, and then, as if she'd felt the Gods
were listening, she opened her mouth and you could have heard
a pin drop, that is beneath the noise of the freshly installed AC.

'We love you, Bridget!' screamed Trent.

And then she began:

Please be seated
No one ever said
To me

Neither at weddings
Or lectures
Would they dare?

I have something to tell you

He said
Will you please sit down?

Take a seat, Bridget, said the psych
Now tell me
What seems to be the problem?

I was nineteen, and it was no one's fault
Drunk guy, crazy guy, hit and run
Who knows if hell is fun?

And it hurt
And it hurts
The pain

But you gotta love like you never been hurt
You fuck with Ernie
You fuck with Bert

And you know what
What you got
It's just the same as me
Even if you stand up to wee

So I'll swap with you
If you swap with me
Swap with you, swap with me?

Who cares who hears me now?
Islam, Jesus, Hillsong, believe it
They're just Gods
We're all Gods

And these are just wheels

And inside my chest are just feelings
And inside my feelings it's just envelopes
And messages
That the brain sends through as pain

And I'm afraid of the cold
And I'm afraid of sharks
Cos the pain the pain

But you gotta love like you never been hurt
You fuck with Ernie
You fuck with Bert

So
Are you sitting down
Cos I wanna ask you something

If I swap with you
Will you swap with me?

Do you hear me, brother?
Do you hear me, sir?
Do you gather my meaning, Willy?
Do you all concur?

I said I'll swap with you
If you swap with me
I dare you do the deal?
And no I don't watch the Paralympics

In my garden I have a plum tree
That bathes in the October sun
And come March or come July
It sprouts red purple fruit
Yum, yum, yum

A plum tree. A plum tree. If she wasn't talking directly into his soul already, she had found the tunnel now. Plum had to hold his chest to keep it from exploding. What is this?

It says, hello Bridget, I am plum
Says reach for me, I am plum
Squeeze me, suck me till I die plum
And what I'd do to climb out of my paraplegia
And into your mobility
So I could walk towards that tree of flirting plums

Oh plums
Oh fucking
Fuck you – you sweet unreachable plums
What I'd give to pick a plum

But this seat picked me instead
And so I must wait until you drop
Spin my wheels and pounce
To beat the insects

And so as the night draws to its close
And it is time for us to leave
Let me pose the question once more my friends:
If I swap with you, will you swap with me?

Through the tears that welled in Peter's eye-sockets he thought he could make out Bukowski, leaning against the opposite wall beneath the speakers, sipping from a Budweiser and nodding at the gifted, brazen poet who had just killed the room. But he couldn't be too sure and so he went to find out, went to ask the prick why he'd just left him high and dry in Parramatta the other night. But he didn't make it far because Trent grabbed him and twisted him round, shaking both his

107

shoulders and beaming, his chardonnay breath vehement to say the least.

'How fucken good was that, Plum!? Did you hear that? Did you fucking not love it?'

Plum looked over to where Bukowski may have been and there was nothing there – just space and just the pole. Suddenly, Plum's anxiety was soaring. He felt like his head might cave in and the poets may well feed on its contents. He had to get out of there. So he did, he got out of there, taking Jupiter and Tug's arrival at the bar as his chance to smoke bomb.

'Did you know that kids these days find the full stop offensive?' he heard Tug say on exit.

Outside, Pete lit a dart, exhaled, looked left and then zigged right, only to find Bridget there, by the tulips, also smoking.

'Oh, it's you,' he said, a little star-struck now.

She took a long drag. 'Security, you don't know where I can get any drugs, do you?'

Squeaky had a bloke, but the last time they'd dealt with him, they'd had to get in the car and the guy's baby was in the back *and* his grandmother, it was fucking weird – plus, he couldn't make that call now, not with how he'd let Squeak in on it all, and it being whatever time it was *and* a Monday night. 'No.'

'That's a shame. I feel like getting fucked up. Do you know what I mean?'

'Historically, yes.'

'Oh, speaking of shame spirals, here's your rope.' Bridget took the twine out of her bag and held it up in the night air. Pete, expelling smoke from his lips, walked over and took it from her.

'How'd you do that?'

'What, how'd I get outside? There's a door behind the stage that leads to an alley – push –'

'No, I mean … how'd you do that poem?'

'How'd I write it or how did I perform it?'

'Yeah, how'd you do it?'

'Ha, well, I don't know, Security. How does any poet? I just looked inside, I guess.'

'Inside where?'

'Myself,' said Bridget, nodding at him now.

'How old are you, Bridget?'

'Twenty-nine.'

'Well, you made me cry. And I gotta say, I'm forty-nine, and not much does.'

'Here,' she said, reaching into her handbag and pulling out a small green writing pad, still in its plastic. 'Have this.'

'What is it?'

'It's a gift.'

'A notepad? Why would I want this? I got pens at home.'

'Good, you can start writing right away then.'

'Ha, no way. I'm no poet. I used to play footy, me.'

'Everyone's a poet who has a notepad. And from the brief time I have known you I have gotten the sense there may well be a poet's soul within you. So write a poem.'

'Look, sure, whatever you say, but I can't write good, not like you.'

'All words are good if you mean them. Poetry is just a window to the soul. It's a way of getting to the truth. Don't worry if it's good or not, just get it down, it's *for* you.'

'It's for me?'

'Yes, poetry is art in a vacuum. It is for the poet only. Not for the people.'

'If poetry is for the poet only then why read it out in front of other people?'

'Because people's secrets are the best entertainment, right?'

'Huh?'

'Because we relish in spying *on* others. Poetry is spying *in* others. Out in the open.'

Pete laughed

'Just let yourself.'

This young woman in a wheelchair. Where the fuck has she come from?

'Can I give you a push home? Or whatever the right thing to say is?'

Bridget laughed out loud at this. 'Goodnight Security. I look forward to your offerings,' she said, rolling off down the alleyway and into the suburban moonlight.

When Pete got home from Lost for Words, the teen couple had clearly gone to bed, he could see their phones in the hallway stacked on top of each other like an ad for an iCouple. Charmayne, well, naturally she was still nowhere to be seen. Nor should she be; he hadn't bothered to call, nor had he texted or messaged her. He was too full of shame and, also, he had no idea what had happened Saturday night when he got home. All he knew was that Brick had come to collect all her stuff while he was at work, because he'd texted to tell him that exact thing: 'Plum, popped in to get Chars shit. Talk soon ay. Chin up'.

Pete arrived in the bedroom to find that all her stuff was indeed gone. It reminded him of when his dad would come home at 4 am and they'd have to do just that, shove clothes into garbage bags and go.

And so, with no one about and nothing to lose that he had not already lost, he did what the girl in the chair had said to do – he unwrapped the notepad, flipped the lid off a pen and tried to express himself.

At first nothing came.

He drank the OJ left over from Gavin and Ainslee's homemade bircher.

Nothing came again, and again.

But then he rolled his shoulders over and back a few times, took a breath, thought of the way she had said 'plum' so many times and then a word fell onto the page, and then another one after it, and pretty soon he had nine lines of words:

Nothin to write down about
Cept my son
Poetry in motion
This arvo we were in the ocean
And I coulda cried the same amount of water
Never had a daughter
Woulda liked one
Maybe she'd have helped me
Soften the fuck up

Having written his first ever original poem, Pete sat there, still as a vase, until it was nearly three in the morning ... which was when another eight lines fell out:

Soften up
Hard man
Soften up
Plum
Soften up
It's picking season
It's time
To soften the fuck up

With poetry softening his thoughts the fuck up, Pete decided that in the morning he would go to Brick Wall's gym and tell his 'Saffa', Charmayne Slocombe, what had happened with Qantas that day. He would tell her the whole tarmac thing. And whatever she decided to do would be alright. He wouldn't get angry. He would stop sinking piss and he would get his shit together. He would say sorry to Gav, and to Ainslee, and find the money for Bali somehow and then, when all of this was done, he would go to Liz the brain woman for the 'bo-peep' thingo. Because, as the great Spudd Carroll used to say, as he stuffed his face with boiled potatoes pre-game, 'DON'T LET FEAR HOLD YOU BACK!'

Pete pegged the rope into the bin, placing the empty Rude Health Bircher bag on top of it so his kid wouldn't see it and raise the dubious topic over muesli.

He slid the green notepad under some bills in the fourth drawer, brushed his teeth, flossed and went to sleep, thinking of that song in the musical *Annie* that his mum used to play all the time on weekends, the one where she keeps singing the word 'tomorrow'.

Three

It was only after Gavin had arrived in the form of a newborn baby that Renee became afraid of flying. Before then, she'd been more than happy to zip up her overnight bag and hop onto a plane, accompanying Pete to Tassie or Perth or Eden Park for games. When they were living in Lancashire, they'd pop to Italy, Spain and Portugal a fair bit, but the moment she became a mum she could barely say the word 'airport', like something had clicked in her: she had to *not* die. When Pete started working for Qantas, he got her into the Fearless Fliers course, but she ran out of the simulator when the engine started up.

But nearly seventeen years had passed since Gav was born and he told his mum in no uncertain terms she had three weeks to get her shit together because Frank Ponissi, GM of the Storm, had said they'd fly all four of them – Gav, his girlfriend and his parents – down to Melbourne on a VIP charter plane, purple on the outside, them on the inside.

For Gavin, it was a chance to show his older girlfriend how big-time he was now. For Ainslee, it was a time to pretend she was dating an American basketball player and that they were on their way to Vegas in their jet, lathered in bling, Insta pumping. For Plum, it was a chance to get outside his bubble, take a breath from the world that was clearly doing his head in and get a dose of Victorian perspective. For Renee, it was about connecting with her first family and freeing herself of the second.

'Ollie said take one Valium now and then one on the plane with a G and T,' she said as she made her way across the tarmac to the aeroplane, which looked about as big as a station wagon.

'And this guy is a GP?' asked Peter, feeling sharp in a brown suit and tie.

'Oh my God, Plum, I'm so nervous.'

'It's only forty-five minutes in the actual air, Mum.'

'Oh my God, the sunrise is so good – look, babe,' said Ainslee, re-playing her Insta video as she took the fold-down stairs to the aircraft backwards and with pace.

'Riders on the Storm!' sang Plum.

Renee shrieked. 'No storms yet, please!'

There were about fifteen other people on the twenty-something seater and from what Pete could tell they were either finance types, surgeons whose area of speciality meant they were rushed places and at odd times, and a couple of other young footy players from Jersey Flegg, also travelling down with their guardians to tour the premises after putting in a sterling performance when it counted.

'G and T for me, please darling. Peter, a nice cold beer for you?'

It had been three weeks since Pete had had a beer, so when the trolley came rolling down the aisle, it took him a second to think about it. 'Oh no, it's a bit early for me, thanks. Just a diet coke.'

Plus, the GP had him on the Ritalin now, after the anti-depressants failed to provide any sort of 'anti', and had been unequivocal in his advice: 'Do not *ever* drink alcohol with this drug, Peter.'

'Always cocktail hour somewhere in the sky,' Renee said, recalling the person she used to be when she was child-free. This was to be her first trip away since she'd had baby Tallulah and she wasn't going to miss out on a second of joy. She would drink gin, shop large and chat away her fear of flying.

Gavin, nostrils flared, leant across the aisle. 'Can we have an alcoholic drink, Dad?'

'Course you can,' Renee answered, mixing the gin into her glass with a little red stick.

'Why don't you wait till after we do the meeting this arvo?' Pete said. 'Have a few to celebrate tonight at Jim's Greek Tavern? Ainslee, can you please stop filming everything?'

'It's just Instagram, Mr Lum. Plus, I'm on private, so it's like ... only two hundred people or whatever that can see my content.'

'Well, that's a hundred and ninety-seven more than I want,' Pete said, turning his attention to the flight attendant as Renee cracked open both his and her complimentary pretzels. 'Two OJs for the kids, thanks love.'

'Since when did you become so sensible, Mr Lum?' asked Renee, beaming at him – a mad mix of fear and freedom having a party on her face.

Pete shrugged, unsure as to if it was even true. But ten minutes later, when Renee had her earpods in, he looked over the aisle at his son sipping OJ and watching *Ozark* on Ainslee's tablet, and nearly exploded with things like pride and things like joy. He remembered the time he'd been asked to the ACT to play in a trial match in front of NRL scouts – and at the exact same age of sixteen.

Getting the call-up was so huge for him, his mum and his sister, Sarah. But it was short-lived cos they got another call ten minutes later saying he had to make his own way to Canberra. The facts were that, at the time, they just didn't have the right amount of dollars to get him on the bus, suited up and registered. And with his mum being as stoic a working-class woman as she was, there would be no accepting the generosity of neighbours, schools and/or friends. They had to be the ones to solve the money problem internally, and they had to solve it in less than two weeks or stay home.

So they went for it. His nineteen-year-old sister worked twice as many hours at the milk bar up Engadine West, his mum did the same at the dentists where she was already a three-day-a-week secretary, and Peter doubled his hours for Waratah Meats, working before and after school hooking up the carcasses and mopping the bloody floors.

With the penultimate Saturday morning looming, and the family still $24.45 short, Pete's mum was left with no choice but to contact Albert and see if he could cough up the difference. Finally, via a brief phone booth phone call, Albert obliged, saying he would train it down from Lithgow and meet his son outside Caringbah McDonald's at 10 am Saturday with the last of the money, giving Peter plenty of time to make the 5 pm bus that afternoon from Sutho station to the nation's capital. The game was on Sunday, and Pete would be staying overnight with a host family in Queanbeyan – and for a kid his age who, after his first ten years in Orange, had rarely ventured out of Caringbah, Canberra may as well have been the moon.

Pete arrived at Maccas in his reps tracksuit at 7.30 am. For the first hour and a half he sat in the playground, figuring his dad wouldn't be coming in by car so this would be the best vantage point for pedestrian arrival. When it got to 10 am on his watch, Pete moved inside, thinking maybe his dad was waiting for him in there, plus he needed a slash like no bloke ever had. At noon Pete bought six nuggets. He felt guilty spending some of the bus money, but he seriously thought if he didn't eat he'd faint. And if he fainted, then his dad might not see him cos he'd be lying on the floor behind the statue of Ronald McDonald.

At 2 pm Pete wondered if he should go home. He felt weird hanging out at Maccas this long. The staff had asked his intentions on more than one occasion. And Peter thought if he could just talk to his mum, he'd know what was up with his dad.

He started walking home, shattered, angry and thirsty. But then, remembering how pumped his dad had seemed on the blower, he turned round and walked back, returning to the family restaurant, thinking, *Nah, me old man always comes through; it's me china plate, and even though he doesn't live with us no more, he isn't a liar. He never lied, he just didn't always come home or turn up …*

Pete spent the next few hours sitting up against the yellow Maccas fence line counting cars and watching families going in and out of Clark Rubber, emerging with pool ponies and pool bananas of all shapes and colours. He couldn't believe how happy and together all those families seemed, pool-bound and perfect, realising, perhaps for the first time in his life, that his family situation was not as good as most.

At 4 pm it got cold so Pete stood up again, thinking he was likely getting piles. At 4.30 pm he kicked the fence, said 'Fuck' and 'This is rigged' and 'No way' a couple of times each, then started walking home again, resigned to the fact that he wasn't going to ever make it as an NRL player because his dad hadn't turned up with the twenty-five.

Pete knew he was better than all the kids his age. He'd won best and fairest and played in the grade above his age group for most of the year. But, cos of Albert, the bloke he loved and hated equally and at once, he was going to end up runnin Waratah Meats then getting fat like his uncles, drinking piss at Taren Point Tavern and talking about what could have been and what he would do if he was playing the game currently on tele.

But then a voice behind him said, 'Me china plate,' and Pete turned around to see his dad flicking a dart into the traffic from across the road.

'Yeah?' young Pete yelled, about to cry, but no way would he – it was his dad standing just over there.

'I said Maccas, yeah?'

'Yeah.'

'Then why are you walking away from the joint?'

'I just thought –' Pete swallowed '– cos it's nearly five now, that you –'

'Come and get it then. Your bus is in fifteen minutes. You can't friggin miss it, Pete.'

Pete waited for an excavating truck to pass, then walked over the road to get his ticket to freedom.

His dad leant in and hugged him like he was trying to get air out of a pool pony. He stank like not-good wine and Pete thought he saw blood on his dad's white shirt.

'Knock em dead me china plate,' Albert whispered. 'You're me china plate, remember?'

'I know.'

'Say it then.'

'Say what, Dad?'

'China plate. Say it.'

'You're my china plate.'

'Good, now off you pop. You can't miss your bus now I've come all this way.'

'Where are you gonna go?'

'Back.'

'Back where?'

'From where I came down from. Lithgow.

'Mum said you have another family. Is that true, Dad?'

'I came through, yeah? With cash for ya trip,' said Albert, flicking his arms out in unison.

'Yeah.'

'Then get!' Albert said, pointing to the horizon, where young Peter Lum now faced as he walked away from his father, trying hard not to cry hard. 'Never take a backwards step!'

*

The plane landed so softly it was almost an apology.

Ainslee, phone out and filming, dared Gavin to raise his arms up like a rockstar as he walked down the ladder to the tarmac. Pete, sedated, told his son to settle down, reminding him he hadn't achieved anything yet – *Don't go acting like Keith Richards* – and, as expected, Gav asked who Keith Richards was.

Renee, jazzed as on three gin and tonics, took her time saying goodbye to the pilot – taking his phone 'for a sec' then kissing his hand – but then she surprised Pete by asking him if he was ok. Pete didn't know what she meant, losing to her in Travel Uno was not a new thing and, yeah, the choc-chip muffin was alright if a touch on the dry side but as they neared the tiny, functional airport terminal to collect their bags, she gestured to the tarmac behind him with a swirl of her arm. 'Are you ok?' she repeated.

Pete looked back at the concrete basketball court that gave alley-oop to the heavens and, yes, a flutter of nerves and a pulse of that ominous burn did erupt within him again. But this was not new music. Every day he thought of the moment he near killed a bunch of innocent humans. This would be the one that followed him: the day he towed a plane out then had some sort of seizure. Luckily for him he had methylphenidate to drown it all out.

'Go easy on the room service, you two – and you, woman,' Plum said, playfully handing his Mastercard over the counter while sending his ex-wife a wink.

'What time do we have to be back down here?' Gavin asked, unable to hide the epic notion of a big hotel bed and an amorous girlfriend from his parents.

Renee winked back at Plum. 'Well, Ainslee and I are going shopping while the boys visit the facility – from what I remember it's all about Flinders Lane and Smith Street!'

Pete looked at his watch. 'Let's all meet down here in an hour and forty-five minutes.'

'Twelve noon it is,' said Renee, batting away Ainslee's phone camera, which once again was operational, 'and no videoing on the shopping spree. I look like Magda Szubanksi since the baby.'

'Sharon Strzelecki!' bellowed Gavin, and then 'Look at moiiiii,' doing a wheelie with his roller bag towards the lifts, his two-day sojourn of life 'firsts' all about to begin in style.

'And will you two be sharing a room?' the hotelier asked Plum and Renee.

'No, there should be two booked under Lum?' asserted Peter.

Renee was watching her son disappear into the lifts, holding back tears. He was a man now, and she knew that once those lift doors shut, he would not need her as much, he would replace her with his lover, as kids did when they got partners, as she did when she met Pete.

'Oh look, we're in adjoining rooms.'

Pete threw some Asics and a singlet on, smashed out five kays on the runner, then cooled off in the rooftop pool whose top lip hung over the public street below. Meanwhile, Renee was in the bath, texting the pilot and sipping on the complimentary prosecco. Six doors down and around the corner from his mother's room, Gavin lay back against the duck-feather-and-down pillows as Ainslee tore open the packet of non-latex condoms she had bought at Miranda Fair eleven weeks ago, and then with tender amounts of caution and curiosity, the young pair of loving athletes sent their virginity out the window, over Federation Square and down into the Yarra.

Being flown to Melbs, family and all, to check out the facility, well, it was overwhelming – and for the past three weeks Gavin Albert Lum had barely stopped shaking. But thanks to what had just gone down in room 717, in that magical one hour and forty-five minute hotel limbo period, the boy was calm on approach. Not only had he seen AAMI Stadium before, having travelled down with his dad six or seven years ago when Pete was guest commentating a Sharks v Storm qualifying semi, but when Ryan Hinchcliffe walked them into the gym and dressing room facility, what would on any other day have had Gavin losing his bundle and hyperventilating was met with a quiet admiration – for he had just done 'ok' in his own pressure colosseum: Between the Sheets. And the exhibiting images were still flicking past like a mini highlights package on the *Big League Wrap* with Yvonne Sampson in the chair, applauding his artistry. Sex was fun and he seemed to be good at it, even that last bit where he got over the side of her leg, placed his thumb in the dint of her hipbone and started working that little angle – like a hacksaw made of kindness – and she had said she 'adored' it and that it hadn't even hurt that much because he was so considerate. Put simply, he could not wait to go again; strategies and ideas for set-plays were forming in his head like it was game day.

'We've come a long way in our journey with the Storm, from being the outcasts of rugby league with a tarnished name to being the club everyone wishes they could play at. What Bellyache drills into the boys, you can't find anywhere else,' Ryan said as he led Pete and Gavin down the mauve-and-white striped tunnels.

'Yeah, no, even if a player moves on from the system here, it's obvious watching them what stock they're hailing from,' Pete said, and he meant it.

'That's it, that's it, Plum, you get it. Plus if you're lucky, Gavin, you might get to meet Molly Meldrum. The Storm's biggest fan!'

'Who?' asked Gavin, softly to his dad.

'"Do yourself a favour",' joked Pete to no avail.

After forty-eight handshakes with ultra-energised blokes called 'Jase' and 'Nath', whose job titles sounded like power tools, and one firm handshake from Frank Ponissi, Gav felt they'd completed a thorough-enough reconnaissance of the premises.

But when they emerged from the recovery ice baths into the cascading glass offices, there stood Billy-fucking-Slater and Craig-fucking-Bellamy, waiting patiently in lilac suit and ties to greet the father and son duo.

'Jesus Christ,' whispered both Lums at once.

'How was the trip down?' asked marketing force Tayah Bot, on behalf of the Storm.

'Yeah, no, good,' said Gavin, but they were not asking him – Craig, Billy and the next set of power tools were all taking their turns in hugging Plum.

'Who have you got in the big dance?' they then asked, cos they would be featuring as per usual.

Plum looked to his son, but Gav'd lost the confidence to answer this one, so Pete just shrugged and said, 'Maybe Roosters in a tight one,' to which they all guffawed.

'Gentlemen? Quick snap? For Melbourne Storm socials?' suggested Tayah.

Once the shots were in the can and the reveries satiated, Gavin reclined in one of the big black ergonomic thrones in the corner, letting it all play out before him. And as the hour-fifteen passed without him being asked a single question, Gavin began to grasp that the ten-strong posse of Storm stars and staff had gathered not to meet a potential pivot but to walk deathly slow down memory lane with one of the game's greats: Peter 'The Plum' Lum. His dad. *Not him!* Not him at all. And, look, usually, this would not sting the boy – he admired his father more than anyone. But when Billy Slater finally shifted proceedings in his direction, he had formed quite the spiky resentment to his dad, whose behaviour of late had been mysterious, annoying and, frankly, a bit fucked.

'Craig here seems to think you'd make a handy number 6 for the Storm in a few years, Gavin,' said Billy.

The adoring fans finally shifted their lens to him, but it was too late, Gavin's rage had taken possession and there would be no hiding it. Like father like son, in that way.

'If he trains hard and *shows the right qualities*, I said, Bill,' Craig said, forcing a smile.

'What do *you* think?' Billy asked Gavin, expecting the kid to spout forth with what no player his age ever lacked: blind self-confidence.

But the boy didn't answer, he just sat there and shrugged. *Whatever.*

'That would be your dream, wouldn't it, son?' Plum prompted, a purple Storm hat resting diagonally on his skull.

'Would it, Dad? I don't know. You tell me.'

'Sorry?' said Craig, looking over to Billy.

'Hey?' said Billy Slater. 'You wanna play at the Storm, Gavin?'

'Do you not want to sign my dad instead? Peter "The Plum" Lum? I got to say, if you do, he's been lacking consistency of late, and I know, down here at the Storm, it's all about consistency, right?'

'Ya fucken clown, what was that about?' Plum said, once they were outside on the pavement. He was draped in purple merchandise and fuming at his son.

'Hey?' asked Gavin.

And then Plum's phone rang, and it was Renee, mid-monologue. Peter and Renee had an appointment of their own now, and with the Storm session going way over, it was looking like they may be late.

'Rightio, Ren,' Plum said. 'You can show us the shoes then! Oh look, the cab's here. Gotta go love. Ok Ren? I'm hanging up the phone because we won't be long!' Plum ended the call, which was no small achievement. 'We'll talk about it on the way to Coburg,' he said to Gav as they launched into the cab.

'Will we?'

'Hey?'

'Or will we just *not* talk about it, Dad? Cos we're men. Lum men.'

The kid knew something was wrong a couple of weeks ago when they went up to Brick's for a sweat sesh.

As they lifted up the roller door, which was cut out of a greater tin roller door that acted as the front wall of the gym, they could see Brick in the ring, using a foam noodle to train a Sudanese featherweight. A newcomer to the gloves, Kutiote had once been a child soldier so nothing much fazed him, Brick had told Pete, and he had the feet of Fred Astaire to match an innate tenacity, so if he didn't find it in the ring, Brick was confident he'd get a go in the cage.

'Look out!' said Brick, alerted to the scraping sound of the tin door. 'It's the power couple.' Brick had bought the mechanics workshop in 2001 off his brother-in-law and it still had the feel of rusted engines and hubcaps; plus, if it rained you seriously needed earplugs.

'Thought we'd pop up and say g'day,' said Pete.

'G'day Gavin …' Brick said, panting with great affection. Brick's own son Kirk was far from sporty – all into gaming and drones; living in a headpiece online and only eating white food – so the kids he trained, and his mates' ones, well, they were pretty much his kids too. Gavin knew Brick was like his second dad from around the time he turned seven, when Brick told him to stand behind him when it was pissing down on the hill at Shark Park. Not a drip of water had hit him. Brick took all the impact on his yellow windbreaker – gut-first. And from then on that's what Gav did whenever the skies opened: he went and stood behind his Uncle Brick, the human weather shield.

'Uncle Brick.'

Uncle Brick didn't miss a beat. 'This is one of the boys I'm training,' he said as he spun the fighter round with the help of the pink tube. 'Kutiote from Sudan. Kutiote, this is my best mate, Peter, and Peter's son, Gavin.'

'Hello Peter, hello Gavin,' said Kutiote, with the smile of a black Julia Roberts.

'G'day Kutiote,' the Lums said, in unison, hoping they got the name sounding ok.

'Kutiote, hit the bag for twenty and give me some skipping please,' Brick said. 'Gavin, you put some wraps on, you're hitting pads with me. Peter! You're out back, there's a certain lady boxer just might want to have a few rounds.'

'Yes, Uncle Brick,' Gav and Pete said at once, both frightened of what they might well cop.

Gav bolted across the oil-stained floor to grab some used wraps off the hook, making sure he didn't get in the way of Kutiote, who had left the ring and was already throwing rib ticklers into a long red bag hanging by a chain from a steel beam that held together the wire-wild aluminium roof.

Pete closed his eyes, using the familiar smells of men and sweat and tiger balm to calm him, then he mumbled the word 'rightio' and pushed on down the back of the gym, passing a couple of big boys trying to bench one hundred and fifty kilograms.

'Let's start with a seven-punch combination to get things going, son,' Pete heard Brick say to Gav in the ring. 'Jab-jab, right, left hook, right uppercut, left uppercut, left hook, finish him. Ok?'

Gav sprayed Brick's pads with punches. Kutiote sprayed the bag with sweat. And Charmayne, at the back of the gym, accidentally sprayed Peter with a hose.

'Sorry!' she said – *but was she?* 'Just lost my grip.'

'What're you doin?' Pete asked her, flicking the drips off his neck and chin.

'What's it look like? I'm cleaning out a bar fridge.'

'Need a hand? I don't mind getting –'

'No, I don't need … I can clean out a bar fridge on my own.'

The playful tone went away with the closing twist of the nozzle.

'Charmayne, come on, I –'.

'What do you want, Plum? I'm busy. I'm at work.'

Charmayne put her hands on her hips, which Pete knew meant she didn't want whatever was happening at this juncture. He turned around, noting the new bamboo torches and fire pit.

'So this is where you'll be setting up Gym N Trim, is it?'

'Brick's letting me trial the salad bar up front, so we'll see how it goes, but there's already lots of interest from the members.'

'Really?'

'Yeah, people want to eat healthy food straight after a work-out, they don't want to have to wait. And with Gym N Trim you can just grab it on your way out and it's there to consume when you're probably *still* sweating!'

'Amazing.'

'Is that sarcastic?'

'No, I mean it. You're amazing, love.'

'Really?'

'I'm into it.'

'You hate salad.'

'No, I don't.'

There was a gap in proceedings. Plum touched a bamboo pole and coughed.

Charmayne grabbed her thermos and headed over to a bench in the corner. 'Do you even remember the other night, Peter?'

'Not everything. But … I'm sorry. Gavin found me on the lawn.'

'Do you remember the hour you spent inside the house?'

Plum paused, wishing sometimes that women would just say their piece instead of doing this circular navigation thing, this emotional Mr Squiggle. 'Nope. I don't. What went down?'

'What *went down*?'

'Ride the porcelain bus home, did I?'

Charmayne stared at the bar fridge that Brick had brought in; with a good clean she was certain it would work perfectly for storing stuff she was actively using for 'Todays Offerings'. Then she took a massive deep breath. 'Peter.'

'Tell me.'

'You scared the shit out of us!'

'Alright ...' said Pete, glancing around to see a full Form and Function class pausing their jumping jacks and looking right at him and the screaming Charmayne.

'No, it's not *alright*!'

'Are you going to tell me what I did?'

'Do you really want to know?'

'I asked you what went down. Can we do this somewhere else? How about a beer?'

'I don't want to go anywhere else. This is my office. No beer!'

'Ok, fine, then tell me what went down.'

'Ok, well. I was in bed. Lying awake, feeling pretty shit because that day, that day I had gotten in a car driven by a teenager because, I now realise – having been told yet another lie – my partner isn't allowed to drive a car for six –'

'Who told you that?' he asked, knowing full well whose lips had loosened, having sunk ships across the coast of NSW her whole life.

'And so he had lied and got his son's *girlfriend* to drive, and she had never driven out of her fucking suburb but, no, here she was driving on the M4. Yes, and little old Gavin, not knowing who he was on the biggest day of his life, playing in the Jersey Flegg grand final, the game of his life, the game at

127

which his greatest hero and mentor, who also happens to be his old man, gets up and leaves twenty-odd minutes into the first half, just walks out of the row and leaves without even a … anything! Can you imagine how that made us all feel? Can you imagine how embarrassed it made your son feel? Can you imagine the bullshit we had to spin to get the boy in a good mood again? The boy, the sweet boy, who had just shocked the entire stadium with the most spectacular display of athleticism, all for one man, all to show one man, his dad, that he was just like him, that he has it too, that freakish combination of natural talent mixed with the smarts that he has learnt from playing, and from listening, looking up and listening, to the guy now spouting bloody Shakespeare in his ear –'

'Band of Brothers is a good –'

'So later we're all in the Parramatta Leagues Club, and the officials, and the coaches, and the scouts are all looking for that same one man, by the name of Peter Lum – oh yeah, where is he? Where is the father of the hero? The man of the moment's man-behind-the-man? He's not in here, is he? No, why would he be here?'

'Sounds like Brick covered for me.'

'Yeah, he did. He turned up for the kid.' Charmayne stood up again, taking a sip from her thermos and then breathing deep into her aching chest. 'And for me, you know?'

He didn't know, he didn't remember. And not just that event, not just that night after Parra, Peter didn't remember anything, nothing, not properly anyway. Not these days. Just snippets. Like the pokies, like Trent, like Bukowski. He could barely remember his playing career, or his wedding day, all he could remember was that girl in the wheelchair talking about swapping lives. The rest was a blur, and he couldn't blame it on booze. Because it wasn't blackout, it was greyer than that; it was like playing footy in the rain. 'I'm sorry.'

'We got home and Gav went to bed. I told him it was all ok, and that we were so proud of him. And that his dad was just having a moment. "It happens to old blokes," I said. "It was probably just because he was too proud. That's what I said. "Your dad was probably too proud of you.""

'Jesus, ok ...'

'And then you came through the door. You'd pissed yourself. You stunk of everything that's rotten in the night. You took a beer out of the fridge, and you said, "You can get it milking a cow," and you started milking it into your mouth. And then you grabbed me – you grabbed me in the hallway and you pushed me up against the wall and you held me there, trying to kiss me, and laughing, and you said, "Let's do the luge, Char! Let's do the luge!"'

'I did not.'

'You did too. And then I realised your son was in the hall, and I told him –'

'What did you tell him?'

'I told him to go to sleep and we would see him in the morning.'

'And did he?'

'What?'

'Go to his room?'

'He did the second time I asked him. By God, yes, he did. And I don't like to speak that way, you know I don't.'

'I know.'

'I learnt how to speak that way from my father in South Africa but I do not like to have to speak that way to anyone else, let alone to –'

'I know, I'm sorry, but ...' Pete trailed off, still unable to look up and find her eyes, preferring the comfort of the fake grass as his landscape right now.

'I tried to put you in the shower.'

'What did I say to that?'

129

'You said, "No, Renee".'

'Renee?'

'Yeah, you called me by your ex-wife's name.'

'Shit.'

'Well, not really. Seems like she's still your number one. Your next of kin.'

And now he was proper sprung. Renee had not been able to shut her mouth. It was all out in the open.

'You don't ever change do you, mate?'

'Char –'

'What happened at the airport, Peter? At Qantas. Peter, fucking look at me.'

He finally looked up from the fake grass. Her eyes had been one of the first things he noticed about her. They were brown but they were also a dark green in the (Parisian) moonlight, and, over time, they had become the safest place for him to gaze into, for him to truly disappear. But now he couldn't hold that gaze. He couldn't even look towards her face. His eyes were on fire and his brain was crackling again. 'I'm going to go for a walk.'

'Yeah, go drink some beer. Hang out with your mates. Put on a few bets.'

He had so hoped she had not checked the balance of their joint account, but the 'bets' jibe concerned him so he didn't turn to go, he simply stood there facing her, wishing she could feel just how afraid he was, and that he had always been this afraid, and that the fear that drove him to win, was the same fear that drove him to hide, and that he loved her, and that if she left him, he would be as good as dead – because he'd never had to deal with heartbreak before, he'd never let anyone into the bloody thing to expose it. With Renee, well, they were so young, but this, this was real.

But instead, maybe because he *was* scared, maybe because he was ashamed and vulnerable, he turned it back on her, just like his dad had shown him, with all them drunken screaming matches in the kitchen somehow ending up his mum's fault. 'You'll be right. You got Brick now, right?'

'Don't be a pig. Brick is helping me.'

'Yeah, sure he is. Sure he is.'

'I care for you, Peter Lum. But until you've done the work, on whatever your father did –'

'Fuck you,' Peter said, pointing at her now, enflamed. 'How about *your* dad, ay?'

'I have done the work on my dad.'

'You say that but you still date older fucked-up men who are never going to give you what you want. Right?'

'Fuck off, you prick,' she said, throwing her empty thermos at him.

Pete turned and walked back through the gym, past the dispersing class – some of whom were clearly weighing up their exhaustion with their desire to get a selfie with the great man – past Kutiote and towards the tin doorway he had helped Brick cut, refusing to look to his left for fear of seeing his son once again excelling in a way that he had shown him, the gentle art of boxing, the beautiful art of self-defence, the pugilist ballet.

'Peter, turn around,' Charmayne said, having rushed to follow him. 'I know that you and your dad had a really hard –'

'You know nothing about my dad!' Pete yelled, silencing the entire gym. With an open hand, he slapped himself on the heart and then the forehead. 'He was *my* dad!' he said, his voice cracking like he was sixteen again and waiting outside Maccas. 'My dad!'

Was it the tears in Gavin's eyes, the shock on Brick's face, or just the hurt in Char's crumpled posture? Perhaps it was the multi. Suffice to say, the very next day Pete was at the Gymea GP at 9 am, banging on the door, asking for a prescription. He didn't care about himself but he had to get the sadness sorted, because messing with loved ones was not in his playbook.

Peter had asked Renee to accompany him to the consult in Melbourne, not because he wanted her there to hold his hand again – quite the opposite – but because this time he *had* to. The specialist, Liz Lombardo, had said on the phone that it was *protocol* he have a 'witness' with him when they did his 'character analysis', so at the hotel they'd left the kids to it, with little objection, and cabbed it to the Brain Centre as a pairing.

'The results of your tests are all Plum Normal,' said Liz, shuffling freshly printed-out pages into a manila folder. 'Pun intended!' She had deliberated on that joke way too much; she'd actually asked her wife about it. Sharon was an ex-AFL player turned physio and, yeah, she'd thought, why not say 'Plum Normal' – whether the patient appreciated the gag or not, he'd surely be happy to know he didn't have dementia.

'All three tests?' asked Pete, leaning in.

'What tests did you get?' Renee said, still upbeat from her shopping spree, and the bottle of natural wine that she and Ainslee had enjoyed in the hotel bar while waiting for the boys to get back from AAMI Stadium. 'I didn't know you got tests. You didn't tell me.'

'Yeah, I saw the GP three weeks ago. I had tests last week. Why is that –'

'Dr Cameron made the appointments for us and issued the referrals,' added Liz, grateful to have got her previously blasé patient in action mode.

'That's very diligent of you, Peter.'

'I went about anxiety and depression.'

Renee's eyeballs went diagonally up and left with confusion.

'I went to see the doctor about anxiety and depression.'

'You've got anxiety? No. You're the most laidback bloke I know.'

'Perhaps he hides it well,' Liz said.

'Hmmm. To Be Discussed. What tests did you get?'

'Peter got an MRI, an EEG and a CT scan,' Liz said, in full support.

Renee leant back into the wall, nodding at her ex with rare approval, and Pete had to shake his head at the woman, sitting there so overt and smug – *like seriously, Ren.*

Liz shook the manila folder, straightening up proceedings. 'Seizures can cause secondary damage so it's a nice thing for us that none of the tests have shown any abnormalities.'

'Great!' Renee said, ready to go if he was.

'Now, this doesn't mean we're out of the woods, but it's a good result.'

'I'm happy with it,' Pete said, almost cracking a smile. 'Plum Normal: could be the name of my autobiography.'

'Yeah, look out, Dymocks,' Liz said, relieved the joke had landed. 'But, still, the report is that you had a major epileptic seizure a month or so ago, and so I would like to characterise that by asking you both a few questions, if that's alright with you two?'

Renee said, 'Shoot,' and took off the coat that she had nabbed only hours ago on sale for $680 at Saba.

Pete said, 'Sure,' but sat back in his chair, confused by her medical tone so soon after the 'plum normal'.

'Now, on the phone we went through the witness account of what happened at the airport, and I have spoken with your GP about it, and I am aware that your memory of the day is blurry and that you don't really know what happened. Is this still correct?'

'Yeah,' said Pete, not offering an abundance. When neither woman said anything he realised he'd need to elaborate. 'I was just, yeah, leading the aircraft out … and next thing … that's it … gone … and I didn't even know … about it all … till I was told –'

To Plum's relief, Liz interrupted him. 'Exactly, so I'm not going to drag you back through all that, but what I would like to know from you, Peter, is that, hmmm, can you recall or have you noticed in the past little while, since the airport seizure, any funny types of feelings or curious sensations? I like to call them "turns". Have you felt in any way, any alterations or different things from time to —'

'No,' Pete said, a little too fast. 'Everything's been good.'

'Ok, ok. Now, it's my understanding that you two are no longer married, but you share a child and still spend time together in your weekly lives?'

'Yes, Peter and I are very close still,' Renee said, flicking the hair that she'd had blow-dried at Show Dry for $87 not that long ago. 'I mean, I was the next of kin on his work sheet, which should give you some idea …'

Liz leant back. Oh, how she did love herself a precious white woman ex-girlfriend; she'd had plenty of them in her own history, which only endeared her to this client more.

'Well, good, then would you mind me asking you, Renee, if you have noticed, even over the past year or two, any alterations or mood shifts, behavioural type changes in your ex-partner?'

'I don't really see Peter as an ex-partner, I see him more as a confidante and a friend. To be honest with you. I know Peter better than anyone, and I'll tell you, if Peter was going to show his true self to someone, then that person would be me.'

Peter scoffed, wishing he could say sorry to Liz because Ren was always like this. Whenever there were people of a certain authority or media power or any stature about, she'd lean back and act like she was on a television show being interviewed by Tracey Spicer or something.

'Yes or no?'

Renee gazed off into space, giving the moment everything she had. 'So has he acted different? Is what you are asking me.'

'Yep, that's it, Renee.'

'He seems distracted of late, Liz. He seems like he is looking through me a lot of the time. And at our son's grand final recently — instead of sitting through the whole game he just — at like one point in the game, not that far in, mind you, I just sensed him, staring at me, from three seats down, with blank eyes, and then he just … got up and walked out of the place. Gone baby gone.'

Pete held up his hand, wishing he could send her to the sin bin. 'Which then led Renee to, you know, head on down to the leagues club where she had a few wines and told my girlfriend all about the incident at the airport, even though I asked her to give me time to tell her and Gavin myself.'

'Gavin doesn't know,' Renee said.

'Oh, and you want a medal for that, do ya?'

'Frankly, yes!' Renee twisted her head so sharply it nearly came out of its socket, and Pete nearly went tits up at this, remembering the night of their wedding when she'd crinked her neck blowing out a candle; it always came down to that sharp twist of her head.

'Now, as much as I appreciate the honesty,' Liz said, 'I must remind you I am no therapist or couples counsellor. I just do brain science.'

'Sorry,' the exes said in unison.

'Peter, nothing more to add?'

Pete went to affirm the negative, but then he recalled what Trent had said to him at Lost for Words last week: *About the health stuff, mate, if you're going to go spend the coin, you may as well use the time.* And so he did. He told her what was up, that he had been feeling really quite strange ever since the fit at Kingsford Smithy, he really had, and about how familiar the lighthouse had seemed at Kurnell the day before the episode, like he'd seen it a hundred times before, and the headaches, and the double vision, and the crackling, shattering static of the snowstorm, and his inability to remember recent stuff like where he had put Gavin's forms for the Storm, etc, and that the reason he never wanted to see people in the street was not a yearning for privacy but a fear that he would not remember their name. He couldn't remember anything. Especially when he came back from the fit. He didn't know he worked at the airport, or who Renee was, or even what apple juice meant.

'And what is that like for you, Peter?'

'It's like I'm a baby again, Liz. It's like being a newborn baby.'

It was pouring out of his mouth and Liz couldn't write in her workbook quick enough.

Renee, well, as much as she was impressed by this outpouring, she had also just remembered she hadn't yet texted back the pilot. He'd sent her a pic an hour ago but she hadn't wanted to reply in front of sweet little Ainslee, so she'd better do it now …

'Thank you, Peter,' Liz said, nodding, 'that is all very plum normal, so please don't feel embarrassed, and it's also … well, it's an incredible help for me to hear the experience.'

'Ok, so that's not a sign of anything worse than what you said I had?'

'Risk factors for seizures come in many shapes and sizes. We know you were a professional NRL player, and that playing lock forward for nearly twenty years comes with numerous head clashes, knocks and collisions.'

'Yeah, spose it does.'

'I watched you and admired you. You didn't hold back, Peter.'

'Yeah, well. My dad taught me. Never take a backwards step, Liz.'

'But can I ask you to think back now and tell me if there was any epilepsy in the family line. Did your mum or dad suffer from any sort of similar thing, that you can recall? And do you know about your birth and if there were any complications when you first came out into the world? Do you have any knowledge of these, Peter? Family history or your birth story?'

'Mum and dad?'

'Did your mother tell you if you had any seizures in childhood? Or if she or your father –'

'My mother died. Not from brain stuff. Dunno re: Dad.'

'I'm sorry,' Liz said. 'My own mother died last year, so I feel your pain.'

'Yeah, well, it's that age, isn't it?' Renee said, shoving her phone back into the bag that she'd bought on sale at Ted Bakers for $440 just three hours ago. 'They all cark it round now.'

'Peter, you mentioned, quite eloquently, the depression and the negative thoughts. I mean, this is an incredibly stressful experience for you to endure.'

'For all of us,' Renee added.

'Do you use alcohol or drugs, in excess, or any particular type of substance, be it drink or drug, to cope with what has happened to you ... a lot ... or a little ... of late?'

Peter looked down at the striped linoleum floor, wondering how many other sad pricks had sat in this room, head down, hearing the verdict: that their head had failed and soon they'd be a flat-out mong, dribbling into their shirts.

'He smokes, drinks and uses drugs on the regular, has since I met him,' Renee said. 'He did when he played, but then he had footy to break it up. Now he just basically does that, only that, broken up with those three days at the airport shifting planes about.'

Pete looked at his ex. 'Who invited you?'

'You did. I bear witness. *And* I'm the next of kin.'

'You find it eases the stress?' Liz asked.

'It's depressing, Liz,' Renee continued. 'It's so sad. They're all alcoholics.'

'Are you working at all now, Peter?'

Renee scoffed. 'Is gambling at 11 am on a Tuesday working?'

'Pete?' asked Liz.

'Nah, Qantas was me,' he answered. 'And they've severed ties. Which is fair play to em. I don't have an issue there. During the league season I do the odd spot of commentary – TV or radio, some talks and corporates, but I'm not a big public … I don't like public.'

'Do you find it hard to concentrate, Peter?'

'Not really, I mean, yeah, it is harder.'

'Do you find it harder to use your brain now than, say, a few years ago?'

'Every year you get older it gets harder.'

'But does your brain feel different to you?'

'I'm on Ritalin now, because the Zoloft did nothing, so I feel less stressed.'

'Right.'

'I don't want to stay on Ritalin, though. It's not how I want to feel.'

'No, I don't imagine you would, cuz.'

'It says anti this and anti that but I don't feel no anti anything.'

'Well put!'

'Sounds like your doctor is using you as a guinea pig!' Renee said, over it now.

Pete thought of how he used to feel when he got stressed, and how good beer was, it was his go-to release option. The only thing that had ever helped that was sports and hitting and sweating and sports, or writing the poetry thing down. He recalled how good it felt to write those words down in that journal Bridget had given him, and he was just about close to admitting the fact – with real relish too, like yeah the poems helped – when Renee relaunched a campaign. 'Peter! Please? Answer the question – our son is with us as he is being headhunted by the Storm, so we have to –'

'I said it's harder,' Pete said, standing up now. Like that day he let rip on Paul Sironen, the gasket was now blown. 'I said my head hurts. I said about the De Ja Vu.'

'Ok,' said Renee. 'I'm just saying that we are not in Melbourne every other day!'

'I said I get dizzy. What else do you want me to say? That I think about death? Yes, I do – and if it wasn't for a certain gentleman I probably would have died! I'm fucking scared, ok, Renee? I don't know what's going on inside my head! I'm scared!'

'Plum … Plum … Plum,' she said, at the same time as Pete said, 'I tried to die. Ok, I tried twice to die. I tried.'

'Time out, time out!' Liz said with force. 'Renee, can you leave us. Peter, here's a tissue.'

Slowly, and not without a pointed scoff or two, Renee left the consult room.

When her presence was no longer felt, Pete felt the need to explain. 'Sorry, Liz, Renee means well. She's just –'

'Don't apologise.'

'It's hard on me, facing all this, but I can see that it's hard on her too.'

'Correct.'

'It's just, like … This thing is … It's bigger than all of us.'

Liz leant over the desk and grinned at him, and the love she emanated from her wonderfully open human face made him feel happy but most of all she made him feel safe. Safer than he'd felt since that day on the tarmac, safer than he may have felt ever.

'Peter Lum. Trust me, as a black gay woman in neuroscience, I know what it's like to feel out of your comfort zone and terrified. But the good news for you, and me, is that it's not all doom and gloom – that is, if you take it all very seriously and do the work. Ok?'

'Ok Liz. Thanks Liz.'

'Let's crack on, shall we?'

And then Liz checked his reflexes and did some basic neurological tests, while Renee waited for him in the hallway outside, sending the pilot an open-blouse selfie and then googling 'concussion and suicide'.

If the cab to Liz's office had been filled with nerves, the ride back was filled with umbrage.

'It's not a death sentence,' Renee said, wondering if Peter had any cigarettes on him.

'I know,' said Pete, 'but it might as well be, with all the restrictions.'

The last twenty minutes in that little room was a blur. Pete could only concentrate for sections of time, just like in Year Ten when he kept finding his mind wandering to visions of green and blue, of fields and sky, beaches and breasts, of hitting and diving, of mud and sand. And it was the same in there; after Liz had called Renee back in from the corridor, she'd done her best to explain to them, through a series of images and graphs, what a 'Seizure Disorder' was but she'd baffled him with the introduction of the term 'Temporal Lobe Epilepsy' and lost him at 'Very Treatable' ... because it certainly did not sound fucking treatable. Temporal lobe epilepsy and seizure disorder! An ACL was treatable, syndesmosis was treatable, a busted thumb, sure ... but not that whole Latin-sounding bonanza. The whole thing was an ominous poem – writing itself in his head:

She said if I could get control of the seizures my life could be good
She said she would prefer me to get off Ritalin
and onto a drug called Lamictal
She said no driving for twelve months is right,
them scrubs were right
No swimming alone – especially in the ocean
No surfing, no boxing, no soft sand jogs
No more than one or two drinks at a time
No smoking anything

Peter was to stay on the new drug for two years, unless it gave him a rash. He was to report back if it gave him a rash because that meant it was not for him. Liz had told him that the dizzy spells and funny turns were all seizures, minor seizures, and she promised him they'd all go away if he took the drug as prescribed. And if he didn't? Put simply, he'd die. She suggested yoga and bushwalks and decaffeinated teas, to which he said, 'So, Liz, what you're saying is, fun is dead or I am dead?' And it wasn't Liz, it wasn't that his ex-wife was there either, it was this feeling of being smothered that was killing him now, because Plum only knew one speed and that was faster, he only knew one approach and that was never take a backwards step.

And minimise stress, don't gamble, don't put yourself in situations
Get spiritual, find calm, change your life
I said, what's spiritual? Is that religion?
She said religion is for people who are going to hell
Spirituality is for people who have been there
I said, yeah, spiritual then please

How was he meant to transition into someone he was not? And how would everyone perceive him, leaving the pub or the Tradies after just one or two lights, letting Brick run ahead in the soft as he walked behind in the hard, standing with a juice and watching the sparring sessions instead of jumping in the ring and throwing some big stuff himself, saying no to Gavin when Gavin said, *Let's swim out to the buoy*, and putting the surfboards away. The BMXes away. Putting the punt away, which was probably smart – but the rest of it? Well, if he wasn't suicidal then, he certainly was now, because life with a seizure disorder was embarrassing, unmanly and frankly DEVOID OF ALL JOY. This stocky little firecracker named Liz had stolen his toys and burnt down his treehouse in one fell swoop, and all he could think of to think of was, *Get me a beer and get me a fucking dart.*

'You right?' Pete asked Renee, taking her by the hand.

'Yeah, you?'

'I'm thirsty.'

She smiled at him.

With the voicemail in from Ryan at the Storm saying that if Gavin was 'feeling better', the pathways option was still on the table, Pete dropped a whack at the bottle shop on Smith Street, figuring the kids deserved a few beers and ciders. Renee, well, she guzzled prosecco like it was coconut water after a Zumba class, and now that he'd flicked that Ritalin into the bin, a few Yarra Valley pinots would do just fine with the lamb chops. *Giddy up!*

'What's on the menu for tonight?' Renee asked the rotund Greek waiter, who had just emerged through the proscenium arch of this bustling old white-stone eatery like he invented the odometer.

'There is no menu,' Pete said, having told her this a few times on the walk over.

'What do you mean-a there's no-a menu?' Renee asked, attempting an Italian accent.

'You like fish?' the waiter asked them. 'You like lamb? You like chicken? Why don't I just bring some nice fish and lamb and chicken out for the family, ok?'

'We trust you,' said Pete.

'Bellissimo,' said Renee. 'La Dolce Vita!'

'That's Italian, Renee.'

'Oh, is it not Italian here? Oh, it's Jim's Greek Tavern, my bad. Greece is nearby!'

Ainslee took an aerial photo of the bread basket. 'I love fish. I reckon it's the best thing you can eat.'

'Me too,' Gavin said, hoping that did not sound like a euphemism.

The big old waiter was swiftly replaced by his daughter, appearing from behind him with four plastic cups and a bottle opener, which she left on the table before leaving them to it.

After pouring out the plonk, Pete raised his glass. 'Cheers to my son. The new Billy Slater –'

'Very good-looking man,' Renee noted.

'Who is?' asked Gavin, slicking back his hair in jest.

'Up your bum!' said Plum.

'Plum!' said Renee. 'To Gavin!'

'Cheers,' said Gavin and Ainslee in unison, happily glued together by the palm.

God, I hope this girl doesn't break his fucking heart, thought both parents at once.

Renee twisted the foil above the cork and winked at Ainslee. 'Lovely day had by all!'

Ainslee blushed. She had found Renee's male anatomy class at the bar quite intimidating, especially when it was Renee's own son's body she would be experimenting with.

'No, yeah, it's been a good day,' Peter confirmed.

The drinks flowed – with Peter sending the young waitress back and forth to the communal fridge for their BYOs – and the food was equally pleasing in both pleasure and proportion: Gavin loved the dips, Pete the lamb chops, Renee the freshly grilled perch, and Ainslee took a thousand photos of the saganaki.

'Greek cheese doesn't melt!' she proclaimed, typing in the hashtags.

'People think I'm not interesting because I don't work but I am interesting,' said Renee.

'What was Gavin like as a baby?' asked Ainslee, sipping on her pear cider.

'Gremlin,' Pete replied, wondering if Renee could tell he'd just had a cigarette. He'd said he had to call back the Storm but really he'd been lunging back two darts in a row.

Renee laughed. 'He did, he looked like a gremlin when he came out, it's true.'

'He *was* a gremlin.'

'What's a gremlin?' asked Ainslee, her hand beneath the table. She knew exactly what one was – she was grabbing one right now.

'They made horror movies about em in the 80s. They're these slimy little bastards.'

'Thanks Dad!'

'Oh yeah, you were a disgusting creature – slimy brown and green.'

'There was complications, see, Ainslee?' Renee piped in. 'My placenta stopped working. No, not my placenta, my … oh yes it was my placenta. I was going to say fallopian tube, but that was more of an issue with Tallulah.'

'Renee and I used to joke you were an anal birth.'

'Peter!'

'Anal, really?' said Ainslee, putting Gavin's cock in-between her thumb and index finger, then sliding it up and down feeling his gremlin thickening – everything was on the table tonight.

'Premature, you see.'

'I was too keen to get amongst it,' Gavin near squealed.

'I can imagine,' Ainslee said, and the boy had to knock her hand away or he might have created his own variety of tzatziki, premature himself.

'What were you like as a baby, Dad?' Gavin asked, trying to focus things back to normal and flaccid. 'Do you know?'

Peter looked at Renee, who was smiling to herself and doing some covert texting under the white tablecloth. It wasn't the first time he'd been asked about his childhood today, and he knew Renee wanted him to fill the kid in on all that had transpired with Liz, but they both knew it would not be tonight. It was all too ripe now, and they weren't down here for his brain disorder, they weren't down here for epilepsy –

they were here for the young star and the beautiful future that awaited him, if that was what he wanted to do, of course; if his dad's footsteps were the ones he wanted to follow in.

'I don't think I've ever seen any baby photos of you, Dad, have I?'

'No, I don't think we did those sorts of things. Probably didn't have cameras, we were that poor. No, I don't really know the answer to that, son.'

'What do you remember? Like, about your dad and stuff? Was he around when you got going into footy like how you're around to help me?'

'I don't, um, yeah, no there's not much ... To be honest, um ... Dad was ...'

'Did Albert go to games?' Renee asked.

'Well, he took off when I was ...' Peter leant forward in his chair, removing his jacket again – having slid it on to have a dart out there on the path. It was always freezing at night here, even when it was fucken hot it would soon be fucken cold.

'Did he give you pump-up speeches like you give to me?'

'While your girlfriend was driving!' said Ainslee, nodding at Renee – *You know, sister ...*

'No, he was never like that, me dad,' Pete said. 'He didn't say a heap.'

'Did he turn up to your grand final and then leave?' said Gavin, suddenly snarling hard.

'Gavin Albert Lum,' Renee snapped.

'You right there, son?'

'I'm just asking. If it runs in the family or not. Does it?'

The awkward pause was filled by the arrival of the bill.

'I'll get this,' Renee said.

'What's the rush, Renee?' asked Peter.

'Nothing, just keen to get a good night's sleep before we fly home tomorrow.'

'Is that it?'

'Yes, and before you two tackle each other over the table, I might add.'

'I'm fine,' said the father and son.

'Well, I'm not. I'd like to go.'

'Before we do go,' Ainslee said, 'Gavin and I wanted to tell you both that, um ...'

'You're not fucking pregnant, are you?'

'No, Renee, but ...' Ainslee looked to Gavin for they had decided, after their third sexual encounter this afternoon, which involved all areas of the room, and their first declarations of 'I'm in love with you', that *Gavin himself* would be the one to break the news to his parents. She had alerted her own parents by text message and they had not seemed too distressed at all, sending back a simple thumbs up emoji followed by a cottage house.

Gav cleared his throat. 'We're thinking we might try living together for a couple of months, before I head down to Melbourne, if that's what I end up doing ... club wise ... cos Manly are –'

'Hey? But you live with me! Why would you move –'

'Ainslee's getting a flat with a pal. I'm going to move into her room for –'

'But you got a room.'

'And so do I now,' Ainslee contributed, with the sharpest of whispers.

Plum poured himself a very full glass of wine, spilling some of it. 'Gavin. You're sixteen. And you live with me.'

'Used to live with me also,' Renee added, typing in her PIN.

'I'm old enough to move out, Dad, and so I'm going to, after the Bali trip.'

'I think let's not get into this now,' Renee said, keen to do a hop, skip and a jump out of there. The pilot was waiting for her at his hotel bar and if she was going to have an affair then she had to do it *now* before the prosecco wore off and she realised she was just high on freedom and the feeling of *not* being a milk bar twenty-four hours a day, seven days a week. 'Don't you think, guys? Now is not the time!'

'We're going to Bali and then we're going to move in together. Ok?'

'Never take a backwards step!' Plum said. 'That's what my dad said to me.'

'For God's sake,' Renee said, whipping on her new coat.

'He wanted to know about his grandfather. Well, that was his grandfather's saying.' Pete stood up, guzzled his full glass of pinot and then threw the remaining amount of wine in the bottle right down the hatch for all to see. 'Never take a backwards step!'

With the motivated youth going straight up to the workshop – room 717 – and Renee proclaiming that after all that unnecessary drama at Jim's Greek Tavern she 'felt like a walk on her own around Fed Square', Peter paid the cab, smoked a durrie out the front of the Adelphi, then made his little way up to level seven for some Plum-time.

The bed had been turned down, a service Peter failed to understand – surely even the fanciest of guests could pull a sheet back. And what was with the tiny chocolate on the pillow? It always ended up smeared on your back; it was enough to make him want to call down and give them a serve. But instead he dragged off his trousers, poured himself a whiskey from one of them little bottles on the top shelf of the minibar, ripped open the Kettle Chips, the jubes and the Maltesers, and declared it on.

He scanned the bedside radio and just like that 'Kiss' by Prince came on, and who would have thought it, pretty soon he was dancing in his undies in room 706. And did it not feel good to just swing the hips, literally like no one was watching, because no one could be watching, so he didn't even have to dance like it! And then his favourite dance song of all time came on, taking the old thug even higher into dancefloor delirium: 'September' by Earth, Wind & Fire – fucken try and sit down.

Pete was cutting loose, until his breath caught up with him, and he had to stop. He sat on the edge of the desk wishing there were drugs in the room. Just a little bumper to give him something. A little distraction from the inherent weight of family, the unbendable dynamic, the too-much love.

It was at the Tradies, three weeks ago, actually, that he'd last put something up his nose. The boys had gathered together – dressed in safari suits and playful ties as if it was Spring Carnival – at 11 am on a Thursday to watch their beloved Floodlight run his third-ever race. It was to be a coming together of sorts for the boys, who hadn't been drinking together as much lately, and Squeaky thought a nice all-dayer would galvanise the crew after a disruptive period and return a restless Plum to the Coxless Four tribe.

Floodlight's trainer, Nancy Tighe from Gunnedah, was no Gai Waterhouse, and so when she said the horse would struggle in the wet over two thousand metres, the boys' overconfidence had to settle at mere confidence.

'I'm going to box her up with the two favourites,' Pete said, having had to tighten the belt since he risked the Bendigo Bank on Jewel of the Nile only four days before.

'You, Matt?' asked Brick, jumpy in more ways than one today.

'I dunno, my gut says be cautious.'

'Your gut says Maccas drive-thru,' quipped Squeaky, and the laughing was on.

'I have been known to stop a horse by simply putting money on it, so …'

'I'm putting a grand each way on her,' Squeaky said, confirming what he just proclaimed to be true with a simple tap of the iPhone.

Pete looked up from his beer. 'What the fuck?'

'Yeah, mate, you gotta believe in your horse. This is Floodlight and if the floodlights are going to come on, it has to be because its owners are giving it a power source.'

'I'm with Squeak, hundred each way for me,' decided Brick.

'Ask, believe, receive,' Matt said, quoting Damian 3-Oh Keogh from back in the day. 'Bugger it, I'm goin five hundo on the nose.'

'Now we're talking.' Brick tapped some new numbers into the app. 'Floodlights are on!'

'You blokes are dyed-in-the-wool,' said Plum, aware that if they only knew the truth – that he, the tightest of the tight, had blown his entire wad on the lowest of all gambling formats: the pokies, the slappers, the idiot's pinball – there'd be havoc.

'I can feel it's going to be a good day for us, gentlemen,' Squeak said, putting his arms around Matt and Pete and lifting himself up off the ground to kick the air.

'Yeah, but you'd bet on the weather if you could,' remarked Magic Matt, dressed in a safari suit and sipping on his fourth beer of the morning.

Yes, the boys had met at Squeak's flat at 10 am, had a few Four X Summers on the balcony, blown a hash joint, watched Floodlight's first two races on Sky Recorder, then taken an Uber X to their place of rest and relaxation for the ensuing ten hours: the Gymea Trade Union Club, once a floor-squelching dump, now the place to be on this side of Tom Ugly's Bridge.

'You got that razzle dazzle on ya, Magic?' Brick asked, placing his phone face down and emptying his latest Canadian Club and dry.

'Yeah, course,' said Matt, sliding the pack of cigs out of his inside pocket. 'Here, I'll go smoke one, you take Plum in for a snifter, then me and Squeak can go in after.'

'Yeah, that sounds good,' said Plum.

Brick took the bag from within the deck. The big man seemed nervous suddenly, looking around like the fuzz was scaling the walls with a 'hut-hut'.

'It's alright, Brick, we're not famous anymore,' Plum said. 'No one's watching.'

'You'd be surprised,' Squeak said. 'Everyone's a Big Brother these days.'

'Cept for you, cos you're just a tiny little jockey with a dick like a crayon,' said Matt, slapping Squeak on the back of his head and hobbling outside to smoke a Dunhill.

'How's he know what my dick's like? Jockeys may not be good for a tip, but they know what they're doing in the saddle.'

In the dunnies the two burly ex-leaguies filled the cubicle to the point where the toilet wondered if it should be the one to leave.

'Tap out a big one. I think that'll do me,' said Plum, staring through the gap in the cubicle door, remembering that time there had been a bust in a pub in Adelaide, and how he and Brick had quickly unzipped emselves and torn at each other's hairy chests as if they were lovers only just discovering their true selves. The young coppers looked so shocked they'd happily stepped away without asking for open pockets.

Brick wiped the cistern with his sleeve, then spread out a couple of greyhounds with his Brick's Boxing membership card and snorted one of them. His rush was always quicker than for the rest of em. With his face moving about like it had no scaffolding and his eyes threading like saffron, he couldn't hide a bump from no one, and so it was only certain occasions he let rip. Plus with what he did, he couldn't risk it – people relied on him to be fitness on brand. 'You're up.'

'Rightio then,' Plum said, ducking his head and hoovering up the powder.

'Plum, before you go, I just wanna say something to ya,' said

Brick, grabbing his best mate by the shoulders and holding him over the toilet like he was getting measured up.

'Yeah, all G,' said Pete, no idea where 'all G' came from.

'With your bird and everything coming in at the gym and that.'

'You don't have to mention it. It's a non-starter, pal.'

'No, no. I need to get it off me chest.'

'Ok, ok.'

Brick took his hands off Peter and rubbed his own face for a minute. When he was done, he chopped both his hands in front and spoke from the heart cos this shit was not easy for a man of his man-ness. 'I know you two are not having the best time of it. And you know I count you as my best mate. Not just footy, but like all the funny shit we got up to off the field. What with us being drilled with mace spray in France by that French hotel woman and having to run around the hallways naked not knowing where we were going.'

'Yep.'

'And, as you know, I say to everyone – you are the best player I've ever seen, and ever played with and, to my own detriment, against.'

'Alright.'

'Let me finish.'

'I am letting you finish but, just, finish.'

'Also when things have fallen apart for me, I always look around, and even though you don't say much, you're the constant, your head is the constant.'

'Ya poor bloke then.'

'Jokes aside, I just want to say that I think the world of Charmayne, and I like what she's got going with Gym N Trim. I want you to know that there are two "w" things I don't mess with. One's a mate's wallet, and the other's a mate's woman.'

'Yeah, pal. I know that.'

'I just had to say it.'

'Why, what has *she* said about it all?'

'Huh?'

'What did Char tell you?'

'Nothing!' Brick said too loud, the drugs rising up in his forehead like a protest. 'I make sure she knows, that me, Brick, is not getting involved in the dramas.'

'Ok, ok.'

'Yeah.'

'What dramas, though?'

'She just knows that I'm your mate, and even though I love her ...'

'You love her?'

'No – yes. I mean I love her smarts.'

'You love her arse?'

'Smarts!'

'She's a smart arse?' Plum said, enjoying the stitch-up.

'I'll fucken put you to sleep in a second, Plum.'

And he would, Plum knew. His mate was big these days, but watch him go on the pads and in the ring, in the bar, in the carpark: he would still take any prick. ANY. PRICK.

'I hear you,' Plum said, 'and I appreciate your honesty.'

'Good,' Brick said, realising he was in love with his mate's woman. 'All good then.'

'Can we go have a beer now?'

'Holy Grail' by Hunters and Collectors was battling its way out the speakers as Pete returned to the main auditorium, and with the drugs in his system, and the beer, and the abandon, he felt like he too was in that army, and it was as big as the singer said.

'Racing now!' squeaked Squeaky as the boys returned to the table and the penultimate fixture sprang to life.

'We win this, we're off to Thailand,' said Magic Matt, issuing Brick a handshake complicated enough to transfer the bag of white powder back to its rightful mule.

'Let's go eighth,' said Squeaky, having lined up a trifecta around a horse named after the infamous Knights number 7.

'Go the eighth!' said Brick and Matt together, as it pulled out to a wide third.

Pete threw half his beer back and looked up to the TV, but, instead of seeing said horse race, he saw Bukowski's face, filling the entire screen like a TV show host, adorned with that shit-eating seppo grin, and it felt nice to think that the bloke had not only remembered to pay him a visit but had taken it upon himself to deliver a message during this most crucial of times.

'Hey cock. Look, I'm sorry I left ya high and dry the other night. But, to be honest, you were starting to weigh down on my soul. And, you know, being a poet, and a womaniser, and an alcoholic, well, I like to do that myself. I have my own shame, my own fear, my own beer. And also, when it comes down to it – I like to leave that stuff to the Gods, that kind of … ennui. Cohen talks about it, yeah, I just hand that to them up there …' Charles erupted into a coughing fit, then lit up a lengthy Cuban cigar.

'Ok,' Pete said out loud, but the boys didn't notice, too busy cheering on their selections.

'So yeah,' continued Bukowski, 'I gotta say, I been liking what I been seeing from you lately. But all this stuff with women, well, asking me for advice on women, it's like asking a fat guy how to lose weight. My contempt is lyrical, but there's no clues in there. So I believe my job is done here, and that you may well be more suited to my friend Sylvia.'

'No,' Pete cried, as his mate's face started to crackle and dissolve into horses.

'You'll know her when you see her. She's a sweetheart; a little dark, a little neurotic, I won't lie to you – all the best ones are – but she's a lot better regarding matters of the heart. Dads and sons, love, forgiveness – all that schmaltzy crap – which is where I believe you're at.'

'Hank, no!'

'I'm good when you're down and out, but if you want to get better – closure, all that – I can't be nearby. I'll fucken hurl. Too positive for me.'

'Charles!'

'And so, as I bid my farewell, remember these two words, Pete. Are you ready?'

'Hey, no no no!' screamed Pete, as Bukowski's face was blurred out in an exhale of cigar smoke and was replaced by the chaos of the gee-gees. 'Where'd he go?'

'Don't Try,' said the ghost of thin air.

Pete looked around the sports bar. 'What happened to my man?'

'What happened?' Squeaky asked, in all realities jumping for joy. 'What happened was we got the boxy up, my boy, and she ain't going to be paying peanuts either!'

'She'll be paying peanut and cashew stir-fry!' screamed Matt.

Plum blinked a few times. 'We won!?'

'I can't believe that,' Brick said, standing back from the table. 'It all just came together'.

This was the stuff of dreams, and it had just taken place right in front of the Coxless Four and now 'Flame Trees' was playing on the stereo. *How on earth?*

Squeak slapped Plum on the back. 'Let's wait for the stewards, but I don't think it'll be a photo. I think it's "Eighth Immortal".'

The boys had won over sixteen grand from just eight hundred bucks, and Matt was immediately on song with the financial management, suggesting they all take a grand each to punt with, then use the remaining twelve as initial cash-flow for their Aussie Pub, Thailand. Brick, staring down the barrel of a debilitating divorce, Squeaky, who was at least 100K in the hole, and Plum, who had just done his arse on the slappers, had other ideas – but for now all that was irrelevant.

Now was the time to rejoice in the glory of gambling and the fact that, like love, luck always reared its ugly head when you least expected it, and they all least expected it, most of all Plum, who didn't even see the race, he was too busy getting dumped by Bukowski, who felt, in their few interactions, like a real life coach.

'It's like a guardian angel was watching over us,' Matt said, raising one of the twelve shots Brick had just bought. 'To a box trifecta *and* a quinella!'

Brick threw back his Sambuca. 'Fuck my arse I needed that.'

'Speaking of arse, isn't that that journalist that used to start shit, whatshername, over there?' Matt pointed to the corner of the Tradies, where a woman was sipping on a glass of white and reading.

'Oh yeah!' said Brick, before bending over for a quick bump off his wrist under the table.

'Dana someone. Writer,' Matt said. 'She was working Fox Sports for a bit, but then they shafted her cos she kept ruffling feathers.'

Pete looked over. 'Yeah, I know that face.'

'She's the one threatening to write a thing about you, Plummo.'

'Apparently,' Squeak said quickly. 'Apparently.'

'Hey?'

The Coxless Three just stared at their mate. They'd all caught wind of something brewing online, but like the Australian males they were, none of them had bothered to mention the rumours to the man himself.

'It's just keyboard warriors,' said Squeak.

'So what's she got to do with it then?'

'It's like Matt said — she's the slut who's thinking of going public with it,' said Brick, pointing over at Dana with a little too much vitriol than necessary.

Pete downed his third shot. 'I'm going over.'

'Plum!' Squeak said, fearing his coked-up state could land him in more trouble. 'Why are you going over?'

'Friendly hello,' Pete replied, snorting his nostrils and collecting his half schooner to go.

And go he did, all the way over to the eastern wing of the Tradies, to find out what he had just heard and now believed: that this worn-out failed journo was hunting him down for a scandal. His family had already had enough of The Plum's antics, they did not need another burst of trouble, so like the footy player he was and always would be, he took the ball under his arm and leapt at the defence with Albert's pre-game words ringing in his ears: *Don't you never-ever-ever take a backwards step!*

'The one and only,' Pete said, arriving at the bar table across from the journalist.

She looked up from her mini Kindle. 'Peter Lum.'

'What's the happs?' he said, having never said that ever before.

'Have you been online and had a look?'

'Geez, I, what?'

'Sorry, but you know – elephant in the room and all.'

'No, not really.'

'It's not pretty.'

'What's not pretty?'

'What's out there. On the socials.'

'The socials?'

Dana laughed. 'Rightio, ok. Not a fan of technology then, Plum?'

'Oh, I like Google Maps. But the rest looks like a waste of time.'

'True.'

'Get a fucken life, I say.'

She smiled at this, charmed by the legend's philistine honesty. She had always found him amiable, a rare gentleman in that tawdry swag of 80s and 90s players.

'So. Dana Crighton. How've you been?'

'Oh look, it's been a time. I won't lie.'

'Been good?'

'I've been good. Well, since the last time I saw you.'

'Yeah, sorry, when was that —'

'And the time before that. And when we first met. Back in Port Macquarie.'

'Ah, right.' Pete said, knowing there was something there that he was involved in that was far from pretty, and that it was either fear or brain dysfunction keeping it distant.

'It's all good. It's all good.'

But it was not good. It was far from good. And Pete, looking over to Brick, who suddenly had his chest up and was peering left and right like a psycho, well, he could nearly drag the memory back.

'All good?'

'You know me? I'm a survivor.'

His brain beginning to blink once more, Pete shifted focus to the smallness of talk. 'And work stuff? How's that? How is sports journalism?'

'The scene has changed a lot over the years. I don't seem to be able to get a leg up with the *Tele* or the *Herald*, plus it's the same ex-players swapping shirts night by night on the talk shows, and if you're a woman, well, you have to be bubbly and thirty-one with nice titties, willing to ask the questions only, and, well, I'm a decade past that in both forms.'

'Look, I don't really pay much attention to —'

'I got a dog, a Pomeranian named Roycie — as you know, I'm a Panthers gal, not one of the new recruits either. I go way back, born and bred in Plumpton, and so, yeah, Royce keeps me busy.'

'Nice one, nice one.'

Pete was doing his best to stay in there — but the drugs were falling out of his forehead — and he now wondered why he was here — Dana was friendlier than he remembered — but what the fuck was he doing drinking with her? She was still the enemy after all.

'I'm sorry,' she said.

'What for?'

'For what's happened to you. Your brain disease. And your epilepsy.'

Pete reached for his beer but it was empty. The headache and the dizziness, again, knocked on his door. Pete was seized by it and bent in half, but he didn't react, he just breathed, and thought of his son's face when he was in the ocean and that time they went camping in Hill End out past Bathurst and how they caught fish with hand lines and didn't even sleep in their tents, just outside beneath the stars, making stories up and laughing.

'Peter?'

'It's been tough … um … fishing is … yeah?'

'Pete, I've always liked you a lot,' she said, leaning in now, and placing her hand on his wrist.

'Good?'

'You were the one on that night … you stopped it getting even more out of hand.'

'Huh?'

'You helped me. Don't you remember?'

'No, well. I was just really young. What was I, nineteen?'

'No, you were twenty-three. So was I.'

'Yeah.'

'Yeah.'

'Ok, yeah, the boys were –'

'I was along for the ride, reporting on the tour, remember?'

'Yeah,' he said, meaning *no, not really*. He knew who she was, but he had a fog in the corner of his temple where that night lived and he couldn't wipe the windows on it still.

'You know I got pregnant from that … event … don't you, Plum?'

'What the fuck?'

158

'Don't worry – it wasn't yours,' she said, applying lip balm from her handbag.

'Jesus,' he said, clicking his neck left and right.

'Thanks to you, it wasn't as bad as it could have been,' she said again, and with the eventual admission of absolute truth, a thing he could recognise these days, he remembered the hotel room, and the boys all round and above her, and him storming in with the backs coach.

'Any New Year's resolutions, Dana?' said Pete, as the waitress collected their glasses.

'Yeah, I want to write a book.'

'Really? What about?'

'About you.'

'Oh right.'

'So that's the proposition I am here to present to you.'

'Let me have it then,' said Pete, stinging for another bump, another beer, another break from the snowstorm.

'The sports media mafia want to tear you a new arsehole – they're just waiting on clearance from the defamation lawyers, then ouchy.'

'Really?'

'Yep. They got you. Alcohol, drug use, gambling issues with debts all the way to Wichita. Concussed maniac shits himself on the tarmac and nearly kills two hundred people. Then there's stuff with ... stuff that's more interpersonal ... let's just say it's juicy, mate –'

'If this is all so juicy then why is it not already out there, Dana?'

'Because I told them I was in talks with you about an exclusive and that stops them dead, see – a press release from Plum cancels em out. It's a mic drop.'

'Ahhh.'

'They want to go you, champ. Not just a little editorial. They want to show how a past hero can fall so far. They're all spiders in news, Plum.'

159

'Oh right. And what do you want to write?'

'Truth.'

'Oh?'

'Warts and all.'

'And how is that better?'

'Better?'

'Yeah, how is you doing a whole book on me better than them doing some pissy article?'

'Because I know you're more than that shit. Because I am on your side. Because I care.'

'Ok.'

'So give me the go-ahead to write the bigger story, and I'll send the wolves away.'

'Do I need to call my lawyer, Dana?'

'You won't need a lawyer if you go with me. Just agree to the book and that's the news story.'

'Is that right?'

'I'll write you from the inside. I'll write about the head knocks on and off the field. I'll write about Plum the soft fruit with the hard stone inside. I'll tell them to look deeper than just "all players are animals". I'll show them what a gentleman you are, if a little lost in post-footy life. Concussion is a big issue now, as is men's health – this could be not just redeeming but important, Plum. This could be game-changing, and you'd be the reason why.'

'And what if I don't?'

'Then I can't hold em a minute longer. And trust me, there's some blokes in there that do not like you because you never played the game.'

'What game? I played the game. I'm Peter Lum.'

'No! The media game. You never walked up to the commentary box. You didn't put your face on like the rest of them do.'

'That's not my go.'

'You didn't network, you didn't mingle, and that offends them.'

'That's not my go either.'

'I know.'

'Neither is having a book written about me.'

'Fine, then don't,' Dana said, accidentally slamming her glass down a bit.

'I won't.'

'Burn your house down instead.'

Pete looked around: the boys were all watching, the Tradies was all watching. 'I don't care.'

Then Dana came clean. 'I need a career moment. To get back in. You need a safety raft.'

Pete scoffed, shaking his head at her, *what a journo ay*. They always played nice, then once they had you warmed up, went in behind the ribs with a biro machete. 'How are you going to stop them, Crighton? You don't have any power left. Let em write what they want.'

And with that Peter turned to return to his mates, crossing the carpeted floor of the bar, trying to walk like he wasn't shit scared of the spiders she spoke of.

Pete sat on the desk in room 706 of the Adelphi Hotel, thinking there was a chance he could have dealt with that Dana dialogue better. There were a few things he could have said, and a couple of things that maybe he should not have said, but they were said now and so whatever would be would be. Dana wasn't a bad broad – she meant well, as far as journalists *can* mean well – but Plum had always got by with his head down and mouth shut: why change that now? But what did she mean the spiders were out to get him? *Fuck it!* Should he call her? Nah, he didn't want no book on no Dymocks shelves.

He turned off the radio and filled his glass with another one of them tiny bottles, hurled some complimentary ice in and wandered over to the windows to see if a dart was at all possible through the gaps in the suicide wind-up window.

He could just get his head through. The air was crisp and alive, and his thoughts drifted like smoke down Flinders Lane, when a voice from the eastern ebb caught his attention, drawing his head back up to find a head jutting out of a window a few feet away.

'Heya, hello, hi,' said the girl, or was she a woman? It was hard to make her pale face out in the silhouetting moonlight, but her accent was American, with the slightest hint of educated English, and she was pretty, smiling at him as she smoked.

'Hi,' said Pete, smiling back at her.

'They don't make it easy, do they?' she said, gesturing at the tiny diagonal gap they were both contorting themselves through.

'Nah, you got to want it,' said Pete, lighting up and inhaling.

'Life?' she asked, 'You've got to want life?'

'Well, yes,' he said. 'Or there's death if you don't.'

'Dying is an artform of sorts, don't you say, Peter? One would want to do it well.'

Pete didn't have an answer to that, so he just smoked and looked out, hardly fazed by the fact she knew his name.

'How was your night?'

'Oh, yeah, it was ok. Down from Sydney with the kid and the ex-wife, so ... you know.'

'Children are a mirror, don't you think?'

'A mirror?'

'To ourselves. When I had mine, well, Ted was not always there. It was very much me alone with the children, in the country house, in Devon, trying to write or just ... stay afloat. And the whole time I played with them I felt I was playing marbles with my own soul.'

'I like being a dad.'

She laughed, and then coughed a bit. 'Sorry, I better be quiet. Ted has a big lecture tomorrow, and he gets mad if I interrupt his sleeping.'

'Right.'

'Yes.'

'Is Ted your husband?'

'Yes, of course. Have you read *Birthday Letters*, by any chance?'

'No, I haven't.'

'It's all in there,' she said.

'Sorry, do I know you from somewhere?'

'No, but you'd know me if you read me. Though in the early days I was much maligned.'

'Excuse me?'

'I'm a friend of Charlie's. My name is Sylvia. He said he told you about me.'

'Sorry, Sylvia. I'm not sure what you are on about. Which is not a huge surprise, I have a brain disorder, you see. A degenerative ...'

'Charles Bukowski sent me. I'm here to deal with your −'

'Oh, Charlie sent you?' Pete said, his eyes lighting up as his cigarette lost its head to the cruel breeze of Flinders Lane. 'Yes, he said I'd know you when I saw you!'

'And do you?' she asked playfully, her gold hair hanging over one eye.

'What?'

'Know me, now you have seen me, Peter.'

'No, I'm sorry. I only know about sports.'

'Well, we're not so sure about that.'

'We? Who's "we"?'

'And I'm sorry to hear about your temporal lobe epilepsy. Though, from my experience, it's not the worst way to go. The drowning − which I believe you tried − no, thank you.'

'You know about that?'

'Of course, Peter, we see all of it. I mean, all of *that*.'

'Any advice, Sylvia?'

'Get your act together, embrace all children and don't forget to put pen to paper.'

'God, you're pretty.'

'I really should go.'

'No.'

'You know these little winding windows are called suicide windows?'

'Do you really have to go?'

'Yes, it's late! Plus your wife's about to fall in the door. Go go, sweet Plum.' She took one last desperate suck of her cigarette. 'We rise, Peter Lum. With our golden hair. And eat you up like the air.'

'Jesus!'

'Plum,' she said, exhaling towards him. 'There's approximately one hundred and thirteen milligrams of potassium in a medium plum, managing your blood pressure. They protect your heart.' She flicked her murdered dart into the air. 'Plum wine, I do love a plum wine, in the mania of Tokyo.'

'Tokyo?'

The doorbell rang, and he twisted back into his room to see the smart TV lighting up with the efficiency of French farce: 'DOORBELL MR LUM.'

'Plum!' came a voice through the door. 'Wine!'

Peter looked back out the window but Sylvia was gone. He rushed to the door and opened it, hoping it would be her, hoping he could call up room service for some cigars and another bottle or two of pinot noir, hoping she'd stay.

'Peter, do you have a wine? I'm in a state,' Renee said, careering into the room and throwing her handbag and jacket onto his bed. 'Oh thank God, you have cigarettes. I didn't know you liked Maltesers. I need to piss.'

Renee waltzed into the frosted glass bathroom and did what she said she would. 'Pour me a big glass of red!' she screamed.

'Is everything ok?' he asked, the sound of her piss taking him back. He poured the half bottle of pinot noir into two glasses, and it was as if his ex-wife's piss was in cahoots, finishing its audio stream at the precise moment he emptied the bottle, down to the last drip-drop.

'You have no idea,' she said, re-entering the room in just her blouse and jeans now, having discarded the cashmere sweater behind her in the bathroom.

Pete handed her a glass.

'Up your bum!' she said and guzzled half the pinot in one gulp, panting from the effort.

Pete could tell she was already hammered: she had that mad glint in her eye and her teeth were Rothko red. 'How was Fed Square?'

'What?'

'Fed Square. You said, "I'm going to walk around Fed Square on my own."'

Renee sat on the bed and ripped off her heels, and her wine would have spilled over if Peter hadn't rescued it on the downswing.

'Make yourself at home,' he said.

She unclipped her earrings. 'I didn't go to Fed Square, silly. I went on a date.'

'A date?'

'With the pilot.'

'What pilot?'

'The pilot from the plane!'

'Aren't you a married woman?'

'Wine!' she screamed, and Pete pointed to the table where the wine was now, sitting right beside her earrings.

'Oh,' she said, reaching for the glass, and with her thighs now stretched out in those blue jeans, Pete couldn't help but remember how much he used to enjoy it when he got to watch her in the shower, pleasuring herself as she put on a water show, and going down on her when she was young, how she'd just arch her back and wrap them pins around his throat till he near choked.

'So how was it?'

'Don't you judge me, mister,' she said, sipping on her wine. 'We all know you're no cleanskin. "What happens on the tours stays —"'

'How was the date?' he pushed on, not willing to open that can of hearsay wormfarming.

'Good, he was a proper gentleman.'

'Really?'

'No. He was a prick!'

'Oh, why?'

'What's it matter? You don't care, do you?'

'Nah, but you're gonna tell me anyway, aren't you?'

The pilot was lovely, Renee told Pete. He lived half in Melbourne, half in Sydney, and flew charters for football teams and doctors and some Labor politicians. He was also married, but he and his wife had opened their marriage up after their thirtieth wedding anniversary, so much so he had told his wife on the phone that he was meeting someone from the flight for a drink at his hotel bar and had then sent her a selfie of him and Renee before they went upstairs. Renee had been somehow calmed by all this and followed him up to his room for that 'second bottle', but he couldn't get hard. He said he'd only been with one other woman since the protocols were decided on and the same thing had happened then. He begged Renee to be patient. He just needed to focus on her, he'd said, and it wouldn't be an issue. To which Renee had replied, 'Aren't you meant to be a pilot? Fly the fucking plane!' She'd got dressed and was all set to go, but the pilot turned nasty and blocked the door and said, 'You're not going anywhere. Not now I've told my wife.'

Of course no one says that to Renee, and her nails and her heels were very quickly in play – but the moment had scared her and on her walk back to the Adelphi, she felt more shame than if she had just gone through with it.

As she recounted the story to Pete, he managed, via fortune and familiarity, to get a water into her and pull her jeans off, and then she passed out beneath the throw, snoring chainsaws into the pillow.

'Goodnight, beautiful,' Peter said.

He sat up watching televised table-tennis on mute. When he was tired enough, he brushed his teeth and went to bed, curling up on the left edge so as not to wake her. And everything went smoothly ... until around 4.30 in the morning when Renee turned over in her sleep and took his naked body in her arms. Whether at first she thought he was Ollie, the pilot or Chris Hemsworth, it didn't matter – because pretty soon she was fully awake and grinding him, her left hand gripping his arse cheek, and Pete, well, he took on the nocturnal wrestle, plunging in and out of her with rhythmic need, unsure of why and how this had come about, but one hundred per cent positive it had to be given the necessary treatment. Renee flipped on top without losing him, just like she used to, a move they liked to call 'NYPD Blue', having seen it in an episode in which Janice Licalsi, who had just come clean about murdering a mobster, and the ranga, Detective Kelly, now in sordid cahoots, had first made love; it was effortlessly erotic their flip round, and it was begging for impersonation.

'I never stopped loving you, Peter Lum,' Renee said, covering his mouth with hers, using her hips and her tongue to support the statement.

'Yeah.'

'I can feel you.'

'Yeah.

'Can you feel me? Gripping you? I'm always gripping you.'

167

'Yeah.'

'Deep.'

'Yep.'

'Do you still love me?'

'Yeah,' he said, as he lay back, looking up at his ex-wife. 'Always.'

Reception called Peter's room at 9.30 am to alert him that his family were waiting for him downstairs.

'Fucken hell, ok right, oh shit.'

Gavin and Ainslee were thirds-deep in the much-maligned breakfast buffet that the Storm had thrown in, having worked up quite the appetite overnight.

'Hey gang, sorry, slept through.'

The wait staff were wrapping up service, but luckily Renee had saved him a plate of his go-to buffet breakfast items: bacon and eggs with barbecue sauce, raisin toast and an apricot tart.

'Thanks, love. I mean. Ren.'

He was confident life could go on as if nothing had happened; he and Renee both needed some loving, and they both knew where it would stay – in the vault with all the other deplorable shit they had seen each other do.

'How were the rest of both your nights?' Gavin asked his parents.

'Fine!' they chorused, stuffing pastries into their faces.

The secret was safe.

Well, it would have been, if only young Gavin, on his way back from the gym at 6.47 am, hadn't seen his half-naked mother coming out of his dad's room carrying her heels in her teeth. The young man was so bewildered by the image he hadn't even told Ainslee about it yet.

Four

Have you ever had a son
Just one
A colossus, agile God boy
A log
A frog
A meteor
Have you ever had a son?
A boy who
Once named
Will shit himself four times a day
Filthy little mongrel – soiled sheet
He screeches and he whimpers
Pathetic in his breeches
No man, no cry
Can't even catch a ball
Then my God
A moment later
Turn your back to mash the pumpkin
God is tall
God will maul
God is eight foot in a toga shawl
God is throwing you from the decking
Gravel voiced and necking
Take that, Daddy, and that, and that
Ping-pong and boxed beer

Welcome to the fear
Of your successor
Have you ever had a son?
Puts daughter to the slaughter
Says I'm hungry, Dad, I lost my wallet, Dad, can I stay at my
chick's house, Dad
Have you ever had a son?
No algorithm
No idea
No one else's
His face shape
The curl of his chest hair
The patterns of his pores
It's like looking in the mirror
But instead of you — there's hope still
There's more
Have you ever had a son?

'Ok!' Trent said, coming in through the back of the Old Bike Shed carrying a large tin of gasoline and some fire sticks. 'Time to blow up a car!'

'Righto,' said Plum, putting the mic back on its stand and hopping down off the stage before his mate could see what he'd been doing up there.

'We gotta get there just as the sun sets for best results.'

'Bang for your buck, T-Dog.'

'T-Dog? I like that. No one ever gave me a nickname, always had to make them up for myself.'

'That's no good.'

'Your mate here yet?'

'Squeak? Should be. I said five bells.'

Trent locked up the tills and grabbed a cold six-pack of IPA as Plum flicked the lights off and ran the alarm codes. At the door, he looked back in, and letting his eyes drift over the empty chairs to the stage, wondered if he could do what he just did but with the mic on next time, and them seats filled. Every time Trent had turned his back over the past month or three, Pete found himself popping up there and having a bit of a faux recite, but the notion of performing one of the stupid poems he'd been writing in that little green book Bridget had given him filled him with the same level of fear and terror as the day he turned up to Origin camp in Coffs Harbour as a 21-year-old, looking round at Steve Rogers, Mick Cronin and Terry Lamb and thinking, *I'm going to get laughed out of this place …*

Trent pumped the happy hardcore so loud from within his well-woofered Kluger, you could hear it two cars back, which was where Pete and Squeaky were positioned, following in the doomed Forester, joint going back and forth. Plum was almost going to drive himself, figuring one journey couldn't do too much damage, but then Trent stepped in and demanded Pete get a driver.

As they neared the National Park, Trent took a left onto a thin and rocky path. Squeaky, suddenly feeling a whack of paranoia, looked to his mate in the passenger seat. 'Plum. This Trent bloke, he's not going to kill us both, is he?'

'Mate, I'd say no.'

'It's just – I've seen a lot of those Danish murder dramas. And it's often the millionaires who have the fucked-up fetishes.'

Plum pulled hard on the reefer but it was nearly dead, so he licked the sides and trayed it.

'Seriously, Pete! And this is exactly the type of side road they pull off onto. That's all I am saying.'

'Trent's a bit mad but he's not murderous.'

'He just wants to blow up your car?'

'Yeah, that's all he wants to do.'

The stoned partnership pushed on, down the rocky laneway into the deep forest.

'Oh look, he's stopping now, Peter, we're stopping.'

'Squeak, chill.'

'Hannibal has stopped!'

Bent out of shape, Pete wondered for a second if indeed Squeaky was onto something, and if all this was just an elaborate plot of Trent's to murder the duo then eat them raw on the sand. It would make sense, the convenient way in which he seemed to turn up every time Plum was in need. Had he been stalking him? Was Plum about to discover the lonely man's perversion?

The tall and wiry enigma got out of his 4WD and walked round to the boot. He got out a pair of bolt cutters and turned to face them.

'Shit,' said the two men in the Forester.

'Back it up, Squeak. Back up the horse!'

But by the time Squeak had fumbled with the gears, revved it in neutral and finally got the stick back to reverse, Trent had gone over to the locked gate, destroyed the chain and swung open the barriers. He sent the Forester a big thigh-spread thumbs up and then jumped back into his car, where 'Wish You Were Gay' by Billie Eilish was now playing.

'Seems sweet actually,' Plum said, and they pushed on.

'Can I ask you a question?' Trent asked.

'Shoot,' Pete said, looking out over the beach. It was like something out of that movie Leo was in about a beach – the one where he got stuck out there but didn't mind it because everyone was attractive and they were away from society; the one where he punched a shark and stole the French bloke's lady who was hot as fucken Darwin. Pete couldn't think of the movie title, even though he was sure it was not that complicated. *Blue Escape?*

The bonfire he and Trent had built with cub-scout enthusiasm was blazing. With the back down on the Kluger, they sipped from the sixer and watched Squeaky swimming from one end of the tiny cove to the other – and with the sun calling it a day, it was hard to believe this tiny oasis was theirs and that they could be this lucky.

'You'd tell me if you thought I was like … you'd tell me, wouldn't you?'

'What?'

Trent hopped down off the boot-shelf and onto the sand between the fire and Pete's Forester, so he could face the music he was playing solo. 'I just, you know – my ridiculous house and my bar and, like, all the shit I've been saying to you at work about my dad and piping and my head …'

'Yeah?'

'I mean this is a mid-life crisis. Isn't it? What I'm about to do, what I'm doing? Everything I'm about these days is Champagne Mid-life Crisis 101, right? Or is it a nervous breakdown? I thought it was a nervous breakdown, but it seems deeper than that, like it's a full personality … identity crisis. Like, if I'm honest, Plum, which I feel like I can be with you, I've always felt more like a chick than a bloke growing up.'

'Sounds fair.' Pete was only half-listening. He was thinking about these last few weeks and how much he had enjoyed training Chloe over at the soccer oval. Stuff like that, the stuff where no one saw you, the one-on-one stuff, that was the stuff of living.

'I love watching men play sport but I never wanted to play myself,' Trent continued. 'I always wanted to be in the girls change room but, like, not in a sexual way. My dad always kicked me when he saw me playing with dolls, see! Sometimes I think I might just, you know, look into it. See what it entails.'

'Yeah, do that,' Pete said, not quite sure what he was endorsing.

'I'm just saying, I could try it.'

173

'Try what?' said Squeaky, emerging from the water like a shrunken James Bond.

'Try setting fire to the sky!' Pete said, jumping off the car and getting the petrol, as Trent took the towel from around his own waist and held it out for Squeaky to disappear into.

Trent's idea had seemed perverse to Pete at first, but the more he'd gone on about it, the more Pete was convinced. Pete couldn't drive anymore and he needed 8K to fill the hole his arvo on the slappers had burnt, so Trent was willing to buy the car off him for said amount on the proviso he could set it on fire. After half a dozen pale ales at Trent's, neither of them could see an issue with the event. It suited everyone, even Squeak, who was always up for a random one, and random it certainly was; Pete dousing the Subaru with gasoline, Squeak howling like a wolf, shirtless and face-painted with charcoal, and Trent lighting the wicked-sticks from within the bonfire and walking, ever so slowly, towards the sacrificial station wagon. This was Trent's school concert and all the roles were his, including that of Firestarter, and who was Pete to stand in the bloke's way, this bloke who'd saved his fucken life and offered him friendship with zero expectations, this bloke who wouldn't even notice eight large dropping out of his account, it was a drop in the ocean to him.

'There goes the neighbourhood!' said Trent, and threw his fire stick at the car.

Pete waited till Trent's had caught some action, then did the same, hurling his own wicked-stick at the car and running backwards to be out of striking distance.

'Oh man, she's about to blow!' Squeaky hurled his stick on the reliable wagon, running away from the car to escape the blaze, clumsily tripping into Trent's torso.

'The present moment is the divine moment,' Trent said, putting his arm around Squeaky's shoulder, then letting it slide down to just above the hemline of his boardshorts – and Peter, fetching a beer, caught the boldness of it, and how Squeak didn't flinch.

'Here she goes ...' Squeaky said.

'Let there be light!'

Pete loved that car, and as it burnt to cinder before the ocean, he felt a wave of nostalgia: memories flooded in of trips away with the boys, of making love to Char in the backseat, and of the thousand pep talks he had given Gavin on the way to footy. But, really, it *was* just a car, a collection of parts, pipes and petrol, and soon enough, as the sun set and the flames did their work on the roof and engine and – *kaboom!* – the Subaru Forester was now just a bonfire, an artwork of tortured protrusions, and a vehicle no more.

'I don't know why I'm so emotional,' Trent said.

Squeaky lit up another joint. 'Maybe you're just happy?'

'Thank you, Trent,' said Plum. 'You're a good friend. You both are actually.'

The three of them remained in a line, watching the car burn, till it was 10 pm and cold.

When Gavin was home the place smelt like Lynx, sweaty shorts chucked off after a weights session, and Milo. When Char was in the house, it smelt like flowers, garlic and vegies in the oven, or just that female lightness smell. When there was no one else home it was Plum's smell: it was David Beckham Intimately for Men, it was Kettle Chips and Tooheys New. But now, as he stood in the hallway, turning to lock the front door behind him, the house smelt different. It was a new musky, smoky smell that he was detecting, and it was emanating from the front room, from his son's bedroom.

'Helllloooo?'

Gavin was in Bali and he definitely wasn't rushing home, not with the way things went off at Rustic Ribs, so Plum could safely and sadly rule him out.

But, still, Plum was not flustered for there was something gentle and delicate about the scent; the deeper he inhaled, the less wary he felt. He knew he wouldn't be up for a scuffle, so he turned the handle and entered his son's room, palms wide open.

'Daddy?' said a voice from the bed.

'Hello?' Pete could see a figure bundled in his son's NSW Blues sheets, beneath a fog of water vapour.

'Daddy, we should have called the doctor,' the voice continued in a whisper. 'Daddy, they could have done something. Daddy, Daddy, you went and di –'

'Sorry, I'm just going to turn on the light –'

'I've fallen quite a long way.'

'Haven't we all,' said Plum, approaching the bed.

'The Nazis are coming ... Do we have linen?'

'Who the fuck ...?'

A face emerged from under its wrapping.

'Sylvia?' he said, suddenly thrilled.

She propped up on her left elbow: pale and distraught, a long fall from the confident Melbourne darling he had met a month ago. She stuck a pen-like vape in her gob then exhaled rose-coloured air. 'There are dark things living in me. Dark angels sleep in me, Peter.'

'I know, darlin, I have the same affliction,' Pete said, 'but there's no smoking in here.'

'I'm not smoking. I'm vaping.'

'Come with me to the deck out back. This is Gavin's room.'

'Fucking patriarchy,' she said, waving him away so she could pull herself together.

Peter sat out on the timber stairs that he and Gavin had sanded down and lacquered together. He lit a cigarette and settled in. As the moon disappeared behind a scrunched-up apologetic cloud, Sylvia finally appeared next to him with a bottle of red wine she said she'd stolen from Ted's cellar. She was wearing Char's white terry-towelling robe, and she seemed to have also helped herself to a shower without asking, as her damp blonde hair was slicked back on her head.

'I told Ted I'd never drink his new wine, just his old wine,' she said and laughed.

'Is that right?' asked Pete, not getting her joke.

She tilted her head, examining him. 'You have a brute's face, yet a gentle aura, much like Ted.'

'Who's Ted? Oh Ted. I think you told me.'

Sylvia drank from the bottle until Pete fetched some glasses. The 1963 vintage Bordeaux wine tasted like plums and dust, as hard strips of rain started to fall on the backyard.

'Where is Ted?'

'Ugh, Peter. Where do you think? Off with some Cronulla girl.'

'Really?'

'An "influencer", she calls herself. And he is under the influence of her. He met her at a bar named after a postcode.'

'2230? No. Isn't that called Drift nowadays?'

'Her tits drifting up and out of their lycra lodgings, and no pants to be seen. Her eyelashes so sharp and tall they could poke both of your eyes out.'

'Gotcha.'

'She said the word "like" so many times I thought *she* was an allegory.'

'Or an alligator.'

'Well, exactly!'

'Did he not go home with you?'

'We had a fight outside Charcoal Chicken, then he said he was going to walk her home. She lives with her mother – the influencer. I'm sure her schoolbooks are only just in the garage, I'm sure her tam o'shanter is only just in the hand-me-downs.'

'Why do you stick with this Ted guy if he treats you like that?'

'Because, well. I have … daddy issues. And because I love him.'

Sylvia's beauty was otherworldly, and Pete knew he was no chance, she made him shiver from the inside every time she uttered a word. 'Is it the sex?' he found himself asking.

'Men are kind till sex falls out,' she said.

'You don't really think that, do you, love?'

Sylvia shrugged, exhaling a vapour cloud in the shape of a heart. 'It's a situation for me, Peter,' she said, and sipped her wine, flicking her wet hair to the side.

'What is your situation?'

'The way my father died.'

The way she said the sentence – so plainly – it shanked him in the chest. He had no idea if his own dad was dead or not, let alone the way he went if he did die. All Pete knew was that Albert took off twenty-something years ago, the same day Pete made it into the Kangaroos. Why did he never call or write? Why did he pop in on Sarah in Darwin six or seven years ago and not even ask about Peter and Gavin in Cronulla? And where did he go from there? Living in an endless limbo of shitness with one's father was worse than if they were just dead or repudiated.

'I write well when Ted has caused me pain. Because it reminds me of my father's death. And how my mother just let him die. She didn't call the doctors in.'

'Oh, right.'

'Understand? Pain is ink. Think!'

'I bloody … I dunno.'

'Ugh, you're so primitive.'

'Easy.'

'That is why they call us "tortured poets" and "hopeless romantics", because, Peter, the good stuff comes from the suffering. From the abandonment, from the reminder that we are rotting like leaves on a tree. You never hear us referred to as doing well in our line of work. "That thriving poet." "That prolific romantic." It's because it would never be true: the fiction from the affliction, the words from the hurt; we write things down so as to make sense of it all. Comprendre?'

'Oh, so you're a poet, are ya?'

'You tell me, Mr Plum, you're a poet too.'

'No, I'm not. I'm an ex-athlete.'

'Do you know the alphabet?'

'Yeah.'

'Do you own a pen?'

Pete nodded.

'And a piece of paper?'

In response, he lifted the little green book out of his back pocket. Sylvia screamed and stood up, raising her wine glass to the moon. The robe opened just enough for Pete to catch a glimpse of her pale right breast, but he took not the luxury, instead turning to face the cheese plant beside the pool. 'Then I'm sorry to tell you, arsehole,' she cried, 'but you are a fucking poet!'

'Ok, I'm a poet,' he said, and he nearly believed it too.

Sylvia sat back down. 'May I stay awhile? I don't want to leave without Ted, and it may take a fortnight for him to destroy that poor local duckling.'

'Yeah, sure. But when my son comes home, you'll have to go.'

She mocked his gruffness. '*But when my son comes home, you'll have to go.*'

'Not a bad Aussie accent, Sylvzies.'

Sylvia nodded, blew rose-water vapour into the night sky, and then kissed the mortal man on the side of his head, right where his temple lived, right where four skull bones fused together: the frontal, parietal, temporal and sphenoid. 'Too right ya bloody cobber fair dinkum up your bum shrimp on the barbie cunt!' she said.

Then Sylvia stood up again and, her speaking voice returning to that unteachable amalgam of Boston and British, she proclaimed to the class of one: 'We have some work to do. Tonight, the Sylvia Plath extension course in poetry and inventory begins with an assignment: *'A letter to our fathers that shall never be sent.'*

Ever since Gav was a kid he'd loved ribs. So, the night before he took off to Bali, there'd been no other venue for him and his old man to have a final session than Rustic Ribs Restaurant: bibs on and fingers dripping with tangy sauce. Plus, there wasn't going to be a rib in Indo. Plenty of geckos and henna tattoos, but no ribs.

'You got your, um, shots?'

'Yeah, we got immunised last week, Dad, remember?'

'Yeah, yeah, just seeing if you got the paperwork.'

'They email it.'

Pete ripped into a rib, spitting out the bone. 'That Typhoid needle in the bum don't tickle.'

'Can I have another diet coke?' Gavin asked, not knowing which way it would go. They'd had a one sugar item a day rule since forever, and it wasn't negotiable.

'Yeah, ok then, Gav. Just ask the waiter when he comes past.'

'The ribs are so good here but the service is shit.'

'That's cos they're all your age. Don't know what hard work is.'

'Hey, I did the lawns and the edges today.'

'After I begged ya – five times, was it?'

'I still did the job.'

And it was true, Pete thought. He did. He always did. The lawns were a big job and Gav took it on. 'You got your travel cash?'

'Dad, we went through all this. I'm ready to go to Bali. So is Ains.'

'Rightio.'

Gav held his empty can up, and catching the waiter's attention, pointed to it for another.

'You nervous?'

'No, are you?'

'No, but I'm not going to Indonesia at 7 am.'

'I'm not scared of anything. I won the grand final. I got man of the match.'

'Ok, settle down.'

'Just saying.'

'Yeah, but don't get a big head.'

'Look at your head. It's massive. It's like a watermelon.'

With the mention of his head, Pete remembered that he was supposed to take his anti-convulsant with food. He tapped his pockets to check the tray was there and then stood up.

'Going for a piss,' he said, half a rack of ribs left for the return session.

'Nice one,' Gav said.

Pete pushed open the door of the bathroom, popped the pills then put his hands under the faucet and, with great difficulty – considering the size of his 'watermelon' – cupped the necessary amount of water into his mouth to get the dusty discs down. He then took his member out, thinking, *Even though I don't need a slash I'll take the opportunity at hand*, and dribbled out a bit of whatever until things were sorted. He zipped up his denims, washed both hands and pulled open the door to medicated freedom.

'Yo,' Plum said, startled. Because young Gavin was waiting for him just outside the dunny.

'What are the pills?'

'Hey?'

'I said, what are the pills?'

'No pills.'

'What are they, Dad?' Gavin asked again, too calmly to actually be calm.

'We can talk later about it; you have a piss.'

'I don't want to piss. You already piss on me.'

'Come on, mate,' Pete said, gently taking his son by the shoulders and attempting to redirect him back to the table.

'You're not stronger than me anymore,' Gavin said, immovable.

'What's wrong with you, son?'

'What's in your pocket, Dad? Stop lying to me.'

Pete went to go past him but Gavin used the momentum of his dad's body and slammed him into the door, the shuddering impact startling a waiter who was seeing to a newly arriving couple at the nearby entrance.

'Son, look, we can talk when you get back fr —'

But Gav wouldn't hear it, he had his father's tenacity, and his father's father's stubbornness, and so again he slammed Plum into the door.

Pete looked down the hall to the restaurant area. He was dizzy again, seeing blurred images of people taking out phones — so many rectangles of light identifying narrow faces.

'Dad!'

'Son.'

'What's going on? I know something's up. Tell me!'

Pete closed his eyes, then opened them again, thinking, *Just give up, Pete, give up, the game has been won, the other team won, the other team are just better this time.* And they were, they had him by both the balls and the brain. They were the St George side of the 50s and 60s, the Storm of 2006–12, the Sharks of 2016 with that fifteen in a row.

'I have epilepsy,' he said to his son. 'I have a head thing. Degenerative.'

'Are you going to be a vegetable?'

'A what?'

'Ainslee's uncle took the wrong medication for his migraine once and now he's a vegetable. He had a reaction.'

'No, son.'

'Are you going to die?'

'I don't think so.'

Gavin took a deep breath, getting himself back under control. 'How'd you get it?'

'From playing footy.'

'Is that right?'

Yeah, the concussions.' Then Plum realised who he was talking to. His protégé. Gavin Lum, who thought of nothing but the great game. 'But not just footy I don't think. Ones from when I was young and clumsy. And ones just from life.'

'Just from life?'

Gavin stared at his father. A different person in the same skin. A vulnerable alien.

'So, yeah, that's it. Now, go and have a wash up, ok, pal?'

Gavin, shattered to the core of everything he knew to be true, nodded and obeyed, pushing past his dad and closing the dunny door behind him.

'He's ok,' Pete said to the waiter. 'Big night.'

He made his way back to their table, ignoring the whispers of 'Oh, it's *him*,' and was about to sit down when Gavin reappeared – and with his body so too arrived the ferocity.

'Are you going to tell Charmayne?'

'Tell her what?'

'That you fucked Mum. In the hotel.'

Gav's voice was footy loud. Pete could see people climbing on their seats to watch the show – phones out to record act three.

'Where'd you hear that nonsense?'

'Didn't hear it. Saw.'

'Hey? How?'

'Charmayne is the best parent I have,' Gavin said. 'She actually asks me questions, and tells me things about herself. Not like you two, you and Mum, you're just ghosts!'

'This is not the time or the place, Gavin.'

'Never is, Dad, never fucking is,' Gavin said, and stormed back into the dunnies – and he didn't cry this time but he did punch the bin, and then the silver door, and then the curved metal drier, and if he'd kept on going they might have called the coppers for there is nothing more impactful than the fist of a young man let down by his hero.

'The Godmother and the Godfather please!'

After a challenging and yet ultimately beneficial few days in isolated workshop together, Plum had invited Sylvia to Tallulah's christening at St Aloysius Church, Cronulla – but she'd politely declined, stating simply, 'I haven't the frock.'

With Gavin still in Bali – having sent a short email to Pete, Renee, Charmayne and his Flegg manager Warwick Bream to let them know that he and Ainslee were pushing on after Ubud, keen to see some canyons – godfather duties rested with Peter, although Gav would take the title when he returned.

Missing his son like all hell, Pete ambled heavy-hearted up to the altar where Renee and Ollie handed him the child to do the dunking part.

'May God bless this child.'

As the organ played a song that may have been more suited to a funeral, Pete saw Charmayne up the back, sitting next to Brick. Pete dunked Tallulah in the marble basin and then handed her back to Renee, and that was it – God had another recruit.

Outside the church Pete nodded and said hi to people. He stood diagonally in a few photos, then found himself stuck talking to Ollie's kids and oddly enough they were quite chatty. Tyson proffered academic ambitions for the next year, and Zoe asked Peter if he had ever seen a hurricane in real life.

'No, I have not, Zoe. Why do you ask?'

'There has been a proliferation of them in Northern America,' she said, looking up at the sky as if they weren't two minutes from Cronulla station and a hurricane might just be on its way. 'I think they're just so wild and so beautiful. You know?'

From the corner of his eye he could see Brick and Charmayne doting on Tallulah – Brick's hand often arriving on Char's back or shoulder but never staying for long. And even though Charmayne had blocked Plum's number *and* unfriended him on Facebook, the contact barely riled him; be it the presence of God, or the delayed effects of Lamictal, Peter felt at peace, drenched in sun, as Zoe talked him through the Okeechobee hurricane of 1928, and Katrina, and the Great –

'Peter Lum,' blew a baritone bellow just behind him.

'Present,' Peter said, turning on his heels and flipping up his shades.

It was the parish priest, Father Emmanuel Pepple, beaming at him from within his tortoise-shell spectacles. He had a prayer book in his hands and he was sweating through the obligatory get-up that came with welcoming the new flock.

'We met at the rehearsal on Thursday.'

'Yeah, g'day Father.'

'Call me Manny,' said the priest, looking Plum over like he was an artwork. Pepple had been a fan since he moved to the Shire in 1989, and now the legend was before him.

'Good service,' Pete said, sliding the sunnies back down to cope with the glare.

'Would you mind taking a walk to the garage with me?'

Once a Catholic schoolboy always a Catholic schoolboy, so Pete followed the missionary man, hoping he wasn't in for the cane.

Out of sight of the others, Father Pepple slipped a hand into his cloak and lifted out a deck of Rothmans. 'Lighter?'

Pete lit the priest up and then took one for himself.

'I was there, you know.'

'Where?' Pete asked, thinking he was in for a war story – and with the bloke being African and all, Pete dared not move nor check his phone. The horror was real in them parts and he wasn't about to disregard any of that.

'At Brick's gym. I was there when you … left that day. Your son in the ring.'

'Oh, true?' said Plum, suddenly cold.

'The boy who was training, Kutiote, he lives with me until the department of immigration issues him his lodging.'

'Oh, yeah?'

'Good boy. Good speed.'

'Yeah, he looked fit.'

'I used to fight too, out of Nigeria, for money.'

'Right. How'd you go?'

'Well, I am a priest now!' said Father Pepple and let out a laugh that was so big and deep Pete reckoned it'd be heard down at Gunnamatta Bay.

'True that.'

'Yeah, I had a few scuffles in my time. But my opinion is changed now, the best fight is won from down the road.'

'Oh, yep. Especially these days. Hooligans with shanks.'

'A coward's game.'

'That is it, that is it.'

'I was here the day of the Cronulla Riots. Suffice to say I called the parish and said, "Maybe only white priests give service today."' And he ripped out the same huge laugh.

'I hear ya.'

'I am sorry, Jesus, but I am not as brave as you. You are the righteous man, I am the frightened one.'

'Exactly.'

'Anyway, anyway – I will not waste any of your time longer, Mr Plum. Except to say that this is my card. It has my email, Twitter and phone numbers on it, mobile and parish.'

'A priest with a business card. That's a first.'

'I do this for the money. I am a priest because it is a job. The card will prove you this.'

'A money priest?'

'A professional man of the Lord.'

'You don't believe all the stuff you say then?'

'Of course I do. Because it is my job. And it's how I can stay here.'

'Practical.'

'So was Jesus. He invented the table. All his miracles were based on need – it's just that he went a bit over the top parting seas, you know?'

'Right.'

'Water into wine, that's going to get around.'

'Yes, not subtle.'

'Anyway, I would like you to call me and come over one night. We can watch Fight Pass. Do you like UFC, Mr Plum?'

'Sure. My son and I watch the odd cage fight. Conor McGregor ...' Pete said in some sort of Irish accent and flapped his hands out like Conor did on his way into the arena.

'I think it would be good for you to talk to me,' said the priest, and his tone was different now, his smile all but disappearing with the tilt of his head; Pete could have sworn the offer was pretty much a threat.

'Sure. Couple of beers?' Plum said, knowing he would never go.

'No, no beers. Not for me. I am a recovering alcoholic.'

'Oh, right. Sorry.'

'Like I said, we do what we do to survive, you know?'

'Yeah, I hear you. Nah, look, I've been laying off it too, since my house guest –'

'Ok, see you then,' said the priest, unmoved.

Pete took his cue and walked off, wondering if he should do the sign of the cross.

*

Sylvia lived like there were no clocks, no bosses, no society; day was night and night was long into the day. She worked harder than anyone he'd ever seen and, seriously, Pete had never met anyone that intense. She was always muttering and waving her hands around at the kitchen table till she found that exact right word: 'Nonchalant!' Drinking wine then OJ then cola then wine again, screaming at the ceiling fan – 'I am *not* a fan of the ceiling fan!' – taking a two-hour shit, and then falling asleep on the carpet crying, only to wake an hour later like she had just been born, crawling outside to the garden for signs of life: she was a tiny gibbon. Grinning and swimming and stroking the cheese plant, she then moved inside to write again, putting Bob Dylan on for inspiration, then Chopin for mood, then Biggie Smalls to push through.

One afternoon while writing his letters, Pete heard a scream coming from the backyard. He raced outside thinking Sylvia might be drowning but found her instead under the basketball ring, weeping about the birds lost to the bushfires and the match-fixing and the Syrian orphans trying to get into Greece. It turned out she'd been lying by the pool reading *My Year of Rest and Relaxation*, when she'd overheard fragments of the next-door neighbour's news radio program. She could barely cope with the horrors. And the reality shows Pete liked to watch made her breathless.

'Why would these people let everyone watch them?' she asked.

'Well, for money,' Pete replied.

Then she leant back, inhaled deeply on her Marlboro and said, 'I guess it's just like poetry, reality TV: take a knife to my soul then, here, eat the entrails.'

After that he started shielding her from all the stuff that wandered in the windows and through the screens – and he needed it too, phone off, beret on, writing in his green book in the backyard, eating delivery Nando's for dinner, laughing at each other's stupid ways, both of them enjoying the flat share they'd never had; both of them gratefully ordinary on an ordinary suburban street in early December. After ten days of literary lockdown, they knew each other. Writing a different letter to a different person from their lives and reading them out loud at night, it was bringing them close – like how magnets work. And their letters had been similar, especially the dad one, and the son one, both racked with equal amounts anguish and anger. And in the act of writing a letter like that, Pete had learnt, not only do you see what you're like in relationships, like pattern wise, but you also get to let go of a lot. Writing stuff down was easier than saying it. And more informative. Plum read back over his letters and it was often like someone else had written em. He wondered if the stuff he was reading would have stayed hidden forever, if Sylvia had not forced his biro.

'What's your favourite word, Peter?' Sylvia asked him one morning as she chopped up a grapefruit with a butter knife.

'Hey?'

'Word, what's your favourite word. Or words?' She put the fleshy stuff in her mouth and winced.

'What's yours?' Pete asked, pen in hand at the dining table.

'I asked you first.'

'I don't think I have one.'

'Everyone has a favourite word. Favourite colour. Favourite food.'

'Favourite colour is blue because … the sky. Favourite food is steak sandwich.'

'Oh my God, you are such a brute.'

'Really?'

'A Neanderthal.'

'Ok.'

'What word gives you a thrill? What word have you written, or – hmm, let's put it this way: what word sums you up, or drives you? What is a word that says this is me, this is Peter.'

Pete spun the pen in his fingers, thinking of all the things he dug. He liked food and sex and contact sports. He loved the feeling when you hadn't had any of them but you knew you were about to have lots, and he liked how that made you feel, that relaxed sort of lust sensation when desire met expectation and they got on well. 'Appetite!' Pete said, thinking yes, that's three syllables and not at all dishonest.

'Pathetic!' said Sylvia, almost immediately, walking out of the kitchen and onto the deck.

Pete kept working on his letter to Sarah, asking her to forgive him for all them years when he thought the sun shined out his arse, like how he iced her for ten years for not wanting to come to games, calling her selfish to their mum and saying she must be jealous of his fame – whereas she never was jealous at all, Sarah feared the limelight more than he did. She just didn't like watching league, she only liked netball and quizzes. He also thanked her for how she used to hang with him after Albert had left again, admitting he had been scared in the house all those years, and that she had provided true comfort after the noise. Pete couldn't write it all fast enough, the words pouring out, and he would have delved further if Sylvia had not re-entered, somewhat sheepishly through the sliding door. She stood above him and caressed his thinning scalp, moving the strands of hair about. It was clinical, almost maternal the touching, there was definitely nothing sensual about it.

'I'm sorry, Peter. You're so right.'

'Right about what?'

'"Appetite" is an incredible word to pick. Appetite is everything. Appetite is why we write, why we hunt, why we fuck. Everything is appetite.'

'Yeah, I thought –'

'Without appetite we starve. Without appetite we die. Without appetite we are skeletons.'

'Yeah, I mean I was mostly thinking about ribs and —'

'I demand we both write a poem on the topic of "Appetite", and then drive to the lighthouse at 4 am on Saturday morning and read them aloud.'

'How do you know there's a lighthouse?'

'Because I was watching you, the morning you got lost in the Kurnell sand dunes. Ted and I were there fishing in a small cove, and we saw you touch it.'

'You saw me touch it?'

'Yes, we both did. Ted Hughes and Sylvia Plath. Witnessed you touch a lighthouse.'

Peter had four days to write a new poem, one that could rival his lodger, and the equal amount of days to work out how he was going to get them both to the lighthouse. He couldn't call his mates for a lift, there'd be too many questions, plus Squeaky was working as the 'muscle and hustle' at the Old Bike Shop now, so he'd be sleeping, or more likely drinking in the jacuzzi at Trent's, which was where he last saw him, arms beneath the bubbles. And Sylvia was deadset against taking an Uber: getting in a car with a stranger from within one's phone seemed ominous to her. He'd have to think of something, because he wasn't about to get Brick involved, or Renee – God, you can only imagine …

The lead-up to what Sylvia was now calling the 'Lighthouse Sessions' wasn't entirely filled with poetry and letters. For the past however many weeks since Gavin had vacated the place, Pete had been waking up at 6 am and popping over to Woolooware Oval to kick the ball with Chloe. Ever since he'd spotted her that day walking home, he'd been thinking about the purity of effort she displayed – and so one morning he went across to see if she was there, which of course she was, and after a few silent sessions of grubbers, witches hats and suicide sprints, they had formed a sort of unsaid bond. But the thing was, Chloe had no idea who Pete was, for she was only fourteen and her NRL planet featured heroes like Harry Grant, Latrell Mitchell and Josh Addo-Carr. To her, Pete was a dinosaur, an unknown Pete-osaurus, and Plum never thought to fill her in, because this too was a clear gift from the heavens. What Sylvia was to him, Plum was to Chloe, and they got as much out of their time on the paddock of poetry and practice as the other did.

That was until the morning after Sylvia proposed the Lighthouse Sessions, when he and Chloe were practising spiral passes left and right, and Chloe's dad appeared in a singlet and trackies and started carrying on about how she was meant to walk her brother to school. Pete just stood there, spinning the Steeden in his hands and thinking how much easier it would have been for the man to have simply walked the kid there himself instead of bounding up here and blowing a hole in the joint. But the mega-fella didn't stop, he was tilting over the girl, and for a second there Pete thought he might well strike her then and there on Seagulls Oval, which inspired Pete to say, 'Easy'.

'Oh no,' said Chloe, sensing the familiar.

Her rotund father turned to face the only other onfield adult and everything in his manner said he was readying to throw hands, but the rage was swiftly diffused with recognition, menace twisting into sycophancy with a single bat of the eyelids.

'Plum?' the big man asked.

'Yep,' said Plum.

The big man turned to his daughter. 'Chloe, do you know who this is?'

'I don't care,' she said, keen to just keep training – having nailed two out of three of her passes down the line to her coach with a skip to catch and a skip to pass.

'This man is the greatest player of our time. No, Chloe, serious, I used to worship this man in the 90s. Ain't that right, Plum, cuz?'

'I don't know,' Pete said. 'I don't know you.'

'My name's Manu. What an honour. Man, you're fucken huge in Polynesia. We call you Plum Warri –'

'Ok, Dad!' said Chloe, kicking the mud with the front of her foot.

Peter laughed, and he could see in the girl's shoulders that she was ashamed to have her dad up here on the training oval, embarrassed that Pete was seeing him in the flesh. But Pete knew nothing this guy did would make him stop coming here to help her; not since Glenn Lazarus had he seen someone train that hard, and be so hard on themselves; Chloe was far from talented, but Pete could see she had the effort and leadership qualities to go far in footy – and it was just like writing a poem: you had to give it everything. It was all about honesty, or, perhaps, as it now seemed, it was all about appetite.

'She's not annoying you, Mr Lum?'

'I think I'm probably annoying her.'

Manu stood there for a second then, suddenly aware of himself, tried to pull his too-small singlet over his too-large gut, but then he gave up and just chortled at the grass. 'Well, I'm going to go and walk my son to school. Chloe, you can have a day off school if you want. What you learn from this man is more important than any algebra.'

After the session Pete suggested they walk down to the Caltex and get a soft drink. With her day now free, Chloe said yeah, and pretty soon they were sipping Fantas and chewing on Flakes on the bench outside the local physio.

'No other chocolate does it to you like Flake does,' said Plum.

'What the hell?' said Chloe.

Their friendship was better without banter, but now they'd stepped out of the training arena for the first time, it felt apt that some sort of conversation take place and involve something other than 'hold the ball this way' or 'end-on-end' or 'drive with your legs'. The problem was, neither of them were natural chat-starters, so they both waited for the other to kick off, and traffic lights went red and then green a dozen or so times in suspense. Finally, Chloe found herself at the edge of her own lips, with the sugar content of the fizzy drink giving her just the right amount of energy to step into the unknown. 'You know how, like, you keep saying to me that what you're teaching me to do will come in handy in next year's season when I play girls' rugby league, Mr Lum?'

'Yeah.'

'Well, I don't think I can play for a team.'

'Why's that? You're good enough. Strong enough.'

'Because we have something wrong with our visa. Which means I can't enrol in high school properly yet, which means I can't join a team if I don't have Year Eight.'

'What's up with the visa?'

Chloe was pepped up in her body now, her voice reaching higher than ever before. 'Well, my dad has just stuffed up another job! He said it was a personality clash but, like, how many personality clashes can one guy have, Mr Lum?! Like, seriously, you only have one personality!'

Pete burst out laughing. The candid way in which this girl spoke, plus the joy she was giving him in letting him coach her – he could've bottled her. 'Does he need a job to get an extension?'

'Yeah, but, you know, he's already had six hundred jobs since we got to the Shire eighteen months ago and every single one of them ended in a –'

'Personality clash?'

'Yeah, it sucks.'

Pete swivelled his body towards Chloe and pointed at her face, her spray of brown freckles and her light brown eyes revealing the fact she really was just a child still. 'You are born to play this game, girl. Ok? And I believe that with the right amount of hard work and a sprinkling of luck, you might just be able to do something. Righto?'

'You can't get my dad a job, Mr Lum. You don't even have one yourself.'

'Ha!' said Pete. 'How do you know that?'

'Because you're always over here training with me when normal people are getting the train to the city.'

'This is true. This is true.'

'But anyway, it's all good. Maybe I am just not meant to play footy.'

'Hey!' said Pete, still pointing at her face. 'Don't you ever say that nonsense again.'

'Sorry.'

'You think I train people not to play?'

'I thought maybe you were just lonely.'

Pete stopped pointing right away, the word 'lonely' cutting the strength from his neck. He crunched the can of Fanta in his hand and then looked back up at the girl, and for a second it was like he was back in the Subaru, and Chloe was Gavin at fourteen, and the world was all innocent again, and he was still a God in his son's eyes, not the lying, dying, piece-of-shit dad he was now. 'See you tomorrow morning, Chloe. Eat clean and get some sleep, ok?'

She spun the ball into the air then fumbled it and they both watched as it rolled and hopped to a stop against a ute wheel in the gutter. 'Yeah, it's all good,' she said.

'Go the Sharks!' said Sylvia.

'Huh?' said Plum, asleep on the couch with Rage blaring.

'Get the fuck up, fat boy, it's time for the Lighthouse Sessions!'

It was 3.17 am and there she was on the front lawn, leaning against Gavin's BMX, ready to go. She had a Sharks hoodie on over a flash pair of compression tights, and by the time Pete had locked up, crossed the lawn, extracted his matching BMX from the garage and rolled the door down to the ground, she was already on the Kingsway popping a modest wheelie and flicking out a sleek back-wheel skid.

'You don't want a helmet?' asked Peter, clipping up the strap beneath his chin.

'Really?'

It was one of those rides that made him wish he did things like it more often. Without a soul on the road, the poets travelled to North Cronulla, passing the cop shop and Red Rooster, then, as they reached Northies, tacking left at The Alley and accelerating up the esplanade past The Wall towards Elouera.

The weather was exactly as it should be for a morning of poems by the lighthouse: depressing and evocative. The waves were crashing in three directions beneath a grey and gloomy sky that opened up in fleeting moments.

'When you get to Wanda,' Pete yelled to Sylvia's back, 'take the path to Kurnell!'

'I know where to go! You don't have to mansplain everything!'

They pushed on like BMX Bandits in 1987, traversing the more difficult terrain with noiseless solidarity, and the closer they got to that lighthouse beyond the caves, the more Peter hoped this woman would never leave him alone again.

'Bloody ripper!' Sylvia said, dumping the bike on the dirt, inspiring Pete to do the same.

Pete opened his bag and withdrew the two tall plastic bottles of Evian he'd put orange Beroccas into and placed in the freezer the night before. 'Here, rip right in.'

'I can't believe you thought to do this.'

'That's how we roll, Sylvzies,' said Pete, looking out to sea.

'How we roll where?'

Pete howled for all cub scouts past and present. 'Dib-dib-dib, dob-dob-dob, Akeyla, we'll do our best!'

'Ok, please stop that now.'

Sylvia spun around to face the lighthouse steps, then folded herself down onto the ground in one clean movement and came to stillness, cross-legged on a sandy patch of grass in the still-moist morning dew. 'No more nonsense – it's time for your poem!'

'You're the professional, shouldn't you be the one to kick us off?'

'First to the lighthouse gets to choose, and I was here first,' she said, shaking her bottle then slugging down a startling chunk of it.

'It's just fair to let someone know that you're racing them.'

'I was racing you.'

'Before you race them.'

'I won! Soft-cock! Now read me your damned poem!' she said, clicking her fingers.

'Don't click at me,' he said, climbing the two tiny yet seemingly unscalable steps to the ancient, looming stage.

'Clicking is a poetry club thing, it's cooler than clapping, you see?' she said, clicking in a jazz-ish way. 'And it makes less noise so the poet is never interrupted.'

'But I haven't started my poem yet …'

Sylvia was done with the preamble, closing her eyes and vaping in a cloud of herself now.

Pete took a deep breath and inhaled all the seagulls of the southern beaches.

Sylvia, eyes still closed shut, spoke from the diaphragm. 'Ladies and gentlemen, our next contribution is from former Aussie legend Mr Peter "The Plum" Lum. A gentleman whom I have come to know and love and, if it were indeed possible on this earth at this time, would surely thrust my daddy–daddy on, but alas, as it is mostly, all we have are words, words words … Ladies and Seagulls, please, now, give it up, for "Appetite!"'

Peter Lum breathed deep into the page of his little green book, closed his eyes and thought of the tarmac. Then opening his eyes, he looked down at his scrawl and started to read.

'*This is a letter to my mouth*'
By Peter Lum

Mouth, it's me
Pete

Are you free?
Can we speak

Sorry
Of course you can speak
You are my mouth
It is your job, week on week

And while I am here
I'll say thank you larynx
Thank you teeth
Shout out to my cheeks and tongue
But today I'm talking mouth
Because to be honest, it's the one

I just
I guess
In this time of poetic isolation
I been doing this thing
Called contemplation
With this chick Sylvia

Red-hot, writer sensation
And so in her American terms
I've been 'unpacking all my stuff'
And what's come up mostly
Is that being you
Mouth
Historically
Honestly
Must have been – must be – pretty fucken rough

Mouth,
My mouth
You soft moist pillow bench
You wide-open avaricious fussy-not-fussy munching suck garage
Your curvy luscious bend
It's me, here, Peter
And I am keen to make amends

When I was a kid I made concoctions
Swallowed for ritualistic indoctrinations
Into clubs and private groups
That no one wanted to join, called like 'Peter's Club'
I'd stir up vegemite and plums
And glue and soy sauce and some of my sister's hair
Grass, dirt and bits of rubber
Into your mouth
Don't care

Mouth, for this I am sorry
Sorry mouth

I'm sorry for the thirty years of binge drinking
Whiskey to beer back to whiskey margarita fried chicken
cigarette back to beer wine vodka Champagne margarita vomit

in the pot plant put it in again
Vomit in the alleyway, tongue down a throat
Make room
Repeat

But mostly I am sorry
Hence the dread
Mostly I lie awake at night
Thinking of the things mouth said

You're a fucken shit of a mum
And dad
Don't even bother, Dad
I don't ever want to see you again, Dad
And ex-wife
I can't even write down

Fuck I miss her mouth
Charmayne the pain
If only I used you and explained

I love you, mouth
And I see you, mouth
And I promise
From here on in
I shall listen before I spout
Or treat you like a bin

So let's us say this one-word prayer together
And within it, drop the fight
One two three before and after me
Let us scream
For APPETITE!

Heart pumping, Pete looked up from his page to meet the panel, but she was gone.

Just the 1.25-litre bottle of frozen-Evian-Berocca remained but on its side, half killed. There was no sign of her, and Gavin's bike wasn't there either, just his.

He looked around to check the lighthouse was real. He laid his palms on the cool white concrete pylon – and, yeah, it was as real as rent – and once more he got that déjà vu feeling.

He looked down at his notebook.

Was it that *appalling*? And, well, where the fuck was hers? They were meant to do a poem each. That was the contract.

'Morning Plum! Go the Sharks!' said a passing jogger.

'Fuck off!' said Plum.

When he got home Sylvia was not there either, nor was any of the stuff she'd scattered about. Gavin's room looked like Gavin lived in it. On the bed she'd left a tartan scarf and black beret. And her vape.

Pete picked up the scarf and beret, smelt them, then put them on. Then he took the vape to his mouth and inhaled. Exhaled plum plumes. And from that moment on, his appetite was different, and Peter 'The Plum' Lum felt more like a poet than a player.

Five

Peter Lum, 'one of the toughest ever to play the game', had lived by the 'good doctor' philosophy his whole life. You self-administer, you google-MD, you take matters into your own hands. And if your head is attached to your neck, then *up and into it, son!*

In 89, he'd needled up against St George to play with a shoulder slap tear, knowing full well October to Feb would be spent beneath a sharp knife. In 93 he went against doctors' orders and played Easts with a cracked jaw and split index finger. In his final years of footy, in England for St Helens, he didn't even bother listening to the cloaks, figuring he was a long time retired and that with enough aspirin and smelling salts he could rustle up a threat. This was where he suspected the brain thing came about, when he really thought about it, which, with Sylvia around, was quite often. Them juice heads up there in the North, the Wigan and the Hull boys, they were after Plum; having heard he was the 'toughest to ever play NRL', they wanted to make a name for themselves by knocking him out. In Plum's final game in England, held up in a tackle, George Preston, more steroids than sense, came running in as planned and caught Plum with a shoulder charge to the skull. Plum played on, and they won the final, but he still couldn't remember the last thirty minutes, and watching the highlights, he didn't remember throwing that winning try assist. When he'd gotten back to the house, Renee was standing in the kitchen with her big belly and he didn't know what it was. He didn't know what pregnancy was. He just vomited in the sink and cried, vomited and cried, asking her why she had expanded and what it meant.

And so, after a few good months on Liz's anti-epileptic – the infamous Lamictal – Pete thought, well, let's see what happens if I just don't take it. The last couple of weeks had been so epically beautiful rolling round the joint with Sylvia; the phone off and only a few drinks a day, Pete felt super good. Nineties good! So he dropped down from two pills a day to one, then by the time Floodlight was racing in the Handicap against a beatable field, he was off em – he was clean – and ready to re-engage with the world as the new and improved Peter 'The Plum' Lum, having recently graduated from the Sylvia Plath Personal Recovery Course, the past was now his power source.

He wasn't about to fit or fuck-out, he was a poet now. And with the scarf and beret on, he leapt out the front door like it was the first day of World Expo 88.

'Scarf,' said Matt, as Pete entered the Tradies, the usual amount of locals turning round to ogle the myth, the man, the master.

'That's it,' said Pete, issuing Squeak an all-in-one handshake, hug and back pat.

'And beret,' said Matt. 'Aren't you hot?'

'Nah, I'm in a T-shirt and shorts.'

'Yeah, but –'

'You're in a safari suit, Magic,' said Squeak, pouring out the beers.

'Yeah, but it's light fabric. Scarves are wool.'

'It's nice around the neck.'

'Where'd you get it? France?'

'A friend gave it to me.'

'Which friend?'

'Geez, Spanish Inquisition.'

'You got it in Spain?'

'No, I'm saying your line of que –'

'Hey?'

'I'm not sure where she got it.'

'She?'

'Yeah, a female friend –'

'Is she Spanish? What's the go?'

'She's American. Just a friend. Her name is Sylvia Plath.'

Matt, with one week to go until his hip operation, leant over his walking stick as pained as he was confused. Next to him and a hundred foot below was Squeaky, smiling up with no idea either. The silence leaked on, for the name was familiar but not quite enough.

'Nope, don't know her!' Matt said. 'She sounds hot.'

Matt went to pour out the jug three ways, but Pete put his hand over his own glass, just as Sylvia often did when she'd had her glass and a half. 'Not for me today, legends. I'm on a moderation kick. Plus I gotta say, I prefer the old rouge vin these days – Bordeaux or even a Cotes Du Rhone – to the beers, which as I get older tend to make me feel a little bloated and dizzy. Youse follow me?'

This floored the boys. Never before had the great man turned down a free beer. You could fill his mouth with razor blades and toothpaste, Plum would still pour it on in, whatever hour.

'I'll get you a wine then?' said Matt, happy to smash the jug himself if need be.

'Anything but merlot,' said Pete.

Magic Matt's phone lit up and started singing 'Enter Sandman' and just like that he was off on his walking stick to see a man about a dog instead.

'So you good?' said Squeak, after forty-five seconds of mutual looking around.

'Yeah, pal, I'm flying.'

'Flying?'

'It's taken a bit of time,' Pete said, beaming at the jockey from beneath his beret. 'But I no longer fear the past, you know? Because I've cleaned house now, and it was about time I did.'

Squeaky wasn't impressed. 'Speaking of time, where the fuck have you been, ya cunt? Trent's needed you, I've needed you, but no – no return call, you just send down Manu the Polynesian to the Old Bike Shop for a job, and think everything's going to be ok. What's with this Sylvia? What's with you? What's with the beret and scarf?'

'I just took a bit of time out to re-set.'

'*I just took some time out to re-set.*'

'Yeah. So kill me.'

'Maybe I fucking will,' said Squeaky, wishing he had the balls to tell his mate what had been going on in *his* life and how his house had been getting a certain makeover too, but he couldn't quite fathom the courage. Maybe eleven beers and eleven lines would help …

'Where's Brick?' asked Plum. 'Is he coming to watch the race?'

'Yeah, he's on his way – said he's dropping Charmayne down at Endota first.'

Plum lifted off his beret. 'Endota?'

'Yeah, Endota.'

'Endota? What the spa joint, Endota?'

'Yeah, what other Endota is there?'

'What's Brick taking Charmayne to Endota for?'

'Probably a spa. Endota is a spa joint. As we've established.'

'That's not right.'

'Endota's not a spa joint?'

Pete sat restless in the silence that dripped like candle wax onto an open thigh. 'She hates spas. She hates hot water. Her dad used to scald her in South Africa.'

'TMI.'

'Hey?'

'Trent says it all the time. TMI, it stands for Too Much Information.'

'Endota, ay. En-fucken-dota.'

'Jesus fuck me. What's the go?'

'Is there something someone wants to tell me?'

The headache Pete had come to know and come to see go was back. Having burrowed in, caterpillar quiet, it now lodged itself just above the right ear, clamped against the temple walls – warming up to cry out, a fully formed cicada.

'Hey Plum,' Squeak said, and leant in. 'Before the boys bust back in on the scene, have a look at this.' He took out his phone and with a few taps was showing the lock forward through a few tweets and retweets he'd saved to the dashboard, all variations on the same theme, the theme being 'Plum Pariah'.

'I told you last time I don't care what the keyboard warriors are say –'

'Just, look, beret man. It's not words this time. It's video.'

Pete had never had a profile on Instagram, let alone Twitter. It all looked like nonsense to him *and so much effort* – but as Squeak pressed play on the insidious, boxed-up little videos, this swiftly changed meaning. Plum watched himself collapse in the buggy on the tarmac then get driven back to safety, groin damp, spread-eagled and helpless, over and over again, cut in with montages of his playing days and mocking memes and music.

'Fucking hell. Squeaky? This is disgusting.'

'It's bubbling, Pete, and there's people circling. Some bloke from Brick's gym got footage of you giving Charmayne a serve and all.'

'Hey? Show me that one, that's bullshit.'

'It's not up.'

'Then how do you know about it?'

207

'Whispers. You know the Shire. It's all that.'

'What are we doing then? Squeak? Where is the prick?'

'Brick's sorting it, but I suggest, well, Trent and I believe ...'

'I've got a brain disease,' said Plum, and suddenly felt like a kid again, looking for his dad, wondering if he should get those nuggets or not.

'I know.'

'I could die.'

'I know.'

'From playing.'

'I know, Plum. I'd say I got it too. From falling off horses.'

Pete refilled the beers. They clinked glasses. They drank. 'What are they saying? These internet blokes. These big brave whisperers.'

'Some people are saying you're a druggie, some are saying you've got amnesia or that you're narcoleptic, you sleepwalk and shit, somnambulant, but the worst ones are saying ... and this is what I think we need to discuss –'

'What?'

'Well, they're saying, they're saying you hit your kid at Rustic Ribs, which is why he's gone to Bali, and that you hit your bird, which is why she's gone to her mother's.'

'No!'

'Yeah, and the boxing video, the one the bloke took in Brick's gym, it doesn't look ideal for you, to be honest, not with these sentiments already out there.'

'Hey?'

'You look like you might throw hands.'

'But I don't.'

'DV.'

'Never!'

'I know.'

'Fuck.'

'Yep.'

'What should I do?'

'Firstly, start answering your phone when your mates ring.'

'Ok, sorry,' Pete said, and he hadn't said that, to anyone, for a long time. 'Ok, ok. Sorry.'

'Does Trent know?'

'Anyone with a phone and an interest in sport knows.'

'Australia.'

'Yeah, mate, Australia knows.'

'Right.'

'Answer your fucking phone, Plum!'

A wall full of missed calls and unanswered texts was his phone's happy place, and every type of relationship he had going – friend, professional, family, lover, media, fan – had all resented it; the bloke was always a myth when it came to getting back to anyone, but even more lately.

'This is heavy shit, Plum. Like *CSI: Miami* shit. You gotta smarten up now.'

Pete nodded, ripping into the beer, wondering why he'd ever stopped drinking the stuff – beer never let him down, beer didn't have 4G and spite.

'Sorted,' said Matt, limping back to the two men and handing the goods to Squeaky under the table, the other two bags safe in the inside pocket of his safari jacket. There was never any point getting just one gram. If you're risking a prison sentence, go Aldi bulk style.

'Kids!' said Brick, slamming his phone, keys and wallet down on the table. 'Let's drink piss and punt, what do you say?'

'Brick!' the friends rejoiced.

'What's with the scarf and beret?' asked Brick.

'What's with Endota Spa and Relaxation?' said Pete, heading to the bar and leaving the others to sort through the small stuff of *how's it going, what's the Floodlight update* and *who has gear* … Waiting for the barmaid to pour the jugs, with the cicadas starting up again in his head, Pete squinted at his three friends in all their naive glory. He noticed firstly how different their body shapes were. He saw the pain in the way Matt hunched over, having never recovered from the death of his brother on a kayaking trip ten years ago, which was when the cocaine went up a notch. He saw Squeaky's gambling obsession, and how his detest for women was likely a closeted gayness. And Brick Wall, whose lacerating self-opinion was reflected in the way he looked up from under his own eyelids, always on the ready to push another bloke down. Plum wondered in what order they would all die, and who would miss who the most: he settled on Squeaky as the loneliest, figuring Brick would always be popular due to his gym, and Matt, well, he could always find comfort in the affordable arms of Thai culture.

He looked around the bar at other sets of overweight, under-loved men, also standing in small circles, lifting beers to their mouths like cult members – up, down, piss it out, and in again – all at differing stages of running from their lives, of burying their regrets inside the stinking carpets, trying not to think of what would be next: bankruptcy, prostate, coffin.

'I might start a brewery of my own in a sec, Plum!' bellowed Matt, wildly parched and anxious at the lack of piss before him.

'It's all the rage these days,' said Squeaky.

'Yeah,' said Brick, 'all you need is a twisted moustache and two-hundred grand.'

Plum picked up the two jugs and wandered over, having completely checked out for whatever amount of minutes and seconds it took to do all that daydreaming. With Floodlight running in the last there was plenty of time for the boys to realign themselves, drinking two jugs at a time in quick rounds, with a counter meal the rock to build a house upon, and races, tennis or Big Bash available on the plethora of screens and the snort on offer if you felt like some pep in your step. What could go wrong? Seriously? But for some reason, as they went about their business like a hundred thousand times before, something about the timbre of the day felt spiky. The well-oiled in-jokes seemed forced, the laughter an interruption to another sentence just beginning, and the booze, well, was it even working or was it just making everything feel heavier, like it could all just sink?

'Plum, what do you think, are you in?' Matt asked, after his Thailand Pinterest slideshow ended. 'I emailed you all the breakdown and texted you the payment plan, but I didn't –'

'Yeah,' Pete said, 'I've been off the comms a bit.'

'It's fifty each,' said Brick, sounding more and more like it was his idea and less and less like he gave a fuck what Plum's vibe was this week or next. He was the King now, he was the one booking Endota for Char, he was the one she called when she needed something.

'Yeah. Fifty large,' said Squeak, flicking his eyes up from his phone, but today it was Trent's banter he was tied to, not so much the betting apps.

'Is it? Fifty seems a lot? What about the win?'

'Fifty, yeah,' confirmed Matt. 'Well, the bits from the recent win that are left ... well, that's all in place for travel and hotels till we're sorted and of course a touch up to the venue ...'

'Right ...'

'We want to make it a good pub to be in, like good good, not some touristy thing.'

'And the pub is *ours*; we run it, we drink in it, we root in it.'

'Right.'

'So are you in?'

Pete took a step back, cradling his beer beneath his chin. He looked to Brick, who was still not looking at him, flicking his eyes between the beer and the TVs instead. 'Brick, don't you run a business? How are you moving to Thailand full-time?'

'Your missus,' Brick said.

'Huh?'

'With Char's café, and now a Zumba and Pilates studio up the back, I think I might sell her in and she can take a load.'

'Take a load,' Squeak giggled, then stopped just as quickly.
'Charmayne's doing Pilates?'

Brick took a deep breath. The gear was running hot in his bloody system and with it the grand plan that could just solve everything in one fell swoop. 'She has a friend who teaches Zumba and Pilates – ex-Sharkette, powerhouse. So yeah, Char'll run the scheduling, Lexi the Zumba and Pilates, I'm training up two young blokes to do the boxing side of things – these forearms are buggered from pads – and Father Pepple says he and Kutiote are keen to run some MMA fighters through there so, yeah, doctor's orders is to go easy on the heart and, as a result, Brick Wall's Boxing Gym is expanding, with a healthy café up front.'

'Well, that all says Thailand to me,' said Matt.

'Char sounds busy, Brick. No wonder she needs a bit of Endota. Workin her hard, mate.'

'She's a good egg, your missus.'

'She is,' said Pete, unsure whose missus she was these days.

'Floodlight in an hour and forty-five minutes, men,' said Squeak, angling for a subject change.

Pete caught the drift, leaning back and letting his voice thicken. 'Can I ask you blokes a question?'

'No, she didn't have a cock!' said Matt, then burst out laughing.

'At least she told me she didn't when I got on her motorbike,' said Squeak, who, in a tight V-neck and distressed skinny jeans had expected the gents to note a difference tonight. 'Shoot,' said Brick, growing confident in direct eye contact now, his hand on his heart, just to check the pace of things since that last bumper in the men's.

'What's your biggest regret? And what's your best memory?' asked Pete, and he may as well have tasered them, with the boys just standing there stunned.

'Geez, Plummo, that's a bit heavy for a boys' afternoon.'

'Nah, I'm into it,' said Brick. 'We should be talking about this stuff, it's good.'

'Yeah,' said Squeak, 'what else are mates for than to say shit to?'

'Righto, righto,' said Matt, 'but let me get a couple more jugs first.'

'No, now,' said Pete. 'Best memory, biggest regret.'

'I'll go first,' said Squeak, flipping his phone over so as to not be distracted by the T-Dog texts.

'Good boy,' said Pete.

'Best memory is probably winning the Cup and the Slipper in that same year.'

'Yes!'

'Yep.'

'Yeah, no, exactly. Fuck, I still forget you did that. Fuck.'

'And biggest regret – probably cashing in my super and pissing it all up a wall and punting it.' There was a stunned silence. Pete had never thought the small man would admit this big issue, but he was, but he had, and now the other three were casting their minds over their wallet history, wondering how much they'd blown on the tappety-tap elixir.

'I'll go second,' said Matt. 'Best memory was playing against Magic Johnson at the Olympics, that whole USA team really, but mostly Magic.'

'And regret?' asked Plum, on the offensive boards now.

'Not asking Leslie Keagan to the debut in 87. Fuck it. Caught up with her at the 25-year school reunion a while back, and over a few too many of those and a walk down to the shop to get cigs, we both admitted there was a sliding door there, so yeah.'

'Fuck, Magic, I'm gonna cry.'

'It's all good. But, yeah, if I could go full Cher and "Turn Back Time", who knows …'

'Brick?' said Pete, smiling to his best and most loyal of mates.

'Best memory is probably playing alongside you, mate,' said Brick, and you could have heard a pin drop, that is if the rest of the bar wasn't so rowdy.

'And the regret side of things?' said Magic Matt, still shaking off Leslie, and what could have been, and the kids they could have had, his brother meeting his kids …

'My marriage and my kid, yeah. I wish I could go back and rescue all that. I wish I hadn't been so stubborn at every turn. I wish I was more, um … listening? To their needs.'

'Fucken hell,' said Matt. 'We can't get to Thailand quick enough. Can we get another jug yet?'

Brick shook his head. 'Not until Plum does his ones.'

'Yeah, Pete hasn't gone.'

'Let's go, Plumster. Beret and all.'

Peter put the beret back on. The headache had cleared as he'd reached that sweet spot of two to three beers where everything made sense and nothing really mattered; it was the ideal time to approach a bird and/or play a game of pool. 'Best memory would be the day Gavin was born.'

'Ah, Gavin. You spoke to him?'

'Let him finish!' said Brick. 'We can talk about Gavin and that after.'

'Biggest regret would be telling my dad that I never wanted to see him again. The day he turned up pissed to see me get my Australian jumper. I told him to fuck off and then pushed him into a hedge. Me old man. Last time I saw him.'

Outside on the smoking deck you could hear birdsong from the far-off gum trees and discontented Labradors longing for a walkies, their music chiming in with that of the pokies and the rabble that drifted through the metal bars from inside. It was a concert of now, reminding Plum of freedom and regret both at once.

'Biggest regret would be ever taking up smoking,' Brick said as he joined Plum in the enclosed outdoor area, having just made a detour to the dunnies.

'Cancer stick?' said Plum, flicking up his pack for Brick to pluck one.

'Put it down, dickhead,' said Brick to a bloke just inside whose phone was up and videoing the two of them having a dart. 'I said put it down or I'll shove it up your arsehole!'

The bloke spun and disappeared, but Brick and Pete could hear him laughing.

'Phones, ay,' said Plum, lighting em both up.

'Mouth breathers, mate.'

'That's it.'

'Makes you realise, with the phones, how good a time it was for us coming through, you know? We grew up in the best time anyone could.'

'How so?' asked Plum, blinking to cope with the old dizziness again.

'The freedom! We got to do whatever we wanted. We didn't have to worry who was watching. The shit we did in the sheds –'

'You remember nude chin-ups at the Bourbon and Beefsteak?'

'Do I ever!'

'See how many you can do while blokes are trying to grab you on the old fella.'

'No one was fucken looking, no one got harmed. It was an innocent time.'

'And now everyone's paranoid.'

'Spying and –'

'You think they're spying on me?'

'Could be.'

'You think I should be worried?'

'You'll be right. Gav'll be back soon. You can get things sorted.'

Plum looked up at his mate. Brick's left nostril was moist, and his eyes were window-cracked. His green Lacoste shirt was doing its best to contain the gut that had been growing week by week now that Plum had kyboshed the soft-sand sessions. The Brick was spilling, but at the same time Plum knew that he could still do over any bloke in Cronulla, any day of the week. He had old-school fitness and he'd be near impossible to kill. He'd nearly killed Plum a few times in the ring, laying a few on his ribs and then, as Pete fell, not missing him with a left hook to emphasise. Brick'd take any inch he could get with Plum because he knew he'd never be as good skill-wise, he knew he wouldn't be talked about on the shows in twenty years, wouldn't be immortalised. When they played against each other in 91, and Brick was front-rower for Manly, he'd not only thrown a few upper cuts in the scrum but later put a knee to Pete's face in the ruck. Luckily for Brick the rain was teeming down and no ref could see a thing. But Pete remembered, he'd stored it like winter linen, and in the last few weeks he'd been wondering just how many of Brick's head slams had contributed to the present state of affairs.

'What ya sayin?'

'Plum?'

'You said Gav'll be back soon?'

'Yeah, well, he's not going to relocate to Bali, is he?'

'Have you heard from him?'

'I haven't, no.'

'Right.'

'But Charmayne has,' said Brick, sucking on the dart like it was a life source.

'Huh?'

'He called her, said he'd lost his phone. It was from an Indonesian number.'

'A what?'

'A Bali one? Plus 6 or 06 —'

'Oh.'

'We assumed he'd rung you too.'

'Yeah,' Pete lied, exhaling smoke. 'He phoned me.'

'So you knew about it?'

'Yeah, Ainslee and him.'

'Yeah, she went on ahead.'

'Yeah. Oh, is that …?'

'And then he got his phone stolen.'

'Along those lines. But that's travel, mate,' said Plum. 'Kids lose shit.'

'Right.'

'And there are so many thieves in India.'

'He's in Bali, though?'

'Yeah, I know, but culturally.'

'I think he's ok now, right? But he sounded a bit stressed. According to Char that is.'

Pete felt trapped. Lit up another dart. Why hadn't Gav called him?

'He's a good kid, Plum, world at his feet too, and I tell ya, the priest who trains my boys, Nigerian fella …'

'Father Emmanuel Pepple?

'Yes! I think you met him at the christening, He's been watching Gavin, and he reckons if footy doesn't work out, the kid could kill it in the ring – in the MMA, in the cage.'

'Is that right?'

'He could make a squillion. If he wanted to. I mean, I think he's the next Laurie Daley.'

'Do ya?'

'Is everything ok, Plum? You're looking at me funny.'

'No?' Plum said, twelve beers and the rest scattering his intent.

'Maybe you should take it easy.'

'Maybe I should go to Endota for a spa treatment.'

'What're you sayin, mate? You wanna air somethin – air it. I'm all ears.'

'I'm fine.'

'I've missed our morning jogs.'

'Me too,' said Plum, finishing his beer – which didn't have enough beer in it.

'Why don't we say in January, only a week or two away, we get the soft-sand jogging back in the iCal? It'll be good for my heart condition.'

'Yep.'

'And your brain.'

'Hey?'

'Char told me. And Squeaky. It's ok, mate.'

A long-haired guy appeared on the other side of the bars, holding up a phone, videoing Plum. Plum didn't even think – he just reached through the bars and grabbed the guy's arms and pulled them towards himself. The kid's face smashed into the metal and erupted with blood.

'Get away from me!' said Pete, releasing the guy.

'Plum,' said Brick, reaching to his mate.

Plum pushed off Brick and charged through the door to the bar.

'Plum, mate, where you goin?'

On the way through the kaleidoscope of grunt, grope and gather, he saw his mates waving at him; he saw frosted bar taps calling him, he saw men and women with phones up videoing him; he saw the pokies screaming and the ceiling fans spinning in opposite directions; he saw his own face on the TV, some kind of nostalgia story he assumed but then there was footage from Rustic Ribs, of his son pushing him against the wall, pleading to know, pleading to understand.

'Gav!' he screamed, bolting for the fire exit.

On the grass outside the carpark Pete looked through his missed calls. The same 062 number had tried him half a dozen times but he hadn't considered it might be his son.

'Gav,' he said to himself, leaning into a shady part of the concrete wall.

He pressed on the number but it was 'no longer available', and then something in Indonesian. Pete called Gavin's Aussie number but the same thing happened here: a long silence then a beep and then 'this number cannot be blah blah ...'

'Fuck it,' Pete said, in paternal panic.

He looked left to see a well-dressed family getting a photo taken in front of a brand-new Toyota Hilux. He looked across the road to see a line of greyhound buses ready to take the day-punters back to their housing facilities. He looked right and, wiping the sweat from his eyeballs and brow, made out the words ENDOTA DAY SPA.

Pete walked towards it, slapping his pockets to make sure his scarf and beret were connected to his person and not back in that drinking, sinking facility of shame. He wasn't going back inside that place now, now or ever. *It ain't my church no more.*

If Pete had any idea what he looked like at this moment, he would have been grateful he never made it to the entrance of Endota, having stopped on the corner of Manchester Road to see if he could spot her through a gap in the soft curtains.

'Char.'

He pressed his face against the glass and bang, there she was, walking through a vine-framed doorway into some kind of relaxation room.

'Spa.'

It was her, yes it was: Charmayne, settling herself back on a lounge, dressed in nothing but a white robe, framed by palm trees and drooping candles. She could launch more ships than Helen with a twist of her hips, but she didn't, she just lay there, head to the side, curly blonde hair setting the suburbs on fire.

'Ahh.'

Pete watched on, face smeared apart on the smudged glass, wishing he could transmit how sorry he was and how much he wished they could go back and do it all differently. And then a young woman in grey slacks and matching Endota shirt came in and rested her hand on Char's stomach, as if there was something being preserved in there.

'Fark …'

Dizzy with disbelief, Pete slid down the glass.

'Kid.'

A couple his age passed him round the bend, gasping at the sight of the famous lock forward sprawled outside a suburban spa retreat. 'Oh my God, Hamish,' the lady said.

Pete's bum erupted with buzzing – his phone was in his back pocket and from here on in he would answer it. But, sadly, this time, it was not his son, just his tall mate Magic Matt with a text: 'Floodlight Snappeds a fetlock!! has to be put DOWN?!> Will need to keep da 4k for horse ADMIN + Thaild AYSSUE pub! Cum Squeak'sfighNight o Da boys!! On it!! l,UFFFC! nose'.

'UFC,' Pete said out loud. 'UFC …'

Still quite drunk and high, he sifted through his wallet and located the golden card that read, 'Father Emmanuel Pepple: Boxing, MMA, Alcohol Councillor and Servant to the Saviour.'

'Do you have anything stronger?' asked Pete, blowing the steam clouds off the surface of his milky tea.

The basement of the parish house was more like a man cave, with framed photos of Jorge, Connor, Diaz and Israel outweighing those of Jesus and his pals. There was a huge TV on the wall, a couple of recliners and a shrine that featured three photos at its altar: Sugar Ray Robinson, Muhammad Ali and Jesus Christ, all in triangular harmony above the rosary beads and white candles.

'Too much milk?' asked Father Pepple, firing up the Apple TV, and sliding across to the UFC Fight Pass app, and just like that it was octagon time in Las Vegas.

'No, I mean booze – *the demon drink*. All you men of the cloth are secret pissheads, aren't ya?'

'At one time or another, very possible, Peter.' Father Pepple reclined, pointing at the identical chair opposite him in the hope Plum would see the light and join him in watching Daniel 'DC' Cormier start setting things up for the stellar undercard about to unfurl.

Still hankering for a whiskey, Pete remained upright. 'Sugar Ray Robinson ay, what a fighter.'

'The best boxer, pound for pound, in the history of pugilism.'

'I'm not about to disagree with you.'

'Nor should you. If there is one thing I know, it is black boxers.'

'Jack Johnson went alright?'

'Oh, yes. You know, a bit. He knew how to live too, that man.'

'Yeah, he liked the fast cars and the prostitutes.'

'He liked life,' said the priest, craning to face the ex-footy player.

'He just kept fighting, didn't he? Jack Johnson. Fought till his head fell off.'

'Yes, well the brain is two and a half pounds of electrified pulp. There is only so much it can take.'

'It's true. It's a fragile thing, the brain,' Plum said, listless. Why had he come here? He could be knee-deep in piss and packets at Squeaky's now, barking at the big screen and moving magically towards a sustained oblivion.

'You know Sugar Ray Robinson killed a man in the ring, and the night before he did it, he had a dream that he did that exact thing – killed his opponent – and so he tried to call the fight off, but no one would allow it. And so it happened, the dream, the nightmare, it took place – he killed his challenger, just how the dream had said.'

'If I'd had that dream, I would have laid down a few bets. Then killed the guy.'

'Oh, yes. Gambling. It always comes back to this in Australia, yes?'

'Nothing wrong with a wager,' Pete said, turning towards the tele where two women, about five foot high and carved out of stone, were kicking each other in the legs.

'Please, do sit, Peter. These recliners are very comfortable.'

'I'm fine up here. You sure you don't have any whiskey?'

'I don't keep liquor in the parish house, no, but I can call for some if you like?'

'Why don't you keep liquor?'

'If I have a single drink I am compelled to have more.'

'That's the general idea, isn't it?'

'Sets off the phenomenon of craving.'

'No point having one or two.'

'How many have you had today?'

'Just the one, officer!' said Pete, raising his teacup and spilling the contents down his already stained T-shirt.

'Well, I'm sorry. Perhaps you should visit the Irish priest in Caringbah, Father O'Reilly, he's more red-faced than I. With me, it is UFC and tea. Ok?'

'Right.'

'Take it or leave it.'

'I'm not a big UFC guy, to be honest. It's all cheap shots.' Pete wondered if the cheap shot he took at the pub had killed the guy. Surely not? No, it was just a little tug forward, a mozzie bite. Brick Wall woulda sorted it all out.

'And rugby league, your game of choice, is this better?'

'I can't drink this. Please, Father, can you turn tea into whiskey?'

Father Pepple got out his phone and started shooting off a text, as Plum planted his arse on the arm of the parish recliner.

'Rugby league is the greatest game of all, it's tough, but it's also an art form.'

'Ok.'

'You think Tina Turner would sing a song about any old game?'

'Ok.'

'Rugby league gave me everything.'

'And did it take anything away?'

'Hey?'

'Did it take anything away?'

'Take what away?'

'Do you think the game affected your life, later on, after you stopped playing?'

'Look at those women, that one on the top is elbowing her temple – no art in that.'

'There is every art in UFC!' said Father Pepple, nearly climbing off his chair.

'Nah.'

'Boxing, muay Thai, kick-boxing, Brazilian jujitsu, grappling, judo, wrestling, karate, luta livre, taekwondo, capoeira, sambo, kung fu, what else?'

'Capoeira. That's not a martial art. That's just dancing in fisherman's pants.'

Pepple's laugh was big from the belly and its sincerity was disarming, making Pete not only laugh himself but find himself now at home sliding down into the opposite recliner.

'Well, that was, yes, very funny, Peter. Oh, it's good to be laughing.'

'You said you fight. Fought? Father.'

'Yes, I did, I did fight.'

'In Africa?'

'All over the world.'

'No?'

'When you are an addict, you are always at war, wherever you are.'

'Right, oh. No. I meant *fighting* fighting.'

'So did I, Peter. So did I.'

The doorbell rang, and then the young boxer Pete met at Brick's gym, Kutiote, came inside with a calico Rebel Sports bag. He was the fourth wise man who had brought something useful: a bottle of Jim Beam for the restless soul.

'Speaking of the war inside, Peter, the church has answered your call.'

'Saint Jim!' Peter filled his cup with brown spirits.

'Goodnight!' said Kutiote and disappeared into the hall again, nodding and smiling at the Lord, at the priest, at The Plum.

'Have I met him, Father?'

'Yes, and your son has met him too. Gavin?'

Peter so wished his son was home. Wished he could sit down with him on the couch with beach towels over their laps and eat burgers, drink diet cokes and watch NRL 360. Then take him out onto the deck and read him the letter he'd written. The one Sylvia had helped him with. The one that had all the info in it, about how much he loved him, how proud of him he'd always been, and how sorry he was for abandoning him. He knew what it was like, because that's what his dad did, and never for a second did he think he'd do the same …

'This man, this man right here, the Russian man, Kabib, did you see him, he was the one who beat up Conor McGregor and then leapt into the crowd to take down Notorious's jujitsu coach – you see this, Peter?'

'No.'

'Utter chaos, and very stupid, especially when he had won so spectacular.'

'Yeah, man, Connor's good, no?'

'Connor is good standing up but not so good on the ground.'

'We can all relate to that!'

The next few hours drifted by with relative ease, the violence on screen allowing the men to indulge in significant silences, and as Plum worked his way through the bourbon, Father Pepple sipped on a refilled Mount Franklin beside him, happy to join the conversation when Plum set one up but equally as happy to watch the card roll on through without interaction, and this was what warmed Plum to the holy man: the way he had embraced the drunk's sudden arrival, not once asking Pete why he had turned up to the parish gates plastered, but instead seeming to be grateful for the company.

'Here is my man, Israel,' Father Pepple said as his favourite cage fighter stepped into the ring. 'You know he trains out of New Zealand?'

'Is that right?'

'Yes, mixed martial arts, his story is very uplifting.'

'So many good things happen in New Zealand.'

'I must go, I would like to see the Fox Glaciers —'

'Write us a poem! Go!' screamed Plum at the fighters, spilling some bourbon on himself.

Father Pepple stood, went to the kitchenette and then calmly came back with a roll of paper towel.

'Ah, right, good stuff. Mop up the self.'

Plum dabbed at his shirt, wondering if the priest would be alarmed if he just took that bottle of Jim Beam down single-handedly tonight.

'Do you think you are one of us, Peter?'

'I'm all good,' said Pete, watching as Israel swept his opponent's leg. 'Fucking spider!'

'No, I mean with alcohol. Like how I do. Do you think you do too?'

'Couple of my mates, I'd say yes they are.'

'And what would they say about you?'

'Take off your scarf and beret, you poof.'

'Have you ever thought about going to a meeting?'

'An AA meeting?'

'Yes, I could take you.'

Pete refilled his teacup then cradled the bottle into his moist chest like it was a small shitzu. 'I can stop at any time. I just like it.'

'That's what Michael Jordan said about gambling.'

'Huh?'

'I just like it.'

'Maybe he just did like it. MJ Air Jordanio.'

'Do you think it has an effect on your life? Negative and/or positive?'

'Both my exes,' said Pete, slurring now, 'they'd say a not good one.'

'And what do you say to them?'

'I say, you are my exes.'

'And what would you say to them about your drinking, if you could say anything you like? If they were seated here before you?'

'I slept with my ex-wife recently. While I was still with my current ex.'

'Oh.'

'What's my penance? Three Hail Marys and an Our Father, Father?'

'What about your father? Did he drink?'

'My father was a terrible drinker, he could only have two, you see, and the mood would turn, he'd be another man, after two, gone, and you would not think this would happen because he was so tall and so strong ... he was a happy, funny man.'

'Funny?'

'Yeah! He'd always be making stories up. Do you remember *Monkey Magic*?'

'No.'

'Didn't make it to Algeria?'

'Nigeria.'

'Well, that's a shame. Well, my dad, Albert, every Friday night after dinner he used to get up and, you know, half-cut he'd do a show for us.'

'What kind of show?'

'It was called "Albert the Expert" show. We'd say a topic, like a country or something, and then Dad'd pretend he was the expert on it.'

'Do you remember an example of "Albert Expert Show"?'

'Yeah like, when my sister said, "Dad, you're an automobile guy."' Pete started chuckling. This was his favourite memory of his dad's performances, or was it just the only one he could remember properly? 'Dad said to my sister, real serious like straight outta *Monkey Magic* was how he'd said it: "Man under car with tool in hand not necessarily mechanic."' Pete laughed even harder.

The priest remained unmoved. 'You love your dad?'

Pete's eyes and chest boiled with wetness and yearning. 'He was my dad. But he wasn't good. He was more bad than good.'

'But when he was good?'

'Fuck!' Pete said and looked at the TV just as Israel annihilated the white wrestler with a reverse elbow to the head, the place where his brain lived, where he learnt to read and write and fly a kite and count to one-two-three-you-are-out ...

'Are you still angry at your father, Peter?'

Pete switched his gaze to the priest and the more he stared, the more Pepple started looking like a full black God, sent down to fix the earthlings, one by one, beginning with the broken-est of them all: Peter 'The Bruised Plum' Lum. 'I need a piss,' he said, but he really didn't, he just needed the outdoors.

Out on the front porch, the moon was good. Trees still. Sky dark purple.

He lit a cigarette and smoked it, trying to blow smoke up and away, thinking that young fighter must be sleeping in the room just to the left of his left elbow and maybe his whole family was in there ... but for how long ... who knew? Australia liked to pretend it loved everyone, but it was never permanent, it was conditional on winning.

Looking up at the sky, blinking away the electric white dots, he couldn't help thinking about his dad. And that last time he had seen him. How he had invited him to the Kangaroos brunch where he would be getting his jersey for the first time – issued to him by the one and only Jack Gibson. And just how excited he was that his dad said he *wouldn't miss it* and that he had his train booked and all. And Albert had turned up early, too, in a woollen suit and tie, but he was shitfaced again, unable to hold himself up.

'Dad,' Pete snarled at the moon.

Pete got his dick out and pissed in the garden, tears in his eyes. He looked to the star at the base of the frypan and muttered, 'You're a cunt, Dad,' thinking surely one of them stars was him, was Albert Lum.

'Peter?' said the priest from the front door.

'Shit,' Peter said, and with his pride still swinging in the breeze, he turned too fast to hide it, not only spraying the deck but slipping on the wood and falling into the gardenias face first, strides now down by his knees.

If the priest had seen the face of God, he had now seen that of the Devil too – in the form of Peter Lum's pink moon competing with that of the one above.

'Father, you've seen into my soul, now,' Peter said, his cock and balls dangling about in the night air as he rolled around and sat up.

The wooden blinds on the front room parted and Kutiote peeked out with eyes as wide as the moon that lit the scene. 'Holy Moley,' he said.

'Acceptance is the first step to renewal,' said Father Pepple, unfazed.

Peter stood, did up his pants and held out his arms in defeat. 'Father, I think I may have fucked up my life, and I am really scared.'

And then the priest took the poet in his arms and held him. 'I know,' said the priest. 'We are all scared men.'

'I'm so scared.'

Pepple held the man as he cried.

Kutiote took Plum back to Cronulla by motorbike, and with the wind whipping up off the beach, and the pace at which this kid liked to ride, Pete was well sober by the time he took his arms from around the young boxer's granite waist and handed back his helmet.

Inside his own house Pete took a left to Gavin's room, hoping that Sylvia might be there, vaping under the covers. But she wasn't. No sign, not even the whiff of her. Pete put his scarf and beret on the bedside table and got under the covers, and thought of his son and what he might be doing right now in Bali.

He looked up at the framed photo of him and Gavin heliskiing in Queenstown, and at the one of Gavin and Ainslee on paddleboards at Bundeena, then across to the photo Gavin loved so much: a young Renee, holding her newborn baby up in the ocean pool at Shelley.

Eventually, Pete fell asleep in his son's bed, where he slept, motionless in his jeans and socks, until the next morning.

Six

'Push up onto your feet not your knees,' said Pete, spinning the footy in his hands. 'You'll do your back getting up like that.'

It was wet out but Chloe had still materialised, and with her fitness improving since he'd bought her the protein shake set-up, Pete felt it was time to give her some old-school Glenn Lazarus drills. And so he'd made a box out of water bottles and jumpers and had her running all the three-metre lengths of it, hitting the ground and getting up at every corner.

'Hit the deck then snap up. There you are. Better, girl!'

As Chloe went about it, Plum looked to the box he had made, and thought about his brain. Over the last week he'd spoken to Liz on FaceTime every day and she had taught him heaps about what was going on: about the patterns inside the skull box, and how his ones were pulsing and the waves of degeneration were trying to take over. And even though he had never thought to look after the thing, now he had to see it 'like country', she'd explained; he had to water it and protect it and love it. Hearing this metaphor had initially made him feel sick because, looking back, all he could see was bushfires, with him as chief arsonist.

'Chloe, have a minute off, sip of water, then round five.'

'That's too hard.'

'You want to play front row for your state?'

'Yeah.' Chloe was blowing, bent in half. She reached for her water bottle in the soggy grass.

'Then sip of water and go again when I tell you, please.'

In between reading the stuff Liz had sent, he'd started writing down – under Liz's guidance, of course – all the collisions he could think of 'on country'. But he couldn't do it for too long because, running through them again, well, it made him feel nauseous a lot of the time – so much so he'd actually gagged over the writing pad.

Some of the clashes and smashes weren't even from footy. Some of them were from falling off the back of a moped when he was crazy pissed on tour; some of them were from fights in pub carparks over nonsense some idiot said; some of them were from his childhood when he got between Albert and his mum – fists and saucepans, garage door, kitchen floor – or that time his dad dropped him on his head when he was pissed at the Orange community fete.

Living with Sylvia, he'd also come to see that his brain was not all that bad. He could remember a lot of things when he concentrated, and he'd soaked up stories, myths and parables with fervour, remembering all them books his mum had read him when he was young. The big noise of footy had stopped all that reading, but before that he'd be across-ways in his mum's bed every night and they'd read a paragraph each – and it was all still in there, it just needed a bit of Windex and some love. It just needed an apology. As did his son. Gavin needed a big one and not a shit one, one from the heart.

'Ok, Chloe. Round five, go! Hit the deck and run!'

The leaner, meaner prop popped up and spun for another set. 'Ok, Mr Plum.'

And so, as he'd cleaned the joint from top to bottom in preparation for Gavin's imminent but not entirely certain arrival home, he'd spent the nights drinking water and crafting not a poem, nor a letter of apology, but an email to his son. And by the time he pressed the send button, this was how it read:

Peter_Lum_70@hotmail.com to gavwhatittakes@gmail.com
Subject: China Plate.
Son,
How is it going in Bali? We miss ya here! All good though.

Looking forward to having you back in the house. Have been bit worried about you so far away from me and Im sorry I missed the calls. No excuses!

Mate got lots to talk about. Not just footy offer from storms who have emailed and called me about management everything,. but more important stuff.

I hate thinking back over ribs night. And want you to know Im sorry for not telling you. I been stressed and scared basicly, and I didnt want to let on. This is crap stuff from dad. Your my best mate, and I know I hurt ya.

The place is looking good and the pool is good to go so cant wait to pick you up at the airport when you fly in. We all miss ya. So give us a text or an email back because not knowing your whereabouts is killing me. Ok mate? Tell me what's going on and Ill come get you wherever you are. Just get home.

And Go Sharks

Your china plate, dad

1 am. 2 am. 3 am. Pete lay awake, shuddering, his nerves on fire. He had not had this long off alcohol since the 90s, his body was making its protest. He could smell the drinks in the centre of his hands. He could smell the drinks in his sweat-drenched T-shirts when he woke up every morning. He could taste the beer in his insomniac tears. He dreamt of beer bottles chasing him. He couldn't watch Channel Nine for fear of a beer ad. He'd underestimated beer, and just how deep it goes, and how it runs you.

Christmas Eve he hadn't slept a wink. Just walked round the house, checking his email and phone, feeling like he had gone mad. The DTs had him by the nuts and the waves of illusion were rapid; all he could do was clean the house.

Renee had popped in with some ham and presents, plus some sleeping tablets she'd got from her husband; Peter was going crazy, he'd told her, and if he was going to roll out of this detox alive, he needed to rest.

'Do you think you're an alcoholic?' she'd asked him, pouring herself a wine.

'Nah, I can stop any time.'

'You just can't sleep when you do?'

'It's just my body is adapting. Have you got the fucken pills, Ren?'

'Ok, ok. Hold your horses. I thought maybe you'd wanted to see me, too?'

Pete gave her a letter (a five-page handwritten poem that he had written in a time of Sylvia and asked not to be read until she was alone and away from others) and a voucher for a clothes joint in Melbourne she and Ainslee clicked with. Renee gave him some budgie smugglers and liquorice and a card from her kids with a volcano on the front. And of course, the most precious stocking filler, a sweet tray of Christmas diazepam from Ollie.

'Have you heard from Gavin?'

'No,' she said.

'Is he coming back?'

'Yeah, a week ago he texted and said he was en route.'

'I've got nothing. I'm checking every ten minutes.'

'Well, if you weren't such a brute he'd be right there on the couch opening a present.'

'I know.'

'But you had to scare him.'

'I know, ok? I'm trying to not be as shit.'

'I know, Plum.'

'You know my brain is the size of a plum? And just as soft? A plum in a glass box?'

'I have to go,' she said, her voice cracking, 'or I'm going to start crying again.'

The diazepam had worked, and Pete had woken up on Christmas morning from an epic couch nap heaving in moisture, his Rip Curl T-shirt drenched and clinging to his chest like lager-lava. But he'd slept more than two hours at a time, and that was something.

When Pete walked into the kitchen to get a glass of water, he saw a note beneath a wine glass. The paper was from the Adelphi Hotel, and on it, in cursive writing: 'We will always have room 706, R.'

He wasn't pissed off at himself for what happened, nah – they were both adults, and she wasn't about to tell anyone. This was one secret she could keep. Because, let's face it, she didn't want to lose her mansion on Woolooware Road and all the shit that came with being married to well-to-do local GP Ollie. They had needs, whatever, how it went, and the old connection was right there, and they moved well. But he never wanted to do that again. He could see that real clear. He could see nearly everything clear now, with the booze and the fog that comes with it slowly exiting his internal structures, albeit with great reluctance.

Thanks to modern medicine, Plum started to sleep in four-hour bursts, even managing to make himself a sandwich, and go for a jog around the block in the afternoon. He thought of calling the police about Gavin, but Renee texted him to just chill out, that if he wasn't back for New Year's Eve, then they could panic.

On the seventh day of detox Plum called Father Pepple, who – aside from asking if Peter had watched any of the UFC YouTube links he had texted him – made some not-so-ridiculous suggestions. 'Clean up your side of the road,' said the priest.

'My house is spotless!'

'No, you fool. Your side of the street. Internal!'

'What do you mean?'

'Good health and a clean conscience.'

'Oh, I hear you.'

'Then leave the rest to God.'

'I told you, I don't believe in God.'

'You are a God, Peter. And we believe in you, man.'

'I'm confused.'

'Higher power, my friend. Now repeat after me —'

'I'm not sure I know what this higher p —'

'It could be music. It could be wind. It could be Phil Gould. Ask for Him and He will reveal Himself to you. Remember, it's just a force that loves you and wants to guide you to the Promised Land. God is Love, your higher power is waiting to show you this!'

Pete could not think of anything worse than having a God.

He could not think of anything worse than having a beer.

That was until Friday around 5 pm.

Always, 5 pm Friday.

And he had not thought to prepare himself for it.

Magic hour.

Beer hour.

Hell.

He'd just finished mowing the lawns in the sun – Gav's job.

He'd just finished edging the lawns – Gav's job.

He'd just finished raking up the leaves – Gav's job.

Thirsty work
Crack a cold one
A gap in space and time
Better fill it
Thirsty work
Being a bloke
Tip a beer in
Like filling silence with a joke

Plum could hear the sunshine screaming at him everywhere he went. The air was dry, the offshore breeze was delicate, as the week ached for a release valve. It was beer time. It was beer o'clock. There was nothing else to do in this sweltering heat but drink beer.

And a glass of water would do nothing.

Shove ten cucumbers down your throat they'd do nothing.

God had made 5 pm on a Friday evening in Australia for beer.

BEER O'CLOCK

Even though he had popped out the other side of a *Trainspotting*-level detox – albeit free of a baby's head spinning on the roof, but, like, not by a lot – beer o'clock had him so tight by the short and curlies he could barely breathe. With the need raging in all arteries and pathways, he'd thought about turning the phone off from old Liz Lombardo's constant caretaking and ducking down to Cronulla Street Cellars and nabbing a carton, lugging it back home and hurling some ice over it, giddy up.

He'd thought about it to the point of walking in a circle. He'd thought about it to the point of taking off his footy shorts, putting undies on, then putting his footy shorts back on again. He'd thought about it to the point of grabbing his wallet and keys.

But then, halfway down, spring in his step, he remembered what he had promised himself. What he had promised Renee, and indeed what he had promised their son, without Gavin even knowing about it. And these promises, the weight of them and the force of their inner compliance, finally, stopped him in his tracks.

He was forty-nine and, finally, he was making wholesale changes. Especially – God, he could barely consider it – if he was to be a dad again, to a woman who'd blocked him, with a son who already hated him, a son to a woman who said she still loved him, well, it all seemed so hard. Beer would definitely help take the pain of all this real-life shit away – but in the long term? In the long term, beer would just make him bloated, fattened by his own unsolved mysteries.

So instead of sinking two dozen throat-snappers he crossed the six lanes to the Elephant House, walked through the doors and, as Pepple had instructed him, took a pew, hit the knees and prayed to a higher power. He felt like a dickhead doing it, and he'd gone into the corner of the church to do so, ducking his head so the other three prayer-heads couldn't see who he was.

'Jesus fuck me,' he whispered to Sylvia Plath but she wasn't there. Instead there was just a crucifix, so he prayed to that, on his knees, palms together.

> *Dear God*
> *Or whatever higher power*
> *Thanks for everything you gave me*
> *Especially in my playing days*
> *Talent, and courage, and strength*
> *Thanks for my son, and for my wives, and friends*
> *Thanks for not killing me yet*
> *Please, I know you have a bit on, but please*
> *If you have a spare ten to fifteen*
> *Could you help me on my path*
> *To reclaiming my relationship with my son*
> *And Char, if possible?*
> *God? May I ask?*

'Cheers,' he said, in closing.

When he got to the park the next morning Chloe was already into her stretching. He teared up a bit at the sight of

238

her, so much skinnier and more muscular now – she resembled a proper athlete. Thank fuck it was raining a bit or his protégé might have seen the pride.

'Good girl,' he said. 'Warm up the body, then it's a thousand skips.'

'Thanks Mr Plum,' said Chloe, as they packed up the gear.

'Pleasure, Chloe. You're going good. Eat clean and I'll see you Thursday.'

'Ok Mr Plum.'

'Oh, has there been any word from your PE teacher on whether you can play or not?'

'He said if Dad can get the visa stuff through then it's possible for March.'

'And what did your dad say?'

'He's not living with us at the moment.'

'Why not?'

'Mum started hitting him again. He's staying at Trent's. When he's not at the Old Bike Shed.'

'Hustle and Muscle.'

'He loves it.'

'Well, Trent and Squeaky are good people.'

'He says all they do is talk about you. In the jacuzzi, every night. They sit with their arms around each other drinking beer and talking about their mate Plum.'

'I'm not sure I believe that.'

'Believe what?'

'What you just said.'

'Which bit, Mr Plum? Haven't you met a gay before?'

'Course, but ...'

Plum was lost for words and Chloe knew it, smiling up at her coach and enjoying the switch in power.

'Just don't believe they'd be talking about *me* is all. That's all that I can't believe.'

'My dad says that there are so many incredible stories about you from when you played. My dad says he can't even believe that no one has ever written a book about you.'

'Maybe you can write a book about me one day, Chloe?'

'Nah, I can't spell for shit. See you Thursday, Mr Plum.'

Three things crossed his mind as he walked home in the light rain.

1) If anyone ever messed with Chloe in life he'd kill em.

2) If Squeaky was with Trent now, would he stay in the Coxless Four? And ...

3) He needed to see that Dana Crighton and sort the book before Gavin got back.

It was three days till New Year's and Cronulla was already loading up. As soon as Peter turned onto the strip, it occurred to him that *now* was probably not the smartest time to meet a journo in a public café. You could hear the ten count already. Lines to the bottle-o were long and heaving; the young people already half naked, screaming down their phones at each other to not forget mixers and cigs. Time did not mean anything to these kids yet, Pete thought, passing the Payless with his head down. They could burn another year or three on Snapchat and cider – no one would say a thing and they wouldn't feel it slide past either! It wouldn't be till they were twenty-eight and no longer welcome at home that they'd realise that everything that happened from then on would be a result of effort, and that if they didn't get their act together soon they'd be working at the RTA and it would all 'totally suck', that was, unless a parent suddenly died and left them the house. Or they'd get the best idea ever for an app. If one of them things happened, it'd be easy always; if not, they'd get what was coming to them, the big drop.

There were only four or five tables in the tiny café, and luckily the one Dana had picked was up the back, but really it didn't matter. The clientele were too old to care about another footballer in hot water; their concerns were well purified into grandkids getting married, the new priest's robust sermons at Star of the Sea, and access to the latest hip joint relief.

'The one and only,' said Pete, taking a seat across from the journalist.

It had been a while since he'd spoken with Dana at the Tradies, and again he was surprised how happy he was to see her; he wanted to reach out and hold her hands, but he wouldn't, not now, that'd be weird, and, as he kept telling himself, she was *still* the enemy.

'Peter Lum,' she said, putting away her mini Kindle.

'Hot out there,' he said, using the paper napkin to wipe his raging forehead.

'Hotter than a snake's ass in a wagon ride,' said Dana, offering up her best Adrian Cronauer.

'What was that one?'

'*Good Morning Vietnam?*'

'Ah! Yeah.'

Dana changed topics with a furious head shake and a flutter of her left wrist. 'Thanks for coming. Do you want a tea? Guess it's pretty hot.'

'I can order something.'

'They do say hot tea cools you down.'

'I might get an apple juice.'

'Get an apple up ya,' she said, and Peter nodded.

The crass comment came more as a surprise to Dana than Peter. She had found the balance tricky throughout her career – how to be 'one of the boys' while at the same time holding her own as a woman in sports journalism – and was yet to iron out the inexorable duplicity. 'Have you been online and had a look yet?'

'No, and I don't want to know. I just want to talk a bit.'

'No, no. I don't blame ya. We can talk.'

'Yeah, been spending a bit of time on my Pat Malone. So –'

'That's the only time I spend.'

'Well, let's try a conversation then. Cool?'

'That is all I have ever wanted from you, Peter Lum.'

'Then play on.'

Pete ordered an iced coffee, Dana refilled her pot of peppermint tea and got herself a slice of lemon cake, which Pete took a corner of and was quietly blown away by because never in his life would he have thought to ask for that. Amid this indulgence of sorts they covered the obligatory topics of Sharks recruitment, the recent rule changes, the comings and goings at Nine and Fox Sports, the rise of the mobile forward and, lastly, the innate stupidity of certain players in the off-season.

'Seriously, rugby league players should be put in an enclosure, *Big Brother* style!'

'Oh, I feel for em. I mean, after playing *that* game, what do we expect them to do?'

Dana was in a type of heaven, sitting here with one of the greats and going at it. They'd always got on well when they'd crossed paths over the years, and they were getting on well now too. He'd only folded his arms once, and that was when she'd mentioned the talk about his son and how the Storm were still waiting to hear back on their 1.6 million dollar offer over four seasons. But other than that his body language was looking more and more at ease, and she felt she had licence to dig a little further so she got to the meat and potatoes of their meet-up.

'So the book.'

'So, ok, yeah, Dana, rightio, ok, well, let's see, I have a question, right, then, so ok here goes. Say if – *if* – you did this book, what'd be the go with it?'

'What do you mean?'

'What would it be for?'

'If we announce it ASAP, which I suggest we do, then we can probably stop the other stuff, which is already out there, really. One of your friends, or someone claiming to be a "close friend", is telling all. So the book announcement would quash some of that and, well …'

Plum wondered which 'close friend' would say anything about him. Surely it was some fifth-tier wanker looking for a pay day. 'What would you write in it?'

'Well, that would be up to us. We can do a standard Cameron Smith "I'm so misunderstood" type book, or a Tiger Woods "I'm so sorry to everyone", or take a Ray Warren "I'm just a kid with a dream" angle …'

'Or?'

'Or we could write about Plum …'

'Me.'

'You.'

'What about me?'

'About your life. About your sport. About your country. And about an issue, the issue of concussion, and that now you know what the dangers are, would you do it again and with such abandon, and what do you say to your son who is clearly going to follow in your footsteps? What's your opinion now of him playing league? How does it affect you, as a parent and a player? Would Gavin talk to me about it, do you think? And about CTE –'

'CTE. Hey? Who said that I have –'

'How much does Gavin know? And Renee, and Charmayne? How much are they aware of?'

Peter could smell the sea from inside the café. It was calling him, and he wasn't listening to Dana anymore. Now that the detox was smoothing itself out, he longed to be in the ocean. His body, which had not stopped going at it since he'd learnt to pull himself over the side of the cot, had been lazy of late and he could feel the overflow on his waist and hips. He wasn't quite a 'ham sack', as Charmayne had coined it, but since his world went askew he'd turned away from the onslaught of fitness and, for the first time ever, he realised he didn't feel confident in his skin. His house was fucking spotless – even the windows – but he was a mess.

'I reckon that'll do me, Dana?' Plum said, swirling the ice around with the remainder of the cold coffee, then pouring its sweet and grey medley down his throat.

'But we were just getting into it.'

Pete stood up to pay. 'Have a good one.'

'Can we speak again?'

Pete left a twenty underneath his spoon. 'Happy New Year.'

The cold water flicked at his nuts. He took a breath and launched in like a human spear. Perhaps if he'd tried less over the years, he wondered, he wouldn't have had a brain fail. If he had only phoned it in a bit more he might have lived to have a straighter nose, a sharper cranium life. God! As he swam out the back, the conversation with Dana still ticking over in his head, he pondered what would have happened if he'd gone easier in play and in pub. Maybe, just maybe, he would have even crept up to the commentary box; maybe, just maybe, it would even be 'Thursday Nights with Peter Lum' – 'The Peter Lum Podcast' – 'In the Scrum with Peter Lum'. But it wasn't him, that stuff.

He duck-dived into the bowels of a two-footer left-hander, the kind of wave Gavin would crush with that goofy stance of his. The thing was, Pete just did not think like them other blokes. And he did not *want* to think like them blokes. Or sound like em: *Hahaha, stats and gossip. No, you are, oh that's a stitch up, gee up, we touched on it earlier, hahahaha falcon, what's with your haircut mate, ah come on legend, fair go, that was a massive night.*

Thinking about footy these days made him jumpy and anxious to the point of wanting to be sick, and he wondered if that was because he couldn't get out there and fix what was going on. He couldn't bolster the defensive line or get some go-forward in place when it was needed, couldn't dominate the defender and then spin for an offload. Watching league – well, it was like one of them nightmares where you find yourself in a fight in a carpark but you don't have arms to swing with. He loved seeing them Fijian wingers dive into diagonal air and place the ball down in the corner, but anything that involved a forward pack was like watching someone root your ex-missus, and you couldn't get in to stop it – and if you did, you had no old fella anyway so what was the point.

On his back now on the surface of ocean, splayed out like Jesus of the Horizontal, the sun belting into his face, he wondered what to think. He could see his thoughts, like products ready to be lifted from the shelf at the supermarket. What was it men were meant to think? When they were alone, in between doing the things that men do? Or even when they were doing them? What did other men consider, and not just on the last day of the year? Did they look back? Did they plan? Did they fantasise about some chick? Did they think of fucking, or slow-cooking lamb over sixteen hours, or beer from Uruguay, or that multi you simply cannot back out of? As the waves got pregnant around him, Pete thought about thought, thinking his own headliners were Char and Gavin and Renee, then there was money and fitness, then his mates, then pub, which was his mates, so that was done with pub. He didn't ever worry about food – Char did all that, and Renee before her – and Brick did his fitness and/or Gavin. Oh Gavin, that sweeter than sweet boy. That weirdness at the Melbourne Storm was the only time he'd ever caused a ruckus – before that nothing, nothing until then. Did Gav think he was an idiot? Was he an idiot? Was he an embarrassment? Was he a lost cause? Was he going to die soon? He lay on the ocean's super-foam mattress, letting the sun charge him like a chubby smartphone, and the thoughts started tripping like lines from a poem. *When I die will people cry?* He thought about his funeral, and whether people would turn up. Whether his life was important. And he thought again about his dad, thinkin that pisshead must be in the ground by now. Thought about his mother and how when she was on her death bed, she kept asking for Albert. Fucken that was it, that was what hurt the most! She'd asked for her cunt of a husband and not her son. 'Albert? Albert is that you? Albert my love.' Can you fucken believe it? Not a single Plum in there. Fucken moved on from this earth to the next one yearning for a prick who never came through.

Pete flipped his rig upright, swam a bit and then finding the sand below with his tippy-toes walked himself to shore, thinking: *I want to die not feeling how I used to. I want to die having done something with my mind too.*

He knew his mind worked and that it had always worked. He just hadn't opened the channels. He'd been too busy smashing into walls and lifting blokes up and then driving them down again into the earth. He didn't want to die of liver cancer, or schooners and ciggies and fear. He didn't want to pour the devil's elixir on everything that was good about him, everything God issued his rig at the registration desk.

> *I want to die a good dad.*
> *On my own two feet having done a bit more.*
> *I want to die with my words, the words from myself.*
> *I want to die myself.*

Peter ran up the sand *Baywatch*-style, feeling lighter than when he was in that café an hour ago, hearing about his downfall in print. Plum turned to the ocean, shadow-boxing the air now, sparring with it, saying stuff like 'yeah' and 'uss-uss' and 'come on', and it was clear to him now that the blue thing laid out before him had always been his higher power, he just needed to make it official, just needed to surrender.

'Hey, you!' said a voice. 'Hey!'

Carrying his T-shirt, towel round his waist, Pete looked for the faceless voice, all of a sudden eager as to engage with his fans, his people, his community. 'Who calls me?' he said, hunting with his eyes.

'I'm over here – or shall I say, down here!'

It was her, it was Bridget, the pommy 'swap with me' girl from the poetry night, sitting facing the sea on a perfectly chosen angle, as if she was about to be painted or photographed.

'Oh, g'day Bridget!' he said, wildly happy to see her.

'That's me!' she said, coping with the large man's enthusiasm. 'I wasn't sure you'd remember me.'

'Yeah, course. I've thought about you even.'

'Wha?' she said, recoiling just a little.

'No, oh shit, I mean –'

'I'm flattered!'

'I just mean, that chat we had, after I saw your poem.'

'Sure.'

'I saw you there again, when I've been, but I've not said hello.'

'I called your name.'

'I didn't forget you, is what I'm sayin. How could I?'

'I guess you don't meet that many posh disabled girls in Cronulla who perform original poetry?'

'Oh, you're posh?' he joked, and to his unfathomable relief she bought it.

'Very good.'

'But no, it's true,' he said, 'you don't.'

'That's ok.'

'Is it?'

'Do you know anyone else confined to a chair?'

'No, but I have put a few blokes in a wheelchair,' he said with a laugh, and then immediately wished he could chop his own head off with a machete.

247

'Funny,' she said, and it became abundantly clear to Pete, that even after such acute consideration out to sea, he still did not know what to think, nor what to say once he had thought of a thought to think. He was a child, and he had so far to go. 'Did you actually?'

'What?'

'Put men in wheelchairs.'

'No, and I am so sorry for saying … that was awful.'

'It's ok.'

'It was a shit joke, I'm absolute brain –'

'Is that an Aussie phrase?'

'Yeah. Well, yeah, in footy.'

'Maybe there's a poem in it. Do you think? Aussie phrases of hilarious violence.'

'Could be.'

'Are there more?'

'Um …'

'Go on.' She took out her own little green book and a pen, and waited.

'Ok, um, bend em in half. Put em to sleep.'

'I see.'

'Put him in a wheelchair.'

'Got that one.'

'The rest are not metaphors. Just like "smash the cunt". You know?'

She sat up in her chair, beat her chest. 'Going to put that cunt in a wheelchair.'

He was taken aback, shaking his head and stifling a laugh.

'Going to paralyse the arsehole.'

'Ok.' It was too much now, and it was he who had made it so.

'Sorry, it's just funny to me.'

'It's not, it's shit. I'm fucked. Sorry.'

'It's hot today, how was the water?'

'Beautiful, yeah. Felt good on the skin.'

'I can see, and I must say, as a poet, don't think for a second I don't appreciate what great form you present on the esplanade at this point ...'

'Come on,' he said, blushing into his own hair. She reminded him of Sarah, and how she would rib him as a kid till he spun on his own two feet like a ballerina. He put his T-shirt back on, suddenly self-conscious of his 49-year-old body.

'I do applaud you; you're ripped.'

'Nah, I've stacked it on a bit –'

'The body wants to die once it is fifty, and you are surely fifty –'

'I am forty-nine, so, yeah, soon enough ...'

'See? And look at you, defying nature before us.'

'Well, my eating has gone off the rails ever since –'

'Since?'

In the silence the seagulls made themselves known.

'I had an accident at the airport,' he said.

Bridget's left palm shielded her eyes from the burning sun as she smiled up at him. She was dressed in denim shorts and a black singlet, her hair tucked up under a straw Bunnings hat, and if you hadn't heard her clipped speaking voice, you'd think she was a true-blue Aussie.

'What happened?'

'My brain failed. I had a fit and, um, I nearly killed all these passengers.'

'Fuck. You're a pilot too?'

'No,' he laughed. 'I work in baggage.'

'Don't we all.'

The clouds blocked the sun. The wind arrived. He felt the chill of truth. 'What brings you down here, Bridget?'

'I come here when I'm not working,' she said, giving him her own truth. 'Look at the waves. Imagine surfing or swimming out there.'

'You don't swim?'

'No, I don't.'

'Never?'

'No. Doesn't that just blow your mind, that I'm not out there carving up a tube.'

'Ha, well, kind of.'

'I am not a swimmer. Though in England as kids, my mother would takes us wild swimming. Which is basically just swimming in lakes and ponds that you discover on foot. And it's wild because it's fucking freezing and you launch in naked.'

'Ok, wow.'

'But here in Australia. I just prefer to watch the water. That's enough for me now.'

'Well, we're about to change that.'

'Change what?'

'You'll see.'

'Huh?'

'Let's roll,' he said and started walking, beckoning her to follow.

'Where are you taking me, bully?' she asked, popping up and twisting the wheels to follow.

When they got to the hill outside Northies he thought, *Fuck it,* and grabbed the handles of her chair and started running. Up the hill, past Red Rooster, Cronulla Seafoods, the cop shop, 7-Eleven, out of the general Nulla area, through the BP and fast by the old Elephant House that sorted out your higher power stuff if you were that way inclined; they could make out the soccer park, where he and Chloe had made an impact over time, turning right onto Kurnell Road, where he lived on his own these days, where it was just him, the new deck, and the out-of-ground Blue Haven pool, waiting, crystal clear, for her.

She had resisted at first, claiming it annoyed her, the

pushing, but once he had his pace up she chuckled, and then rested into the neck brace, even closing her eyes once or twice to feel the wind hitting her face at speed, imagining being a kid in a stroller again, and not having legs that didn't feel anything, and her life open wide.

When they got to his front lawn and he snapped open the side gate, she followed him down the driveway to the backyard and things became more urgent.

'How's these?' he said, chucking her a leopard-patterned one piece. 'They're my ex-girlfriend's.'

'I'm not swimming,' she said, without even the slightest gap of *maybe* in her voice. There would be no humiliation, *not today, not again*, please and thank you.

'Well, you will be or you'll fucken drown.'

'You don't get to tell me what to do.'

'I'm going to put you in the drink, so it's your call if you sink or swim.'

'Peter.'

'Whack these on.' He hurled the togs at her, and they landed on her throat. 'Come on. *Adversity brings adventure. Lean towards the uncomfortable.* All that shit.'

'What self-help books have you been reading?'

'None, just phone calls with a dodgy priest from Malawi.'

'What else does he say?'

'Give In to Win.'

Bridget held up the one piece – the size and shape seemed accurate. 'She won't mind?'

'She won't know.'

'Ok.'

'Should I ...'

'No, I can put them on, thank you very much. Is that an outdoor loo?'

'Yes.'

'Before I change, forever, Peter, I think we need to make an agreement.'

'I won't drown you.'

'That's not it.'

'Ok, but get on with it, the pool's waiting.'

'If I get in your pool –'

'*When* …'

'Then you will read a poem out at Lost for Words.'

His confidence and swagger left the yard in swift succession. 'Fuck off.'

'Fine, I'm going.'

'No, wait …'

'I'll put this disgusting leopard-print one piece on, if you read out one of your works.'

'How do you know I even have works?'

She pulled the little green book out from under her left thigh and held it up.

'Because I read a few while you were in there rummaging through your ex-wife's clothing and crying or wanking or whatever brutes do!'

'Ah, man.' He went to lean in and swipe it but she put it in her lap between her legs.

He stood there, nodding in his Sharks shorts, thinking, *This is what you get when you bring fruit loops into your life.*

'So we have a deal? One swim, one poem?'

'I'm not really going to bars. I'm not really drinking anymore.'

'Man up, cunt, or I'll put you in a wheelchair.'

'Ta da,' she said, pushing out onto the deck.

Pete was down by the pool plucking leaves out of the scoop, and when he turned to see her he nearly didn't recognise her. 'Does it fit?'

'It's on me. Or I'm in it.'

'Play on then.'

He lifted her down the steps and hauled her over the rocky terrain of the backyard, then pulled the chair to the pool edge and spun it round.

'This is just like the sea,' he felt like saying, but instead he just leant down and picked her up, claiming her weight in one fell swoop – one arm around her back, the other under her thighs, his forearm looping around like a safety brace. He felt her body falling limply into him. They ascended the six steps to the edge of the water as one.

'You right?'

'Yeah, just don't drop me or I'll die.'

'Ok.'

'Bridget Rose Boothby, twenty-nine, from Primrose Hill. Found dead in a rugby player's backyard. Reports claim the leopard-skin swimsuit may have not been her own.'

'It's a strong headline. And likely not the first time.'

'Huh?'

'A girl found dead in a footy player's –'

'In your backyard? I'm sure it's not.'

'Well.'

'If you kill me, I'll kill you. Ok?'

'At this time in my life I can just about run with that.'

He knelt into the water till he couldn't take it on his joints anymore, then, out of his depth, pushed into the pool, kicking for dear life until he found the bottom. The Blue Haven had a lump in its centre so kids could always find a safe spot if they needed it, and for the first time in his adult life he was fucking grateful for the design.

'Shit,' Bridget said.

'Cold?'

'No, it's nice.'

'Why'd you say shit then?'

'Just thought of a poem and I don't have my book with me.'

'Never stops with you, does it?'

'Well, you know, poetry is what happens when nothing else can.'

He held her body like she was a serving plate on his forearms. 'You right?'

'The water is nice,' she said, splashing with her left arm.

'You can probably stand up if I hold you.'

'I don't want to stand up please.'

'Why not?'

'This will do, ok?'

'Yeah, I was just saying. If there were other positions.'

She leant her head back, her hair meeting with the surface of the water and separating out, and Pete smiled to himself, stoked with how clean the pool was, and how good a day it had turned out to be already.

She flicked her head up to look at him. 'Don't you want to know?'

'What?'

'What happened to me?'

'What do you mean?'

'How I came to be in a chair.'

'Oh.'

'I can tell you.'

Their faces were close now. And her green eyes were like nothing he had ever seen before. So open and powerful and good. He wanted to look away but he feared if he did she would know that he was not as brave as her. And to look into her eyes, in this pool, on this day, he knew it was higher power stuff.

'I see you,' he said, 'and I carry you.'

'I met a boy when I was quite young. He was travelling through London. His name was Klauss and he was from Munich.'

'Oh yeah? Guten tag Klauss.'

'And when I met him he was staying with the family of a girl I was really good friends with, so I was over there a lot, at their place, because my place wasn't fun.'

'Yep.'

'And it was like, when I first saw him, I knew it was …'

'Love?' said Plum, the weight of the L resting heavy on his tongue.

'No, it was like – I knew he was my ticket out of where I was, and I so wanted out of my world. My brother was just this dick, a real bully to me my whole life, and my mother let him do it because she didn't know how to stand up to men. She never stood up to my dad.'

'Ok.'

'And also I was abused when I was fourteen. By a friend's dad. He put a pill in three girls' drinks.'

'Fuck off. At your house?'

'No, at a sleepover. I didn't have the worst night of us three, but it was still bad.'

'Oh my God, Bridget. Is he still alive? I'll fucken kill him.'

Bridget shook this off, the line of a poem coming in to her mind unbidden: *Why do men always have to think you're asking them to save the day?*

'At sixteen I had to face him in court. Which I did. But my mum said it was too stressful for her so she didn't come. My dad said it was too complicated for him so he didn't come. And my brother just laughed and said us girls were all sluts anyway.'

'Healthy.'

'So after the trial was done, and I was eighteen, I tracked down Klauss. He was working at an Angus Steak restaurant in Leicester Square, and basically I said, let's go. And we went. We drove across America in a white Chevy, and we went skiing in Colorado – and it was right when they had decriminalised marijuana so everyone was going downhill in bras and knickers or in tuxedos. It was so funny to be there. And then we worked in the ski shop for a bit saving money to fly to Indonesia and Fiji, which was maybe the greatest three months of my life, and where I completely fell in love with him. Which was also when we thought to take a year and drive around Australia in a combie.'

'Ha!'

'What?'

'No, I just like the way you said combie,' said Pete, 'it was cute. Cool. *Combie.*' He put some water in one of his hands and let it fall down her forehead, and she did not flinch; she let him bless her with dripping chlorine.

'But Klauss got cold feet about Australia, and I think his football team got into the European Cup Final or something, and he went back to Germany.'

'Fucken Klauss.'

'But I kept going, because that is all I know,' she said.

'That's it, you gotta keep going – and was that to Australia?' he asked.

She splashed both hands into the water and then clapped. It made quite a sound, and the sound rang out into the suburbs, where dogs needed more than just a walk a day, and kids played Halo 6 on their Nintendo despite the crashing waves. 'I went everywhere. In a combie. On my own.'

'Wow.'

'Coast to coast. Uluru, Kangaroo Island, Darwin, Great Barrier Reef – you name it, I drove it.'

'I always wanted to do that.'

'Then of course I met a guy riding camels at sunrise on the beach in Broome. He was from South Australia and within three months we were married, Ben and I, half for love and half to keep me here. We moved to Sydney and he got work as a chef in the Rocks and I did a writing course at night and worked in the day at a call centre selling education courses.'

'Nice.'

'Then this one night we went out, in Kings Cross, and we had a fight, and he said some things, and I knew he was lying because I'd seen him with this girl, and there were other ones. So I threw my drink at him and called him things in front of everyone and went storming out onto the road and down onto William Street. Crying, drunk, in heels, trying to cross all those lanes into Darlinghurst and I was hit. By a car. Going into the tunnel.'

Peter needed to move his arms, needed some blood flow, but couldn't, not right now.

'I broke my neck and collarbone right away. And my shoulder here still needs constant acupuncture, but it came back. Just my legs never did, never will.'

'I'm sorry.'

'Yeah,' she said, arching her back so first her forehead then her eyes went under the water, with just her nose and lips above the surface, and her breasts, which he was using all his inner strength not to take a peek at, heaving and breathing beneath him. 'What we cannot have in life is what makes us who we are.'

'You think?'

She propped back up. Her face close to his again. Wet, red and open. Her face was round and it was beautiful, and she had never been so beautiful as right now, and she knew it, God knew it, and Peter knew it, her gorgeous cheeks. 'Yeah, everyone has something they can't have.'

'True.'

'I am glad it happened. I am glad this is me today. I am glad, I am grateful, to be in this pool right now, legless and limp with you.'

She was more brave than any player he had run at or tried to put in a wheelchair. This broad had gone above and beyond, with no power where it should be, and she had lifted him out of his chair more than she would ever know.

257

'And Ben?' he asked, wishing he could kiss her, but not like sexual.

'He was sweet. He stuck around for six months. I said to him that it was ok if he wanted to go, and, yeah, just like that – well, three days after that – he moved to Eden Valley and started working at his dad's winery.'

'Fuck. That's pretty ... Was that ok with you?'

'We email sometimes. He has a wife and a kid now. Like I said, I am glad I met him, he got me my Australian visa – and Australia is my emotional home. I love Australia so much.'

'You're amazing to think like that.'

'What do *you* think about? When you think about what you could change? What is the sad part of your heart that I can see in your blue eyes right now?'

Peter inhaled water and sun at once, thinking back over the 70s, 80s, 90s, 2000s and now – it was a blurry slideshow of too much but not enough. 'Probably my comeback. Mostly.'

'What does that mean?'

'Well, when I was thirty, I went to England to play, and then I retired from the game at thirty-two. But then I came back. I made a comeback at thirty-four.'

'And you regret that?'

'Yeah, well, I was voted the game's most over-rated player in *Rugby League Week* and in the *Daily Tele* two years running. I was no longer a starting player but an "Impact Player", coming off the bench to spark something. I only went out in the thirty-third minute, socks up, needled up and the salts, and I just wasn't being cheered the way I was used to, and it was just so much harder to get up for games, for training, and –'

'So why did you make a comeback? If you didn't feel as strong?'

'I dunno. That's the thing. To this day I don't know why I did it.'

'If you *had* to say –'

'My boy was still young, and Renee was all over that. I didn't need to be involved – or at least I didn't know how to be that involved. So I just felt like, after footy, I didn't have a purpose, and that was starting to make me feel sad and, like, numb or whatever, like I wasn't a man anymore, and I was getting in fights because, you know, you spend your whole life not taking a backwards step – *Don't take a backwards step, Plum. Don't let the other guy get on top of you. Smash him, go.* I spent my whole life in that mindset, but that doesn't work in normal society, people don't accept it, and the police intervene, and drinking comes in, and the drugs. So I signed back up, thinking if I don't play, I'm probably going to go downhill, my body and then my mind, you know what I mean? And that could be dark for everyone. So I went back and played again, even though I knew, physically and mentally – and concussion-wise – yeah, I knew that I was cooked. But I kept going because I think I was too scared to stop, you know?'

'I would like to stand now please,' she said, coyly looking up at him from within his impermeable grasp.

'Yeah?'

'I mean, not on my own two feet. You will have to hold me up.'

'That's cool.'

'I will be an impact player only, in this.'

'And that is more than enough.'

'It is enough, I do agree, to make an impact.'

Peter took his left arm out from under her pale thighs and let her legs flop into the water world to do their best on their own. They flopped and then shook and then found their way to the pool floor. He spun her around to face him, half releasing her as if she was a toddler learning to swim, playfully pretending he would not be back to catch her, and when she placed her hands on his shoulders, he took her by the hips and together they were dancing, face to face, in the backyard pool, beneath the blaring midday sun of another year now done.

'That was seamless.'

'Torvill and Dean.'

She smiled a smile she had not smiled in years, tears and chlorine blending in her eyes, making one stinging liquid of yesterday, today and tomorrow, and the pair remained like that for minutes, staring into each other's eyes as they shifted round and round the pool in a slow circle, like some kind of plastic toy, that would never run out of batteries. As the clouds shifted over, Bridget's face grew closer, and Pete felt for a second that he could, and should, just kiss this girl right there and then, and she was not far from the notion either, their lips centimetres apart now, her breath in his mouth, her pain in his pain; their struggle and their swapping now swirling into one whirlpool of want.

'Peter' said a voice from beyond. 'Pete.'

His eyes half-closed, Pete turned towards the house, where he could almost see a woman, he thought, yes, a woman, a tall woman with curling blonde hair? No, but who was she, calling his name, and how did she get out the back?

'It's me,' the woman said.

'Who is it?'

'It's me, it's Charmayne.'

'Oh! Char?' he said, blinking madly and half letting go of the girl to go see about a girl, then realising the possible results of such a negligence.

'No!' said Bridget, feeling helpless again, longing for her chair, longing to be back in her flat, propped up with a Yorkshire tea watching *BoJack Horseman*.

'I'll come back,' said Charmayne, keys flicking round the back of her hand.

Before he realised how it must have looked she was gone, into the yellow archway of sunlight that scorched the corrugated-iron fence and bounced off the cement driveway with a vengeance.

'I better get us out of here,' he said to Bridget, looking for an easy way out, his cock hard and yet his brain softer than the clouds.

'Yeah, it's getting cold.'

A person who, historically, always had a plan in place beyond the plan at hand, Charmayne didn't know what to do or where to go. The image of her man in their pool up against a girl, a wheelchair by the steps, was all too much. The humiliation reminded her of the Cape Town school yard, and with that and the heat and the hormones she found herself vomiting in the fern prongs beside the letterbox out front. With a throat full of hot acidic sick, she turned left off Kurnell Road then power-walked, Kerry Saxby style, past the series of identical dark-brown brick houses with neglected speed boats towards Shark Park because that's what felt familiar, because that was a place she knew and because, well, they had good toilets there.

'Char!'

But she didn't quite get to the members lounge because the lock forward, who was known for chasing down a speedster in his time, had done it again – elbows up, bolting in bare feet – he appeared out of nowhere just as she got to the golf course.

'Nope,' she said at the sight of him, and pushed herself through a gap in the fence.

'Ay!' he yelled, nearing the corner. 'Where you goin?'

Char didn't run. She couldn't really. A spin class was about all the cardio she could manage, feet on the pedals, low centre of gravity. So instead she just hurried across the seventeenth green and slid down into a steep, shielding bunker, hoping Plum hadn't seen her.

'Charmayne?' said Plum, looking down at her from above.

'Oh, it's you?' she said.

Plum was puffing hard. He too had been off the cardio and it was showing, air seemingly not on offer to his chest. 'What're you doing in the bunker?'

'Just ... felt like a nice place to stop. For a bit. Why not, Plum?'

Plum walked round the sizeable green into the trap and, by habit, flopped down beside her in his wet boardies and T-shirt, back up against the wall of raked sand. 'Hey.'

'Hey,' she said, wishing she had never visited him today. Her mother, her therapist and her beautician had all said it was the right thing to do.

'How's work been?'

She looked to him, then away, baffled by the normalcy with which he was approaching this. 'Good. Have you spoken to Brick?'

'No.'

'Well, I'm probably not meant to say, but his heart reading, it's gone through the roof.'

'True?'

'No longer the high end of normal but the high end of high.'

'I better call him.'

'He is your best friend.'

'I know, I've just ...'

'Just what?'

'Well, I've been doing stuff.'

'What kind of stuff?'

'It's hard for me to say.'

'Just say it?'

'Maybe you won't like what it is, though, Charmayne.'

'What? Sleeping with an invalid?' she said, and the world stopped. The grass on the playing field stopped growing. Sports all over the world ceased to exist. Charmayne's golden hair stopped growing too, for there would be no future now.

'Fuck, Char.'

'I'm sorry,' she said, shaking her head, and reaching into her bag for a tissue, but she couldn't quite free the thing from its tiny plastic bag, so she tore it and then shoved it into the corner of her eye where the tears were boiling up the blue shadow. 'It's so hot today, and this time of year, it always makes me feel –'

'Feel what?'

She stood up and dusted off the sand. Sitting next to him, her fortress walls had gone down, but, standing above him, she felt she had a better chance at keeping them in place. 'The night you came home from Parramatta.'

'I'm so sorry, Char,' he said, standing up himself, so they faced each other in the middle of a golf bunker across from Shark Park.

'Why? You don't remember what happened. You were shitfaced.'

'I've tried to call.'

'Have you? I didn't notice that.'

'You blocked my number!'

'Well, try harder!' she said, screaming at him. 'Try fucking harder! Just for fucking once! Fucking Australian men! Can you not make an excuse and just try fucking harder!' Char reclaimed her breath, rested her hand on her stomach, then pulled it away.

'Why'd you come to the house today?' Pete asked, reeling from the onslaught. 'Why'd you just turn up out of the blue?'

'Why, was that an inconvenient time?'

Pete laughed a harsh cough, and so Char took a water bottle out of her bag and handed it to him. He took a mouthful, then handed it back, like a thousand times before.

'I'm going to have a baby, Plum,' she said. 'And I don't know if it's yours or Brick's because the night you came home from Parra, I went to Brick's. It's not something I am proud of but that's what I did. And it wasn't that long after you forgot the Redfern rule, so it's anyone's guess whose kid it is. But what I know for sure is that it's mine and I'm keeping it, and both of you can just deal with that because I'm sick of you both, and how you never do anything other than just suit yourselves. So I've built a fortress round my baby, and at the doors of this fortress will be some security guards, and those guards will decide who gets in to said fortress. Ok?'

'Are you and Brick together, Charmayne?' said Plum, blinking in the blur.

'Why don't you tell me your news, Peter?'

'Who else knows about the baby? Have you told Renee? Does Gavin know?'

'Gavin knows. Not Renee.'

'How does Gavin know?'

'Because I told him.'

'When?'

'When he got back.'

Plum's throat went cement. 'Huh?'

'Yep. He's been living at Brick's gym in the massage room for a week. He's going to be the godfather.'

'Fore!' called a voice from around the bend just as a golf ball landed right at Charmayne's feet, digging into the sand and dying with a thud.

'Who fucking hit that?!' screamed Plum, scrambling to the top of the bunker, ready for a fight, ready to protect the fortress too.

But Charmayne didn't need that from him anymore, so she left the bunker the way she'd entered it, taking her own deep footprints out of the trap and onto the green fairway of freedom.

'Char, where you going?'

'Don't follow me!' she yelled, crying now, yet with joy.

'But ...'

'Fortress!'

Seven

Instead of taking on four elderly golfers, Pete left the course and crossed the highway to Shark Park. The gates were open on the club side so he snuck in by the turnstiles and walked towards the empty field. It was late afternoon so the boys must have just wrapped up their ball work. Pete hopped himself over the boundary fence and just like that he was back on ground and every blade of grass was happy to see him. He walked to the centre of the oval, where his team had kicked off a hundred times, and opened his arms out wide. Opened his eyeballs to the air. Opened his mind to the memories. But nothing of any clarity arrived. Just a blur of blue and black. A blur of elbows and filth. A blur underscored by the fresh panic Charmayne has just injected into the marrow of his bone structure. *Fucking Brick. Fucking kid. And fucking what about Gavin? He was back in town and hadn't told me?* This hurt more than any knee or shoulder injury incurred on this field. *This field.* This field still his playground, still the shape that loved him, still the holy land.

'Plums!'

Plum pretended he had been passed the ball and ran at the pretend defence line for a pretend hit up. When he got to the line he leant in for impact, for the collision, but no one was there. Plum fell, a pretend head-high, he ate dirt. Pete rolled onto his back, kicking out, then he got up, dirty and distraught and started swinging at pretend blokes. Uppercuts and lefts and headbutts. Pete fought a hundred ghosts in the middle of Shark Park till he could no longer breathe good. Till he'd pounded a hole in the ground with his right fist, screaming 'I'm comin, I'm comin.' Till his head was hung over and his chest heaving. Then he left the oval and walked home, past the infamous course, where the elderly golfers were just riding off in their buggy towards the eighteenth.

Back at the house Bridget had clearly gone, Char's swimsuit and a towel draped over the fence. The whole place felt off now. Then his phone rang.

'Where are you?' said Squeaky, with tinny music behind his voice.

'Hey?'

'Are you on your way?'

'Where?'

'Matt's out of surgery. We're all going to visit him. Remember, the group chat?'

'The group chat?'

'Yeah, the Coxless Four. We all agreed to meet there now?'

'Righto.' Plum hung up, showered, whacked on jeans and a polo, then booked a cab to Sutherland Hospital. And if the call was not a sign in itself that something was brewing, the cab driver Phat was originally from Thailand!

When he got to the ward, Pete did not switch up, for he was leading the charge on the life that lay ahead for all of them now. 'Cold beers and tuk-tuks, Matty! Fishing and freedom! Let's go, Thailand!'

Magic Matt was fresh from the knife, benched with Endone and barely intelligible, but if anything could startle him to attention it was talk of the Thailand escape. 'Young girls and golf!' he slurred, blinking at the roof.

'I'm tipping my super in – fuck it, I'll sell my Kangaroo jumpers.'

'Heeeyyeyy! You don't need much coin, mate, that's the … thingggg … wif da Toy lannnn … Ddd, isss …' Matt fizzled, drips and blood lines tangled around the beast like highways in LA.

'I'm yours, Magic. When can we leave? Let's go to Thailand!' said Peter, circling the hospital floor, manic with the need to just leave it all behind.

'Ko Samui!' Matt moaned through the muck, the opiate haze, the honey drop.

'I love you, buddy, big buddy. We're going to look after each other.'

Matt somehow sat up, headbutting a pink balloon. 'Magic Matt and the Plum, with a cocktail in one hand and some tail in the other,' he said. His hip still had a hole in it but it would heal faster now that a brother had seen the light, the light he had always known but couldn't get a follow on.

'Aussie Pub!' said Pete, nearly gone.

'Aussie Pub,' said Matt, yearning in sedation.

'What's that about Aussie Pub?' said Squeaky, from behind the curtain.

Matt fell back into the bed, which was only half as long as it needed to be to hold the former centre. 'Australia's greatest-ever jockey?'

''Tis he!' Squeaky materialised, wearing a sleeveless pink V-neck and white jeans. Beside Squeaky was a tall, slim woman in a short skirt and crop top. Pete nodded at the high tower, who smiled right back at him, and the familiarity of the smile pulled Pete out of his own sedation. Trent? *Trent!* Not only dressed in women's clothes but wearing a wig too, and holding himself in a new way. That tilting way that a woman does.

'Gimme a kiss, my friend,' said Trent, reaching for Plum.

Plum held his friend, who smelt of white musk and foundation. Here was Plum thinking *he* was the one who had changed when Trent had gone the full 180! 'Hi there,' he said, and he could have stayed in that hug all day. His mate holding him in the cold unfriendly light of Orthopaedics was exactly what he needed right now.

Squeaky handed some wine and chocolates to the wounded warrior. 'How was the bludgeoning, Matthew?'

'I can't feel a thing. But that's drugs, ay.'

'You got any left?'

Trent held Plum at arm's length. 'I've missed you.'

'Looks like you've had your hands full,' Pete said.

'Oh, Pete! Yes!' said Squeaky. 'We're hosting New Year's at the Old Bike Shed. Everyone is coming –'

Trent chimed in with the pitch. 'Yes, we're going to have all the nights smashed together into one event, including Lost for Words! So come early and stay late.'

'I think it's going to be massive if we can keep the cunts out.'

'Manu will do that, darling,' said Trent.

'Will you be there, Plum?' asked Squeaky.

Plum looked to Matt, who knew exactly where he would be: on a connecting flight to Ko Samui via Bangkok and Darwin. But Matt was too morphined-out to give the game away, and Plum was grateful for this – so he just nodded to Squeak and said, 'Of course.'

'I'm going to have to get my hip done eventually,' Squeaky said. 'I get these spasms in my bum. From wear and tear. They last about three or four days and I have to sit on an angle. I can't sit straight. My physio says it's just from bumping up and down a million times over twenty years. It's not the big falls, it's the little jolts. Anti-inflammatories barely do a thing these days, so I'm going to have to have the hip bone shaved off the bum bone.'

'Sounds like you're having your bum bone shaved down already,' said Matt, his eyes closed, seemingly out of it.

'Where's Brick?' Plum asked Squeaky, breaking the tension from Matt's off comment.

'I don't talk to him,' Trent said. 'The guy freaks me out. Energy-wise.'

'His heart's fucked,' said Squeak, with concern. 'It's not good, they said, heart-wise. Told him to stop gambling right away.'

'Gamble responsibly, ay Squeak?' said Matt, who took a sip of his water, farted and then passed out again.

'I don't gamble anymore actually, guys.'

'No, how is that possible?' asked Plum, his body heating up with recognition.

'Love of a good woman,' said Trent, who was in the process of becoming Tatania.

As soon as Plum got home he slammed the door behind him and went to work. By nightfall the lawn was mowed, the pool emptied and covered, and the house so clean it could feature on *Grand Designs*. Plum threw his mobile phone and his little green book full of poems and musings into the recycling out front, and, from above, pissed on them all with his eyes. In this life, he thought, you're a poet or you're not, you're God-fearing or you're not, a footy player or you're not. And he was, he was an ex-athlete, not the others, not this bullcrap of idle imaginings, long sentences and allegory. Creativity was a fake phase caused by a brain spasm while working for Qantas. It had taken his sanity too, it seemed, that fateful day, that hostile tarmac, taken the lot. I mean, who even were those people he was talking to? Now he would let it have its way, let the sun set, let Thailand decide.

Plum cleaned out the fridge, put a load on, packed all his shit into boxes, had a diazepam and a wank, and went to sleep in his bed for the last time ever.

When he woke up the next morning he wrote a note to Renee and Gavin saying he was off to Thailand with Matt, booked a silver service cab to the airport and had a long hot shower to close.

Everything was so cheap in Thailand there was no point in packing the wardrobe. He'd only need a pair of boardies, a polo and slacks for golf and a handful of briefs. Anything else he could pick up at the markets for less than what a flat white cost on Cronulla Street. Plum knew this intel from experience, which meant he hadn't bothered with a suitcase. He'd just filled his duffel for carry-on and – *boom* – customs cleared.

Pete made his way to the airport bar. It was not yet 10 am but that didn't matter in this building. It was always time for a cold one here, the taps were always frosted. Pete ordered a Stella, a bag of chicken Twisties and a glass of water. No one in the bar seemed to recognise him, which was good because the last thing he needed was another fuckwit with a smartphone blowing his escape plan just when he'd gone the full Shawshank and ducked out through a hole in the prison wall. Which, in his own special Plum way, was exactly what he had done.

Pete flipped through the *Tele* and sipped his beer, letting the froth settle on his top lip. *Maybe I'll grow a moustache in Thailand*, he thought, chuckling to himself. Nothing on the first few pages seemed to appeal and he didn't recognise anyone in the gossip section, so he flipped it over to Sports. Which was where he saw his own face, full page, smiling up at him under the headline: 'Plums are back in season'.

It was an article about Plum's incoming 'tell-all' book, which would, the journo said, put to rest the 'disgusting rumours' about one of the 'most humble and hard-working forwards to *ever* play the game'. *Giddy up! I always rated the Tele.*

Dana had done what she'd said she'd do. She'd silenced the haters in one fell swoop. Plum smiled and took another sip, and as he drifted over the paragraphs, it seemed she'd also done a good job of spinning the evidence while creating a sense of anticipation for the release. Plum just hoped she didn't mind him Skype-ing the sessions in from Thailand. God, maybe he could fly her over? He'd always enjoyed her company. And as far as he could tell from the write-up, she was officially on his side.

'We celebrate alone and we sing alone,' said a big old booming voice from beside him.

Pete turned to discover an extremely old man croaking beside him at the bar, his beard long like a furry white scarf. He was wearing a felt hat and dark grey woollen suit, walking stick in hand.

'What's that, fella?'

'Mind if I take a stool? Those stairs down from Star Alliance do not sing the body electric.'

Pete pulled out a stool and helped the ancient man onto it.

'American, are you? I've been meeting a few of them recently.'

'Yes, well, we are all the same one really.'

'Oh no, there's different Yanks. I'd say two kinds.'

'And what would they be?'

'Loud and very loud.'

The old man laughed and then ordered himself a port, and Plum wondered if he had ever met someone so old. This bloke seriously looked like he died a hundred years ago.

'Pete is my name, Peter –'

'Lum, yes, I know.'

'Oh, right, how'd you –'

'I always read the back page.'

'Ah. You read the, um –'

'I read and I write for no other reason than that I am a member of the human race.'

'And what would your name be?'

'Walt. Walt Whitman, is me.'

'Hang on, I know that name. You were in *Breaking Bad*, weren't you?'

'And *The Notebook*.' The ancient man wheezed out a chuckle.

'Dunno that one.'

'Poems, love, beauty, film, art – these are the things we stay alive for.'

'Right.'

Whitman leant in and whispered to the mahogany, 'At this bar I tell things in confidence, things I won't tell everyone but will certainly tell you.' He stank of cigars and forests.

'You headed back to the States?' Plum said, leaning back a bit.

'I'm going with you, Plum. There is only one plane, really.'

'Well, I'm going to Thailand. And I gotta say, Walt, that woollen suit is probably a bit much for the climate there.'

Walt sipped his port, staring Pete in the eye. 'Are you running away? Or running to?'

'Thailand? I'd say that I'm … I'm running away. If I'm honest.' And it hurt Pete to admit it, but ever since he'd found out that Brick had rooted his missus and that his son had been home a week without even telling him, the pain inside had told him to get the fuck out; it was only now that he could see this, that he wasn't thinking well, that he was just avoiding everything again like he always did.

'You can be honest. And the world will not fall apart. You can speak your truth. You can love who you want to love. You can love everyone that you want to love, and you can be who you are. Clear and sweet is your soul, Plum. Do you understand my meaning?'

'You don't have a ciggie do you, Walt?'

'I have cigars. Duty free.'

'Fancyyy!'

The two men made their lumbering way to the Indo-themed smoking section, an open-roofed bar with fake grass and a view out over the tarmac. This was where the enormous men stood, facing each other by the enormous windows, smoking enormous Cuban cigars, as planes parked and others ambled out for departure.

'How do you think the plates of the earth will position themselves?' Whitman asked.

'Huh?'

'When you flee to the tropical beaches of South East Asia, you will upset the weight of your world, and those who love you may spill and slide.'

'Um.'

'The gravity of grief.'

'I hope you don't judge me, Walt, but I honestly believe that if I go then everyone I love and that loves me will be better off. I do nothing but make things worse –'

'You cannot make things worse. Things are only what they are.'

'Oh, no. *I* can.'

'I can postpone my acceptance of things, my realisations, and scream at my own eyes.'

'Hey?'

'In all people we see ourselves. We are the glass windows in this smoking section. And the good or bad I say of them I say of myself.'

'So what are you saying?'

'Peace is the most beautiful choice.'

'Sure, but there is also my brain issue, I don't want to take pills for the rest of my life, in and out of consults reading up on CTE and dementia.'

'You embrace your mind and your body.'

'Always did.'

'You knew the dangers and you played on?'

'I found something worth dying for.'

Whitman nodded his head. 'Valorous. Virtuous. Valid.'

'I just want to be set free, you know? To die knowing I did a pretty good job, that I made an impact and yet I never overplayed my hand.'

'Let me tell you something.'

'Please.'

'I am two hundred years old today.'

'You certainly look like it, Walt, my boy.'

'Thanks.'

'These cigars have had their way with you.'

'Ok.'

'Ever thought about cutting down?'

'You run because of fear. Fear of your own son. But you should not fear your own son because your own son is you. You are your son and your lovers and your friends. In fearing them you are fearing what lives inside your own skin, Peter Lum. Run to Thailand, to Mars, or, to where I am from, New York —'

'Fun city.'

'It doesn't matter. The past and the present. Look to me, Plum. Look to Whitman.'

Peter put his cigar down by his side and stared into the man's medieval face. He looked like Albert, but softer. He looked like evolution, but closer. He looked like love, but harder.

Then Whitman said, unexpectedly, 'Let's take our shoes off.' With great difficulty, he bent down to undo his boots, refusing to let Peter help.

The two men stood, their feet unshackled by socks and shoes.

'Can you feel the grass beneath your feet?'

'The synthetic turf?'

'Loafe with old Walt, across the grass, and feel the blades between your toes.'

Walt and Peter walked in a circle, feeling the sharp blades between their toes, only stopping to suck on their cigars.

'Your flesh will one day be a great poem, Plum.'

'Poetry is too indoors for me.'

'No one else can travel the road for you, Peter. But if you go now you cannot come back. And if you don't come back you will still be you. For wherever we go, there we are. So tell me this, are you happy on water or land, knowing you never spoke your truth?'

'What do you expect me to do?'

'Do whatever you like. But make it produce joy.'

'I'm just so sick of hurting everyone.'

'Your son aches because you ache. Your son hides because you hide. Can't you see? If you run, it is because your father did the same. If you face up, it is because your son will one day too, to his son. You are the world, the way, the wisdom.'

Walt Whitman, this smelly old fossil dredged up from a swamp six million miles down, well, he was right. And Plum knew it. Once he'd got to Thailand, had a hundred Singha beers, a couple of six-handed hand jobs and a surf, it would just be him again – and the other thousand overweight Aussie men running from financial ruin. From the women in their lives, with their complexities and needs. From facing up to the wreckage. It would just be him and Magic Matt, and the shame and them stinging nettle caterpillars.

'You *are* love, Peter Lum.'

Pete took another swirling suck on his cigar and broke into a smile. He peered at the old man through wet clouds, tears falling down his cheeks. 'If I go back to Cronulla, will I ever see you again?'

'If you want to see me, then look for me down there, beneath the soles of your feet.'

'In the sharp and unforgiving leaves of astro-turf?'

'I could not have said it better myself.'

'Thanks, Walt.'

'Multitudes, my friend. Multitudes.'

Once Pete decided to about-face, he couldn't get back to the Shire quick enough, hauling the duffel over his shoulder and running, lopsided, towards the exit gate. But, alas, being an international flyer in a time of terror, the ex-footy player was stopped by officials and asked to explain himself. They wanted to know why someone would purchase a one-way, premium economy ticket to Thailand, clear customs without checking luggage, drink a schooner, smoke a cigar in the lounge while talking to the air with their shoes off, then leave the airport without looking to regain a credit for losses incurred.

'Oh, look,' Pete told them. 'I can understand your confusion at my actions. But I assure you I just had a change of heart.'

An official took Plum and his duffel bag into a cold-blue room and asked him to unzip it. 'I'm going to lift out the items one by one – at which point, sir, I would like you to name the items as you understand them, ok?'

'Ok,' said Plum, needing to piss as much as he needed to piss off out of there. 'Um, undies, undies, undies, slacks, boardies, shirt, singlet, undies, photo of my son, photo of my son and his girlfriend, photo of my ex-wife, zinc, undies, socks, thongs, speedoes ...'

Out of the interrogation and innocent again, Plum took an epic slash in the men's by the carousels then sailed out onto the arrivals deck and straight into a cab.

As it carried Plum's spirit back the way it had come, past Sans Souci, past Botany Bay, past Sylvania and Miranda, Caringbah and then Woolooware into Cronulla, Pete began to realise just how appalling his decision to leave was, and as the driver turned up the Kenny Rogers, Pete swore to himself that he would never do such a thing again.

He pushed through the tin door of Brick's gym like a million times before. But once he was inside, he had to turn and check he'd got the right place because the whole set-up seemed suddenly unfamiliar. Where the ring used to be was now Gym N Trim pop-up café, featuring a teenage girl making a smoothie. Where the bags used to be was now an MMA octagon: black, red and tall. Beside that was a studio section, where a dozen or so ladies were finishing off a relentless Zumba class.

'Shit,' said Plum, dropping his duffel at the door.

This gym felt more like home than home to Plum. Gav grew up here under the ropes and weights benches. Renee used to come here after work with a book and a wine, as Plum and the ex-Sharks boys would just go at it, often long into the night.

But now it was like somewhere he'd never been, and for a second he thought about just turning round and going home. He could convince Renee to ask Ollie to give him a script for Nembutal and just end it all, float out to sea and let the real sharks have him. But Walt would have scoffed at such weakness. And Pete knew he couldn't run off anymore. He had to face up to the way things were …

'Mr Plum!' said a voice from beside him. It was Kutiote, locked in a grapple with another fighter on the octagon floor yet somehow still managing to say hello.

'Morning, Kutiote. How are you today?'

'I have been better,' said Kutiote, straining under the hold.

'I'll leave you to it.'

Kutiote smiled at him then slid through the knee lock, flipped his opponent over and choked him out from behind like a snake. Three taps it was over.

'Fucking hell,' said Plum, passing the cage.

'That was for you, Mr Plum!' said Kutiote, before helping up his opponent and giving him a hug.

'You alright, son?' said Plum to the opponent.

The opponent shook it off, wiped his eyes with a towel, had a sip of water from a bottle beside him, took Kutiote's hand as if to dance, and then – *whack* – they hit the floor as one to practise the hypothetical until he got it, until he didn't cop the same fate. This was UFC: you got it wrong until you got it right or you got concluded.

A woman emerged from the studio, sticky with sweat. 'Peter,' she said. 'What do you think of the changes?'

'G'day Lexi. Well done, yeah, no good.'

Pete wondered if Char was here. He could feel her presence, her disappointment in him. The scene that had played out the last time he was here was pulsing through the walls and the open red faces of her confidantes – every step through this gym was more and more treacherous.

'Looking sweet!' said Lexi. 'Isn't it, Plum? Did you hear I'm running the Pilates side of things?'

But Plum was off.

There was nothing in his head to speak of now.

He was silenced, emptied, floored.

And frozen to the spot.

At the back of the gym by the new row of bags, was a long sinewy figure hingeing back and – *snap snap snap* – kicking into the waiting pads of an agile Father Pepple, dancing round the mats then lifting his left arm and inverting it backhandedly for another set of – *snap snap snap* – kicks to the pad. Gav collected the centre of Pepple's mitt every single time. *Snap snap snap.* Finally, a bell went ting. And the boy, who had shaved his head since Plum last saw him, turned and faced his father. 'Dad.'

'Gav.'

Priests are piranhas. Pepple had clearly known the boy was back when they spoke, he was moulding him behind closed doors, and yet here he was playing the patron saint.

'Peter.' Pepple took his pads off and walked gingerly upstairs to the offices, leaving the father and the son to greet each other: one breathless, the other heaving with effort.

'I'm going to go for a swim,' said Gavin, walking off towards the courtyard at the back.

Plum followed his son into the massage room off the courtyard. The massage table had been replaced by a mattress on the floor, and the corner table where the towels and oils used to sit was now covered in fitness clothes.

'I only have half an hour, then I have to eat again, then come back to train.' Gav was curt, focused, nowhere near his father's eyes.

'Ok,' said Plum, watching the boy change. His son's body was so much skinnier and stronger since he'd last seen him, and his demeanour much less open and vibrant. 'Is this where you've been staying?'

'Yeah, why?'

It was the pointed 'why' that stung him. He'd heard other parents' kids talk to them that way. Responding to their requests with a blunt 'huh?', a jabbing 'hmmm?' or a whiney 'what?', but not Gavin. Yet here Plum was, copping one to the face, and he didn't have a leg to stand on. If anything he was the kid being scolded, so he took it, doing his best to respond like it hadn't touched the sides. 'Yeah, why, Gav?'

And as much as it felt good to offload the 'why', brat did not suit Gavin, even in a tizz. So he returned to head down and mumbling instead. 'Brick was in here for a bit. But he's back with Suzanne and Kirk now so I said I'd take it. That's the story.'

'Right.'

'Just until Ainslee gets back and we move in together.'

With boardies, UFC Fight Pass singlet and matching cap on, Gav slid into his Sharks sandals, took a towel from off his bed, and headed out of the room he now called his home. 'Comin or not?'

'Yeah,' whispered Plum, staring at the pile of his son's clothes, wishing he could just collapse into them, and inhale.

North Cronulla Beach, where Pete'd had such a holy swim just yesterday, now bristled in a mood. There was no light sparkling off the surface, no soft, curling waves crashing politely against the perfect shoreline. Instead there was wind, cutting up the waves and making them separate before they found themselves, squawking seagulls asking where the good times went, and sand lifting off the surface and blinding the eyes of the deluded few.

But this did not stop Gavin. Because Gavin, like forever, approached the nature of life and the life of nature without expectations. He went to the kitchen for food. He went to the toilet to piss. He went to the sea for the sea. And that is exactly what he got. He got the sea. Ducking down beneath the waves, he swam right out past the buoy until he'd got his fix, turned and swam back, finding three waves melding into one with enough formation in which to carry his muscular, narrowed body back to land. There was no joy in it, Plum noted. There was no fun and games in his spirit, Plum noted. This boy had changed in Bali, Plum noted. He was all business now.

'Have you got keys on you?' asked Gavin, drying himself.

'To where? To our place? Yep.'

'To *yours*.'

Plum felt the left jab implicit in the statement and he took it on the chin. 'I do. Yep, got em right here. You wanna go there now?'

The boy was coming home.

'I'll come get some stuff.'

The boy was not coming home.

'Yeah, no, of course.'

Pete followed his son as he marched up through the sandstone park, past Northies to the Kingsway, and all the way home, albeit from three metres behind, and in silence.

'Why is it all so clean here?' Gavin said as soon as he stepped inside the house. 'Looks like you're moving out.'

Plum had gone in ahead of him and barrelled down the hall into the kitchen, pocketing the note he'd left out for Renee and Gavin. 'Just, you know, bringin in the new year with a clean slate?'

'Right,' Gav said and went to his bedroom.

Pete meandered back down the hall, his bases covered, anxiety held at bay. The noise of his son rummaging in his room reminded him of Sylvia, and how much she went on about the importance of children, and how we have to learn from them not the other way round.

'Need anything, son?' he called from the hall.

'Nup.'

But by God he wished things were different. Wished he could rewind things back to the day he spoke at Sharks Leagues. When they were all out the back, eating trial salads and having a laugh. Fucking innocent and fucking family. Nothing wrong with it. But Pete didn't know then what he had. Didn't know he had it all. He would ask for help. From now on, he'd bring it in. Like how he did on the field. So much stuff he did on the field, he realised, he didn't do in the walls of his own house. Pass, support, encourage. But he would now. Connect the youth with the experienced group and run as one at the defensive structures.

Plum peeked round the corner of his son's bedroom door. 'You sure?'

'Yeah, just filling a couple of bags. Been wearin the same thing for two weeks.'

'Well, you didn't have to do that, Gavin. You could've come back here.'

'Didn't want to come back here,' said Gav, stuffing the contents of the third drawer into a sports bag. 'Too toxic.'

'Too toxic?'

'Yeah, it is,' said Gavin, refusing to look up.

'What happened in Bali, Gavin? Where's Ainslee?'

'She's still there.'

'Did something go down?'

'What do you mean?'

'You came back early without her.'

'She's her own person.'

'Answer the question. Come on.'

Gav stood up straight. He had filled two big sports bags and he'd put a football on top of it. The football gave Plum hope – it meant Gav hadn't forgotten about the Storm altogether. Maybe he wasn't going one hundred per cent into the world of snap-kicks and choking blokes out. 'I gotta get my toiletries and shit.'

Gavin passed his father in the doorway and pushed on down the hall, turning right into the bathroom.

'Did Ainslee do something? Charmayne and Brick seemed to reckon that something went down over there? Son.'

'What do you care?'

'I care a lot.'

Gavin shook his head, forcing his deodorant into the too-colourful toiletries bag his mum had given him for his last birthday.

'Son?'

Gavin looked at him, releasing a huff of honest air. 'She just wanted to go somewhere else. And I wanted to stay where I was.'

'Why'd you want to stay where you were?'

'I found this sick Balinese MMA gym in Ubud, and the guys there said they'd train me for a week, and for like nothing. The guy who ran it, Mikey, was a Muay Thai champion.'

'Right.'

'But the group were all geed to see this hidden canyon in the Sukawati jungle. And I couldn't be bothered with that. I'd already seen a canyon in Ubud and so I was like, why would you go see another one? It's a canyon – it's the same. Ainslee called me selfish for wanting to stay in Ubud. Said I was just like you actually, in that I only thought of myself, not others. And then I told her she was a sheep, just wanting to do what everyone else was doing, you know? And we had this massive fight out the front of the hostel and then she left, and I stayed in the hostel on my own. Yeah.'

'Oh, son. I'm sorry.'

'Not all bad. I learnt so much in that week of training. And Ainslee got to see the canyon.'

'Ok.'

'It was all good. We just didn't communicate good.'

'So you didn't break up?'

'No, no way, Ains is the ducks nuts.'

Plum went to touch his son on the shoulder but the boy flinched. 'You looked good in the gym, Gav. The Bali week must have paid off? Father Pepple's got you looking sharp on the pads.'

'Long way to go if I'm going to get in the octagon.'

'Is that what you want? To get in the octagon?'

'What's it look like?' asked Gavin, spreading his wings and revealing his UFC Fight Pass singlet. 'Doesn't say NRL on it, does it?'

'Pretty dangerous sport, mate. A lot of blokes get carried out of there.'

'Least if I get a brain injury I'll know why. Playing league you don't know until it's too late.'

'Sorry?'

'If I get hit in the head in the cage it's because I made a mistake. I can control what happens to my brain. You've got no say in the matter in footy.'

'You don't want to play rugby league, son?'

'I don't want to play for the Storm.'

'Ok, ok, well, no one can force you.'

'Ok, good. Thanks. Can you move out of the way please?'

Gavin went down the hall and back into his bedroom then dragged his bags out front, as if his assistant was about to turn up and load them into a cab for him. Then he came back in, had a bit of a text in the living room, took a beach towel from the linen press, and then decided he'd scope the kitchen to see if anything took his fancy from the pantry.

'Hungry, mate?'

'I can't eat any of the stuff you cook. Pepple has me on a diet – with Charmayne's help. Just eating good fats and smart proteins now, like salmon and asparagus.'

'Ok.'

'Not that there is anything *to* eat in this kitchen,' said Gavin, staring into the open fridge.

'I did a clean-out of the fridge too, as you can see, sorry.'

'There's only yoghurt, Dad.'

Just the sound of the word 'Dad' gave Plum hope. 'Yeah. Have that. If you want?'

Gavin, confused and fucking starving now, and well out of Pepple's eyeshot, took a big spoon from the drawer and started ripping into the strawberry Ski yoghurt, knowing full well his nutrition team would shake their heads at the high sugar content.

'Good?'

'Read in the paper today that you're doing a book.'

'Yeah.'

'Do you not even have a banana?' asked Gavin.

Pete shook his head. He'd buy a banana for a thousand dollars if he could, just to chop it up and throw it in that yoghurt tub. 'Sorry, son. Like I said. Clean-out.'

'Looks like you're *moving* out to me.'

'Why would I move out?'

'Who knows, Dad? Why does Peter Lum do anything? You're a man of mystery.'

'How's the yoghurt?'

Gavin shrugged, remembering a topic he wanted to bring up. 'I'm not going to talk to her.'

'Who?'

'Dana Crighton. If she asks. Things are going to be different for me now. Social media wise. Private account for my personal, public for my fighting, because Twitter and Insta are big in MMA and UFC. Kutiote has 440K followers and he's only had one fight. Plus, yeah, with the book, Dad, I don't want shit out there about me. So don't talk about me in your "tell-all", ok? Tell that journo that Gavin's not saying nothin. And leave out family. Same goes for, like, Charmayne too. We spoke about it and we don't want our names involved. Just talk about yourself and your successes or whatever shit.'

'You been seeing a fair bit of Charmayne?'

'Sure have. And if UFC goes well I can give her some backing. She's doing her Masters in Food Science and she wants to buy Brick out, see. His arms are gone and his heart had a bad reading. He's heading back up to the Gold Coast with Kirk and Suz in February. He made a bit of fast money on a thing and bought them all a beach shack in Currumbin.'

'He made some fast money?'

'Yeah, said he got a quick hit from somewhere. Don't think it was on the punt, though, because Suzanne doesn't allow that anymore.'

'Certainly not.'

'They're patching it up, Brick says, for Kirk's sake.'

A car horn beeped outside and Gavin shifted in demeanour, hurling the tub into the bin and the spoon into the kitchen sink in one swift, swirling movement. 'I gotta go.'

A shiver moved through Plum's spine. He had to shoot now, or it would be busted with his son forever. 'Gav, just gimme a second, please.'

'Pepple's out front. We're going to get a steak. Then train some more.'

'Well, Pepple can wait. God can wait. Gavin, just stand still.'

'Pepple's —'

'Fucken just a minute. I'm still your father, ok?'

Gavin looked at him, eyes wet and hot with feeling.

'I want to say to you that … Well, that … I was very worried when you were in Bali.'

'That's why you didn't answer my calls?'

'Just let me say something, alright?'

'Alright.'

'Alright.'

Plum released the boy's shoulders, and, knowing the kid wasn't going anywhere, he got himself and his son a glass of water. 'My dad made a lot of promises to me when I was your age. And he fucken didn't come through with them. If anything, he abandoned us when he said he'd be there.'

'Right.'

'And I did the same thing to you. I said I'd be a dad to you and I failed. I shut you out. And when you got a dad like that, it's better if they die. Which I thought I was going to. I still might die with what I got. But I don't want to die with you thinking I'm not there. Because I am here. And so you're not in limbo like I was. Ok? You have a dad. Father Pepple may be a father in his church but I'm your father in this kitchen. In this life. You hear me?'

'Is it yours?'

'Hey?'

'Charmayne's baby. She thinks it's going to be a girl. I'm going to be godfather.'

'You're already godfather to Tallulah.'

'Yeah, but this is different. Charmayne's always been there for me. I want to —'

'You're a good kid, Gavin. You know that? Even with a shaved head.'

Gavin laughed, leading Plum to open up his arms.

'I'm not going to hug ya, ok?'

'Ok.'

Gavin was older now. He'd survived a scare in Indonesia, having gotten so lonely and scared in Bali on his own, feeling like the ground beneath him may just fall in without Dad and Ainslee, without the food and the language and the comforts he relied on to survive. But he had punched on, and he had loved it, and as he got on that plane to come home he felt he didn't need to be mollycoddled anymore. He had his own back now, he could get himself through regardless of who was in his corner or what it said on the menu. 'Just don't lie to me, Dad. That's all I ask. Don't lie to me or to Charmayne.'

'I'm so sorry. Son, I'm sorry. I can't say that enough.'

'You hear what I asked?'

'I'll never lie to you again.'

The screen door flung open, revealing Lexi, carrying Plum's duffel bag. 'Plum, thank goodness you're here. I tried to call but your phone's off. You left your duffel bag at the studio – and, sorry, I rifled through it to find out whose it was. It has your passport in it so I thought it best I deliver it! Are you off somewhere nice?'

Gavin, beyond despair, threw the remainder of his water in his dad's face, whipped the beach towel round his neck and left.

Plum fell into a slump. He had never felt this powerless. Like a dream where you don't have arms. Drifting through a depressing sort of treacle, he tried to write stuff down but he couldn't remember where he put the little green book. He thought about opening up the shed and whacking the Kreepy Krauly in for a cleansing lap of the out-ground, but again he didn't have the energy. He found himself on the couch, or even on the kitchen floor, simply lying there on the horizontal, for hours at a time. Plum went so deep into this cave he forgot his other service positions in life, namely training Chloe over at Seagulls FC – and he would have missed the entire week of sessions too if her less-than-subtle father hadn't banged on his front door with a reminder.

'Plum Warrior! It smells in there!'

When Peter finally got to the field, rubbing his eyes and burping, Chloe had already lined up the four witches hats to start her interval sprints. Run up to one, tap it, then run backwards to the start. Up to the second, tap it, run backwards to the start. Up to the third, tap it, run backwards to the start. Run up to the fourth, tap it, turn and sprint all the way home. Rest for thirty seconds. Repeat.

'What's next Mr. Plum?' she said, red-faced and blowin.

Plum went to call her on but the words didn't come out and he felt his legs buckle beneath him. He flopped over one knee and sobbed into his wrist.

'Don't cry,' said Chloe, patting his head. 'The new season starts up soon.'

New Year's Eve arrived like a parking fine in the mail and Pete, not willing to dispute the infringement, took to the roof for some long-overdue maintenance. It was a job Gavin usually did but, in his absence, Pete unlocked the three-tiered ladder and by mid-morning was shining up roof tiles with his shirt off. Having barely slept since that conversation in the kitchen with Gavin a coupla days ago, this was the perfect task for distraction. As Pete worked away at the mouldy spots and engrained seagull deposits, passers-by beeped their horns at him. Some offered the odd 'Get a real job' or 'Show us your tits!' standards – but most of them just pointed, then put their heads down and pushed on. His fans were no longer fawning, he realised. He'd felt it at the BP getting milk that same morning, and at Cronulla Seafoods the night before: people were seeing him, spotting who he was, but instead of asking for a photo or hitting him with a hundred questions, they ducked their heads and got on with filling up or picking out medium prawns from WA, whispering and shaking their heads. And it was getting to him, finally – this hissing dislike was melting his soul. If only that Dana book was hitting shelves now and he didn't have to sit and share it all. The only upshot from his time on the roof was spotting his phone and the little green book in the recycling.

With the tiles mostly cleaned, Pete got down off the roof, had a shower, rubbed in some aloe vera, drank a milo and then sat down at the kitchen table. Dana had asked him to scribble out a few things, anecdotes he wanted in the book, facts he wanted known that might assist in defusing the media firebomb. That was his homework. But sitting in the kitchen with his little green book, he began to feel a sense of imprisonment in his own house. Everywhere he looked, he felt watched, judged, stifled. Unable to kick the weight of it, Plum took a walk around the place, inspecting the floors and walls and shelves for what it might be, this silent gaoler. Finally, it dawned on him: it was the images and memorabilia of his playing days that was making him feel trapped and suffocated. It was those days that caused his brain injury, and it was his brain injury that caused his relationship issues, so if he took down the triggering emblems, perhaps his brain could go about manifesting the 'love for country' that Liz had spoken to him about.

So, instead of journalling his life, Peter spent the final arvo of the year cleansing the house of posters and framed photos, signed jerseys and success shields from his rugby league career. And as they came down and the blank walls revealed themselves, he did feel a certain lightness come over him, he even found himself smiling at a wall without anything on it. There was no way he was going to get rid of them all completely, they were too meaningful, but for now they could spend some time in the back shed, stacked up against the rods and kayaks. He did feel like totally getting rid of *one* of them from the premises, though: the one from Game Three at Lang Park, when Brick's knee got him in the face. Proper head knocks like that one reduced him to an eight-year-old; they made him want to drink milk and be near his mum. He needed to be warm, safe and held by Renee in the caring darkness. He'd wear sunglasses inside even though the blinds were drawn and he'd beg her not to leave him alone ever. And Renee, she would dab his head with a wet washer and say, *Of course, I'm right here ... I'm right here, Plummy ...*

Pete leant over the couch and lifted the heavy frame off the living room wall, laid it down on the carpet and took the sought-after ornament apart with a Phillip's head and some patience. Then he lifted the still-stained number 13 jumper out of its setting and brought it to his face. He inhaled the grass of yesterday and, just like that, like clockwork, the snowstorm awoke in his head. He had come to know his illness so well of late, it was like he could summon it himself now. He was the conductor of his own sordid symphony.

Plum decided, as he showered and dressed, that he would take that jersey with him tonight. *Happy New Year!* he would say to Trent, and he would mean it. He'd gift that rare sportifact to the Old Bike Shed, and Trent could raffle it, burn it on a beach, do what T-dog wanted. Pete didn't care. He just wanted it gone, and in killing a seagull with a single stone, he could also show his appreciation to the person who had literally saved his life this past year.

If there was an ominous energy in town three days ago there was a nuclear one brewing today. Eight o'clock and Cronulla Street was already a cauldron of desperation and vomit. Pete had to tuck the jumper under his arm and duck his weary head, burrowing through the scattered limbs of young women wearing nothing but flimsy wisps of fabric, flailing flesh in all directions beside rectangular males just standing there, hearts open, eyes empty, hurling their stunted, video-game confusion at the night. It was hot and it was happening, and they still had four hours till midnight without any apparent plan of attack. The young coppers in overalls and caps seemed no match for the punters with muscles climbing out of muscles.

What on earth was in them protein shakes? From any distance, on any day, Pete could tell the difference between men who won arm wrestles in country pubs after loading granite onto Mack trucks, and those metro kids who built their biceps in expensive gyms; their bumps amounting to nothing when the moment arose. Them policemen, lined up like mannequins against the glass walls of the shut-up, boarded-up juice shops and gluten-free pizzerias, seemed to be ogling the semi-naked girls more than making an umbrella for their safety – and the boys' buff bodies in munted motion had Pete on his toes, but, as always, he found his go-forward to break the chaos line, wondering how his own son would fare in this mess of jizz and joy. But as he neared the Old Bike Shop, it was the screeching voices, punching staples into his already taped-together brain, that nearly had him drop his gift and look to buy a gun on eBay. Can't a sentence just stay down at the end? And why not have a BBQ in your mate's backyard and get your passion out there? Leave society alone. That's what he did when he was young, dumb and full of rum – drank facing a bonfire with other blokes until you could not stand and then three hours later woke up under a panel van.

Pete entered the Old Bike Shed, Origin jersey round his waist, gel in his hair, black denims on. Jupiter was onstage, dressed in a purple space suit, reading out instructions to the audience on where to go when the world ends.

Unfollow me to the next life
Where you will be retweeted
And all those who blocked you
Will explain themselves, naked
Then you will be led by Kanye and Kim
To a pink room made of dolphin skin
Where all the likes and comments you ever got
Will build up and explode like fireworks

Jupiter's tone was so coy and assured that the audience, jazzed as they were on resolutions and natural wine, dared not stir.

'This one is on the house,' said Tatania.

'Thanks Trent!' said Plum, taking the frothy off the bar.

'No, my dearest Plum,' said Tatania, pointing at him playfully. 'I've never actually been Trent. My name is Tatania.'

'Titanium?'

'Tatania!'

'Rightio then. Tatania. All good with me.'

'I wasn't asking. But thank you.'

'Do we still hug, Tatania?'

'Fucking of course,' said Tatania, coming round for a big one, arms fully wrapped, and she may have become a chick but the strength was exactly the same as the person who lifted him up from the ocean floor that near fateful morning.

'That feels better,' said Pete. 'Love ya.'

Plum took position against a pylon as a bloke called Les, a cantankerous fat bastard from Melbourne, or from hell, got up with a schooner and spoke of talking minds.

'Speaking of talking minds,' said a voice from below, and there she was, his mate Bridget, the virgin swimmer. She looked really pretty in her black dress and lipstick, and Pete couldn't help feel like a complete prick about the last time they hung out, having lifted her out of the pool into her chair and then bailed, bolting to the golf club after his jilted girlfriend.

'Sorry about the other day,' Pete said.

'Duty calls.'

'I'm a good friend, but a shit boyfriend.'

'I'm sure there are more options than that.'

'What do you mean?'

'People do themselves a disservice thinking in binary terms. *If I don't get the girl I'll be lonely. If I don't get that job I'll be a failure.* Trapped by two options – it's a living hell. If you think of life as more of a journey, as a collection of experiences that you learn from then, it doesn't have to be so cut and dry. Maybe you weren't the best to her, now you know that, you can go be what you want to someone else?'

'Or to her.'

'Or to her, exactly. Or to her,' Bridget said, deciding in her head at that very moment, that they would never be more than friends, but God would they be friends.

'You look really amazing tonight, Bridge.'

'What? No. Ok, I do.'

'Do you want a drink?'

'Are *you* drinking?'

'What? No. Ok, yes I am.'

Pete took his hand off Bridget's shoulder, only just noticing it had been there this whole time, with hers on top of it, and turned to the bar to get them some refreshments. 'My shout.'

He ordered them a couple of champagnes because it was New Year's, waiting patiently at the bar for Chloe's dad to unwrap the cork foil.

'I never got to say this,' Tatania said, slipping in beside him, 'but thanks so much, Plum, for sending Chloe's dad my way.'

'Oh, he's worked out?'

'A few teething issues with stealing from the till and drinking all the stock, plus he basically moved into my house when his wife hit him with a fire extinguisher, but once we sorted all that out it's not been an issue. Plus he's great at keeping the more narrow-minded hoodlums away from the Old Bike Shed.'

'Hustle and Muscle!'

'Haha, that's it! "Hustle and Muscle". You coined it, my darling friend.'

Plum was all set to hand the jersey over when a voice lit up from on stage:

This is poem about when I used to get fucked up.

The portly, forty-something actor with a fierce beard, who kept reminding the crowd he was based out of London, was kicking off a bit of beat poetry on the topic of when he used to drink:

The mornings are getting earlier
The slap in the face is beginning to sting
It simply cannot be − day
That man cannot be running past my window
Cos I'm still in that bar, I'm still in that car
I'm still in that sambuca, black as tar
My guts are still moving to the beat
I haven't divulged every secret in my head
There's more to throw to the floor
I'm still standing
I'm not dead yet
I wanna crawl back inside the spewy carpet
I wanna sleep in a woman's handbag

And Plum could do nothing but relate to the sentiment, as the rugged thespian wowed the audience with his self-deprecating tale of post-Bukowskian destruction − if only Sylvia was here to meet him! He completed the mad howl with the stanza:

And the morning scribes the warning:

Don't abuse the night
It loves you
You must love it back.

'Thank you, Cronulla!' he said. 'And go you mighty Sharks!'

Pete looked down and around for Bridget. He wanted to see what she thought of the poet but she was not where he last saw her, she was not anywhere on that eye level. Plum panicked, he didn't want to be in this place without her, but then a voice answered the query – as Jupiter announced Bridget as the new poet on stage, and there she was, already in place before the lowered mic stand, book in her right hand, champagne in her left.

'This is a poem I wrote recently, and the title pretty much um, explains it … it's called, um, "I swam with a thug and I liked it".'

The crowd chuckled then howled, and Tatania whistled till the mirrors thought of cracking, but the poet had her crowd under complete control. She sipped her fizz with poise and brought the room to silence with a crack of her neck on both sides. Plum's heart was pounding – knowing that this one was for him – about them.

I took a swim with a thug
And I liked it

Perhaps it was because it was New Year's Eve, perhaps it was because of her coy delivery of the second line, or perhaps it was just because this woman was owning her own shit and getting what was hers. Whatever it was, she was killing.

'Enough!' she said, and the crowd did what they were told. Pete remained by the pylon, sweating, still wondering how on earth she got on stage.

I said I took a swim with a thug
And I liked it
I spotted him, the thug
His jeans spread out on the sand like a late-night murder drama
His rippling rectangle shape, gathering speed, sending tremors
On the loose, on sand, on song

Pete stood there, shoulders relaxed, empty-handed, listening to the distance between her breaths. He narrowed his eyes, wondering if anyone else in the bar felt what he did when someone – in particular, this someone on stage right now – recited a poem.

> *And as he dove into the open sharks-mouth wave*
> *The frothing, curling, sweet left-hander*
> *'Closing out'*
> *As the surfers say*
> *I wished I could too*
> *Penetrate the sea, free, like a thug*

Plum looked around and saw Brick, sipping from a bottle of water in the corner and looking lonely. Plum, living in Bridget's breath patterns, turned back to the stage.

> *He spotted me, the thug*
> *Seated, like a good girl, in my chair*

Peter's eyes then darted to Gavin, sipping on a diet coke next to Father Pepple and Kutiote. The two men waved to Plum, but Gavin was watching Bridget like he was about to be called into the octagon, his eyes beneath the hoodie focused, his body rocking from side to side.

> *'You want to come for a swim?' he asked.*
> *'You don't need a costume, just be yourself.'*

Pete took his little green book out from his bum pocket and opened it to the page, the page that held the offering he had ready. He was never one to back down from a bet, and now that Bridget had taken her plunge, he had to do the same. He had to read out an original poem. She'd sent a text that morning, saying she would call him up after her 'swimming poem', and this was clearly that. Peter 'The Plum' Lum was next on at the

Old Bike Shop's New Year's Eve poetry slam and he had never, ever been more terrified in his life.

> *Where I shall be blessed*
> *Anointed, a virgin dipper*

The jumped-up audience howled, a chorus of groins in urgent voice. They couldn't wait for the fireworks' either, and the fireworks after.

> *His arms under my pits*
> *Lowers me in and holds me there*
> *I think fuck, I think God, I think shit*
> *I think woah, Bridget, this is it*

Pete's rig vibrated with the roar of the crowd. His eyes wet with emotion, he knew full well that what was happening up there was everything life could be. Peter Lum, the thoughtful thug, was in love with a 29-year-old Brit. He was in love and he knew it, and the feeling, it was not unlike a head knock, it was sweet and young and delirious, and that was when he realised, that being semi-unconscious was not the place he feared, but the place he lived for. Knocked out and dizzy was the holy land, where the human mind could not take the force: Love. Words. God.

> *I took a swim with a thug*
> *In the pool I am dead*
> *I'm alive*
> *And the thug*
> *His breath in my mouth*
> *His heart in my chest*
> *We are swimming*

It was too much. Pete turned away to find Gavin, with his head out of the hood now, staring at Bridget, engrossed. Brick, standing with Squeaky now, both enraptured. He found Renee at the bar, cradling a red wine with her mouth open. Plum knew there would be consequences, but this time he did not care, finally understanding what Pepple meant by 'acceptance'.

And as I meet the thug
Skin to skin
And come to rest
Beneath his chin
I feel the shudder
And look up to see
That the swimming thug
Is just as scared as me
This thug
He used to hit and spin
Bend em in half, he tells me
Put em to sleep
Put em in a wheelchair

The crowd gasped as one. Pete held his breath, then gulped. He felt the eyes of the crowd on him.

But the thug is a boy
Who learnt to swim too
The thug is a boy
Thugs have feelings too

Peter felt someone nudge him and looked around: Dana Crighton, a bottle of Four X Summer against her chest, eyes wide open, looking to tell him fresh news. And just like that the snowstorm started up again. *She can't be here, she can't know, can't have her hear it.*

'Pete, I need to talk to you,' she said via a thick whisper, leaning around the pylon with her left index finger pointed upwards as if to say 'just one minute'.

To be close to someone
Not an inch apart

'I gotta get out of here,' said Pete, to the air, to the stage.

To connect with another
Heart to heart
That takes more courage
Than killing

Pete moved on 'killing' – and Bridget saw him do so, swallowing pride into the microphone.

But he wasn't staying. No matter what the guilt. For the ghostwriter was here, which meant the media was here, which meant Australia was here, which meant everyone would be laughing at him because he was up next.

That takes more courage
And thug is willing

Shake and bake, duck the stiff arms, off the left foot into clear space. Plum charged for the door. Chloe's dad and Tatania the posts. Exit sign the try line. With his NSW Blues jumper tied around his waist like a silent testimony to strength, he zig-zagged round a handsome man in a white T-shirt holding an endless ream of paper, and for a moment there it looked like the thug might just score – until the second line of defence stopped him in his tracks with a sliding effort. Renee. Peter surrendered in the tackle and played the ball – as taught by his father, forty-four years ago on that rocky, barely bearable backyard in Orange.

'I'm in love with a thug,' Renee said in an aggressive whisper. She'd clearly had a girls' lunch, pushing on to the Old Bike Shed instead of going home.

'Why are you here?'

'I was invited.'

'By who?'

'Fuck off, Peter. I don't have to justify shit to you,' she said, no longer whispering at all. 'Hugo!'

'Did you tell Charmayne?'

'About what?'

'About the – about Melbourne – the Adelphi.'

'No!' she said. 'Of course not. What do you think I'm crazy?' She slugged on her red wine.

'Good,' he said.

'I told Ollie, though.'

'Told Ollie what?'

'About that night. About the whole Storm thing in Melbourne. About how we feel about each other.'

'Hey?'

'The things you said, and the things we did that night, I couldn't keep from him.'

'Renee, what are you talking about?'

'I'm talking about us!'

Now there were two performances going on.

'How does Gavin know then?' asked Plum, feverish.

Renee shrugged. 'Ollie says if Gavin goes to Melbourne then we can go down there too because he can get a practice there. Says it will be a good reboot for us. Gavin will live with us.'

'Gavin doesn't want to live with you.'

'How do you know that?'

'Because I know him.'

'Oh really?'

Plum nodded, staring into the face of his ex-wife, his best friend through it all, his next of kin.

'He's coming to Melbourne with us.'

'How?'

'I'll take you to court and win.'

'On what grounds?'

'You had an affair!'

'With you, though. Renee. I slept with you.'

'Oh,' Renee said, her neck jutting backwards with realisation. 'True.'

'Happy New Year,' said Plum.

'If he ends up in the UFC with a brain disease like you then it's all your fault.'

Pete took a breath. The familiar rage grew within him, but he let it pass, preferring to smile at her instead and nod, slowly. 'I'll take that on board, Renee.'

Renee took a breath too, then, with a smooth arcing movement, threw her red wine on his white T-shirt and left for the ladies room. Like a header harvesting this year's grain, she ploughed through the field, passing the thrust stage where Bridget was ready to introduce her chum. 'The final poet for the New Year's Eve gala presentation of Lost for Words poetry club will be a special debut performance by an iconic Cronulla local. You may know him ...'

The air in the lane was thick and hot, and the noise of Cronulla Street just around the corner was that of an army coming over the hill for warfare. Pete tightened the jumper round his waist and headed for the cab rank that nestled in beside the station. But just as he went to cross the lane, a murder of mid-teen skaters flew past, with a roar of their cockroach wheels over the pavement ridges. Plum, his awareness on high at this juncture, snarled at their transit and then noticed a boy and a man chucking stacks of newspapers off the back of the truck just by the noodle joint. Thinking he couldn't be seeing what he thought he'd seen, and feeling dizzy and off-balance suddenly,

Pete stepped out into the lane. Just as he did, the skaters doubled back and streaked past him again. Pete said 'cunts' to the bitumen and then walked over and dragged a copy of the paper out from within its plastic restraints. And, yeah, there it was. Beneath the urine-yellow streetlamp, Pete saw his printed face and the words 'Rotten Plum!' and with them a collection of blurry images, clearly taken on smartphones, and other bylines: 'Dumb Plum', 'Peter the Cheater', 'Shark in the Dark'.

'What the fuck?' he said to the cement. He flipped through to where the meat and potatoes lived, page seventeen, the punish page. Photos of him and Bridget. One of him on a stretcher at the airport having fouled himself. One where it looked like he was punching his son. One of him by the pokies screaming at a bouncer. One in Parramatta, screaming in the rain like a madman. One of Charmayne and Brick, holding each other close outside Hog's Breath. One of him as a young player, beautiful and agile. One of Gavin, moving out of the house. One of Plum coming out of the toilets at the Tradies, looking worse for wear, fingers pinching his own septum. One of him pushing Charmayne at the gym. One of him hurting that kid in the smoking section through the bars. One of him. One of him.

'A close friend confirms Lum's drug use and gambling issues.'
'A close friend confirms Lum has started talking to himself.'
'A close friend confirms Lum's philandering and violence.'
'A close friend,' Pete said to himself. 'A close friend.'
Silence in his head and silence in his heart.
Then a scream.
Plum turned.
It was Bridget.

Jupiter was beside her and on the other side the actor. But them skaters, well, they were circling round Bridget like she was their prey now, intent on seeing who could ollie over the top of the wheelchair. Her dress had blown up in her face, she was covering herself with one hand, the other hand on top of her head – a skin helmet – as skater after skater launched over her using the tail of their boards to snap-up; some skimming her hair, some soaring way above – even throwing out a Judo-air – the others failing to clear the girl, clipping her shoulders or the arms of her chair, or her arms.

'Fuck this!' said Plum, hurling the assassinating paper into the street. 'Oi!' Stiff-arming a passing skater youth to the ground, Plum headed into the swirling circle, ready to die for love.

But he was too slow, and the crew were on wheels, and they were laughing their heads off as their decks carried them away, their goals achieved: humiliate, get sick air, escape.

But there was still one. The one he had coat-hangered.

'Now, sir.'

The boy was on all fours, the thug's Popeye forearm having concussed him somewhat.

'Oi,' said Plum, the ex-player, whom once you'd poked him was a well-renowned bear. He'd fucking bite your head off if you got him going – and he was going now, teeth bared.

The boy was crawling across the pavement, his head peering sideways like he was looking for his skateboard under a car, but there was no car and no escape craft, just a large ex-footy star above him, ready to put a cunt in a wheelchair.

'Get up,' said Pete, but the boy didn't. Couldn't. 'I said, get up, ya little cunt.'

'No, I ...'

Bridget screamed, but he couldn't hear her. He was in the zone, the whistle had blown. Goodnight outside world, it was warrior time now. Time for 'Dumb as a Plum' to get things done. He knew that was what he was: an animal, despicable, uncivilised, brutal. So why not be it, why not let go, why not surrender to your nature? He had arms and legs to throw. 'Rightio then, do it your way.'

'No, please don't. I'm so sorry. My brother made me.'

Plum grabbed the kid by the shirt-throat and lifted him up off the ground. By now there was a crowd emerging from the bar but Pete couldn't see anything outside his target. The rage and the regret had formed a bubble for him and the boy. And the boy was a boy, skinny and just fifteen, pimples breaking out on his chin; he probably hadn't even had his dick sucked yet, he probably left his towels on the floor for his mum to pick up, he probably liked Pokémon Go and chocolate milk and sleeping till 2 pm.

'Please man. Don't kill me.'

Pete took a breath to end the kid. Blinked, thought, *Don't*, and then decided he would.

But because he had paused to consider his conscience, a hand had time to grab the back of his T-shirt and pull him back towards the Old Bike Shed wall.

'Don't be a goose,' said the other force.

It was Brick but it wasn't Brick, because Pete, hurt-crazed and ready to die, could not remember Brick's name. All he knew was that *he* was to blame – this block of a man before him – and not just for what had happened with Charmayne, but for the way his brain was, because Brick, mediocre on field and off, had taken every opportunity to break Plum – be it a knee to the head on his way down, high elbow in the initial contact or a shoulder to the jaw in defence, and now, well, now he would pay, now Plum would end this nameless recreant and it would be evened out, finally; it would be anything but bubbling.

'Pete, it's me.'

'Who?' Pete said, ducking and shrugging from his grasp.

The kid scrambled off into the night. Then Pete saw Dana among the crowd pouring out of the Old Bike Shop, and he looked back at Brick and, blinking, sweating, he recalled Brick's position in that infamous night up the coast all them decades ago. It was Brick who'd picked Dana up at the bar, and it was all fair and well – a mutual play on – but he hadn't kept it one on one. He'd invited players in, and in they came, drinking wanking singing. And it wasn't until Pete caught wind, and got in the lift with the backs coach, that things had dispersed. Pete couldn't remember his best mate's name but the event was suddenly crystal, and once again he was filled with the rage, nostrils flared and pulsing. He could kill proper this time. 'It's you,' he said, punching his own head with his left fist, staring down the Brick Wall.

'Hey?' said Brick.

'It's you!'

'You don't have to hurt anyone anymore, Plum!' said Bridget, wheeling her way over.

'Pete. Please, babe,' said Renee, outside now too. 'It's Brick!'

But Pete ignored the pleas of the women who cared. Instead he just strolled forward, ever so calmly, towards Brick, his life-long oppressor, his best mate, his closest friend. It had to be him – no one else knew all that stuff – and suddenly it was obvious. The quick fix and the sudden move to the Goldie; he'd sold Plum out and cashed in in the process. *What a cunt.* 'This is for Dana.' And Peter swung to avenge her assault.

But no one wins against Brick. He was born to be hit. And born to know how to not be. He slipped to his left, and Pete's reckless haymaker dissolved into the breeze like water vapour. Pete's weight was no longer balanced. Brick leant in to Pete's body, then held him up from beneath the shoulder with his right elbow, and just like that put three lefts into Plum's rib cage – *bang bang bang.*

'Brick, no!' Squeaky yelled.

Pete was tilted to the other side now and vulnerable, his kidneys wondering where breath would flow from, and then Brick ended proceedings with a single right to the jaw. *Pop.*

Pete fell to the ground and for the second time in his life had an epileptic fit.

'Prick', said Brick.

Pete didn't know he was having it. But everyone else did. Everything was clear for them now, including their position in his life, and the reason why things had been the way they had been. Pete's world, by contrast, was a blur, as he spasmed on the ground beside Bridget's wheel. He knew he was dying, and it was ok. He had been trying to escape this whole time and so he stopped fighting it, he just let go, shuddering and spitting and spasming his way to the next life …

'Dad!'

The first thing he recognised was the smell, the fruity cover-up of Lynx Africa, and that breath, still sweet as the day he first held him. It was his son, the prodigal and the only, back from the dead to drag his old man out of purgatory.

Pete opened up his eyes, still shuddering, still at sea. 'Hey?'

'Dad!

'Me china plate.'

Gavin stood back up and spun round, unzipping his hoodie and flicking it over to Pepple, alert in his corner. Pete could just focus enough to see Brick trying to get away. And then his son was leaping through the air, collecting Brick with a fly-kick to the arse and back. Brick hit the wall and turned to face Gavin, the kid he loved more than his own.

'Gav,' Brick said, 'you don't want to do this, son.'

'I'm not your son.' Gavin leg-kicked Brick in the calf, which buckled the industrial-sized Judas, and then he did it again – *snap snap snap*. Brick twisted to avoid more of the same, so Gavin came at him for the knockout right, which Brick caught in one fist while grabbing the boy's face with the other. Gavin twitched out of his clasp, issuing a left elbow to the throat then spinning to a right elbow, and then a snap-kick to the jaw to do it. Brick Wall was falling face first into space. Boof, the world exclaimed, as the huge hippo hit the canvas. Not done yet,

Gavin climbed aboard the bloke, offloading a flurry of open fist punches, both left and right, to the temples.

Plum watched on from the ground beyond, thinking of how Gav used to stand behind Brick in the rain – and here he was raining down upon him. *Now that's poetry.*

'That's my dad!' said Gavin, releasing everything on the deviant skull. And he would have ended him too, if Kutiote hadn't stepped in, pulling his training partner away and over to the waiting priest.

'Shhhh, it's ok,' said Pepple, calming the fighter back into his breath. 'Shhhh, find your centre, shhh.'

'Are you ok, Mr Plum?' said Chloe, handing Pete a bottle of water from above.

He looked up at her, this girl after his own heart, and the moment he caught her eye he knew exactly what he had to do, and so he went to do it. He hauled himself up with all of her strength helping him and re-joined the living for one last play.

Eight

What are the best things you can feel in your time on earth? Like, if you had to say, what feels the best in terms of human experiences? Of all the ones on offer to us in this life? And keep it above board, please. What would be your top three, say? Getting sweaty on the dance floor at your wedding. Skiing out of a helicopter in Colorado. Eating a pizza with your wife in actual Italy. High at a festival and your favourite band are just there, they are right in front of you. Sex with love. Seeing your first baby be born and everyone is doing well. Dunno. They're all up there. Finishing the half-marathon with your best mate from school. Finishing just ahead of him too. Or after years of toiling away at it – sucking it all up and pushing through the tough times and the inadvertent politics of the workplace – finally getting that promotion and buying that house with water glimpses. Sure. That all feels pretty great. But for Peter Lum, well, it was now. It was this moment, the one before the beginning. The moment where the adrenaline of what he was about to do matched with his fear of the unknown. This psyched-up, fired-up, pent-up surrender to chaos, to competition, to collision. The knowledge you could kill or be killed. The want for that perilous limbo.

The busted neon bar overhead lit up his face then didn't, as he slapped himself with both hands and on both cheeks, took a deep breath and then thought about nothing.

'Let's do this,' he said to the carpet, as he ducked into the thin corridor with the roar of the crowd underscoring his hard-beating heart. This was the best feeling ever – knowing you had what it took, knowing the truth was in you, and knowing that your time had come ...

In the backstage mirror Peter Lum took himself in. His top lip cracked and bleeding, his left eye sunken in and blackened from Brick's infamous right cross and his white T-shirt splattered in wine and blood. His potato head dumber than before, his chest heaving, his forehead dripping with sweat. *This is me*, he thought, grinning madly at the steamed-up glass. *This has always been me.*

He ripped the barely coping T-shirt off his body and tied it round his messed-up skull, a makeshift bandage of sorts. Then he took the Origin jumper from around his waist and lifted it up so he could take in its majesty. Pete smelt it because he loved it again – he was proud of what was done inside it – and then dragged it over his head, pushing each arm through and yanking it down over his torso like so many times before in other change rooms in other towns before other battles. He was a much younger, and therefore much leaner, man when he last went to war in this jersey, but luckily back in the day they'd worn them loose, and so the Blues 13 gripped his physique to fit. He liked the look of himself. He was back in the game. He had never left.

'Son,' he said to himself in Albert's voice, 'never take a backwards step.'

Pete turned away from himself towards the curtain, lifting out his little green book. It seemed like years had passed since Bridget had given it to him. He'd changed more in the last three months than he had in twenty years, and it was time to acknowledge that.

Through the cracks in the curtains, Pete could see Australian performance poet and two-time winner of the Nimbin

Performance Poetry World Cup, Tug Dumbly, in mid-flow:

Fill a child like a cup to the fizzing brim
It spills and runs all over your hand
It runs and runs and you, poor mop
come late to understand

He saw Tatania and Squeaky at the bar comforting Renee, who had just bought another bottle of red. Beside her, Gavin was being counselled by the priest. Gavin had risked his own life for his dad, and he had won. That boy, the one thing Plum had not completely fucked up yet. The one thing he could salvage. If he did one thing. Speak from the heart. Now, and then forever, the rib cage would be open 24/7 to G. Lum.

I won't always have you
I haven't got you now

This was his whistle to go. This was the do or die. This was the forward step.

I drew you like a breath

But what if he just couldn't do it? Couldn't read out loud in front of the class, just like at school?

I tried to keep the sketch

He thought of going down to the sea and jumping in again. Tatania would be busy this time round. Yeah, that's the go. Let's just go.

It wasn't mine to keep, you crumpled it
threw it on a heap

'Plum,' said a voice from behind him.

Pete turned around to find that handsome young man with the endless ream of paper standing there with a cigarette hanging off his lips and an ironic smirk on his face. 'Name's Jack Kerouac.'

'G'day Jack.'

'I just wanted to say … when you get out there, blow deep, my brother.'

'Huh?'

'You've scribbled your notes, wild typewritten pages or by pen, and for your own joy, you've been open, listening, in love with your life.'

'Not always –'

'Blow as deep as you want to blow.'

'Ok.'

'You're a fucken genius, Peter Lum.'

'You don't know me.'

'We both are. With nothing behind us and everything in front. Genius.'

'Righto.'

'Accept loss all of the time and believe in the holy contour of life.'

'Why are you talking to me?'

'Because there is nowhere to go. So just keep rolling, my brother. Underneath the stars.'

Jack kissed Plum on the forehead and left. On stage, Tug closed out his moving work on parenthood, then looked around. 'No idea who's next. Is anyone next? What's next? The future is next! Or is it the now?'

Now

Peter Lum took a breath and parted the red velvet sea. With blood pouring out of one eye, and his Origin jumper

312

tight across his chest, he pushed into the blinding light of now.

'A rogue stray?' said Tug, departing the stage at the sight of him.

The crowd went deathly quiet. Quiet and confused and stunned. Not just because there had been a kerfuffle outside but because before them, at a quarter to midnight, was a famous footy player, bleeding from the head and bewildered, breathing grand final energy into the mic, which squealed and shouted in horror at the interruption.

'G'day everyone.'

Pete squinted, closed his eyes, and looked around the bar.

'My name is Peter Lum.'

Pete spotted Bridget, who had rolled herself over to the bar next to Tatania, and that was enough to go on. No one was braver than them two.

If only Charlie was here, Pete wished, and Sylvia. Or that old maniac from the airport. Were they ever really there? He hadn't thought to wonder until now, up here on stage, where they all belonged. Perhaps he had that Lewy body dementia Liz told him about and was hallucinating the whole time. Was he hallucinating now? And if he was, did it matter? Like that American had just said, *the road is endless – just get on it.* Was that what he had said?

'And I um …'

Pete looked at the little green book in his large pink hands. Took deep breaths. And then he read out the words he had written:

> *This is a poem called 'Plum'*
> *About a life I just lived*
> *This is a poem about head knocks*
> *And some things I wish I did*
> *Different*

Head knocks are on another level
Bad head knocks
Being levelled
You don't know

What's what
Is that real
I'm going to cry
Too much to feel

Like everything that ever lived
Is coming out of me
Like everything that ever felt
Is alive in me

Women, you want your man to open up?
Throw him out to sea
Let him crash against the rocks
Let him box, MMA, rugby league
Cos a head knock is a heart knock

Open up the door
The day after a head knock
Your man's weeping on the floor

Ask Renee, just there, she'll tell you
Walk to get a sandwich and I'm bawling
and no one can see, cos I'm Peter Lum
The gladiator with sunglasses on
tough man, tough player, tough era
but I'll tell you this from any distance
the day after a head knock
I'm like a kitten

My name is Plum
And I'm sorry
To all of you
That I can't recall your name
But if you could just lay off for a fucken second
Cos I swear to you, I got my own shame
And it lives here, inside my chest
It lives here, shame, with all the rest

You hear about that bloke
Stabbed himself in the chest
So they could dissect his brain
Insane
But when the time comes
I'll probably do the same
I nearly killed two hundred and eighty-nine people
aboard a plane

And do not get me wrong
I wouldn't change it, wouldn't even dream
What I got to do with the gift I was given
I'm so lucky it's obscene

For the game is in my blood
I privileged the present
Not the future
And, ay, there's the rub

Drink on my own to ease the pain
Of yesterday
Better alone than lonely
They say
But that's not what I am saying now

A poem is not a complaint
It's a window to my obsessions
It's a crippling confession
And so I am here to confess to you
Because we are all Gods
A few things

That for so long have been locked inside
this prison-guarded-chest
That now, like birds, I shall release,
and in their flight, my pain can come to rest

I am a lock forward
A number 13
I am an athlete
a machine
I confess I am a lover
I am a brother
I am a father and I am a son
I am a winner
The only number is one
I confess I am a failure
I am an alcoholic
The secret is within
I confess I took the line on
I confess I have a tough chin
But the real collisions
The ones of the heart
From them
I ran
Time and time again
Yellow card
For there's a coward deep within
And that's why it was easier

To take the line on
Than take this life on

Head knocks
for
Heart knocks

What truly knocks your head around
Is what your heart leaves behind

Unsaid
For dead

My name is Plum
My head is a plum in a jar
Shaken, sugared, scarred
My heart the same
I confess I am an impact player
But have I made an impact?

I confess
My name is Plum.

Nine

Pete considered the staggered stacks of books laid out on the coffee table and carpet areas of his living room – signing them made his head go fuzzy, and he'd done a thousand this morning easy. 'Dana, look, I think I'm done –'

'Okay,' Dana said. 'Just before we wrap it up, though, there's a question that I, um, I always wanted to ask you –'

'I can't sign any more, sorry. I'm going blind.'

'And your party awaits. Of course.'

Pete sipped on his mid-strength, happy the session was concluding but also completely relaxed in here, away from the complications of the mixed dynamics outside. 'Sorry, what was your question? Thanks for coming by the way.'

'Hey, you're the one doing me a favour signing all these copies. This stuff helps sales.'

'More so than a scandal?'

Pete and Dana were friends now. They'd spent so many hundred hours in this set-up, facing each other across a coffee table with an ice-cold beer in hand. Dana had seen him cry, Pete had seen the same, and in that exchange Plum had come to trust her. He was astounded by how she continued to find his story interesting. And now the book was published Plum was happy it was doing well, mostly cos of the 180K advance he'd banked, and then there was the rest easy factor. For Dana, well, it meant she was back in the greatest game of all, working as a journalist for NRL.com and a key member of an all-female footy podcast with Lara Pitt and Emma Lawrence.

'The question?'

Dana stacked the signed books into a box beside the recliner, sipped her beer, then leant back to press her friend one last time. 'That gig you did, on New Year's Eve, when you read out your poem –'

'"The Plum" poem?'

'Yeah! Had you practised it beforehand? Because it was perfect. Or had you learnt it previously? And where did that poem come from?'

Pete fished his little green book from his bum pocket. Though the book was now thoroughly stained and dishevelled on the outside, its insides remained plump. 'It's all in here. The complete works of Peter "The Plum" Lum,' he said, and handed it to Dana. 'Stinks a bit. Because it was in the bin. But time has passed and so …'

She turned the book over in her hands. 'Wow, ok, are you sure you trust me with this?'

'Bit too late for that talk, isn't it?'

Dana held out her hand over the table to say thank you, but he didn't take it. Instead he jumped up and stepped off the left – as he had done so many times on green ovals across the league-playing world – and sliced round the edges towards her, opening up his arms and wholly embracing her. It was his cathartic power move of late.

She smelt of cigarettes and white musk, and when they broke apart, Pete could see her eyes were wet, and that she had been waiting all her adult life for that hug.

'Have a good barbecue,' she said, 'birthday boy.'

Pete wasn't quite ready to join the party yet. There was unfinished business in the living room, and he'd learnt that in this game of life, you have to play the full eighty. 'I spent a lifetime trying to kill myself but now I wanna live forever – and you helped with that.'

'I'll see you soon,' she said, throwing her handbag over her shoulder.

'No, you won't. We got a birthday to celebrate. Come on, mate.'

He put his arm around her and they walked out through the kitchen to the deck, where the new wheelchair ramp was now in play, reaching across the yard to the poolside lift.

The afternoon stretched on with snacks and speeches aplenty. Pete refused to speak, saying that being fifty was 'a sad state of affairs'. But Renee, always on high alert, popped up and did a haiku-ish poem with the deepest part of her voice:

> *Peter Lum 'The Plum'*
> *People think that I'm quite dumb*
> *But I am poetry in motion*
> *Love the ocean*
> *Too tough for suntan lotion*
> *Today I turn fifty*
> *Everyone is here*
> *Hand us a beer?*

Then Gavin did his own speech, using all the letters of his dad's name to express his gratitude and wonder.

> *P is for Parent*
> *E is for Eats like a horse*
> *T is for Terrible at most things*
> *E is for Epileptic and brain disease*
> *R is for Rough and Rugged and Really bad sense of humour*
> *L is for Loyal*
> *U is for Unanimously the best player ever*
> *M is for My china plate*

And then finally Pete's sister, Sarah, stood up at the northern edge of the trestle tables, beneath the Sharks-themed '50' balloon, and told several hilarious and embarrassing tales of when Peter was just a child, and how earnest and polite he was … before he discovered *ladies and league*. Even though there was only a few years between them, Pete realised how much more she knew about everything – all those fibro houses they'd moved in and out of – and how much more she must have seen. He couldn't wait to get up Darwin way with Gavin in December for the *Australian Story* filming and spend some time with her and her kids and her hubby, see if she knew any more about their dad's disappearance or maybe his death, and, for the first time, ask her some questions about when they were kids – with maybe a quick dip in Litchfield springs thrown in somewhere, freshwater crocs allowing!

At around 2 pm the August sun popped its head out so Gavin whipped his shirt off and announced it a 'pool party'.

From Pete's position at the barbecue – heating up the grill plate for the incoming calamari, eggplant steaks and enormous green marinated WA prawns – he was still marvelling at the effortless way in which Gavin and Ainslee had rediscovered things since the incident abroad, and how they had found a way to grow together again, something Plum had always failed at in love. When shit hit the fan in his relationships, that was it, there was no second album. But through his son, he could see that there easily could have been, if only he had left his ego at the door, said sorry, and then let time heal.

'Whack on one of Dad's wetsuits, Chloe!' said Gavin, taking a nude Tallulah from her baby bouncer in the shade. You couldn't say no to this kid. He was too honest, too sweet in his intentions. Gav had moved back home but remained out of school. To Plum's relief, the UFC dream had faded. Pete thought that maybe Gav had scared himself outside the Old Bike Shed. He worked the desk part-time at Cronulla Studios (which is what Brick's Gym had been called ever since Plum had loaned Charmayne the 180K to cement the loan and buy it outright) and coached Chloe's footy team two nights a week. The boy was making the most of his gap year, being a young man for a bit, with his old man, and learning some stuff that might help him be a better man later.

At the head of the table, Renee was filling Sarah in on every detail of her complicated family life. 'We were going to move to Melbourne but we think we might just stay here. Ollie's kids both love swimming and, let's face it, Peter needs me; I am his next of kin after all.'

Two seats down from them Dana rolled a cigarette as she listened to Tatania and Squeaky discussing adoption agencies and whether it would be best to just move to Zimbabwe and explore an option that way. Along from them was Magic Matt, knee-deep in a chat with Father Pepple. With the operation a success and the Thailand plan dissolving on all fronts, Matt had surrendered to his addictions and enrolled in AA; the priest was his sponsor. Pete was proud of the tall man, and often wondered how long *he* himself would last one day at a time. Pete had gone to a few meetings with Magic and Pepple, and he admired the members and their transition from vulnerability to resilience, but he was still at odds with the whole God situation – and felt like he had a good handle on his intake now. He'd found poetry, and his boy was back.

'Hope you're hungry!' he yelled, allotting the prawns across the hot plate.

Down the far end of the table sipping on a James Boag's, Bridget was talking to Kutiote about his ESL studies. Watching her listening, Pete wished he could run over right now and tell her how good his life had been since he saw her read that poem out: 'Swap with Me I'll Swap with You'. And the thing is he *fucking would swap with her*. If he could give her his own hairy, fifty-year-old pylons he'd take hers, floppy and thirty — no consideration, no hesitation, no worries. *Lob em off, oh Lord!*

In the corner of the yard Charmayne attended to her son, Wolfie, who was finally asleep on her chest, having just exhausted himself by way of a 97-minute scream-cry. The baby was undoubtedly volatile, and Renee had not held back in her whisperings about its 'South African personality', which became louder and louder with every glass of riesling. Brick, who was currently in a Gold Coast hospital recovering after another triple bypass, hadn't reached out to the birthday boy. He'd asked Charmayne, quite fervently by Messenger, not to get a DNA test, highly aware there had been a 'crossover' in that week of Gavin's grand final. Brick and Pete would always be at war over something, it seemed, and Pete kind of liked that; it was healthy to have tension in life, to be tested by a constant. And the baby's head was *that* wide — let's face it, Wolfie could be either of theirs. As he watched her with the baby, he felt a tightening in the chest, hoping to God he was in with another crack.

As the clouds came in and a distant rumble spoke of emotional storms to come, Peter felt grateful to be alive, to have a working brain and body, and love all around him. And he did have all that. Especially love. Love was bloody everywhere and if he wasn't in such a good place he would have found it all a bit much, but he didn't freak because he knew later on he would open up the new moleskin Bridget had bought him and write a poem about it all, about how if you can sit in them shit feelings, the shit then passes, and it gets good.

'Peter, your sister is getting me drunk,' Renee shouted to him, her hands in the air. 'I'm going to have to leave my car here. I'm about to finish this entire bottle.'

'Yeah, look, no surprises there,' Pete yelled back. 'I'll shout you and Tallulah an Uber for my birthday, and you can come back and get it in the morning.'

324

'Ok,' she said, already pouring the rest of the wine out into her glass.

He squeezed lemon over the prawns and watched the hot plate sizzle with satisfaction. 'You can give me a lift to work.'

'To what work?' said Renee, winking at Sarah.

'The airport. Didn't I tell you? I'm starting back up tomorrow.'

'Pulling the planes out?'

'Yeah. Back on the tarmac. Felt like it was time!'

He had missed the work, and with his medication sorted now, Qantas had welcomed him back, and it excited him, thinking maybe his next poem could be about the airport and its characters.

'Dad, it's about to rain!' said Gavin from the pool, baby sister in his arms.

'Well, you can't get any wetter!' Pete said, turning the eggplant steaks over on the bars, and admiring their stripes, hoping that Char would approve of the char.

'Peter,' said a voice from behind him and he felt a polite tap on his shoulder.

Plum turned to see a pale girl, skinny as a rake and wearing a black matronly dress from a time past. 'Yes?'

'We have to go now,' she said.

'Who is we?'

'You and me. Me and you. You and I.'

'Really?'

'Yes, I am the thing with feathers, to help you fly away.'

'But we haven't eaten lunch yet. It's about to rain. Who are you?'

'Emily Dickinson.'

'Emily? Are you a friend of Charmayne's from Zumba?'

'Because we cannot stop for death … death has stopped for you.'

'Char said she was bringing a single friend to meet Matt. But I think she meant Lexi –'

'Follow me, Plum. Behind me, eternity dips. Before me, immortality the same.'

'Really? Nah, you stay instead. You look like you need some sun.'

She shook her head. It was too late to get a tan, and besides she had always been an isolator, hiding in her room, writing poems on envelopes and stashing them in her apron under the bed. 'Now.'

Fuck, I gotta go now, he thought, *and the prawns are nearly cooked, and they look so good! But that's life. That is just life.*

And what a time to work that out.

'Rightio then,' he said, dropping the tongs and letting them fall to the ground, at which point members of his family and friendship groups turned and rose from their positions.

'Plum!' they all screamed, as Plum walked away from himself.

Inside the kitchen he asked Emily if he could take some photos with him from off the fridge, but she suggested he better not: it would only taint the lives of the living who featured in them, and as much as it was allowed, it wasn't a nice thing to do to your inner circle.

'I guess that makes sense,' he said, taking one last beer from the fridge.

'Take a look at the litany,' she said, pointing to the ruckus outside.

Plum turned to the backyard, where a familiar-shaped man shook on the grass, surrounded by his family and friends, doing their best with what they had to revive him. The scene was chaos. The scene was tragic. But because it was his scene, there was something beautiful about it. But he couldn't watch it for long or he'd be dragged back out there again.

'Shit ay.'

'You know I was an epileptic too?' Emily said. 'Just like you, I felt a cleaving in my mind.'

'Cleaving or clearing?' Pete said, savouring his last-ever gulp of cold beer on this earth.

'Exactly. They thought I was lovesick when I wrote about it but I wasn't. My brain was split and my thoughts like marbles on the floor.'

'What do I take to where we're going, Em?' he asked, as she led him down the hallway past the living room, where so much of his life had sat and spat itself out.

'Pack like you're off to Thailand. It's quite hot up there. Where you're going.'

'Hell?'

She laughed, because they all suspected it. 'No. Not quite hell. But still warm enough.'

'Is my dad in hell?'

'He is where you are headed. He wasn't that bad a person. He was just ... limited.'

'Like me?'

'It's not for me to say, I'm just here to collect you. They thought we would be a good match.'

Pete stuffed undies, T-shirts and boardshorts into his duffel bag and went out the front door to the lawn, where a driverless shuttle bus was waiting for him.

'I'm sure they'll bring you back down,' Emily said, ushering him onto the shuttle bus, whose steps were lit up by the gentle blaze of Australian winter. 'You're a poet now, Plum.'

Thanks to

Uncle Anthony 'Shadow' Hayes for your priceless insights, Andrew Johns for being so open about concussion and seizures, Chris Levi for your expertise, Yvonne Cowell for your enduring support, Sarah Meacham for your notes at the very start, Merrick Watts for your creativity at the very very start, Hannah Temby for your power read, Justine Goss my brilliant agent who always backs the work, Tug Dumbly the poet laureate of Australia, Fiona Seres for saying this idea had to be a book, Catherine Milne for lifting this book up into the air, Emily and Louis Smith, Lee-Anne Higgins for being all things BC, Sian, Maddy and Lola from HH, The Tip Bowl, Joel 'Sugar' Caine, Madeleine James, Angus Fay, Andy Ryan, the Frasers, Jackie and Hamish, and lastly, to my brothers in this life, Jonathan Duncan and Simon Burstall.